THE SWASTIKA TATTOO

Geraldine Birch

This book is a work of fiction. Names and characters are either the product of the author's imagination or are used fictionally. U-893 is a fictional U-boat. Historically, places and events are based upon extensive research, including military bases named. This includes the prisoner of war camp, Camp Papago Park, located in east Phoenix that housed men of the German Navy from October 1943 to March 1946. If there is incorrect information, it is done without intent to harm.

The Swastika Tattoo is a historical novel about intolerance. Derogatory, even offensive, words referring to African Americans, Jews, and other races or nationalities are used because during this historical time frame such words were spoken with impunity. Unfortunately, these words are part of that history. They are not meant to offend, but to inform.

The workbook for high school students at the end of this historical novel includes a short summary, a discussion of theme, historical terms of WWII, German words and their meaning, a glossary, naval terms, and suggested essay questions.

ISBN: 1500257141
ISBN 13: 9781500257149

Also by Geraldine Birch

Sedona: City of Refugees

THE
SWASTIKA
TATTOO

Geraldine Birch

For Joe

Chapter 1

September 1944
Arizona

The question exploded upon Rudolf Meier like a torpedo hitting the hull of a German U-boat.

His head jerked violently to see who could possibly have voiced such an outrage and then Rudolf's gaze landed on the son of the farmer who owned the fields where he and other Nazi prisoners of war labored.

"Why do the German people still believe in Hitler?" the youth asked, unexpectedly throwing his inquiry into the stifling air. In that terrible moment of frozen impotence, Rudolf knew he would never forget the brazen American kid who stood in the midst of a scorching Arizona cotton field, leaning against the wooden handle of a hoe.

The German straightened suddenly from his bent position where he had been digging fiercely at a tenacious weed. "Why do you ask such a thing?" Rudolf spat out his words, rage soaking his voice. Wasn't it bad enough he suffered such degrading work tending the hated *baumwolle*? Rudolf felt no better than a lowly nigger in this parched American wasteland, and now there was the added injury of a stupid American questioning the German people's love for *Der Führer*. Like the small flame of a match to a cigarette, Rudolf's fury lit the crumpled edge of his German soul.

The teenager answered Rudolf's angry words without flinching. "Well, in school yesterday—in my civics class—we were discussing the war and our teacher said the German people would gladly follow

1

Hitler into…well, into Hades. Of course, you need to understand my teacher's brother was killed in the Normandy invasion…fighting you guys, so maybe that's why she thinks that. I heard you speak English to the guard, so I thought I would ask you why the German people still believe in Hitler."

Rudolf stared at the American with unwavering suspicion. He guessed him to be about seventeen. Rudolf's first inclination was to retort he was a prisoner and not allowed to talk to impudent farmers' sons, but he knew the sluggish guards did not care. Deciding to answer the question after a long moment, Rudolf looked around to make sure none of the other POWs could hear; he did not want to be seen talking with the enemy.

"We believe in Adolf Hitler because he made life better for us," Rudolf said, trying to keep a calm demeanor, but his right eye began twitching. "Before Hitler, under the Weimar Republic, there was no work for the German people because of the injustice of the Treaty of Versailles. The *Führer* brought food to our tables, gave us work for our hands. He is our leader, our strength."

The teenager digested that for a moment and then countered, "Yes, but he's led you into this awful war. Germany is losing…"

Rudolf's face, burned brown from the Arizona sun, blanched. He wanted to strike out against this idiot who voiced such blasphemy, but he knew the trouble he would be in if he did. Instead, in a measured tone, he said, "Don't be so sure of that," and then he abruptly turned from the source of his enmity, his eye still twitching against his fierce will. Rudolf quickly found another patch of weeds in an adjacent cotton row to hack into, hoping it would alleviate his wrath.

Moments later when Rudolf glanced back at the farmer's son, he saw a quizzical look, as if the youth wanted to say more, but the guards called the men together to take them back to Camp Papago Park. Rudolf carried his hoe to the shed at the end of the field and turned it in; he was glad for the end of this day and the disrespectful questions by the American.

Back in his barrack, Rudolf removed his boots and placed them carefully at the foot of his cot, and then he stripped off his clothes, filthy with the dust of the cotton field and his sharp-smelling sweat. He dropped them on the floor, one on top of the other in a messy pile, and then sat wearily on his cot in his underwear. The interminable heat was even more stifling in the small barrack, and Rudolf's longing for the green of his beloved homeland permeated his being. Disgusted with his circumstances, Rudolf's thoughts turned easily to the conversation with the American bastard.

He pondered the heresy of the question about German fidelity to Adolf Hitler and then his mind roamed through his knowledge about democracy. Considering it from all angles—what he had been taught in the Third Reich and what he had viewed himself as a prisoner of war—Rudolf determined the American democratic system was a farce. It was beyond logic that every citizen could have a voice in their government, and the turmoil of the failed Weimar Republic imposed upon Germany after WWI certainly proved that.

Rudolf smiled faintly, knowing the German people would never again want self-governance because only *Der Führer* knew what was best for the Fatherland. With all his heart, Rudolf Meier believed in the *Führerprinzip*, the obligation that everyone must obey the nation's leader. Germany's glory was because its leader, Adolf Hitler, had led the country out of its economic crisis, and spread its military force far and wide throughout Europe. While he conceded the *Wehrmacht* was pulling back now on all fronts, that would soon change, and the world would crumple once again under Germany's might. Rudolf felt certain of the Fatherland's triumph, and when that moment happened, America—this country of mixed races and a foolish belief in individual freedom—would simply capitulate.

Although he grudgingly acknowledged the economic strength of America, he believed it to be a country riddled with Jew bankers and bank-robbing Dagos busy lining their own pockets. Rudolf shook his head in wonderment: Americans had no thought for the national community like Germans—they were too busy stealing from one another other in their capitalistic greed.

Rudolf remembered the celebration a year ago, in the fall of 1943, when he and other POWs heard about a tremendous German victory;

the news passing jubilantly from man to man, like a soccer ball kicked down the field toward the goal line.

Werner Carl, a swarthy torpedo mechanic who had served with Rudolf on *Unterseeboot-893* (known as U-893), ran into the barrack Rudolf shared with other German submariners. Barely containing himself, he yelled, "We just heard over the radio—we took Rome!" Carl slapped Rudolf on the back and there were smiles on all the men's faces. "Field-marshal Kesselring and his airborne troops seized Rome and then they freed Mussolini from a hotel where he was held captive!"

"Such good news!" one of the men shouted. "Maybe our officers will allow us to celebrate!" Rudolf smiled along with the other men at the prospect of cracking open the hidden alcoholic cache made from citrus fruit they secretly brewed under the noses of the American guards, hiding it beneath the altar in the prison chapel.

That was a fine memory, Rudolf acknowledged as he walked toward the bathhouse carrying his clean clothes; he had to keep his focus on the Third Reich's successes, as minor as they may be now. He deliberately kicked at the annoying dust beneath his feet as if he could clear it from his field of vision, an impossibility considering the prisoner of war camp sat in the middle of the Arizona desert. Rudolf sighed. The lack of greenery exhausted his senses; the inside of his nose seemed forever dry and scaly and the pale earth coated his throat.

For some unexplainable reason, the catchy American tune, "Boogie Woogie Bugle Boy" came to mind when he entered the bathhouse and he began to whistle it, wondering if it wasn't verging on treason to enjoy a song that was so blatantly American. He had heard it while his U-boat patrolled the waters off the East Coast; the boat was often so close to shore that its wireless radio easily picked up American stations.

Soaping in the shower, Rudolf jabbed at his American captors. "You know, one German is worth ten soft-bellied Americans. All they want is a comfortable life. They have no will to work hard like us pure-bred Germans. You can see how lazy they are by looking at our guards who never stand properly at attention!"

His good friend, Fritz Kraus, another radio operator from U-893, was showering as well. Over the din of the water, Fritz yelled, "*Amerikaner* morale will surely fall when they try to enter Germany. We will never capitulate!"

Rudolf stepped out of the shower and toweled off, giving special care to his right bicep, the site of his swastika tattoo, touching it lightly with reverence.

Fritz gave his friend a nudge. "*Mein Gott*, you love that tattoo! My father would have flogged me if I did such a stupid thing!"

Rudolf raised his eyebrows and looked at Fritz. "Yes, my grandmother was not pleased. She said I made myself low class."

"Do you remember our graduation day from the Naval Signals School?" Fritz asked suddenly, laughing. "You sure were hell bent on finding the best tattoo artist in Flensburg. I also seem to recall how that harlot kept teasing you. She said you were a perfect example of a true Aryan, that you should have your picture on one of those Third Reich posters with your blond hair and fine nose."

Rudolf, who had moved over to the row of sinks to shave, grinned with the memory. That was a fine day, he remembered while he shaved his face, careful not to cut the deep cleft in his chin. He closed his eyes, remembering the sensation of her, but the feeling passed quickly when he splashed his face with water.

Unwittingly, he whistled the boogie again while putting on a clean pair of denim pants and shirt plainly stenciled with large letters on the front and back of each garment identifying him as a prisoner of war. Once dressed, he stood patiently in strict formation with his fellow prisoners on the dusty field of the compound watching the apathetic guards as they performed the evening head count. He stood proudly knowing one day soon the Third Reich would soon kick the asses of such a slipshod bunch.

When he stepped into the mess hall, the irritating American song returned; it stuck in his mind like a scratched record. Rudolf tried to focus on the *faustball* match that evening, but his thoughts—triggered by the song—returned to that time more than a year ago when U-893 prowled the eastern coastline. He remembered the joy he felt then that the indolent Americans did not have the slightest hint the U-boat lurked silently in their midst, hidden under the sea, homing in on their radio programs, and waiting patiently for the chance to annihilate their ships. But his happiness did not last; Rudolf's life changed forever in one horrible moment when an American plane sighted the U-boat. Bombs were dropped before it could make it into the murky depths. Rudolf escaped with half of the crew only to be picked up by an American destroyer.

The smell of meatloaf engulfed his nostrils and he deliberately stowed away the wretched memory of the sinking of U-893. He was incredibly hungry, more so than usual, but Rudolf wriggled his nose in distaste. How he longed for curried sausage, or a good fried *schnitzel*, wondering if he would ever taste good German food again.

After dinner, Rudolf walked toward the canteen, passing the enlisted men's barracks. He eyed the old stables and supply sheds that had been turned into flimsy living quarters: tan gypsum board covered some of the Great Depression structures, but many of the barracks were wrapped in inferior grade jute paper. Rudolf sighed; buildings in Germany were stout—made to keep out the elements, a sure sign of Germany's superior workmanship over the American slap-dash habit of making do with anything available. Much to Rudolf's displeasure, with the slightest whisper of a wind, sand seeped easily through poorly-fitting windows and doors along with the desert's vermin—venomous stinging scorpions and centipedes that hid under his cot and found refuge in his boots.

Camp Papago Park sat about ten miles from downtown Phoenix, incarcerating approximately seventeen hundred German seamen in a barren area next to the Arizona Crosscut Canal, a large irrigation ditch. The camp hugged close to two odd geologic formations—pockmarked red sandstone hills called Papago Buttes, shaped by the desert wind. One of the formations, called Hole-in-the-Rock by ancient Indian tribes, stood like a watchful sentinel overlooking the prisoner of war camp. The interminable sight of it disgusted Rudolf for it represented his imprisonment by the enemy.

Rudolf earned eighty cents a day in canteen credits working in the nearby cotton fields and citrus groves, not something he wanted to do, but the days passed quicker and lifted the weight of utter boredom. Walking toward the canteen, he hoped there was a new stock of Chesterfield cigarettes he could purchase. Rudolf grudgingly admitted they were much smoother than his favorite German smokes, *Sondermischung No. 4*, but he came away disappointed. Chesterfields were so popular that the canteen was already bare from that morning's stock, so he settled for a Hershey bar.

Stripping the wrapping off the candy, the conversation in the cotton field returned to plague him. Although he knew he could have handled it better—perhaps by ignoring the question altogether—the youth's boldness was insufferable. In Germany, no minor would dare approach an adult with such a blasphemous question; his grandmother would have slapped him sharply on the side of the head.

Rudolf's mood slid further into gloom as he watched the sunset. It was the close of yet another day so far from his beloved homeland. Feeling wretched, he searched for someone he knew among the men milling about the compound's dirt yard, finally seeing another U-893 crewman. Wolfgang Gertzner stood by the barbed wire fence, a cloud of cigarette smoke swirling about his dark blond head. Rudolf walked to him and offered Wolfgang a bite off the partially eaten chocolate bar. In turn, Wolfgang gave Rudolf a few puffs of his Camel, another popular brand among the Germans. The two men stood silently, looking at the Arizona sky as it flung its dying light into unimaginable colors, turning the strange hills nearby into ghostly formations.

"Any news?" Rudolf asked.

"Whatever news there is… it is bad!" Wolfgang said.

Wolfgang, a thin, wiry man who had worked in the control room on U-893, was well-known around camp for his sticky fingers, taking anything the gum-chewing Americans forgot to lock up. It was Wolfgang who stole a radio receiver from the camp supply room, an easy enough task since his assigned duty was to resupply and clean bathrooms in the hospital compound. Wolfgang turned the receiver over to one of the German officers who, in turn, secretly rigged it to pick up short-wave broadcasts from the Third Reich. The news from Germany was a welcome respite for the prisoners wary of American propaganda about Allied victories.

Rudolf's voice sounded dull, sullen. "Is it true what the American newspapers say…that the Russians have captured Bucharest and they are on the march toward Germany?"

"I think it is true," Wolfgang said, his answer a low growl. "Although, my gut tells me our officers are probably not giving us the full story either."

"M*ein Gott!*" Rudolf sucked in his breath. "For Germany to be defeated by the Russians would be far worse than being beaten by the Brits and Americans. Those filthy communists will kill as many of us as possible!"

Rudolf stopped speaking for a moment and then glanced sideways at Wolfgang before voicing his thoughts. "You know, I have often wondered why Americans with our German blood have not risen up to help us in our fight."

Wolfgang looked askance at Rudolf. "Why would they do that Rudi? They are weak now; they have lived in America too long. The races mix easily here; they are nothing but mongrels. The only ones they don't mix with are the niggers."

Rudolf laughed; what Wolfgang said was true. After the capture of U-893, the Americans interrogated the crew of the U-boat at Fort Hunt, a secret center located on the Potomac River near Washington, D.C. After several weeks, when the Americans were satisfied there was no more information to be had, the crew climbed aboard a south-bound train to Camp Blanding where they stewed in Florida's humidity. Weeks turned to months, and then the War Department moved them again by train to desolate Arizona. On those train trips, aside from seeing the vast American landscape with its bountiful farms and peaceful, untouched cities, they also viewed filthy shanties slung along the railroad tracks where only black people lived, and they talked among themselves about the appalling conditions. No one in Germany lived like that before the war, not even the Jews.

Rudolf looked up at the darkening sky. He loathed Camp Papago Park, not only because he was a prisoner of war. It was more than that, so much more. The camp was incredibly bleak for Rudolf's German soul. His vision was accustomed to the green of his native land that stretched as far as the eye could see—pastures heavy with wheat, rapeseed, rye or barley, and forests laced with wide flowing rivers. Rudolf psyche ached desperately for home, for his beautiful Bremen located on the picturesque Weser River. Here, in the middle of the Arizona desert, he felt as if he inhabited an alien world, particularly with those scarred, ugly hills that sat adjacent to the camp. The arid landscape of sand, cactus, and stark rubble-strewn peaks made him irritable. The only comfort Rudolf could summon was that he was imprisoned with his own countrymen in this strange land.

He stuffed the candy wrapper in his pocket and headed for his barrack. He needed sleep to take away his feeling of utter despair.

Chapter 2

May 1936
Bremen, Germany

For Hermann Meier, building U-boats was like a love affair with a beautiful woman.

He knew each submarine intimately, inspected every inch of their sleek bodies, and made sure their wombs could carry German seamen safely into the hostile sea. When a U-boat he supervised was commissioned, Hermann watched the ceremony like a jealous lover, feeling a mixture of emotion. It felt *wunderbar* to see that his beloved boat was seaworthy, that she could carry the fear of Germany to the far reaches of the ocean, yet it was difficult for him to know other hands would now be caressing the lady he helped create.

Hermann Meier was a giant of a man. He was tall, bear-like in his stance, and his voice was deep and resonant like an old church bell, which was made even deeper with the years of yelling orders to his men over the din of sizzling welders and banging riveters at the vast Bremen shipyard known as Deschimag AG Weser.

In 1894, at age 17, Hermann began working at AG Weser, an immense place where tall cranes, heavy steel and sweaty men made mighty ships. The yard was more than 50 years old even before Hermann began working there; it was born on a cold November day in 1843 on the banks of the wide Weser River, about 125 kilometers south from its flow into the North Sea.

The old yard was like home to him with its constant crackle of welding torches and huge cranes swinging in the fog with their heavy loads.

Railroad cars stood next to dry docks waiting patiently for their bellies to be unloaded, and compressed air hoses slithered on the ground like snakes waiting to entangle any unwary worker. The immense shipyard held a multitude of workshops for everything that went into U-boats from periscopes to artillery and torpedoes, and workers ranged from welders, mechanics, carpenters, and smithies to tool and die experts.

The noise at AG Weser was deafening but the smell of the yard—a combination of oil, paint, rust, and strong acids never seemed to leave him. Those odors mixed with his own sweat came home in his clothing. Only a great deal of scrubbing by his dear wife, Luise, could take the odors and sweat out, but not without her bitter complaints.

Every morning for forty-two years, Hermann eagerly woke to face the hard labor of the day. He moved quickly out of bed at 4:30 a.m., patted Luise on her fanny, which he lovingly thought was his wife's best feature, and headed for the kitchen sink where he shaved, being careful not to nick the large mole on his left cheek. When he looked closer in the mirror, he wondered how he, Hermann Meier, this man with such large features, managed to win the hand of his Luise, his bride of 40 years, a woman of great beauty and sizzling temperament. He sighed, reminding himself that her beauty far outweighed her carping. Besides, her cooking was exceptional, which was more than a man could ask considering his station in life.

Cleanly shaved, he trudged back upstairs to the bedroom, where he put on his clean clothes. Only when done with that task would he use the bathroom situated between the two bedrooms, a small room that contained only a toilet and a window. Finished then with his morning duties, he headed downstairs to wash his hands and enjoy a hearty breakfast set out on a clean linen tablecloth. Depending on his wife's mood, sometimes there would even be a fresh flower in a bud vase.

Hermann sat down and Luise placed a small pot of coffee on the table. Her strong brew always required heavy cream, and that, too, waited for him in a small porcelain pitcher.

The table was laden with dark bread, globs of butter and delicious jam Luise preserved every summer when fresh fruits were available. She served Hermann cheese and cold meats on a porcelain dish, and finally a soft boiled egg stood waiting in a delicate egg cup. With his big hands, it was a trying task to crack the shell with the small egg spoon Luise put on the table, but he tried his hardest to be precise about this intricate task. He always wondered how Luise could deftly clip the top off the egg with her knife, a trick he would not dare try on her clean tablecloth.

Hermann savored his breakfast meal and the conversation at the table each morning with his wife and his beloved twelve-year-old grandson, Rudolf. As he ate, he took special care to explain to Rudolf what was happening at the yard, what project he was supervising these past months, and all the complications of making sure the new U-boat was seaworthy.

Today, the sixth of May 1936, was a special day for Hermann. He was tremendously excited as he explained to Luise and Rudolf that U-26, the boat he had been working on for nine months, was to be commissioned.

"Ah," Luise said, as she served her husband more steaming coffee. "Now I understand why you are wearing your suit."

"*Opa,*" Rudolf asked as he jammed his mouth full of food, "What does 'commissioned' mean?"

"It means the U-boat is being formally accepted by the German Navy," Hermann said. "It is an important ceremony and our country's flag will be raised for the first time on my beautiful boat, *Enkel,*" a German term of endearment that Hermann used often when he spoke to Rudolf.

The boy's intense blue eyes opened wide at his grandfather's explanation. Then, without warning, he reached out to grab another piece of cold meat with his hand and his grandmother gave him a resounding slap.

"Rudolf!" she scolded. "Use your fork! What has happened to your manners?"

His eyes filled quickly with tears, and Hermann tried to salvage the situation by putting his large arm affectionately around his wife's shoulders and squeezing her. "He's a growing boy, Luise. Let him eat what he wants!"

A moment of silence was followed by Luise's sharp "humph!" Rudolf glanced quickly at her, then at his grandfather, who nodded slightly. The child picked up his fork and jabbed another thick slice of sausage.

"As I was saying," Hermann continued with a heavy sigh, "during the commission ceremony, the crew will be standing at attention on her deck behind the conning tower and her commander, *Kapitänleutnant* Werner Hartmann, will be on the wintergarden—the platform—while the German flag is raised. Oh what a glorious moment it will be!"

Finishing his breakfast, Hermann looked down at himself to make sure there was no jam on his suit. He wiped bread crumbs from his mouth with the back of his big hand, and then remembering the linen napkin in his lap, he cleaned his mouth again, hoping Luise had not seen his error in manners. Hermann knew it was important to look his best on this day. His position as one of the supervisors on the U-boat allowed him the privilege of being at the commissioning ceremony, and he would mingle with people who were in a social stratum far different from his own. Hermann was forever conscious of having pulled himself out of the ranks of an ordinary welder to that of a supervisor of many men—and burns on his hands and arms from the welding torch proved it.

At the ceremony, Hermann knew there would be various Third Reich and *Kriegsmarine* dignitaries as well as family members of the original U-26 commissioned in 1913. Sadly, with a twinge to his gut, Hermann remembered that boat was lost in the Gulf of Finland two years later during the Great War. He had worked on that boat too, but as a mere welder. Hermann shook his head in wonderment; his job was to make streamlined killing machines, a tube of metal holding sweating men in the depths of the ocean. When he thought about it, in the dark of the night, he questioned how he faced his work every day.

Hurriedly stuffing the last of the cold cuts in his mouth, Hermann stood up and again checked his suit for anything out of order. There was much on his mind as he reached for his hat hanging near the door, and then he remembered his daily habit. He went back to the table and kissed Luise on her soft mouth and Rudolf on the top of his blond head.

As Hermann opened the door, Rudolf asked, "*Opa*, when can I see your U-26?"

Hermann thought about his grandson's question for a moment. "The boat needs to go to sea where the rest of her equipment and weapons will be fitted and tested. There are many hard tests for the crew and the boat to pass before she can be declared a front boat, ready for combat. Once that happens, she will come back to me and my men and we will fix anything that is out of order. It is then I bring you to see my beautiful U-26!"

The door closed and Luise took a last gulp of her strong coffee. She was the disciplinarian in the household, although none of Hermann's yard crew would ever believe the soft spot Hermann had for his grandson and his inability to scold the boy; not this man of great strength who could focus on the most minute of problems in the din of the yard while cursing at a new worker because his rivets went in at a slight angle.

Luise looked at her grandson and her grey eyes took on a shade of sadness. Rudolf was so like his father Erich when he was the same age. He had the same strong jaw, blond hair and sky-blue eyes. It was almost as if her son and grandson were twins, but still, there was something different about Rudolf. Erich's personality had been much like Luise's. He was unafraid to voice strong opinions, and that had caused a lot of trouble in the household when Eric was growing up, particularly when he was a teenager. Rudolf, however, was quiet, introspective. There was a part of the boy Luise could never reach, no matter how much she tried, and Luise never failed to tell Herman that Rudolf's "slut of a mother" gave the boy that trait.

At fifty-eight, Luise's long blond hair showed only a few stands of gray. She had hurriedly pulled it back into a loose braid when she got out of bed and now she absentmindedly reached back, undid the ribbon, and tightly re-braided her thick hair while watching Rudolf slowly eat his bread, his eyes gazing far off into the distance. When she finished fixing her hair, she tapped the table with her forefinger in a silent attempt to show her grandson he needed to finish quickly if he was to get to school on time. The child looked at her and smiled, but she would have none of it.

"Rudolf, quit playing with your food!" she said sharply.

"Yes, *Oma*," he said as he gulped the last of the dark bread. He jumped up from his seat and rushed from the room, skipping stairs to get his coat and books from his small bedroom. Luise made a "tsking" sound with her tongue against the roof of her mouth as she swept the crumbs from Rudolf's chair onto her hand.

"What will become of this boy?" she muttered.

Chapter 3

September 1944
Arizona

Rudolf and other POWs were driven by a camp guard the next day to the same cotton farm about thirty miles south of Camp Papago Park. Another guard traveled in the back of the Army truck with the twenty-five Germans. The ratio of one guard to every eight Germans was an Army regulation, but the Americans often disregarded such rules, usually sending only one or two guards to watch the prisoners—a wonderment to Rudolf. Following orders was part of his German soul. To question or disregard regulations was unthinkable. He sighed as he surveyed the lax guards, reminding himself this was a country he did not fully understand. Rudolf closed his eyes to the barrenness stretched before him, trying instead to envision the beauty of northern Germany.

The guard who sat in the back of the truck was a husky American with a long, sad face. As usual, he struck up a conversation with Rudolf while they bounced over dirt roads to the cotton fields.

"Hey, Rudi," Tom McKay nudged Rudolf. "Where'd you learn to speak such good English?"

Rudolf did not open his eyes, answering, "In *Gymnasium.*"

"What...you learned how to speak English in a gymnasium? Hey, that's where we play basketball." The guard moved his hand up and down like he was bouncing an imaginary ball.

Rudolf opened his eyes and laughed out loud. "No, no! Not like that. It's the term we use for secondary school. In Germany, *Gymnasium* is for those who will go on to university. We learn languages such as English, Latin, or French, mathematics, physics, chemistry, and history."

"Well, why is it called gymnasium?" McKay said, trying miserably to pronounce the word like Rudolf.

"It refers to ancient Greece, where young men were trained both intellectually and physically."

"You speak English so well you could be a spy," the soldier said, his sad demeanor brightening with the idea. "I've seen those movies about U-boats. You guys always have a spy onboard to drop off when you get close to the American shoreline."

"If I were a spy, McKay, do you honestly think I would be sitting here talking with you on my way to work in a miserable cotton field?" Rudolf could not help grinning. The guard's remark was so ludicrous.

"I don't know, Rudi," the guard said, shaking his head in wonderment, "You would make a perfect spy. You could pass as an American any day."

"Thanks, McKay." Rudolf chuckled quietly.

He thought about the recurring conversation among his fellow POWs about Camp Papago Park. It was not strictly run, at least to their Germanic way of thinking, so the Nazi officers chose to test how far their men's behavior would go with the Americans. Two weeks ago, the German camp leader, *Fregattenkapitän* Jürgen Wattenberg, gave the order to stop saluting the American flag when lowered at the end of the day. Rudolf and his fellow inmates stood straight and tall as the flag moved slowly down the pole, then they stretched out their right arms and yelled in unison, "*Sieg Heil, Sieg Heil, Sieg Heil!*"

The Americans responded to this test of wills with reduced rations in the mess halls. The prisoners, who were used to full bellies, went back to saluting the Stars and Stripes.

It was a game, Rudolf thought, like a hard-fought *faustball* game—a form of volleyball introduced into Germany in the 1890s—with all of its intricate strategies.

Rudolf worked mindlessly in the cotton field, hoeing the interminable weeds, day-dreaming about his escape from the prison camp. It was only one-hundred thirty miles to the Mexican border, a fact the Germans knew by heart because they stole maps regularly from unattended military vehicles.

Rudolf considered what he would have to do before hand: hoard food, gather clothes without the hated "PW" printed on them, and find a way to earn some American money. Above all, he needed several canteens filled with water to keep him going until he reached Mexico. Finally, and most important, his plan of escape had to receive approval from the highest German officers who really controlled the men at Camp Papago Park. The Americans thought they ruled the POWs, but Rudolf knew otherwise. All of those factors seemed daunting on this hot September day, and he was bored. He forced himself to focus on what he was doing, wondering how the obstinate weeds could have such a tenacious hold on the roots of the thick cotton plants.

The sun pushed into the apex of the azure sky, and the guards called loudly to the prisoners who moved quickly under large cottonwood trees bordering the irrigation ditch, seeking refuge from the searing heat. An old Ford truck sat next to the ditch with a man inside, his face hidden by a felt hat stained with sweat, and a woman in a printed cotton dress stood at the rear of the vehicle, its tailgate down. She handed out thick egg sandwiches and fig bars. Large jars frosted with beads of moisture held cold lemonade that beckoned seductively to the workers. The woman smiled and nodded as the men moved through the line, muttering *danke* as they took their food.

Rudolf studied the woman who he had seen for the first time yesterday. She was thin, almost pencil-like in appearance, yet she had a bearing that spoke of fine breeding. She wore her dark brown hair pinned in a roll at the base of her neck, but one strand kept falling on her cheek and she repeatedly tucked it behind her ear. Her dark eyes were bright and she looked each prisoner in the face as she served him, as if she were trying to discern the personality of each German man. Rudolf stood at the end of line and when he took his food, he said, "Thank you."

Ruth Feller looked squarely at him. "You must be the one my son told us about yesterday. Bob mentioned how well you speak English."

"Your son?" Rudolf asked.

"Yes, he was working in the field yesterday afternoon."

"I remember him," Rudolf answered politely, but his German soul cried out to tell this woman of her son's insolence. Instead, he turned abruptly toward the ditch bank to find a place to sit, but he heard her voice again and looked back at the woman.

"I apologize if he upset you," the woman said, wiping her hands on her apron. "He told his father and me that you seemed offended. He wanted to tell you he was sorry but the guards took you away, back to the camp. So I will apologize for him. He shouldn't have asked why you believe in Hitler."

Rudolf faced the woman, stunned by her statement. For a moment, his mind could not grasp the fact that the insufferable American youth had realized his audacity and told his father and mother. When he regained his bearing, Rudolf stammered, "Thank you for saying that."

The woman smiled. "He's a good boy, my son, Bob. He's just…well, inquisitive. I guess that's what you would call him. He's interested in most everything, and that includes you and the other men working in our fields."

Rudolf could not resist replying, "In Germany, no young person would dare ask such a question of an adult, questioning our loyalty to our leader, Adolf Hitler."

Ruth Feller looked at Rudolf, her expression serious, then, with a dazzling smile, she said. "Well, I guess that's the difference between Americans and Germans."

Rudolf hesitated for a moment and met Ruth's eyes. Despite his judgment of her son, he felt a slight flush caused by her engaging manner and her surprising response. "Yes, I suppose it is," he said.

He walked to the ditch bank and sat down with the other men. They talked among themselves, some complaining about the brown bread, wishing it was the heavy dark bread of home, but Rudolf said, "At least this is not that nasty white bread they feed us at the camp—that bread made of air and sugar that ruins our teeth. This, at least, has some substance to it."

One of the prisoners who sat close to Rudolf laughed loudly. "Yes, Rudi, you got a pretty smile from the farmer's wife. We all understand why you like her bread!"

Rudolf realized what the other prisoner said was true: She was kind to him and he had stood up for her. Momentarily astonished at himself, Rudolf laughed with the other men but wondered why he would take the side of an American woman—a woman who had spawned a man child that would grow to fight the Third Reich. Still embarrassed, he wolfed down his lunch, carefully watching the woman as she came to the men with more lemonade, refilling their paper cups.

When she got to Rudolf, she said, "Would you please tell the men my husband and I know this is a difficult situation for them... being prisoners of war...but we want them to know we appreciate the work they're doing. Without them, we would lose this crop. The war has taken our pickers..." Her voice faltered and she turned away quickly from the shade of the cottonwood trees, and looked toward the cotton field, her thin hand screening her eyes from the blistering sun.

"You see," she said as she glanced momentarily toward Rudolf with damp eyes, "My husband is ill and it looks like my son and I will have to bring in the cotton with their help." Then Ruth Feller sighed deeply. "It's a hard job picking cotton. The hoeing of weeds is nothing compared to the picking of it. I know you and the other men won't like it. Still...it must be done."

After she closed the truck's tailgate and drove away, Rudolf repeated what Ruth Feller told him, and her sympathy toward the men spread among them like a soothing letter from home. Confusion dogged Rudolf. It seemed inconceivable that an American woman would voice gratitude to German prisoners of war. He tried to imagine a German woman expressing compassion to captured Poles or Russians working in her fields, but he could not. Still, Ruth Feller had done exactly that and she had said it directly to him.

Later in the day, Rudolf noticed Bob Feller working not far from him. They stared at one another for a moment and then Bob walked purposefully over to the German.

"Excuse me," he said.

Rudolf stopped working. "Yes?"

"I wanted to say this yesterday, but the guards took you away before I could...I want to apologize. I did not mean to make you angry. I should have put some thought into my question before it jumped out of my head."

After a moment, Rudolf said, "Yes, I admit you made me angry, incredibly angry."

Rudolf was not sure what to do then, but because the American looked at him in a straightforward manner, he felt the need to acknowledge Bob's words.

"...and I accept your apology," Rudolf added.

The teenager, a handsome youth with dark hair and eyes like his mother, stretched his hand to Rudolf. "I'm Bob Feller."

"Bob, I am Rudi Meier," Rudolf answered, shaking the youth's hand with unease at first, but the firmness of Bob's handshake caused Rudolf to respond in kind. He realized immediately as he looked into Bob's face that there were not many years between them—two or three perhaps and yet their life experiences were so incredibly different. Bob Feller was a free American working on his family's soil, and he, Rudolf, was a German prisoner of war.

The heat of the day suddenly felt oppressive to Rudolf as he let go of Bob's hand and the green plants seemed to close in on him, trapping him somehow in this place where he did not want to be. Rudolf smiled faintly, and Bob returned to his spot in the field but Rudolf stood still, his unflagging German spirit painfully crushed, realizing clearly that the total war Germany had launched against its enemies had not touched this Bob Feller or damaged his country.

At the end of the day as the Germans turned their tools in to the guards, one of them suddenly cried out in desperation. The prisoner searched his pockets, pulling them inside out, and spoke rapidly in German to the men gathered around him. Some of them tried to comfort him, but the man, in his early thirties openly sobbed. They motioned for Rudolf to interpret the problem to the guards who were impatiently telling the men to get into the truck.

Bob walked to where Rudolf stood. "What's the matter? Why is he so upset?" he asked.

"Helmut lost a small Bible his mother gave him—a gift to keep him safe at sea," Rudolf said. "He has had it with him since the war began in 1939. He wants to search the area where he worked, but the guards say we must leave."

"Where was he working?" Bob asked.

"There, about three rows over from where we were," Rudolf said, his voice tight. He pointed to where the prisoner had been working, a spot thick with maturing cotton.

The two guards became more aggressive, yelling at the men. Rudolf obeyed, climbing reluctantly into the bed of the Army truck, but he turned back toward Bob with a look of fury crossing his Aryan features, and suddenly, without warning, he spit violently onto the dusty ground, the force of his anger floating through the hot desert air.

Bob stood thoughtfully in the trail of dust as the truck sped back toward Camp Papago Park. He walked to the area where Rudolf pointed and began his search. He lifted the branches of the big cotton plants, shaking them a little to make sure the Bible had not fallen in between the thick growth. Bob worked methodically, knowing if he moved too fast, he might miss the small Bible.

More than an hour later, toward sundown, Ruth Feller drove to the cotton field. Her son was normally home by this time, hunger drawing him to the farmhouse kitchen. She found him standing at the edge of the cotton field with a troubled look on his face.

"Bob! What are you doing out here so late? Dinner is almost ready."

"Mom…one of the German prisoners was crying. He lost a small Bible his mother gave him—over there in the field somewhere, but the guards wouldn't let him look for it. I thought I could find it for him."

Ruth set the brake, turned off the ignition, and got out of the truck. "Oh, my! There's no telling where it could be, son. It's getting dark. Time to come home now."

But Bob stood resolute. "Mom, you didn't see him. He was horribly upset. I could tell that Bible meant everything to him. I've just got to find it, I've got to!"

Ruth looked past her son toward the irrigation ditch. "Well, Bob, they all sat on the ditch bank eating lunch. Come on, maybe it fell out of his pocket while he was sitting down."

She climbed back into the old truck, started it quickly, and Bob jumped on the running board, holding himself steady as the vehicle bounced over the field. In a few minutes, they were at the ditch bank searching the area, pushing through pungent brown and golden-colored cottonwood leaves that covered the damp ground of the irrigation ditch.

After a while, Ruth sighed and said, "Bob, it's late. Your father will be wondering about his dinner."

"Oh, Mom…just a bit longer. Please! Say, I have an idea! Could you turn on the truck lights for a moment, and I'll search one more place."

"OK," Ruth answered, "But this is it…"

"Maybe he sat up against this big cottonwood," Bob said, more to himself than to his mother. Feeling Ruth's impatience, he hurriedly pushed his hands under the dead foliage caught in the tree's bulging roots, the leaves like golden coins under the headlights. Suddenly, Bob felt something under his hand and picked up the object, moving it into the light so he could see it properly.

The teenager shouted, delight filling his voice. "Oh, my gosh! Mom, mom, here it is! I've found it!"

Chapter 4

May 1936
Bremen, Germany

The day was bright and clear without the usual fog coming off the Weser River. Rudolf and his best friend, Lothar, met by the entrance to the apartment building where they both lived and soon fell in with a group of other boys on their way to school. There was excited talk among them about the upcoming visit to Bremen of Adolf Hitler, who held the titles of Reich Chancellor and *Führer.*

"Oh, it will be wonderful to see how the Nazis decorate the market square with their great red and black swastika flags!" one of the boys, Johann, exclaimed. "My father said there will be music and lots of soldiers marching."

Lothar leaned over to whisper into Rudolf's ear. "My father believes Hitler is a madman who will bring the downfall of Germany."

Rudolf's blue eyes opened wide; he was shocked by what Lothar said. "My grandfather says he has brought us prosperity. Just look at the number of U-boats we are building now. More people are working and we are beginning to stand up to the French and the English. *Opa* says we are becoming a stronger nation, even stronger than under the Kaiser. He believes Hitler will restore our national greatness."

Lothar laughed. "Yes, I know what your grandfather says. But I bet your grandmother doesn't say that. She won't even allow a picture of Hitler in your house!"

Rudolf was silent. Yes, he knew what his grandmother would say. She would begin by cursing the Nazis and Hitler's thugs, the S.A., those men in Brownshirts who brought Hitler to power and then she would carry on about Rudolf's father, but that was a long time ago. *Opa* explained to him that his father's death was an unfortunate accident, and Rudolf believed *Opa* with all his heart. Besides, *Der Führer* had renounced the Brownshirts. As for his mother, Rudolf was unsure what to think because *Opa* never spoke about her and Rudolf did not understand why *Oma* would get such a sour look on her face when he mentioned his mother.

The boys broke into a run as they heard the toll of the school bell, a warning that they needed to get into the schoolyard before the bell stopped clanging and their teacher stepped punctually out from the school entrance. To be late for G*ymnasium* was unpardonable and punishment would be quick from Herr Braun. Lothar, the first to reach the schoolyard, pushed open the gate and the rest of the boys piled in as fast as they could. They were just in time before their teacher came out of the building, a large three-story structure, painted yellow with white columns at the recessed door entrance.

Rudolf stood on the grass in a neat row with the other boys, greeting Herr Braun with "*Heil Hitler*," his thin arm jutting up in unison like a robot. The teacher greeted everyone in kind and began taking attendance. He was a small man with a neatly trimmed pointed beard and thick glasses. He always wore a dark suit with a bow tie and at all times carried a wooden pointer he used to tap on the blackboard to emphasize what he was talking about. Herr Braun exacted fear in Rudolf's heart because of his brutal punishment if homework was not completed. Although small of stature, Rudolf had seen Herr Braun inflict beatings on fellow students with his pointer that left raised welts.

The group of friends stood rigidly, breathing hard from their run into the schoolyard. Herr Braun eyed them suspiciously, but his eye landed on Lothar, his usual target of venom.

"You…Lothar, why are you breathing so heavy?"

Lothar, a gangly boy with sandy brown hair and a crooked smile, took a deep breath and began to explain but his throat was dry and only a croak came out.

"Well, I am waiting, Lothar," Herr Braun said.

Lothar tried to act in a nonchalant manner. "Herr Braun, I am breathing hard because I am out of breath."

A frown came to the small, pinched face of Herr Braun. "You are breathing hard because you are out of breath," the teacher yelled at him. "You nobody! You *pimpf!* Do you understand I want to know *why* you are out of breath?"

The teacher stepped beside Lothar and struck him hard on the side of the head with his pointer. There was dead silence among the students. No one dared make a sound or even look sympathetic toward Lothar for fear they would receive the same reaction from Herr Braun.

"Now, Lothar, are you going to tell me why you are out of breath?"

Lothar stood with his hand to the side of his head where a large red welt was beginning to form and his eyes filled with tears, but no sound of pain came from his throat. "Herr Braun, I am out of breath because I was running to get to the schoolyard. I was late."

"Ah, now Lothar, we get to the bottom of the problem. And why were you late?"

"Because I was talking."

"And what were you talking about?"

"About *Der Führer.*"

Herr Braun frowned, stepped back, and resumed his stance at the head of the class. His voice was a low growl. "And what could you possibly be saying about *Der Führer* at this time of the day on your way to *Gymnasium?*"

"Herr Braun, we were talking about *Der Führer's* visit to Bremen in a few days."

"And what about his visit? Were you making fun of *Der Führer*, you *pimpf?*"

"No, Herr Braun! I was not making fun of *Der Führer*," the boy's eyes opened wide in terror. "Herr Braun…I am…I am excited about seeing *Der Führer*, and I was only talking about his visit!"

The schoolmaster was quiet. Herr Braun considered Lothar unworthy to be a student in *Gymnasium*, even though the boy carried one of the highest grades in his class. *Gymnasium*, which focused on a liberal education, was not, Herr Braun believed, for a member of the lower class despite the display of mental brilliance. The teacher considered it beneath him to teach any student who did not have a decent social status, and besides, the boy's crooked smile irritated him. Lothar definitely was not headed for university, if he had anything to say about it.

"So, you are excited about *Der Führer's* visit? Do you know why our leader is visiting Bremen?" Herr Braun asked in a sarcastic tone.

"No, Herr Braun."

"No, I suppose you would not know since I doubt if your parents—mere bakers—read the newspaper. Well, Lothar," and then Herr Braun turned his head to eye the other students, "the reason *Der Führer* is coming to Bremen is to talk to us about the Nuremberg Laws that were put into effect last September. He is going to talk about the Jews—how they are an inferior, alien race, and how they affect all the rest of us. It is good to know because of these new laws, that Jews no longer are legal German citizens. We, the true Germans, without hesitation can run our beloved Fatherland without these aliens affecting our lives!"

The schoolmaster looked at Lothar. "Now do you understand why our leader is coming?"

"Yes, Herr Braun," Lothar said.

The schoolmaster reached up and adjusted his thick eyeglasses. He had enough of berating Lothar for the time being. It was past time to bring the students indoors for the lessons of the day.

"Boys...line up and march into the classroom," he said as he slapped the pointer against his right pant leg.

Lothar smiled his crooked smile at Rudolf. He saw Rudolf sneak a look at the angry red welt on the side of his head. "Rudi, don't look so worried. It doesn't hurt, not too bad anyway. "

Rudolf and Lothar sat together under a large Horse-chestnut tree in the schoolyard eating their noon meal. Rudolf had a thick piece of ham stuck into a Kaiser roll. Lothar eyed it with envy as he pulled a small piece of white cheese out of his sack. After peaking at his friend's wound, Rudolf handed him part of his lunch.

"Herr Braun always picks on you. Sometimes, I don't know how you stand it," Rudolf said, his voice sad.

"I look at it this way, Rudi: I'm a baker's son and I guess Herr Braun has a problem with that. My parents are proud that I have made it into *Gymnasium,* and they work extra hours because I am not at the bakery to help them. Because of that, I will take whatever punishment Herr Braun gives me just to have him as a teacher. He is the best—you know he is the best—and if I work hard enough I will get into university and make my father proud."

"You don't get any beatings at home when they see you have been hit by Herr Braun?" Rudolf asked in amazement.

"No. Father says I should be proud to have been hit by such an excellent teacher."

Rudolf wondered why Herr Braun had singled out Lothar rather than himself or any of the other boys who were late to school. Although he was the brightest boy in Herr Braun's class, and his hand was always raised to answer questions, Rudolf noticed Herr Braun seldom, if ever, called on him.

Lothar's thrashing could have been me, Rudolf reasoned. What if Lothar had said he was late because we were talking about *Der Führer,* but Lothar did not do that; Rudolf looked sideways again at Lothar's wound and felt a flood of gratefulness to his friend. Just coming home with a lump like that on the side of his head would raise the anger of his grandmother to a fever pitch, and then his grandfather would find out there was a problem at school. He knew he could deal with his grandmother's fury, but he never wanted his grandfather to confront him. Never.

Rudolf was aware he was taking a chance with his teacher by befriending Lothar. The teacher knew a great deal about all of the boys in his schoolroom: their siblings, friends, social standing, and community gossip about the family, and Rudolf had seen Herr Braun interfere in students' friendships.

Since he was five-years-old, Rudolf had heard the continual gossip in the neighborhood about his grandfather: Hermann's position as a supervisor at the AG Weser shipyard would have allowed the family to move into a finer apartment closer to the *Marktplatz*, the stylish center of Bremen near the Town Hall. But Hermann chose instead to stay in the old neighborhood because he felt more comfortable with neighbors he had known for many years, including Lothar's father and grandfather. Hermann Meier was highly respected in the working-class neighborhood, and Rudolf wondered if that was the reason Herr Braun chose not to intervene in his friendship with Lothar.

Rudolf unwittingly shook his head. What would it would be like to grow up with his own parents rather than his grandparents? His grandmother Luise was always unhappy about something, although Rudolf never knew for sure that he was the cause of her unhappiness. It seemed to him, however, that no matter what he did, she was unhappy.

"I wish I were as strong as you," Rudolf said. Suddenly, Rudolf decided he could no longer keep his secret longing from Lothar. "Can I tell you something that I have been thinking about for a long time?"

Lothar put down his food and looked at his friend. "You want to run away from home?"

Rudolf frowned. "No, Lothar, of course not! I want to become a member of the Hitler Youth."

Lothar began to laugh but when he saw the serious look on Rudolf's face, he stifled it. "*Mein Gott*, Rudi, why do you want to do that?"

"Because, Lothar, it will get me out of my grandmother's hands. You don't know what it is like, Lothar! She is constantly on me, giving me directions about the smallest of things; always checking on me. The only time I feel free is when I am outside with you and the others. I was talking to Peter, you know Peter Heinz don't you?"

" No."

"He is about fifteen years old. I'm not sure where he lives, across the river I think, but I met him one day when my grandfather took me to the shipyard. Peter was there with his father who works for my grandfather and we began talking about the Hitler Youth. He has been a member for two years and he particularly enjoys the freedom he has from his parents. He said he loves the precision marching, and the camping out in the forest. Oh, Lothar! There is not only marching and camping, but members learn different sports like rowing, boxing, and they have war games!"

Lothar frowned. "It sounds nice, Rudi, but I am not sure I would like all that marching. When would you have time to play Sardines?"

Rudolf did not have time to answer because the noon break was almost over. But his friend's question made him think about his favorite game of tag. Rudolf wondered if Lothar was right—if he joined the Hitler Youth, would he have time to play Sardines.

Chapter 5

September 1944
Arizona

Rudolf sat between Helmut Kessler and Werner Carl, waiting for the rest of the POWs to file into the recreation building for their Sunday movie. Helmut, a tall, thin man with a friendly face, reached in his pocket and took out the small Bible returned to him by the American teenager. He opened it and showed the inside front cover to Rudolf. Written in Helmut's fine handwriting, was information about the three U-boats Helmut had served on, including the Commanders' names.

"This little Bible means so much to me," Helmut said. "I am grateful that farmer's son found it. I would like to give him something for what he did, but I have no idea what that would be."

Helmut handed the Bible to Rudolf, who looked carefully at the treasured book, turning the pages slowly, reading the inscriptions.

"I am surprised," Rudolf said, "that the interrogators at Fort Hunt did not take this from you, Helmut. It lists every boat you served on!"

Helmut nodded. "Yes, I know. They questioned me carefully, but each boat sank after I transferred off—well, except U-893. Besides, from some of the things they said, I realized the Americans knew more than we like to think! I got it back because they had no use for it."

Helmut shook his head. "I am amazed by the American boy. I cannot imagine why he took the effort to find it."

Rudolf shrugged. He felt confused by the kindness of Ruth Feller and her son, and he remained disturbed by Bob's question about *Der*

Führer. Suddenly, he said without much thought, "Do you have anything from your uniform? Perhaps you could give him your U-boat badge."

Helmut was silent for a moment, thinking. "The Bible means so much to me, and the boy did me a great favor. Still, my U-boat badge is the only thing I have that the American guards have not taken…"

Rudolf could see Helmut mulling over the prospect of giving away his medal and he wondered why he had even suggested it. Perplexed by his own behavior, Rudolf looked down at his newly blistered hands in disgust. He could not understand his muddled thinking regarding the American family. Then, Rudolf felt Helmut nudge him and looked over to see the other man's face lit with a bright smile, "Well, I have nothing else of value," Helmut said. "*Ja! Ja!* What an idea, Rudi!"

Helmut took the small Bible from Rudolf, and rubbed it lovingly with his fingertips. "You know, my U-boat badge was given to me after my first two war patrols when I served on U-17. One of the interrogators at Fort Hunt threatened to keep the badge if I didn't tell him what U-893 was doing off the coast of that place…South Carolina, I think. I felt lucky then not to be an officer or work in the control room. What did I know, I told him. I was just a lowly machinist stuck in the bowels of the boat. I must have convinced him because he did not bother me after that."

Rudolf nodded in confirmation to Helmut's remark. "Yes, I felt the same way. I was glad not to be the chief radio operator. My interrogator plied me with beer and cigarettes, but when he figured I was on the boat only three months, he left me alone."

Helmut, Rudolf knew, was older than most of the men on U-893. The two men shared the same barrack, their cots close to one another, and Rudolf often heard Helmut speak about his wife and two daughters. Whenever there was news on the camp's stolen radio about Allied bombing of German cities, a look of heaviness would descend over Helmut, changing his normal friendly visage to one with deep apprehension. Often, in the stillness of the desert night, when the two men lay thinking of home, Rudolf and Helmut would commiserate softly with one another about their fate and their worry about their families.

"My family considers it lucky I was captured by the Americans," Helmut said, tucking his Bible safely into his pocket. "My wife, Helga, says she doesn't worry about me now like she did when I was a U-boat machinist." Then he laughed. "She knows I'm being fed three meals a day and I'm not going to die here!"

Werner Carl made a noise deep in his throat. "Dying of boredom is what we need to be afraid of!"

Rudolf ignored Werner and spoke to Helmut. "My grandfather and grandmother feel the same as your wife," Rudolf said. "They are glad I am safe with the Americans, and not in the hands of the Russians." He paused and said, half-heartedly, "Well, as safe as we can be I suppose…"

A soft look came to his face as he thought of his grandparents who raised him. His grandfather whose bearing was as threatening as the U-boats he built, yet Rudolf remembered how tender-hearted his grandfather was toward him. His grandmother, Luise, on the other hand, had a fiery temperament, scolding him one minute and then kissing him on the top of his head to make up for her verbal abuse.

The roomful of men quieted as their camp leader *Fregattenkapitän* Jürgen Wattenberg came before the enlisted men. He was a towering man, 6'3", austere, correct and considered old to be a submarine captain at the age of forty-two.

"Men, we need to make good use of our time here," Wattenberg said, "which should not be long because the Fatherland will triumph in the end!"

The men clapped loudly and whistles pierced the air. Wattenberg held up his hand for quiet. "But while we are here, especially for the new men who arrived several weeks ago from the camp in Florida, there are study courses in the evenings in French, English, Italian, history, commerce, law—take your pick. Do not waste your time sitting around and bemoaning your fate. We are proud members of the German Navy and we will survive this period of internment!"

Helmut leaned over to Rudolf, "I have heard that lecturers discuss interrogation techniques in case we are ever sent back to Fort Hunt."

"Is that a possibility?" Rudolf asked.

"I don't know, but they prepare us anyway," Helmut said.

Werner listened to their conversation and leaned over to whisper hoarsely, "I hear they also talk about how to stay free once we manage to escape!"

"Yes, yes," Helmut said with excitement, "The Geneva Convention, you know, recognizes escape. At least three articles in the convention establish the right of every prisoner of war to escape if he gets the chance!"

Rudolf smiled as he imagined slipping from under the barbed wire, heading for the Mexican border where beautiful women waited, but his day dream was short lived when the lights dimmed and the film, *Young Mr. Lincoln,* flashed across the screen. Several men sitting near Rudolf hooted, yelling out for a rousing Western with a climatic shootout.

"Who picks these anyway?" Werner grumbled loudly. "Why are we suffering an American history lesson?"

Rudolf agreed. He had studied the American Civil War in *Gymnasium,* recalling the war as an absurd struggle where Americans killed one another to free men not of their own race. To Rudolf's thinking, it was further proof of American stupidity.

Some POWs left in disgust, including Werner, but Rudolf watched the film carefully, trying to discern the propaganda. Abe Lincoln was depicted as an affable fellow, slow to anger, heroically stopping a crowd of men intent on lynching two brothers charged with murder. As the film ended, Rudolf realized the message was a celebration of individuality as opposed to State control. He shook his head in disgust, and said to Helmut, "The Americans are always trying to foist their individualism shit on us."

"Yes," Helmut agreed. "Well, it won't work. We Germans believe in sacrifice for our beloved Germany!"

Rudolf nodded his assent. He wondered why freedom of the individual was so important to Americans. Was not the State more important? His *Gymnasium* classes emphasized that, and so did the Hitler Youth, and those stalwart German institutions could not be wrong. To Rudolf, individualism—doing what one wanted for oneself—was a sign of a weak society, and America was indeed a prime example with its discordant democracy; a cacophony of voices rather than the single brilliant voice of *Der Führer*.

As Rudolf and Helmut walked toward their barrack after the movie, he again reassured himself that Germany's strength was its State, the national community. With that confirming thought, Rudolf's tenseness eased as he intentionally tucked away the troubling vision of Germany's borders encircled by its enemies.

The wind blew hard from the east, buffeting the two men as they walked across the compound, the powdery earth rising in swirls about their feet. Usually the wind blew from the west and dropped off around sundown. That was when the dust of the day would grip the edge of the sky and twirl it into a magnificent blaze of magenta and orange, but not this night. A strange opaque color permeated the void beyond the camp, making Rudolf vaguely uncomfortable.

Helmut said he wanted to write a letter to his wife before going to sleep, so Rudolf walked alone toward the Crosscut Canal and lit a cigarette he bummed earlier off Werner, cupping his hand over the match, with his back to the wind. Inexplicably drawn to the compound fence where freedom beckoned, he could hear the wind whistling through Hole-in-the-Rock nearby. It was an eerie sound like no other he consciously remembered and, in that moment, a crippling fear gripped his stomach, making him suddenly queasy. Rudolf hurriedly pinched the end of his cigarette—to save it—and put it into his pocket; he desperately needed the safety of his barrack.

As he headed back, he remembered uneasily that this unreasonable fear had pounced on him throughout his life like a stalking mountain lion, in the oddest of situations. He felt the same when he was 12-years-old and had to summon the courage to ask his grandfather if he could join the Hitler Youth. Why the moaning sound in the middle of the Arizona desert would affect him so, he could not imagine.

Chapter 6

May 1936
AG Weser Shipyard
Bremen, Germany

H ermann Meier sat straight in his chair in the bow torpedo room of U-26. He was incredibly uncomfortable, although he tried desperately not to show it by wiping his sweaty hands carefully under the table with the clean white handkerchief he always carried in his pocket.

Someone touched his shoulder, and when he looked up, he saw it was one of the shipyard owners, a man of great wealth and prestige. The man smiled at Hermann.

"She is beautiful, is she not, Hermann?" said Ludwig von Clausen, referring to the 750-ton boat designed to prove to Great Britain the strength of the *Kriegsmarine*, the Third Reich's new war navy.

"Yes," Hermann replied, shyly. That von Clausen would even speak to him was of momentary shock. He took a large gulp of air to calm his nerves, making a mental note to relate the day's events to Luise.

Hermann noticed the U-boat's deadly torpedo tubes were hid behind bright swastika flags. Fine linen tablecloths covered the long table along with colorful spring flowers, and champagne glasses were placed in front of every chair. Hermann nodded to several men he knew who were senior yard managers, but he did not have the slightest knowledge who the rest of the guests were, although he guessed they were dignitaries from the Third Reich and the German Navy.

At the head of the table was a man Hermann had not seen before. To the left of the unknown man was *Kapitänleutnant* Hartmann. Suddenly the unknown man stood and as he did, Hermann realized with a shock he was *Kriegsmarine* Commander-in-Chief Erich Raeder. Everyone, including Hermann stood up.

A prim man, Raeder did not smile but instead seemed to look straight ahead at no one in particular. "This is a momentous day," Raeder said. "I am extremely grateful to the men at AG Weser for their work on this magnificent U-boat. She will be of great pride to the *Kriegsmarine* and to the Third Reich. U-26 and her sister boat, U-25, is but the beginning of a new life for the U-boat arm of the German Navy. The German people need never worry again about the security of their ports."

Everyone applauded and then the *Kapitänleutnant* popped open a bottle of champagne to the roar of the crowd. Crewman suddenly appeared and opened more bottles to fill the guests' glasses. When all was ready, the crowd lifted their arms high with champagne bubbling over onto the tablecloths.

"To the U-26!" Hartmann shouted, and they all cheered.

When they sat down again, the men at the table began to talk to one another, but Hermann Meier did not know anyone and so he focused on the tablecloth in front of him, wishing he could somehow get up and leave, yet he knew he could not commit such a grievous error in manners. If anything, he would be one of the last to leave, most certainly not the first. He looked up and took in the view of the torpedo room, seeing the many pieces of equipment crowded in a small space. There was hardly enough room to breathe with all of these men together and his thoughts suddenly turned to his son Erich, a U-boat crewman on UB-85 during WW I.

He sadly remembered the fierce arguments with Erich about becoming a U-boat crewman. Hermann wanted Erich to become a welder like himself at the yard, a job that would possibly keep him out of the military, but Erich wanted to join the *Reichsmarine*, the German Navy under the Kaiser.

Luise, Hermann recalled, took Erich's side in the argument.

"Hermann, Erich is a young man and wants some adventure in his life," Luise told him as they lay in bed together after their son's announcement. "I am worried, yes, about his safety, but I understand his longing to see places other than Bremen."

"*Mein Gott,* what are you saying, Luise?" Hermann asked. "I build those U-boats, but as I swear to God in heaven, you would not catch me inside one on the open sea!"

Luise laughed despite herself. "Yes, Hermann, but you fear the open sea and Erich does not suffer from that. One way or the other, the Kaiser will get him into the military with this awful war, better it be on a U-boat than in one of those dreadful trenches!"

A cold sweat broke out on Hermann's forehead sitting now on board U-26, almost two decades later. He took out his handkerchief again, wiped his face, and looked slowly around him, hoping no one saw his distress as he remembered clearly his horror when Erich was assigned to UB-85, one of thirty-six coastal torpedo attack boats made at AG Weser during the Great War. Hermann himself worked on that boat, and, at first, he was relieved knowing the perfection put into the building of it, and then a terrible thought crept into his mind. Perhaps it was not flawless after all, perhaps he had made some stupid blunder while working on the boat and in some way, he would be responsible for the death of all the crewmen and his own son.

Hermann's job, unlike those other men sitting at the celebratory table, had consequences—deadly consequences. He looked around and felt a stab of envy. He doubted if they carried home the weight of their work like he did. Still, if he thought about it with a clear head, most of the U-boats he worked on were lost because they had been in the keen sights of the enemy. Yet whenever workmanship problems disabled a boat built at AG Weser, he and his men felt the might of their mistakes. In the shadows, behind closed doors of the Third Reich, they were called *Du dummer Idiots* and blamed for problems the boat developed when the sailors were in deadly situations.

Erich had served on UB-85 from November 1917 until April 1918, Hermann remembered. The boat completed two war patrols, but on the fateful day of April 30 while diving to evade gunfire from the

British Royal Navy ship, the *Coreopsis*, the submarine began taking on water because the hatch malfunctioned. The boat resurfaced and the crew escaped under fire from British patrol vessels; the men, including Erich were picked up, spending the rest of the war in an internment camp in England. Badly wounded in the right arm, Erich never recovered the full use of it.

And Hermann, who continued wiping his sweaty forehead, was never free from guilt.

Chapter 7

November 1944
Arizona

Rudolf cursed his fate. Picking cotton was worse than treating lice and crabs on his shipmates' peckers, a radio operator's secondary job in the absence of a doctor. Searching through intimate body parts made him nauseous, much to the delight of the men on U-893, but picking cotton was far worse; it was a degrading exercise in utter monotony.

It was also dirty work—not because the cotton itself was soiled, but because of the changing working conditions. The first hard frost had arrived in mid-November, popping open the most mature of the cotton bolls, nature's protective cover for the cotton that withered in the cold and turned brown with hard vengeful edges that grabbed at Rudolf's hands. With each successive frost, more bolls popped open. If the ground was wet from rain, Rudolf and the other prisoners worked in mud, slogging from bush to bush, dragging their six-foot-long bags. More often than not, however, the days were windy, and then they worked in constant flowing dust, the pickers resembling giant insects with long tails.

Ruth Feller was always there, early in the morning, directing the men, encouraging them with her ready smile to pick their one hundred pounds a day. She walked often to her truck, parked near the ditch bank, checking on her husband who sat inside with a blanket covering his legs and his stained fedora on his head. By mid-morning, she would take him back to the house not far from the picking fields.

At lunch break, she stood again by the ditch bank, handing out food, and returned at intervals during the afternoon to check on the men's progress.

Catching glimpses of Ruth Feller throughout the day, Rudolf sensed the strength it took for her to guide the workers, tend to her sick husband, and prepare food for the prisoners. There seemed no one else to help her except her son. Unwittingly, Rudolf compared her with German women toiling in the harvest fields while their men were at war, and he felt odd for doing it, equating an American woman with stalwart German women. He had always pictured American women as spoiled, spending time primping while nigger maids tended their households and raised their children. Rudolf realized Ruth Feller did not fit that image and it unsettled him as he moved mindlessly through the thick rows of cotton pulling the white harvest and stuffing it by the handfuls into his trailing bag.

A sharp pain in his hand suddenly made Rudolf yelp like a coyote pup. He dropped the cotton he was picking and turned his hand up and saw a sharp piece of hardened boll stuck in his palm. Furiously, he dug it out with his fingernails, blood running down his arm. Then with his teeth, he tore off a piece of material from the bottom of his shirt, wrapping his hand awkwardly, trying to stop the bleeding, and cursing violently as he did. The thought came to him as he stood tethered to a cotton bag that he should have listened to his grandfather, who urged him to apply to the *Kriegsmarine* as an officer cadet.

"*Mein Gott,* Rudolf!" his grandfather had said to him before he graduated from *Gymnasium.* "You have the chance to become an officer, an officer! Do you not realize what that will bring you? Better pay, privileges, and respect, above all, respect."

But Rudolf, thoroughly soaked in the propaganda of the Hitler Youth, desired only to give his life for the eternal glory of the Fatherland. "I want to be on the front lines of the war," Rudolf said, "fighting now for Germany, for our *Führer*! I don't want to waste my time studying to become an officer. What if the war ends and I have missed it?"

Opa had mutely shaken his head in disbelief, and Rudolf wondered now at his stupidity. Captured officers were not required to work in the

41

fields, according to the Geneva Convention. He could be sitting in the barrack planning his escape to Mexico instead of doing this grueling, demeaning work.

The cold late autumn wind blew mercilessly, whipping the ever-present dust around Rudolf's feet as he dragged his bag through the cotton. He wondered bitterly how a place like Arizona could be so hot and then so cold and then the memory of freezing Soviet weather came upon him, where every movement was a fight against the elements. Rudolf decided his disgust with picking cotton was nothing compared to the compulsory Reich Labor Service where he spent six wretched months on the Eastern Front prior to joining the *Kriegsmarine.*

It was there, on the road to Stalingrad, in the brutal weather, that he and other young Germans supported the *Wehrmacht,* clearing frozen roadways of broken tanks, trucks, and human remains. Rudolf's taste for war turned sour when he experienced rotting flesh and weeping refugees laden with their meager possessions, caught like pawns on a chess board in the wrath of two bloodthirsty armies. He also saw what happened when German soldiers captured Russian soldiers; they were shot on the spot.

Guilt flooded Rudolf. He was alive after all, with a full belly, and for the most part fairly treated by the Americans.

Rudolf looked up from his picking and noticed Bob Feller not far from him, laboring like the other prisoners of war. Bob saw Rudolf and smiled.

Despite himself, Rudolf responded to the American. "I have not seen you lately," he called out. "Where have you been?"

"Playing football, but the season just ended," Bob said.

"You play soccer in America?" Rudolf asked, surprised.

"No, not soccer. We play football, American football."

"Oh, sorry," Rudolf said. "I do not know about American football."

The teenager dropped his bag of cotton and walked over to Rudolf. "Say, I asked my mom and dad if you and the man who lost his Bible could come to Thanksgiving dinner at our house. They said it would be OK. We have to get permission from the camp commander, but we've had men from the camp for dinner before, so I don't think it would be a problem."

Rudolf's blue eyes opened wide in surprise. "Your mother and father would allow us to come to dinner?"

"Yeah, sure. Why not?"

"But we are from Germany. We are fighting a war with your country!"

Bob laughed—it was the wonderful sound of youthful mirth, his dark head thrown back in merriment. "Yes, of course, that's true. But you and your friend are not fighting us right now, you're picking our cotton!"

Rudolf nodded, accepting Bob's explanation. "Yes, I see what you are saying. But what is this 'Thanksgiving' you Americans celebrate?"

"Well, the Thanksgiving legend is that people who came to America from England, the Pilgrims, celebrated their first harvest back in 1621," Bob said. "They wanted to give thanks to God for the food they raised, and they shared their harvest with the Indians. Nowadays, it's a time families get together and eat lots of good food. I can hardly wait. There's a big roasted turkey, sweet potatoes and mashed potatoes, and lots of pies, pumpkin, apple, and mincemeat. Supposedly, we eat food like the Pilgrims ate on the first Thanksgiving—but I doubt that."

Rudolf envisioned a table laden with delicious food and a day away from the confines of the desolate camp. For a brief moment, he wondered if he should reject the American's invitation out of hand, but the growl of his stomach told him otherwise. "I will talk to Helmut. I am sure he would be happy to come to your Thanksgiving, as would I. Thank you."

Suddenly, the old truck driven by Ruth Feller came into view and Bob waived down his mother. "Come on, Rudi. My mom will put a clean bandage on that cut."

Bob Feller climbed into the truck to fetch Rudolf and Helmut from Camp Papago Park for Thanksgiving dinner. He shifted the seat back to give his long legs more room, adjusted the rearview mirror, the side mirror and started the motor, slowly letting off the parking brake. This Bob's first time to drive so far from the farm since he obtained his driver's license, and he wanted to be precise in his driving skills.

He heard a tapping noise on the window and turned to see his mother standing beside the truck. She held a Thermos in her hand, and he rolled down the window.

"Here, son, I thought you would like some coffee. It's cold this morning."

"Thanks, Mom." He reached out the window to get it.

"Now be careful and don't get so involved in talking with Rudi that you don't watch what you're doing," she said.

"Yes, mom, I'll be careful," he said with a sigh.

Bob looked up at the wide expanse of Arizona sky, crystal clear except for a smattering of fluffy white clouds hugging the mountains to the north. As he pulled onto the road that stretched with open arms before him, he took a deep breath of the cool air, so different now from the heaviness of summer heat, and his heart surged when he viewed the beauty of the desert landscape. It was a land he treasured.

Ahead lay the prospect of a day that would allow him to learn more about the German prisoners of war. Excited, Bob headed toward Papago Park, the 1500-acre plot that the residents of Phoenix used as their summer refuge, where children climbed the intriguing rock formations and swam in the Arizona Crosscut Canal during blistering days while parents watched under lacy Palo Verde trees. The internment camp was but a small portion of Papago Park.

When Bob arrived at the camp's guard gate, he presented a letter from the commander which allowed the Feller family to pick up Rudolf Meier and Helmut Kessler for Thanksgiving. The surly attitude of the guard surprised him.

"How do we know you're not going to drive them across the border?" the guard asked with a growl.

Bob laughed. "What, on Thanksgiving? Are you kidding?"

"Well, I dunno. You look too young to be picking up these Krauts. Why didn't your parents come for them?" the guard questioned.

The teen smiled, just like his mother. "Well, sergeant, my mom is cooking dinner, so she couldn't do it, and my dad is too sick to drive. So, I'm the only one left."

For a long moment, the guard stared at Bob, finally saying, "OK, young man, but be careful. These U-boat guys are dangerous. You've got two sure-fire Nazis on your hands. You wouldn't want to be responsible for them committing any acts of sabotage, now would you?"

Bob realized he had never considered such a thing. He sat up straight in his seat and looked directly at the guard. "No, sir."

The guard scowled again at the paperwork and then grudgingly allowed Bob to drive through the gate, pointing him to an administration building. The teenager parked the truck and walked into the structure, again showing the letter to an officer who manned the front desk.

"So, you're taking Meier and Kessler home for Thanksgiving, are you?" the officer asked.

"Yes, sir," Bob answered.

"Well, I wish I were coming along. It would be wonderful to have some home cooking," he said ruefully, then dutifully returned to the business at hand, logging out Meier and Kessler. "OK," he said finally. "They'll be here in a few minutes."

Bob sat down on a bench against a wall, facing a framed picture of President Franklin Roosevelt. An American flag hung from a pole in the corner. He looked at the picture of the president with fondness, and then considered the two men coming to his home for Thanksgiving.

No doubt, he thought, they felt the same about their leader, Adolf Hitler. That was a reasonable assumption, Bob knew, but how could they? Hitler was a mad man and Roosevelt was trying to protect America from Hitler's ruthless domination of the world. Then the thought struck him: Could it be possible these Germans think the same about Roosevelt?

That reflection quickly passed from his mind as the side door opened and Bob saw Rudolf and Helmut dressed in clean PW denim pants and shirts and their gray leather U-boat coats.

Bob jumped up and smiled at the two men, extending his hand in welcome.

"We are anxious to know about this day of Thanksgiving," Rudolf said, acknowledging the offer of friendship.

Helmut nodded and smiled, grabbing Bob's hand with both of his own, saying, "*Ja! Ja!*"

When they left the building, Bob noticed other farm families coming into camp to pick up prisoners for Thanksgiving, and he wondered if the irritable guard was also surly to them. Trying not to feel singled out because of his age, the teenager decided the cause of soldier's short temper was because he had guard duty on Thanksgiving Day.

All three climbed into the truck, Rudolf sitting next to Bob and Helmut next to the door. Bob concentrated on his driving skills while he pulled past the short-tempered guard, then he looked over at the two POWs. "I wasn't sure that guard was going to let me pick you up," he said.

Rudolf spoke in quick German to Helmut, who laughed. Rudolf replied to Bob, "Yes, he thinks we are all Nazis." After a pause, Rudolf said, "Americans do not understand there is a strict separation between politics and the armed forces, carried over from the days of the Weimar Republic. Men of the German armed forces cannot hold membership in the Nazi party!"

Bob's eyes widened in surprise. Oh, how he wanted to delve deeper into what Rudolf said, but he remembered his mother's admonition. Instead, he spoke about Thanksgiving.

"I think Thanksgiving is the best of the holidays. We always had lots of people at the house, more than a dozen," Bob said, his voice a bit forlorn. "But, you know…some of them have passed away, and the gasoline rationing has forced the rest to stay closer to home."

"Are you not rationed?" Rudolf asked.

"Well, we are rationed for gas, but not as much as most people," Bob said. "As farmers, the government gives us an allotment based on our acreage, so that helps…still we have to be careful."

Bob glanced over at the two Germans he was driving home for Thanksgiving, two men who loved Germany and made war on America, and America in turn made war on Germany. He wondered bitterly what it was about war that so entangled the human species.

Rudolf climbed the steps up to the long porch that provided shade along the front of the farm house, following Bob and Helmut. He noticed a swing at the end of the porch, and he suddenly wondered what it would be like to sit there looking over the cotton fields as the rays of the dying sun colored the white crop with a golden tint. Rudolf's longing for a different life momentarily engulfed him and then when he stepped into the foyer, the tantalizing smell of food embraced him in such an exciting way that he was unsure if he were not committing treason in his heart by wanting to eat this Thanksgiving dinner with an American family.

Bob led the men to the living room where his father, Vern, stood up from his rocking chair and smiled, extending his hand in welcome. Rudolf noticed he had been reading a newspaper when they came in and had folded it carefully, laying it down so that the front page war news was hidden. The teenager introduced Rudolf and Helmut and then Rudolf heard Ruth Feller's voice. He turned toward the dining room to see her wiping her hands on her apron.

"Hello, boys," she said, her voice cherry. "I'm glad you've come... just in time, too! Bob, dear, I need some help in the kitchen." She disappeared behind the swinging kitchen door, Bob hurrying to catch up with her.

Vern, a tall, pale man with graying hair motioned the men to follow him into the dining room where he poured each a glass of wine, his hand shaking noticeably as he handed Rudolf and Helmut their glass.

"I'm glad you could come," Vern said to Rudolf. "Ruth and I—and Bob, of course—thought you would enjoy getting away from the camp for a while."

"Thank you for inviting us," Rudolf said and then he turned to Helmut and interpreted Vern's words.

The kitchen door swung open and Bob emerged with a large platter holding a glistening turkey, golden brown. He set the bird carefully on a sideboard for his father to carve and then went back into the kitchen.

Rudolf looked at the dining table with its lace tablecloth and sparkling settings of crystal and silverware. A bouquet of purple and white chrysanthemums graced the table's center, and then he noticed the porcelain. Moving closer, Rudolf's mind reeled. The Feller's porcelain seemed to have the same rose pattern his grandmother cherished. A sharp pang hit Rudolf as he recalled a delicate cup and saucer that sat high on a shelf in his grandmother's kitchen, only brought down on special occasions.

It cannot be, Rudolf thought. While Ruth and Bob were still in the kitchen, and Vern was busy carving the turkey at the sideboard, Rudolf quickly reached over and picked up one of the dinner plates. On the bottom was the famous Meissen porcelain trademark with its crossed-swords, so cherished in German households. He set the dish down immediately, but Helmut saw his action, and raised his eyebrows in surprise. Rudolf smiled weakly, guilt flooding over him for his improper behavior.

The beauty of the table setting tugged at Rudolf's heart for it brought the vision of his grandmother's table, always set properly with a clean tablecloth. If the meal was a special one, she poured her rich coffee into the precious Meissen cup and sipped it gingerly, holding it in both hands as if it were a chalice, then finally placing the cup gently in its saucer when she finished. At the end of the meal, *Oma* always turned the cup over and showed Rudolf the swords, emphasizing that only German craftsmen could make such exquisite china prized by kings and popes. Then she would give him a warning to never touch her precious Meissen. Remembering the sound of her voice, a small shiver passed down his spine and he wondered how he could have that reaction so many years later in a place infinitely different than Germany.

The coincidence of the same porcelain was not lost on Rudolf, although he made no mention of it. Curiously, however, he began to feel some affection for the American family, much against his right-minded German will. Their genuine hospitality softened him, and in that moment of understanding, Rudolf realized the Fellers were not the enemy; indeed, they were simply reaching out to two lonely men trapped in their country. Would he do the same? Rudolf shook his head in wonderment. He did not know the answer to that.

As Ruth placed the last dish of enticing food on the table, Vern invited everyone to sit. Ruth and Vern Feller sat facing each other at opposite ends while Bob sat alone on one side and the two Germans on the other. Then Vern looked over at Rudolf. "The tradition of Thanksgiving is to say a prayer before the meal. I hope you and Helmut won't mind."

Blessed are You, Lord our God,
King of the Universe, who has granted us life, sus-
tained us, and enabled us to reach this occasion.
We thank God for giving us life, for sustaining us, and then
our task is to focus on the Universe and all of its wonder.

The first course was a steaming tureen of soup. Bob carried the large vessel to each person while Ruth ladled the cream of tomato into serving bowls.

A high-pitched laugh bubbled up from Ruth's throat as she filled Rudolf's bowl with the hot bisque. "This was made to open your taste buds, but I don't think you boys need prompting!"

The food's delicious smell overwhelmed Rudolf. He had never celebrated a feast like Thanksgiving, not even at home in Bremen. U-boat provisions were substantial, but portions depended on how long the boat had been at sea. If the crew was lucky, sometimes there would be a restock of food and fuel from a German supply ship, but that was not often. As for camp, Rudolf had little complaint because the helpings were generous, even if it was not always tasty.

But this meal was entirely different. Helmut rubbed his eyes as if he could not believe what he saw, and Rudolf took another deep breath, a way to implant the memory of this special meal.

First, Vern passed the heaped platter of roasted turkey. Along with the turkey came oyster dressing, giblet gravy, cranberry sauce, whipped potatoes, and a sweet potato casserole made with maple syrup, orange rind and chopped nuts. Bowls of green peas and Brussels sprouts swam in butter, not yellow-colored margarine. Large black olives and stuffed celery crowded delicate crystal dishes and hot Parker House Rolls lay in a basket covered with starched linen.

"*Mein Gott*," Helmut exclaimed as he licked his lips, "What a wonderful day this is!"

Rudolf nodded, and translated the comment to Ruth, whose smile of pleasure lit up the room. He noticed Ruth looked entirely different than usual. Her dark hair, normally pulled back in a bun, curled softly about her face and she wore a bright lipstick. Her gray stylish dress with padded shoulders was made of fine silk, very different from the plain housedresses she wore as she walked through the fields encouraging the POWs.

All was quiet except for the clink of crystal as Vern refilled wine glasses and silverware tinkled on porcelain. At first, Rudolf and Helmut politely gave themselves small helpings, but after seeing how Bob and Vern piled their plates high, on the second go-around, the Germans became less restrained.

Amid light conversation, the U-boat men ate as if this were their last meal. Rudolf filled his stomach to excess, and he wanted to loosen his belt but he knew that would be unacceptable conduct. Instead, he pushed back slightly from the table, as imperceptibly as he possibly could, set down his fork and took a deep breath. His feeling of satisfaction was almost as good as his first sexual experience with a woman.

With the clearing of the table, Ruth served everyone a large slice of pumpkin pie and hot coffee. It was then that the farm couple asked their guests many questions, with Rudolf translating for Helmut. Ruth was curious about their home and families, while Vern was particularly interested in their U-boat service.

Bob sat quietly through the conversations, itching to get to the real questions, those that came to him while sitting in his civics class—what

Rudi thought about National Socialism, about Hitler, about the war, and if he questioned the rationale for any of it—but he didn't dare ask during Thanksgiving dinner, remembering again his mother's lecture that morning about being a polite young man.

Instead, Bob closely watched the two Germans as they interacted with his parents. Rudolf was polite, but always on guard, while Helmut loved to talk, glad to satisfy Vern's questions with stories of his perilous life at sea aboard the three U-boats he had served on. Rudolf had a certain aura about him, Bob noticed, particularly because of the cleft in his chin which gave him a he-man look that teenage girls would probably swoon over. If what he saw in Movie Tone newsreels were true, Rudolf certainly fit the stereotype of a Nazi with his dark blond hair and the way he held himself—like he had goose-stepped a thousand miles. That was another question Bob burned to ask. Did Rudolf goose-step?

As they finished their dessert, Helmut suddenly pushed back his chair and stood rigid as if he were in formation before his commander. He clicked his heels together and gave a proud salute of *Sieg Heil*. Stunned by his performance, the Feller family listened as Rudolf announced that his fellow U-boat crewman had something to say.

Helmut put his hand in his pocket and brought out the small Bible that Bob found near the irrigation ditch weeks ago. He spoke with great feeling—apparent by the tone of his voice—about the little book and its meaning to him. He waited while Rudolf translated, and then, with a flourish, he retrieved his U-boat badge from another pocket.

The brass badge was a wreath of oak leaves surrounding the silhouette of a U-boat. Above the German vessel, at the top of the wreath, the national emblem of the Third Reich, the eagle and the swastika, stood in gilded glory.

Before any of the Feller family could comment, Helmut was at Bob's side, bowing politely. Then he presented the medal to the teenager. Bob flushed with bewilderment and glanced at Rudolf, who said, "It is yours, Bob. Helmut is grateful for the return of his Bible, and he wants you to have his badge."

Bob got up from the table and stood facing Helmut. Blushing, he nervously pushed back a lock of hair from his forehead. "This medal means a lot to you, I know. I…I will treasure it always. Thank you, Helmut."

Helmut listened to the translation and nodded his head. He smiled, shook Bob's hand, and returned to his chair.

There was much more coffee and talk—about the cotton crop and the various activities of the camp, particularly the upcoming variety show put on by the POWs that farm families were invited to attend. Finally, by late afternoon, the Germans got up from the table and retrieved their leather coats. At the door, Ruth presented them with packages of cookies, and they gave their thanks and farewell. As the two men walked to the truck with Bob, Rudolf stopped for a moment in the yard and looked back at the farmhouse with Ruth and Vern standing in the doorway. The look on his face told Bob everything: Rudolf longed for home.

On the way back to camp, the men were silent. With the long road stretching ahead, Bob caught himself wondering about the two men sitting next to him, benignly holding his mother's cookies. Did they think about escape? The guard at the gate was certainly concerned about him being alone with them, and Bob realized these two strong Germans could easily overpower him, take the truck, and head for Mexico. Yet Bob refused to focus on that possibility, hoping instead that he and his parents had judged Rudolf and Helmut correctly to be good men caught in a war not of their making. Still, Bob remembered Rudolf's menacing attitude toward the American guards that day when Helmut lost his Bible.

He glanced over at Rudolf who seemed to be lost in thought, and asked without warning, "Rudi, do you like to read?"

"Yes, I do. Why do you ask?"

"Oh, I just wondered if you ever read anything by Ernest Hemmingway," Bob said.

"No, but I know he is a popular American writer. The Third Reich banned Hemmingway's books, so I never had the chance to read him. My grandmother once told me she read one of his novels and she said the sadness of it affected her deeply."

"Do you know which novel that was?" Bob asked, curious.

"It was a war novel, about an American ambulance driver, I think."

"Oh, yes," Bob said, "That would be *A Farewell to Arms.*"

They fell silent through the long miles, finally reaching the camp gate. The guard waved them through and once more Bob drove to the administration building, parking carefully. They all climbed out of the truck and Bob walked them into the building, making sure the men were properly checked in. Helmut said his farewell and moved through the door to the camp enclosure, but Rudolf hesitated for a moment.

"This Thanksgiving day that you Americans celebrate brought back memories of my home in Bremen." There was a catch in the German's voice. "You were right Bob. The food was wonderful. Thank you."

Bob nodded. "Yes, it's my favorite meal of the year."

They looked at one another, and Bob wished he knew more about this German who yearned for home. Then, as Rudolf turned to go, Bob said suddenly, "Can you wait a minute? I have something in the truck for you."

The teenager rushed out the door and returned quickly with a book in his hand.

"Here...it's Hemmingway's *For Whom the Bell Tolls.* I just finished it. I...I think you should read it," Bob said, handing it to Rudolf.

Rudolf turned the book over in his hands, looking at it carefully. "Why is that?" Rudolf asked. There was a curious note in his voice.

"Because," Bob said, "it's about a man who stays true to himself amid the crisis of war."

Chapter 8

May 1936
Bremen, Germany

It seemed to Rudolf as if the whole of Bremen had gathered to see *Der Führer*. There were so many people in the plaza it almost felt like a carnival. He nudged his friend Lothar because he saw their teacher Herr Bauer standing across the plaza.

"Look," Rudolf pointed to Lothar, "Herr Bauer doesn't have his wooden pointer with him!"

Lothar laughed gaily. The two young friends and their families stood together at the Nazi rally, and Rudolf felt goose bumps as a military band marched past. But even at that short distance, the din of everyone yelling *Sieg Heil* drowned out the music.

Following the band were hundreds of goose-stepping black-shirted SS troopers, and close behind were members of the Hitler Youth marching in perfect formation. Rudolf could not keep his eyes off them, their marching looked flawless, and his heart longed to be part of them. Just look at them, he thought, boys my age, marching with the SS!

The day was gloomy with the sun hiding behind gray clouds, yet with all the red and black swastika bunting hung in Bremen's *Marktplatz* there was a peculiar brightness, a reflection from the bold colors onto the old gothic buildings. The crowd was so dense that Rudolf could barely see the opulent façade of the six centuries-old Town Hall. This was his favorite place in Bremen.

Rudolf, Lothar, and other friends would walk to the *Marktplatz* on Sunday afternoons just to see the 10-meter-tall stone statue of Roland, the city's protector, standing in front of the Town Hall. Once there, the boys imitated Roland, who stood tall bearing the sword of justice and a shield decorated with an imperial eagle. Each boy would stand for as long as he could in the same position as the statue, holding a play sword and shield. The one who held the position the longest got a congratulatory slap on the back.

Rudolf stood on his tip toes, straining to see over the crowd. Suddenly, an open black Mercedes touring car turned onto the plaza. With a jolt, Rudolf realized it was *Der Führer* himself with his arm outstretched and a thin smile on his lips. The car stopped momentarily directly in front of where Rudolf and his family stood, and Rudolf rubbed his eyes as if he had seen a vision.

The boy looked up at his grandfather and saw a wide smile on his big face, but to his great embarrassment, his grandmother Luise stood with her arms crossed. Everyone within Rudolf's field of vision was screaming except *Oma*, and he saw people lean out of open windows facing the Town Hall reaching out to this man who had once again turned Germany into a proud nation.

Hermann Meier squeezed Rudolf's shoulder in exhilaration. "You see," Hermann said, "what a great man looks like. How straight he stands with his arm out to us, as if to salute *us*! See how undecorated he is, just a plain coat without military medals. He is truly a man of the people."

It was true, what *Opa* said. Adolf Hitler wore only a plain great coat and tie, his head bare. The boy felt as if he were looking at God instead of *Der Führer*. For a searing moment, Hitler turned his head and looked straight at Rudolf—at least Rudolf thought he was looking directly at him—and it was like a thunderbolt hit the youngster. The boy stopped waving and gasped. *Der Führer* nodded his head slightly as if to acknowledge Rudolf, then the car continued its slow pace down the street to the head of the plaza, in front of the Town Hall. Once there, the car stopped and Hitler climbed out. Rudolf pulled on his grandfather's arm and Hermann easily lifted the boy to his shoulders where he could see Hitler walk with determination to the podium.

The crowd hushed. Hitler spoke calmly about the beauty of Bremen and his happiness to see the people, *Das Volk*. He told of his pride regarding the Bremen shipyards that were again producing great ships for the *Kriegsmarine.*

Then, in an even tone, he said, "The men of Bremen are building mighty ships to protect Germany from her enemies, those countries that lied and said the Great War was started by Germany, when, in fact, Europe slithered into war on its own. And after the war, the financial devastation imposed upon us by those Jew parasites will never happen again—you need never be afraid because my four-year plan to bring Germany back from its economic depths is working! The manufacturing of ships, airplanes and automobiles is putting food again on German tables."

Then his voice rose, and with it, a sort of rasping sound flowed from his throat.

"There is much work to be done, but Germany is making great strides! It is now more than two months since we reclaimed the Rhineland," Hitler yelled, and the crowd went wild. He moved his head downward as if to look at the lectern and waited for quiet. When the crowd was silent again, he raised his head and continued.

"Our troops are safe in the Rhineland in their peaceful garrisons, and I swear to you that we shall strive for an understanding between our European neighbors. We have no territorial demands to make in Europe! The Third Reich will never break the peace!"

The crowd erupted, yelling, *"Sieg Heil, Sieg Heil, Sieg Heil,"* until they were hoarse, arms pumping the air with salutes. Rudolf sat triumphantly on his grandfather's shoulders, his arm stretched out, imitating the crowd.

Once again, there was silence, but Luise leaned over to Hermann and whispered, "I wish there was a place to sit. His speeches are always too long!" Hermann motioned for her to lean against him, and Rudolf glowered down at his grandmother for committing such a grievous error in manners while *Der Führer* was speaking.

Hitler now began to shout: "We must never forget our German heritage, and how great we can become. But a peaceful Germany is not a stupid Germany. We know there are evil people in our midst, the Jews, who will do anything they can to keep us from becoming the strong nation I promised when I became *Führer.*

"That is why I enacted the Nuremberg Laws to keep Germany pure. We do not want these aliens, these Jews, to be citizens of our country and we do not want them to mix with us!"

Hitler rose up his right arm and his fist punched the air with each statement.

"Do not forget those horrible years when there was so little work, so little to eat. The Jews were responsible for that! They were hoarding our money in their Jewish banks with their filthy Jewish hands, and at the same time, they were taking the food out of our mouths. They grew prosperous and we grew thin! We all know what they are, these Jews, they are nothing but Communists, all of them, Bolshevik Communists, and they would wish to do nothing better than undermine the will of the German people who believe in National Socialism.

"Well, let them understand now how it feels to be strangers, to be without a country, without a place to live, without food. That is why the Nuremberg Laws are so important. The sooner the Jews leave Germany, the better we all will be! Let them go to Russia where they can practice their Communism, or to America where they can practice their hooliganism with American gangsters, and we Germans can live in peace without these aliens in our midst!"

Der Führer was finished. As he stepped down from the podium, the crowd began to chant again. Hitler saluted them as he stepped into the black Mercedes, and suddenly, he was gone.

Hermann set Rudolf down next to Lothar with a groan. "You are getting too big for me to do that anymore!"

Lothar looked at Rudolf and gave him a punch in the arm. He leaned over and whispered, "Well...now is the time to talk to your grandfather about the Hitler Youth, Rudi. That is, if you still want to."

Lothar waved as he and his family headed back to open their bakery. Lothar had told Rudolf that his father and grandfather had gone to the bakery at midnight to prepare their delicious almond-tinged strudel and, at this time of year, there were fresh strawberries to make the strudel even more attractive. The Volkmann family, always with an eye toward earning a living, hoped to take advantage of the festive crowd wanting to celebrate Hitler's visit.

Hermann took his grandson's hand and walked toward their neighborhood. Rudolf's grandmother walked on the other side of his grandfather, and Rudolf peeked at her to see if her pinched expression had changed, but she looked straight ahead, and seemed to be lost in her own thoughts.

"*Opa*," Rudolf began, tugging on his grandfather's arm, "*Opa*, I need to talk to you about something." The boy felt suddenly queasy.

"What is it?" Hermann said.

"I…I," Rudolf stammered.

Hermann leaned closer to his grandson and said again, "What is it, Rudolf?"

"*Opa*, did you see how wonderful the Hitler Youth were, how straight they marched?"

"Yes, Rudolf, the *Jungvolk* were extremely good. I was surprised they could stay in such straight formation. How professional they looked."

"*Opa*, I want to become a member of the Hitler Youth." There, he said it at last!

Hermann stopped walking and looked down at his grandson. Luise kept walking ahead until she realized her husband and grandson were not with her. She stopped and turned around, but she could not hear the conversation between them because there were many people walking past, everyone talking and there was much laughter among the happy crowd.

Hermann's deep voice changed. It was harsher. "What are you thinking, Rudolf? You have so much schoolwork now that you are in *Gymnasium* and responsibilities at home to help *Oma*."

"Yes, I know, but *Opa* I can do it, I can! Just ask Herr Braun. I am doing well in school; I do not complain too much about the work for *Oma*—and I will still do what she needs done! But I am twelve years old now and I need to be doing other things…more important things. The Hitler Youth is training us for the future, and I want to be part of that. Please, *Opa*, please, let me do it!"

Hermann's voice became a low growl. "Your grandmother and I need to discuss this, Rudolf. This is not a decision I can make without talking to her."

Rudolf was silent. He could not believe what *Opa* just said. Why must his grandfather discuss this with his grandmother, since *Opa* always made the important decisions in the house?

When they arrived home, Luise put on her apron and while the pot of coffee was boiling, she took a homemade chocolate cake out of the cupboard and cut it carefully, placing the pieces of cake on her porcelain plates, every once in a while licking the cake crumbs off of her fingers as she hummed one of the tunes from the marching band. Hermann picked up the newspaper, *Völkischer Beobachter*, the official Nazi newspaper, and settled in his favorite chair. Although he was not a member of the Nazi party, Hermann tried to stay on top of the writings of those who were in charge of the government. Rudolf sat at the table and tried to engage his grandmother in some conversation about the rally.

"*Oma*, did you see Herr Bauer at the rally? He was standing across the plaza from us."

Luise grunted, but she did not answer Rudolf.

He decided to try again. "*Oma*, can you believe *Der Führer* was so close to us! I think he actually looked at me!"

Luise was in the middle of setting the table and she suddenly slammed down the forks and yelled at Rudolf, "Ah, yes, that stupid little Austrian housepainter, the great *Führer*! If he looked at you, you can believe it was because he thought here was another child he could get into the Hitler Youth!"

Hermann jumped up, and the paper fell from his hands. "What are you saying, Luise? Shut up before our neighbors hear you through these thin walls and turn you into the Gestapo!"

"But *Oma*, I want to go into the Hitler Youth!" Rudolf stuttered. "Couldn't you see how wonderful they were today? I want to be part of that!"

Luise turned white and she began to shake. She wiped her hands on her flowered apron, and pulled a chair from the table, sitting down with a small thud. "*Mein Gott*, this man who took away my son is now going to get my grandson in his clutches!"

Hermann was there beside her, patting her on the shoulder. "Shush, shush," he said. "Luise, calm down, now, calm down."

Despite his grandfather's efforts to comfort his grandmother, Rudolf could see she was terribly upset. He did not understand what she said about *Der Führer* taking her son from her, Erich, his father.

"Rudolf, eat your cake, and then you can go outside with your friends," his grandfather said sternly.

The boy said nothing, and wolfed down the cake with eyes that searched his grandmother's face. Once again, he had upset her, and he did not know why. When he finished, he put his dish in the sink, looked back at his grandparents sitting at the table. *Oma's* face was in her hands and *Opa* was still patting her on the shoulder.

When the door closed, Luise looked at her husband in despair. "Oh, Hermann, when that man was named *Führer*, I knew…I knew somehow he would have an impact on our lives again!"

Hermann was silent for a moment, but then when he spoke, his voice was low, comforting.

"Luise, we cannot live in the past. What happened to Erich, and Rudolf's mother was horrible. But that was then and here we are now with their son and we need to think about him and his future. The Nazis are in charge of Germany, God knows for how long. Rudolf's success in life comes from whom he knows and what organizations he belongs to—you know that, and under the Third Reich it begins with the Hitler Youth." Hermann took a deep breath. "Do you want him to be a welder like me or do you want him to make something of himself?" Hermann asked.

Luise shook her head. "You are not just a welder, Hermann; you have become someone of importance at AG Weser! But no, I do not want him to have a life of struggle like you and I have had—I remember those days when we had to barter away everything we owned to buy food! I know what you are saying about his future, yet to think he will join this Hitler group of marching babies—they are no different than the Brownshirts who killed his father and mother because they answer to Hitler, that Austrian *Schweinhunde!*"

Hermann's eyes opened wide because he had never heard his wife use that filthy word.

The grandmother's face brightened for a moment after she said it, as if it gave her some relief. "Herman," she said, touching her husband's hand, "Maybe we should tell him what happened and then see how he feels about joining the Hitler Youth?"

"No!"

There was a tone in his deep voice that made Luise visibly shiver; still she persisted in pressing her point. "But why not, Hermann? Rudolf is old enough to know." She looked down at her hands, which had been twisting the cloth of her apron. The smooth material now had ridges in it from her nervousness. When she looked up again at her husband's face, she saw an expression she never saw before, one that gave her a small inkling into what Hermann was like while inspecting his U-boats.

"Erich was a Communist, for God's sake, Luise! No one here in Bremen knows that, and as long as I live, I swear to God, no one, not even Rudolf will ever know. He brought shame on us—him and his Maria, that Polish slut who ensnared our son with her wily ways."

Luise looked down, afraid to see Hermann's face but she gave one last push. "Yes, it is true Erich brought us shame but the Brownshirts, no doubt with Hitler's orders, killed them both! He is a monster! How can you not think otherwise?"

There was no response from her husband, so Luise said, "Oh, Hermann, I have fought for so many years to remove that terrible memory from my mind, from the nightmares of how Erich was murdered, and now, here it is again!" she began to cry, and her tears dropped on her spotless linen tablecloth. She tried to rub them away, but it was as useless as her conversation with Hermann.

Hermann left her side and went back to his chair.

Luise could see a coldness in the way he held his shoulders—that he was through comforting her, and she knew there was nothing more to say. She wiped her face with her apron and proceeded to act as normal as she could while serving Hermann her delicious chocolate cake and strong coffee.

Hermann hid behind the newspaper most of the afternoon. He did not want to show his wife how much the conversation upset him. As the head of the family, it would not be proper for him to show such weakness; anger, yes, but weakness, no. Yet Hermann was also overcome with the memory of his son.

Erich may have survived the sinking of his U-boat, but he was a changed man when he returned home. The letters Hermann and Luise received during his time in England as a prisoner of war were filled with angry words aimed at his country and its new democratic government imposed on the German people by the Treaty of Versailles.

One letter Erich wrote in particular tore at Hermann's heart. The words were etched forever in his memory:

"Part of me knows I served Germany to the best of my ability," Erich wrote. "But we are a defeated country now, and my time in the *Reichsmarine* seems to have been a waste. We Germans were victims of the Kaiser's propaganda telling us we could defeat our enemies and, in the end, the destruction of Germany befell us!

"I hear from our prison guards there is no work there, no way to make a living in Germany. There are rumors that hundreds of people roam the streets, looking for food in the garbage dumps, and I am worried about you and *Mutter.* Here, at least, I am fed three times a day. It may not be *Mutter's* good cooking, but my stomach is full, so do not worry about me. Soon, however, they must ship us home—they cannot feed us forever!

"I am concerned about what I will do when I return. This arm is useless! How will I be able to support myself? Who would want me with only one good arm? Even with your influence at AG Weser, they will not hire me, I know.

"As I see it, *Vater,* the only way out of this economic freefall is for Germany to become Communist like Russia. Then and only then will all of us be equal, no greedy Jews will rule over us like kings, and there will be food for everyone!"

When Erich finally returned to Germany, he did not come home to Bremen, but found meager work instead as a day laborer on the wharves of Lubec, the largest German port on the Baltic Sea. Soon, he was caught up in the political free-for-all of the rowdy port where workers clashed in the streets with Hitler's thugs. It was there he met Maria, a Pole, at a Communist rally. Hermann never understood the attraction Erich had for Maria. She was a slight dark-haired girl with rabid political opinions, a trait that men of Hermann's generation would never have allowed in their households.

Erich quit his day labor job, much to Hermann's consternation, and the two of them became Communist agitators, moving from place to place putting together rallies, living on the good graces of better-fed Communist sympathizers. Only once did they come to Bremen; it was a relief to Hermann that they stayed but a few hours on their way to a political rally. Not long afterward, Maria became pregnant, but to the two freethinkers, the subject of marriage was not even a consideration, much to Hermann and Luise's dismay.

Hermann was not sure how Erich was making a living, and he did not ask when contact with his son was so seldom. Once in a while, they would receive a letter, but the details were sparse. He only knew Erich and Maria settled down a bit after Rudolf was born, and they lived in a town near the Polish border.

Then, one day in 1926—a day seared in Hermann's memory—while working in the bowels of a ship, he received a message to come to the main administration building where a policeman was waiting for him.

"Are you Hermann Meier?" the policeman asked, his voice icy.

"Yes," Herman said. "What is this about?"

The policeman ignored his question. "Are you the father of Erich Meier?"

"Yes…yes, I am," Hermann said, fear rising in his throat.

The policemen took Hermann by the arm and led him outside the entrance gate of the shipyard. Turning to him, he said in a brutal voice, "Your son, Erich, and his whore, Maria, are dead."

With the mental shock of the news, Hermann barely heard the rest of the story—only bits and pieces seeped into his fogged mind: A group of six drunken Brownshirts broke into the small cottage where the couple lived. They beat Erich, breaking most of his bones, and finally killed him by strangulation. One of the men, the leader of the group, stepped on his windpipe for good measure. The policeman, a man with hard eyes and a lean face, casually wiped his glasses on a handkerchief and said, "…to make sure he was indeed dead."

Maria was raped repeatedly and then a fireplace poker was used to stab her. "But it appears," the policeman said as he fingered his swastika keychain, "she did not die easily."

Looking hard at Hermann, he said the suspects were free because of lack of evidence. "Those two Communist agitators," the policeman snarled, "they deserved what they got. We knew who they were long before they were murdered. However, Herr Meier, I respect your position at AG Weser, and you have a good reputation. That is why I chose not to tell you this in front of your superiors."

Hermann had only one question. "Where is my grandson?" he asked, his voice tight with grief.

"We found the boy about a mile or so from his home," the policeman answered. "He is not hurt, but it is apparent he saw something. He had blood on his clothing, and he is deadly silent." Rudolf was delivered to Hermann and Luise a few days later.

Hermann sat still for a long time, thinking, the newspaper clutched in his hands. No, Rudolf will never know about his father, Hermann firmly decided. He is ours—mine and Luise's, and I will do everything I can to make sure he will be successful. Germany is becoming great again and Rudolf is going to be part of that.

Yes, he nodded as he began to focus again on the newspaper. I will see to it that he will be part of that greatness!

Chapter 9

July 1936
Bremen, Germany

Rudolf stood ramrod straight. Every nerve of his body tingled, aware of how the bright summer sunshine shone on his precisely combed blond hair. A swell of pride gripped Rudolf's throat as he glanced down at his *Deutsche Jungvolk* summer uniform with the light brown shirt ironed properly by his grandmother and his black *lederhosen*, the knee-britches made of leather. A woggle held the black scarf around his neck, a black shoulder strap crossed his right shoulder, and his belt buckle was adorned with a swastika. Most important, however, was the armband he wore so proudly on his right upper arm. In the center of the red armband was a white diamond field emblazoned with a black swastika.

Rudolf's pale blond eyebrows knitted together as he gripped the German flag and held up three fingers extended to the sky. In a hoarse voice, he recited the words that would forever tie him to Nazi dogma:

"In the presence of this blood banner which represents the *Führer*, I swear to devote all my energies and my strength to the savior of our country, Adolf Hitler. I am willing and ready to give up my life for him, so help me God."

Rudolf could see his grandfather, Hermann, from the corner of his eye, standing at the end of the grassy field, but he dared not even smile at him. The rules of the Hitler Youth ordered members to ignore friends and parents while marching, and although he was not marching at this moment, taking the oath as a *Deutsche Jungvolk* surely had to fall in the same category.

He knew his grandmother would not come to the ceremony because he saw her wet eyes when he went down to the kitchen after dressing in his uniform, but she reminded him to stand tall, and she did something she rarely did, she kissed him on the cheek and softly touched the top of his head, then she quickly turned her back to him and he could hear her stifle a cry.

His grandparents had not been talking a lot to one another since his grandfather told him he could join the *Deutsche Jungvolk*—the Hitler Youth unit for boys 10 to 14 years old. Rudolf did not understand why they were more silent than usual at the kitchen table, talking to one another through him, but it seemed that his grandmother was the cause of the silence, not his grandfather.

Surely, *Oma* must see how wonderful this is, Rudolf thought. He knew she did not like *Der Führer*, but what had that to do with becoming a member of the DJ?

Rudolf banished those thoughts and concentrated on the speech from his *Fähnleinführer*, the 16-year-old leader of the unit Rudolf belonged to—a total of one-hundred and sixty boys. Ernst Ackermann was the son of a day laborer, a member of the lower class that Rudolf—as the grandson of a superintendent at AG Weser—would normally never mingle with.

When Hermann Meier heard Ernst was the leader of Rudolf's group, he roared, "What nonsense this is, that you, as my grandson, have this Ernst as your leader, this son of a nothing! That is the one thing I dislike about the Hitler Youth—making us all equal, like those damn fool Americans."

Rudolf stood before his grandfather with wide eyes, inwardly cowering into his secret hole; but he had no answer for his grandfather's discontent. Eventually Hermann calmed down, went back to reading his newspaper, and Rudolf stopped shaking.

Ernst Ackermann took his position as *Fähnleinführer* seriously, Rudolf knew. Gossip from the other members of the troop told of Ernst's unflagging enthusiasm for the Hitler Youth. He had attended the *Reichsführer* leadership school where he went through a three-week cram course in Nazi principles and German history. The school included leadership training, physical activity, and rifle shooting. Because of his excellent performance, he was named *Fähnleinführer*.

All the boys knew Ernst's ambition in the Hitler Youth was his way out of the dead-end heap of day laborers. Ernst said he wanted to become a member of the elite Gestapo, the Third Reich's secret police, and members of the troop knew he was ever on the lookout to make sure that happened by pushing his unit as hard as possible.

Towering over the boys, Ernst's six-foot frame was lean and hard. His thick dark blond eyebrows grew together over his nose, giving him a ferocious appearance. The young man commanded respect and his unit gave it to him unconditionally.

"This is a momentous day for those of you who have just joined our ranks," he said with a hint of a scowl. "But remember, this is only the beginning. Six months from now, you will be given your test of courage, your *Mutprobe*. You must train yourselves to be strong, for this test of courage will bring you the coveted dagger. You are the chosen ones, the future leaders of Germany. Do not fail the Fatherland!"

After the induction ceremony, Rudolf proudly took his grandfather into the new building, the *Heim*, shared by both the boys and girls in the Hitler Youth organizations. In addition to housing the group Rudolf belonged to, the *Heim* had space for the Hitler *Jugend*, boys from 14 to 18 years old, and the corresponding girls' organizations.

Hermann expressed amazement when he saw each Hitler Youth group had their own meeting room and separate rooms where each group completed their indoor duty. All the rooms had new furniture, blond in color to add to the light reflecting from the large windows looking out onto the green park adjacent to the *Heim*. There was a myriad of shelves filled with books, parlor games on tables, and table-tennis tops propped in a corner.

"I tell you, Rudolf, never in my life have I seen such abundance of things to amuse young people." Hermann made an audible sigh. "There was nothing like this when I was young."

Rudolf laughed, happy to see his grandfather approved of what he was doing. Next, he took him to the cellar where there was a fully equipped workshop and showers.

The boy went to a bin labeled with his name and produced a partially completed chess board he was making in the woodshop. He displayed it proudly to Hermann, who took the piece of wood in his big hands and felt the board's smoothness, looking carefully at the workmanship as if he were inspecting rivets on his U-boats.

"This is quite good, Rudolf, quite good!" the old man said, patting Rudolf on the back.

On their way home, Hermann said to his grandson, "Make sure, Rudolf, when you tell me what you are doing in the DJ that your grandmother is busy doing other things."

Chapter 10

August 1936
Bremen, Germany

As the sun began to set, Lothar and Rudolf sat on the riverbank of the Weser River dangling their feet in the icy cold water, skipping stones across the vast waterway. Each boy tried to throw farther than the other, past a large branch sticking up in the middle of the wide tributary.

"You throw better," Lothar sighed as he half-heartedly lobbed his last stone.

"Yes, but you beat me on your aim," Rudolf admitted. "I may be able to throw it past that stick, but I can never throw as straight as you."

Lothar grunted at the compliment. "Perhaps it is all that marching you do in the DJ that makes you throw so well."

Rudolf laughed. "I am exercising my feet, Lothar, not my arm!"

Lothar chuckled. "Well, just how far do you march, anyway?"

"About 25 kilometers."

"Oh, that is too much! I know I would not like doing that." Lothar said. He stopped lobbing stones, and leaned back on his elbows like Rudolf and they watched the sun set behind a drift of snowy-white clouds.

After a while, Lothar said, "Say, Rudi…the Olympic Games are ending today. I wonder what it must be like to actually see it. I can imagine it while listening to the radio, but to see such a thing in person—that music, so stirring, and the swastikas hanging everywhere."

Rudolf nodded. "I wish I could have seen our gymnasts win their gold medals. I was so excited my grandmother threatened to send me to my room because I was making so much noise! What glory they brought to the Fatherland!"

Lothar was quiet for a moment and then said, "It is amazing that nigger American, Jesse Owens, won four gold medals! I wonder why the Americans would even allow those people to come to the Olympic Games. They are not representative of the American race; they are black after all."

Rudolf took a piece of long grass out of his mouth he chewed like a toothpick. "That's because there is no American race. They are all mixed up in America, people from all over the world, together—you know what I mean, *geschlechtsverkehr,* having sex with one another! They are not strong and pure of race like we are."

Rudolf paused, picked up another stone, and lobbed it into the river. "Just look at us," Rudolf said with awe in his voice, "we have won the majority of medals at the Olympics! But with Owens winning those gold medals, it shows what *Der Führer* says is true, that inferior races are capable of producing brilliant specimens. And that is what makes them so dangerous, like the Jews."

Lothar nodded slowly as if he were deeply thinking. "Yes, I suppose you are right," he said.

The boys got up and headed in the direction of home, across the green fields they knew so well and then toward the neighborhood where they lived, where small shops and restaurants lined the cobblestone streets. The morning had seen a summer cloudburst, but the day ended warm and enjoyable, the air clean from the rain, and the residents of Bremen were taking full advantage of a beautiful summer evening. Rudolf and Lothar passed shoppers laden with baskets full of fresh breads, fruits, and meat, and the smells wafting from the outdoor cafes and bakeries encouraged the boys to hurry home for dinner.

When Rudolf and Lothar rounded the corner near their apartment, they could see a crowd standing outside. A police car was parked near the front entrance and the boys saw their parents, grandparents, and other people from the neighborhood gathered, talking to each other in whispered tones. Rudolf and Lothar stood at the edge of the crowd, listening.

Frau Schweiss, one of the women from the building where the boys lived, stood on the sidewalk, near the police car. A tall woman with a flat face, she was crying so hard her whole body shook violently.

"No, no! You cannot do this!" The woman clutched her daughter, a girl of 16, rarely seen outside by Rudolf and Lothar and their friends. The boys referred to her as "the dummy" because she never spoke; she sat mainly in the hallway of their apartment building, on the stairs near her mother's doorway, and played silently with an old rag doll.

The policeman, a round-faced man with a protruding belly and a nightstick, had the girl, Frieda, by her right arm and was trying to pull her away from her mother. "It is time to take her and you have no right to fight us, Frau Schweiss! You were notified by the Hereditary Health Court that you were to take her to the hospital last week and since you did not, I am here to do it!"

"You cannot do this, please, you cannot!" Frau Schweiss cried, holding as fast as she could to her daughter's other arm. The girl, crying as well, made no sound, but her eyes shone bright with terror.

The policeman let go of the girl, and took his nightstick to the mother's head. Her cries became louder and louder as the policeman beat her, but she would not let go of her daughter. Finally, Herr Manheim, a tall, heavily-built widower who lived in the apartment building on the same floor as Frau Schweiss, stepped up to the policeman and grabbed his arm. He said in a loud voice, "Please, please, stop this! The girl has done nothing, what is this about?"

The policeman, angered and frustrated, wrestled his arm free from the older man and then he raised the nightstick as if he were going to hit Herr Manheim, but stopped suddenly when he saw the old man towered over him.

"Listen, you old fool, why do you want—why do all of you—want to get into the middle of this?" he questioned the group of people who surrounded him, looking directly at Herr Manheim. Sweat poured from his forehead as he stood defiant for a moment and then he yelled, "This is a matter between the Reich and Frau Schweiss!"

The mother still held onto her daughter, but the blows to her head had taken their toll and she was bleeding profusely. A mixture of tears and blood smeared her face, and she staggered for an instant, and then grabbed her daughter's shoulder for support. The girl's anguish at seeing what happened to her mother came gushing up into her silent throat; it was as if the pumping of the blood in her heart could be heard through her mouth—a gurgling sound of shear fright. The agony of mother and daughter was palpable to neighbors, yet all were strangely silent except Herr Manheim who would not back down from the angry policeman.

"Why do you want the girl?" he insisted, standing resilient against this threat to his neighbor. "She is a silent one; she has made no trouble for the Reich. All she does is play with her old doll!"

The policeman could see he was getting nowhere, particularly with the old man standing in his way.

"Listen, you old man, have you not heard of Dachau?" the policeman threatened. "It's a place for people like you who poison other people's thoughts!"

Then he turned to Frau Schweiss. "I will be back, and when I am, you will be very sorry you did not give me your dummy quietly, without a fight!"

As he drove away, Rudolf's grandfather and Herr Manheim took hold of Frau Schweiss and led her up to her apartment. The girl, panic clouding her young face, clung to her mother's dress. Rudolf's grandmother followed behind them.

The clot of neighbors did not disburse; they continued talking to one another about the incident, and Rudolf heard a tenant who lived in his apartment building speak loudly to her husband, a printer by trade whose ink-stained hands never looked washed. "She is 16 years old, after all," the woman said. "There is nothing wrong with the Reich making sure she cannot breed more silent babies. We working people should not have to provide food for more dummies."

Rudolf looked at Lothar. "What is she talking about," he asked his friend.

"My father says it is a government program to save the people of Germany from having to pay for babies born from people who are crazy or who cannot work. They are taken to a hospital where they are operated on…you know… down there!" Lothar indicated with his hand, and then his face turned red with embarrassment.

Rudolf frowned at Lothar, and then the light of understanding came to him. "It seems to me if *Der Führer* approves of it, then the policeman was only doing his duty," Rudolf said blithely.

Lothar looked astonished at his friend's remark, but before he could reply, his father told him to go inside for the night, and he passed Rudolf with a scowl. Rudolf, not understanding Lothar's frown, went to find his grandparents.

The door to Frau Schweiss' apartment was partially open and he found his grandparents in the kitchen with Herr Manheim. Luise stood near the sink, cleaning the blood from her neighbor's hair with a white rag. Once that was done, she made Frau Schweiss sit down at the table with the rag held against the wound, and then Luise put on a pot of coffee. The girl slouched in a corner on a stool, still looking dazed. Rudolf moved closer into the room and leaned against a wall, listening to the conversation between the adults.

Hermann had a concerned look on his face. "George, you put yourself in a bad position with the police. I don't blame you for standing up to him—I am ashamed I did not do it myself—but he will report to his superiors why he did not bring the girl in."

Herr Manheim's face was red and he remained standing with his fists clenched. "Yes, Hermann, I know," he said. "But how could I be silent about such a thing! The trouble is, these days we Germans are silent about too many things! *Mein Gott!* What have we come to that we sterilize people because they are different from the rest of us? When will this madness end?"

Hermann sighed. "I know what you mean, George, and you are right, but there is no way to stand up to the police these days. They are not just our old familiar Bremen police; they are State police now, run by the SS! Everything is run by the book…by the book! Frau Schweiss will have to hand over the girl."

Herr Manheim ran his large hand over his eyes as if to wipe away the injustice of what the State was about to do to his neighbor's daughter.

He pulled out a chair from the table and clumsily sat down, looking sadly at Frau Schweiss who held her head in her hands. The smell of coffee filled the small room, as did the unbroken silence between the adults.

Luise continued to fuss with Frau Schweiss' head wound, and when the bleeding stopped, Luise wrapped a clean cloth around her neighbor's head in a makeshift bandage, and poured everyone a cup of strong coffee.

Frau Schweiss gulped it down with shaking hands and wailed: "What am I to do? What am I to do? My Frieda, my Frieda…they will carve her up like a roast pig, the butchers!"

Very early the next morning when all was quiet in the city of Bremen except for the sound of the Weser River moving steadily within its banks, and the only people working were bakers readying their dough for the first loaves of bread, Luise woke up her husband with a frightened whisper.

"Hermann! I hear sounds on the stairs above us."

He was awake instantly, and put his hand over Luise's mouth. "Sshh…be very quiet!"

Suddenly there was a large crashing sound as if a door was kicked in and then another and then muffled screams. Hermann sat up, moving to the edge of the bed. Luise grabbed his nightshirt as a way to keep him near her. "*Mein Gott*, Hermann, what can it be?"

The door of their bedroom squeaked opened. It was Rudolf.

"*Opa, Oma*…what is happening?" he whispered, moving quickly from the door to the side of the bed.

"Come here," Luise said. She patted the bed and he climbed in, hugging his grandmother.

Suddenly there was the deep voice of George Manheim, yelling. "Let me go, let me go! What do you think you are doing, you *Schwein*?"

They heard the sound of a female crying, her voice reverberating against the emptiness of the stairwell. The Meiers heard more cries, thuds, and the scraping sounds of heavy objects dragged down the stairs. Finally, after the slamming of car doors and engines starting up, there came a dreaded, terrifying silence.

Hermann did not move a muscle as he sat listening while Luise and Rudolf trembled beneath the blankets. Finally, Hermann climbed back into bed and held his family to him. When dawn came, he quietly got up, pulled on his clothes, and went out the door of his apartment and up the stairs.

When he came back, Luise and the boy were sitting up in bed waiting for him.

"They are gone," Hermann said. "All three are gone."

Chapter 11

September 1936
Bremen, Germany

Herr Braun sat at his desk as the boys filed into his classroom. He was reading *Der Stümer*, a weekly Nazi newspaper known for its anti-Semitic cartoons, which usually portrayed Jews as ugly characters with exaggerated features and oddly-shaped bodies. Behind the teacher on the wall hung a picture of Adolf Hitler, and a swastika flag stood in the corner of the room.

Lothar Volkmann nudged Rudolf and whispered, "I bet we get a lesson on Jews today." Rudolf nodded, but did not respond for he was still preoccupied with his previous class, where Herr Mann, who had lived five years in America, was trying to get him to properly pronounce English words without a German accent. As the star pupil, Herr Mann insisted that Rudolf, more than any of the other students, learn to speak English properly. Rudolf never questioned his teacher's reasoning, but simply did as he was told.

Herr Braun moved to the front of the class and stood with his arms crossed. Suddenly, he raised his right arm and shouted, "*Heil Hitler!*" The students stood and responded by repeating the phrase.

"Today," he said as the students sat down, "we will discuss the Jews and their continuing influence in this country even though our *Führer* has declared they are no longer German citizens."

The teacher adjusted his glasses and turned to the blackboard where he wrote in large letters: *Juden*. He turned back to face his class and eyed his students. There was no sound as he glared at each boy individually and then his icy gaze moved on to the next until he knew his authority had been re-instilled. Herr Braun often began his class in such a manner; it was his way of making sure each student gave him his complete attention.

"Now…can you tell me, one of you, how to tell a person is a Jew?" Herr Braun said.

A boy with a wide smile raised his hand. "They are swarthy."

"Ah, good, Heinrich," Herr Braun replied. "Yes, they are often darker than we are, but all of us pure-blooded Germans do not always look like Rudolf." The teacher reached out with his pointer and touched Rudolf who sat in the front row. Rudolf blushed.

The teacher looked around the classroom. "What is another way to tell a Jew?"

Lothar raised his hand. Herr Braun hesitated a moment, but then called on him.

"Herr Braun, my grandfather says the way to tell a Jew is to look at his nose. If it looks like a bulging number six, then that is a pretty good indication that person is of Jewish blood."

The teacher seemed surprised by Lothar's response and gave him a small smile. "Yes, although not every Jew has such a nose and that is why we must be on our guard. The size of the nose is a good indication of Jewishness, although many have mixed with us pureblooded Aryans, and so it is harder to tell. Still, there are other ways to determine someone is a Jew."

Stillness pervaded the school room. Herr Braun stood erect, and slapped his stick into the cup of his left hand. "Well, *pimpfs*, I am waiting," he shouted, growing angry because of their silence.

Rudolf raised his hand.

"Yes, Rudolf, give me an answer that will make me proud of you."

"Herr Braun, Jews are money handlers. You can tell just going into a store who is Jew and who is not by the way they handle their money. It sticks to their hands, and they have a pinched face when they must hand over their money to a non-Jew."

"Ah, yes, Rudolf! Yes, yes! It is true that they would sell their children rather than give up their precious money!"

Herr Braun became visibly agitated as he continued his lecture. Since Hitler came to power, teachers were mandated to instruct their students in Nazi dogma. Herr Braun planned this lesson to teach his students the truth about Jew aliens who had infiltrated the Fatherland. It was his job to impress upon their sponge-like minds the need to be constantly on guard against Jews.

"I am recalling the writings of our beloved Richard Wagner. As I have mentioned to you before, Wagner is a German composer beyond the pale, an artist of the first class who wrote in 1850—in his essay called *Judaism in Music*—'we Germans have an instinctive repugnance against the Jew's prime essence.' "

Herr Braun turned to his desk, grabbed a sheath of papers, and began waving them at his students. "Wagner said—here, I have found the passage," he said as he removed his glasses and scrutinized the words on the paper. "The Jew...'has only been able to maintain his stand beneath the shelter of a twilight darkness—a darkness we good-natured Humanists ourselves have cast upon him, to make his look less loathly.' "

He laughed, a sound that resembled a hen cackling, "Yes, yes, the Jew is a loathsome creature! And Wagner said, 'the Jew—who as every-one knows—has a God all to himself.' "

The little man stood at the front of the room with his legs spread slightly as if he were bracing for battle. "Now, students, can you imag-ine someone believing he has a God all to himself?" he said. "This is such nonsense, such utter nonsense. I tell you this, the Jew may have his God—but pure Germans, you and me—we will have our State!"

The children murmured approvingly. Herr Braun gave them a tight smile. He was just warming up to his subject.

"Again, let us listen to the writing of Wagner." He shuffled through the papers until he found the passage he wanted: " 'The Jew speaks the language of the nation in whose midst he dwells from generation to generation, but he speaks it always as an alien.'

"This is very important, extremely important for you to under-stand," Herr Braun said. "What Wagner is saying is that the Jew does not speak naturally in our beautiful language—he speaks in that distasteful blabber Yiddish—and if he speaks in that foreign tongue, how is it that he could possibly write music, which is, after all, the passion of speech?"

Rudolf, mesmerized by his teacher's agitation, watched the small man move back and forth in front of the blackboard emphasizing his words by vigorously slapping his wooden pointer into the palm of his hand. Rudolf wondered if his teacher was on the brink of hysteria, as his voice became louder and louder.

"Yes, yes! Wagner was speaking about that Jew, Mendelssohn," he continued. "I want you to think, my students: How could someone who speaks in the creaking, squeaking sound of Yiddish be able to produce music comparable to Bach or Mozart? He can't—but it is the Liberals and Communists of this world who would tell you that Mendelssohn is far above other German composers! Do not listen to that rubbish! If a Jew cannot speak proper German with his Yiddish blabber, then how can he possibly compose beautiful music, which is the height of speech?

"The answer is no! A Jew can never do it! Thus, another way we can tell a Jew is that he is not musically inclined—and can never be despite how much money he has or how cultured he thinks he is!"

Herr Braun was suddenly finished. He mopped the sweat from his forehead with a sparkling clean handkerchief he always carried in his pocket, and then he sank down into his chair, exhausted.

The students, including Rudolf and Lothar, stood in unison and repeated what Herr Braun had told them a hundred times—only this time they did it on their own without his encouragement—"The Jews are our misfortune," and filed obediently out of his classroom when the bell rang.

Chapter 12

December 1944
Arizona

Rudolf Meier lit a Chesterfield and inhaled deeply as he slowly moved his head up and glanced at the one light bulb hanging from the middle of the barrack's ceiling, the glare of its illumination reflecting the brilliant red, white and black of the Third Reich's flag tacked onto the wall of the bleak living quarters. The room was empty except for him; the other prisoners of war he lived with preferred to spend their free time in the camp's recreation hall, playing cards, or painting landscapes of the Sonoran Desert. Rudolf enjoyed his time alone—he could read and think without interruption.

The book, *For Whom the Bell Tolls,* lay on his lap; absentmindedly his thumbnail raked the page edges as he absorbed Hemingway's novel about the Spanish Civil War. Robert Jordan, the main character, was an American, tall, lanky, and fair, much like himself. The Spanish peasant girl, Maria, seemed so beautiful to Rudolf: Hemingway's description of her made his heart race. Her lithe figure and beautiful smile haunted him, and in the young man's fantasy, he replaced Maria with the dark-haired girl he kept tucked away in his heart, a girl he had seen years ago on the banks of the Weser River and never forgot.

The love affair between Robert Jordan and Maria hung in Rudolf's mind, plaguing him with its sexuality. As a man, he understood Robert Jordan's emotion whenever he saw Maria: a tightness in the throat that made swallowing difficult. Rudolf felt the same tension when he thought about the unknown girl he hungered for. He ached for her

The Swastika Tattoo

physical presence, imagining her smooth body lying next to his after a night of passion, snuggling together close, and warm beneath a goose down coverlet. Without anyone around, he moved his hand to feel his hardness, but he restrained himself for fear someone might walk in; he would have to take care of his urge later.

Rudolf forced his thoughts to examine the theme of the book—the right of an individual to decide his own fate. What Rudolf fought to comprehend was why a man would go to war for a country that was not his own. Robert Jordan lost his life helping the people of Spain win their freedom from tyranny, people who were not of his blood or race. Rudolf shook his head involuntarily with the wonder of it; such behavior was beyond his understanding.

Rudolf remembered when *Der Führer* declared war on America almost three years ago, telling the German people that as an ally of Japan, he had a clear understanding of America's intention to interfere in Germany's social order, and that he would not tolerate such an action. Rudolf wondered if Robert Jordan was not doing the same thing—interfering in Spain's social order by fighting in that country's civil war.

Unable to resolve his question, Rudolf put the book aside, got up from his cot and walked out the door. It was a cold, windless night. He found Helmut Kessler leaning against the building, looking up at the sky.

"This desert somehow makes the stars seem so close," Helmut said with a note of wonder in his voice.

"Yes," Rudolf agreed, looking upward. He drew in a last deep breath of smoke as he eyed the dark velvet void and then he threw the cigarette down on the ground, rubbing it fiercely into the dirt. Perplexed by Hemingway's ability to bring up unwanted emotions—passion, duty, independence, superstition, even death—Rudolf was not sure he understood the book. He needed to return it to Bob Feller, but he did not think he would see him again.

A sudden feeling of remorse flooded Rudolf when he remembered the conversation with Bob a few days ago. He was sitting on the Feller's ditch bank during lunch when Bob walked over and sat down next to Rudolf under the bare cottonwood trees.

81

"Are you enjoying the book?" Bob asked. His disarming smile made Rudolf feel as if they were life-long friends.

"There are some things I question," Rudolf answered.

"Oh, good! That's what a book is supposed to do, you know, make you think and question the purpose of life." The American chomped happily on his cheese sandwich and settled against a giant cottonwood as if he and Rudolf had hours to talk rather than minutes.

Rudolf relaxed a bit; perhaps he could tell Bob what he really thought; maybe this inquisitive young man would understand his puzzlement. "I do not understand…" he said, with hesitation.

Bob looked up from his lunch. "What don't you understand?"

"I do not understand why a man would fight for another country, a country not of his own race."

The young American put the sandwich down in his lap and a crease came across his forehead.

"Well, the whole premise of the book is based upon its title *For Whom the Bell Tolls*—which was a poem by John Donne, a blind 15th Century English preacher," Bob said. He grinned at Rudolf, "I had to memorize it for my English class, so here goes—'any man's *death* diminishes *me*, because I am involved in *Mankind*; and therefore never send to know for whom the *bell* tolls; it tolls for *thee.*' "

When Rudolf gave him a blank stare, Bob said, "What Hemingway is saying, I think, is that it doesn't matter if the country is not your country—more important is that you are fighting for the betterment of the human race—and since every man is a part of mankind, when the bell tolls, when death comes, it is not just for others, it is for each of us."

Bob took another bite of his sandwich and then said, "I…I think the book also speaks to the cruelties we inflict on one another and that we are each responsible for that insanity, whether we want to be or not. Robert Jordan goes to fight not so much for a cause, but for mankind."

Rudolf sat quietly for a minute, absorbing what Bob said, and then he asked, "But what if a person believes his country, his race is superior to another? I believe my country is greater than yours; surely you think the same about America?"

"Oh, no, I don't think that at all!" Bob said quickly, as if his response had been on his mind for a long time. "I truly believe that no country, no race is superior to another. Our nations—Germany and America—hold different ideals, and I happen to believe our democracy is a better government than National Socialism, but I would never tell you as an American that I am *better* than you are!"

Rudolf stopped eating and looked over at Bob. "If that is so, then can you tell me why Americans treat the niggers...uh, you know, the Negroes so terribly?" Rudolf said, realizing from Bob's sudden facial expression that he should not have used that derogatory term. "The black soldiers I have seen are separated from whites. In the Florida camp where I was before I came to Arizona, one Negro guard told me he understood the plight of German prisoners of war because Negroes feel like second-class citizens, too."

Bob Feller blanched. He took a deep breath before he answered. "That is a problem this country must soon come to grips with. In my view, Negroes are no different than white people—we are all humans trying to live our lives the best we can, to make a home and feed our children."

Rudolf mind ran backward to a time long ago. "How odd you should say that," he said. "That was what my grandmother said to me when she tried to explain her friendship with a Jew merchant." Distain tinged his voice.

Bob gulped down the mouthful of food and turned full-on to Rudolf. "My God, Rudi, are...are you anti-Semitic?"

The German thought about that for a moment. "I think Jews have created many problems in my country, but we are making Germany pure again. The Nazis pressured them to live elsewhere, and I think that is best for the Jews and us. Why do you ask?" Rudolf took a bite of his sandwich as he watched the guards. He knew they would call the men back to work in a few minutes and then he looked again at Bob, whose face was flushed red, and his dark eyes blazing fiercely.

"I am a Jew, Rudi!"

Rudolf choked, the food in his mouth catching in his throat. He bent over quickly, trying to spit it up, but he could not. He coughed roughly, gasping for breath, his face an agony. Suddenly, Bob reached over and slugged him hard on the back, dislodging the food.

When Rudolf regained his composure, Bob had disappeared.

The two German prisoners of war continued to look at the Arizona night sky and finally Rudolf asked in a hoarse whisper, "Will we ever go home, Helmut?"

Helmut's head and shoulders drooped; the weight of the question seemed too much for him. "...I don't know, Rudi."

"Oh, how I miss Germany!" Rudolf said, lamenting his fate.

Helmut did not answer. He was still propped forlornly against the wooden barrack. Rudolf could tell Helmut was thinking about his family, and he suddenly felt ashamed of inflicting his longing for Germany on his friend when he had his family to worry about.

Rudolf's eyes wandered over the bleak wasteland of the internment camp, landing finally on a guard tower squatting ominously at the corner of the compound that was enclosed in a double barbed-wire fence. Home suddenly seemed so far away—an eon, a lifetime. Although he kept as busy as he could—teaching English classes five nights a week in the camp after picking cotton, citrus fruit, or cleaning irrigation ditches, and playing team sports on the weekends—time moved slowly, each day bringing news of Germany's imminent defeat.

At first, Rudolf and other the men refused to believe the news about the war—American propaganda they whispered—but a kind of depression floated over the camp like a sand storm after the successful Allied landing on the coast of France in early June, nearly six months ago. The men talked among themselves, trying to keep their spirits up, but the American newspapers shouted victory for the Allies, and the newsreels seen at the Sunday movies showed thousands of German soldiers surrendering, producing a pall of silence in the recreation hall.

Rudolf waited for Helmut to say something. But instead, Helmut pushed himself away from the wooden building and stood facing Rudolf. The tone in his voice was one Rudolf never heard before.

Helmut was usually a quiet man who spoke little. "What is there to go home to, Rudi? Our cities are rubble; soon the Allies will physically take over Germany. If I had my way, my wife and daughters would be here in America and they would...they would be free!"

Rudolf blinked. He stared at Helmut as if he had never seen him before. A surge of anger welled up and Rudolf nearly shouted, "Free, free from what...from being a German, from living in our beautiful Fatherland? I have heard you exclaim the Americans want to foist their individualism on us. Well, have you swallowed their shit?"

Helmut stuck his chin out in defiance and looked around making sure they were alone. "What I want Rudi, and what I want for my family, is the ability to decide what *we* do with our lives. Maybe what you call individualism, I call freedom. Do you remember freedom in Germany? Tell me, when do you remember walking down the street without the Gestapo questioning you? Oh, but perhaps they never questioned you...you were dressed in your *Hitlerjugend* uniform. Well, they questioned me and I have been a member of the German Navy for years, for God's sake!" Helmut spat the words in Rudolf's face.

"Our beautiful Fatherland is taken over by people who live for the power they possess over the common, ordinary German. Everyone snitches on everyone else just to be in the good graces of the Gestapo. We are all afraid of making a slip of the tongue—a joking comment about our glorious leader will send us to Dachau for two years! Here in America anyone can say whatever they please about their President Roosevelt, and no one thinks anything about it. I ask you in all honesty, is life under the Nazis anyway to live?"

Helmut sighed heavily. "I have given it a lot of thought, Rudi, and when this war is over, I will do anything...anything I can to bring my family to America!"

Helmut left Rudolf standing outside and he walked sullenly into the barrack. Rudolf continued his night vigil, his anger suddenly draining from him as the cold seeped into his bones. He pulled another cigarette out of his pocket, lit it, and leaned against the wall, standing alone in the desert's darkness, its silence swallowing him like a rattlesnake slowly ingesting its prey. He felt battered, as if Helmut had physically hit him.

He had never confronted such ideals like those hurled to him by Bob and Helmut—being part of mankind rather than only being German, fighting for the rights of other men because of a moral code that enveloped all of mankind, not just one race or country. Could it be true, then, that cruelty inflicted upon one person by another was the responsibility of all who let it happen?

Those principles were decidedly different from Nazi dogma: Germany was a national community and no individual was more important than the State. It was a creed taught to him by his teachers and the Hitler Youth; his grandfather, Hermann, never renounced it and his grandmother, Luise, grudgingly accepted it.

Helmut's accusation that Germans were not free filled Rudolf's mind with uncertainty. Rudolf never thought to question why the Gestapo stopped him, asking to see his papers. It was an automatic response, something ingrained, a habit of pulling out his wallet and willingly showing his identification.

Yes, Rudolf knew about the daily questioning of average German citizens, and then a thought came to him about a recent trip he had made into Tempe, a town not far from Camp Papago Park. The camp commander had permitted Rudolf to go with a guard to pick up textbooks at Arizona State Teachers College for the English language classes he was teaching at the camp. It was an amazing act of faith, Rudolf thought as he stood in the darkness—an act he first considered to be American foolishness. While the guard snoozed in the Jeep, Rudolf went into the college bookstore. No one questioned him even though his clothing was plainly marked as a prisoner of war.

Rudolf acknowledged his trip to the college excited him: several young women gave him flirtatious glances—but it was more than that. He simply walked into the bookstore, said he was from Camp Papago Park and was there to pick up the English textbooks. No one asked him for identification, although he expected it; and he was amazed at the friendly treatment.

Suddenly, it occurred to him: the exhilarating freedom he experienced for an hour would never happen to an American POW held in Germany; it would be unthinkable there to let a captured soldier leave a concentration camp and mingle freely with the populace.

His thoughts turned to the daily work program. While the POWs worked, two guards sat unconcerned, their guns propped against the truck, and most of the time they joked with the prisoners or handed out water. When Rudolf was captured, he took the Americans' behavior as one of stupidity—but, as he stood leaning against the barrack, he realized that their self-confidence and sense of independence was not stupidity, it was a freedom of behavior—an ability to think for oneself—which was virtually unknown among Germans. Was that the freedom Helmut sought for himself and his family?

Unsettled, it was as if his Nazi-indoctrinated soul had been ripped from its swastika-entangled roots. He took a last drag on the Chesterfield and stamped it viciously into the ground, hoping that act would stop the subversion infiltrating his being.

The camp was abuzz. Germany had begun an implausible offensive in the Ardennes, a heavily forested area that swept through southern Belgium and central Luxembourg. During one of the coldest European winters in nearly a century, the German offensive began in mid-December and took the British and Americans by complete surprise. On the first day of the battle, the heavy snow and dense fog allowed the German *Wehrmacht* to push twelve miles into Allied territory creating a bulge in their defensive line: it was the beginning of the Battle of the Bulge.

Exhilarated by the possibility that their Fatherland just might push the Allies back to the Atlantic Ocean, the men at Camp Papago Park celebrated, cracking open their secret cache of citrus schnapps made in a distiller hidden under the floor boards of an empty barrack. Rudolf took part in the drunken ruckus, standing with other prisoners near the double barbed-wire fencing, singing the German National

Anthem—*Deutschland, Deutschland über alles,* Germany, Germany above everything!—as loud as possible to irritate and confuse the guards.

It was a bitter winter night and Rudolf cupped his hands over his mouth, blowing on them to keep warm. He stood near Werner Carl, who stamped his feet viciously against the cold. In between the patriotic songs and yelling of German slogans, Werner, who was drunk, yelled, "This place that is so goddamn hot in the summer—why is it so fucking cold in the winter?" Suddenly losing his balance, Werner lurched into another prisoner.

"Watch it!" the other man said, pushing back against Werner.

Werner yelled, "You *Misthaufen!*" and swung his fist with all his might, hitting the man on the side of the head. The man, angered at being called a shit heap, leaped to the challenge and kicked Werner in the testicles. Suddenly, more men flung themselves into the melee, including Rudolf who pushed himself into the throng and took a swing, landing a blow on no one in particular.

Soon the fight was over with Nazi officers gaining control of their men; but it was a wonderful moment for Rudolf—his fist stung as if a hive of bees had attacked it, but the exhilaration made his blood rush and the cold of the night suddenly evaporated. Rudolf needed this small triumph of bloodletting as he sang his heart out again with the other men, all of them surrounded by blinding searchlights stretching into the black desert night and the glowering of the Americans with their guns at ready. The prisoners' insolence got them a day of bread and water, but it did not matter for a sense of victory was in the air— Germany was fighting back!

Chapter 13

October 1936
Northern Germany

As fall tiptoed quietly to the flat, low country of northern Germany and the leaves of the linden and horse chestnut trees changed to golden yellow and bright rust, Hitler Youth leader *Fähnleinführer* Ernst Ackermann announced a camping trip.

The troop would be going to Weserbergland, a hilly region where the Weser River begins its long winding course on its way to the North Sea. The boys, assembled outside the *Heim* for their Saturday Youth Day, began talking excitedly to one another.

"Calm down," Ernst said with a low growl. "This will be a longer trip than usual; each of you will need to miss several days of school. It is your responsibility to notify both your teachers and your parents. We will be gone four days."

He looked through the eager faces of new recruits who had not yet earned their test of courage. Backpacks needed inspecting and Ernst was seeking the best newcomer for the task. He walked slowly up and down the rows of boys, faintly scowling as he did. There was Wilhelm, with his unruly crop of red hair, but Wilhelm did not take membership in the DJ seriously; there was Dieter, a bright-eyed lad who talked too much; and then there was Rudolf who was quieter than most of the boys, yet Rudolf never failed to carry out orders. When he returned to the front of the troop, Ernst dismissed them and then he called out, "Rudi Meier, come here."

The boy jumped as if a slingshot hit him. He pulled nervously on the woggle that held his black tie as he walked toward Ernst.

"Yes, *Fähnleinführer?*" Rudolf said.

Ernst leaned over and touched the boy on the shoulder. "Rudi, I have decided to give you the responsibility of checking all the backpacks for the trip."

Rudolf's eyes opened wide. "Yes, *Fähnleinführer!* I will do my very best."

"Yes, I know you will," Ernst said. "And I want to tell you I appreciate how serious you are about the *Deutsche Jungvolk.*"

Rudolf nodded. "Thank you, *Fähnleinführer.*"

"I also need to talk to you about something else," Ernst said suddenly. "Come, let's go for a walk."

The boy moved his legs as fast as he could to keep up with Ernst who had a long stride and was heading toward a grove of linden trees. Although Rudolf had been granted an important responsibility, he wondered if he was in trouble and his nervousness made his stomach cramp—why else would his group leader ask to speak to him alone. Rudolf looked quickly out of the corner of his eye at the older boy. He noticed Ernst did not look to the right or left, but dead ahead as if he had something serious on his mind and was deeply concentrating on it. They moved quickly to the grove where the wind gently lifted leaves from the trees. When they reached a small bench, Ernst stopped, sat down, and then motioned for Rudolf to do the same.

"Rudi, I have a question I need to ask you," Ernst said after a long, tortuous moment, while Rudolf's stomach churned. He turned to look at Rudolf.

"Yes, what is it *Mein Fähnleinführer?*" the boy asked, croaking as if a large frog was stuck in his throat.

"I have only seen your grandfather, Herr Meier, at our Sunday parades. I would like to know why your grandmother never comes to see you march or to visit the *Heim?*"

The question stunned Rudolf and he felt like a blanket of fear descended on him instead of the softly falling leaves. He shrugged his shoulders and looked up into Ernst's face, knowing the honest answer—*Oma's* hatred for *Der Führer* and the Nazi regime—would only cause his family great trouble, so he replied, "I do not know."

Ernst, undeterred by the boy's answer, said, "Well, then, Rudi, you need to ask her. No—let me say this—you need to *tell* her that as the grandmother of a proud Hitler Youth she must come to our parades and also come to see our wonderful *Heim.*"

"Yes...yes, of course, I will do that," Rudolf stammered.

"Do you understand why your grandmother must do these things?"

A sudden sharp pain came to Rudolf's left temple and he began to rub that side of his face with his forefinger. He never felt so cornered, so overwhelmed. Telling his grandmother to do anything was unthinkable, and he could not even begin to imagine what her reaction would be. His answer was a meek, "Yes."

Ernst's thick eyebrows came together and a ferocious look enveloped his face. "Do you *understand* why your grandmother must do these things?" he yelled so loudly that Rudolf actually jumped.

"Yes, *Mein Fähnleinführer!* I...I! My grandmother must come to the parades and visit the *Heim* to show support for the Fatherland!"

Ernst smiled and his eyebrows relaxed, making his face look a bit comical. "Yes, Rudi, that is right...that is right! We are the future of Germany, and as Hitler Youth, we are responsible to make sure our families and friends are squarely behind us. We must always remember all good things come to us because of our beloved *Führer.*"

He patted the younger boy on the back, got up without saying anything else, and headed back to the *Heim.*

As far as the eye could see, boys in brown shirts and black shorts with swastika armbands scrambled over the green hillside singing the Horst Wessel song as they made their way back to camp for the noon meal.

Flags high, ranks closed,
The S.A. marches with silent solid steps.
Comrades shot by the red front and reaction
march in spirit with us in our ranks.

Rudolf flopped down on the grass next to his tent. His tent partner, Hans Lieberman did the same. Both boys were sweating and dirty from the long trek they took that morning with their fellow youths into the forest while carrying heavy backpacks. Once they were deep in the woods, with the advantage of the trees that still held their brilliantly-colored leaves, the troop divided into two groups and the boys entered into a spirited war game where one side wore red armbands and the other wore blue; the objective was for each boy to hunt down someone from the opposite side and tear off his armband, and the team with the most armbands won the game. Rudolf learned there was no holds barred and he soon sported a black eye after scuffling with a bigger boy from the other team. Much to his shame, his opponent ripped off his armband.

Rudolf and Hans were on the losing side, and they knew from past experience that the *Fähnleinführer* would soon punish the losing team. Rudolf took the drubbing seriously, but it seemed to him that Hans, who was older than Rudolf by a year, never took anything seriously.

"*Du dummer Idiot,*" Hans said, laughing at Rudolf's black eye and slapping him on the back. "What is the point of working yourself up into such a lather over a stupid war game? It is only a game after all!"

Rudolf looked harshly at his tent mate. "Well, at least I tried to fight off my opponent. What did you do to stop them?"

"What else was there to do but grovel in the mud?" Hans retorted. "Rudi, has it ever occurred to you our *Fähnleinführer* likes to put the bigger, older boys on one side and the smaller, younger ones on ours? With that combination, we are never going to win and our leader knows it!"

Rudolf breathed deeply. He realized Hans was possibly right—still, he could not bring himself to believe it, and he did not like Hans' sarcastic tone about their leader, Ernst. After all, under the Leadership Principal, authority moved down the line from the highest leader in the organization, and those leaders could only have achieved their position by being directly appointed from Adolf Hitler; Rudolf believed any order given, even by the youngest leader of Hitler Youth, came directly from *Der Führer* himself and must be obeyed.

"Maybe Ernst does that to test us," Rudolf said, "to make sure we can come up to the standard of the other team if we try harder."

Hans glared at Rudolf. "Are you joking, Rudi? He does it to see how much we get beat up and then he enjoys watching us squirm when he gives us our punishment."

"I cannot believe that, Hans! Ernst is our leader, after all. He is making sure we are striving to be the best. He would not punish us as a way to make fun of us!"

Hans snorted, but did not answer. Instead, he gulped water from his canteen. Rudolf realized the conversation was at an end, and in stony silence, he opened up his lunch pack to find thick chunks of dark bread and sausage.

After lunch, Rudolf stretched out on the ground, leaned on his backpack, and looked up at the sky. Clouds were amassing toward the north, a sure sign that a shower might appear. Some of the boys from the unit were kicking around a soccer ball on a level part of the green hillside. A light breeze lifted the swastika flag stuck in the ground near Ernst's tent. After a while, Hans, who was also resting against his backpack, got up, and pulled a blanket from the tent, saying he was cold.

Rudolf took in the view around him. How glad he was to be a part of this, to be in the beautiful German countryside with its green rolling hills and trees burnished red and gold. Here, he felt liberated from his grandmother's frown. After the private conversation with Ernst about his grandmother's noticeable absence from Hitler Youth activities, Rudolf trudged home with a sickened heart. The only way he could possibly approach the subject was to talk first to his grandfather with the hope that *Opa* could have some influence on the situation.

When he got home, he found Luise busy at the sewing machine set up on the kitchen table. She was making something for herself from material she bought from a Jewish merchant whose fabric shop was not far from where they lived. Luise was always happy when she was sewing; it was her creative outlet and she was known in the neighborhood for wearing better than average housedresses.

Rudolf eyed the thick potato soup cooking on the stove, and he took in a deep whiff of the rich pear cake his grandmother just pulled out of the oven, a wonderful autumn treat she always made for him.

"*Oma*, you have made my favorite cake!" Rudolf said with delight in his voice. He placed his books carefully on the table in the small front room, alongside the radio.

His grandmother gave him a sparkling smile. "Yes, Rudolf, I just couldn't resist the beautiful pears Frau Grabber had sitting out in the front of the market. A little bird told me you would be in the mood for a pear cake after all that marching around."

The boy sat down beside his grandmother and watched her sew. He saw the material was heavier than most of the fabric his grandmother usually worked on, and he reached over and felt the thickness of it. Seeing her grandson's appreciation, Luise smoothed the rich chocolate brown cloth that stretched over the end of the kitchen table where it came to rest on the immaculate kitchen floor she scrubbed every day on her hands and knees.

"It is beautiful, is it not, Rudolf? I am making a new coat—I have had that old rag of a green coat for years. I just couldn't help myself when Frau Weiner marked the material down—I have been eyeing it for weeks! She would never give such a low price for it, but she needs to get rid of everything in her shop—that poor woman and her family are being run out of Germany by *Der Führer* and his lackeys because they are Jews! What will I do without Frau Weiner, after all these years of buying material from her? What *Dummköpfe* will take over her store? No one but a Jew—with their eye for the very best—could know so much about good material."

Astounded by what his grandmother just said Rudolf's mouth dropped open.

"*Oma*," he said with exasperation in his voice, "Frau Weiner is a Jew, after all. It is better for Germany there is one less Jewish family in our beloved Fatherland!"

Luise looked up from her sewing and her eyes became hard. "What do you know about Frau Weiner? She is a good woman, for heaven's sake. She never cheated me, and she always put away the best material for me all these years. We are friends and I will miss her terribly! If I hear any more of this nonsense from you, I will throw away the pear cake and then see how angry your grandfather will be!"

Rudolf gulped and muttered he was sorry. But the boy, badly shaken by his grandmother's outburst, wondered if he really knew her. How could it be that she was friends with a Jew? Was she not aware of all the problems they created for the Fatherland? Now he was sure it would be very difficult to get her to attend his Hitler Youth rallies and visit the *Heim* because of her attitude, and then he would be in serious trouble.

To Rudolf's surprise, Luise stopped her sewing, put her hand over his, and looked him square in the eye. Her voice was soft, very unlike her earlier harsh tone and her face no longer held the sharp look that could make him wither.

"*Enkel*," Luise said, "listen to me for a moment. I have a pretty good idea what they teach you in the Hitler Youth. These people who run the Hitler Youth are Nazis, after all, and their explanation for all of Germany's troubles have always been laid on the Jews and the Communists—as if all Jews are Communists, for God's sake, which they aren't!

"Someday, Rudolf, you will learn Jews are the pretty much like everyone else, they are people who are just trying to make a living, trying to raise their children the best way they know how. As for the Communists, they wanted to change this country in their way, and the Nazis wanted to change this country in their own way. The Nazis won and now no one can have a different point of view." Luise's voice choked and she looked down at her hand which was covering his.

When she recovered a moment later, Luise said something that forever bored itself into Rudolf's brain: "But remember this, Rudolf— the Jews may have different ways about them, but they are human after all, with hopes and dreams like the rest of us."

Rudolf's blue eyes opened wide. He got up abruptly from the table, unsure what to say to his grandmother. She was refuting everything taught to him by Herr Bauer and the Hitler Youth. *Mein Gott*, the boy thought, she is an enemy of the Fatherland!

"I have a lot of homework to do, *Oma*," he said as he picked up his books from the front room and began walking slowly toward the stairs.

Luise was undeterred by his abruptness. "I hope you will think about what I just said, Rudolf." As the boy walked up the stairs, she began sewing again, and called out to him, "Yes, Rudolf, get your homework done. Your grandfather will be home soon and we shall have a wonderful dinner."

Just the memory of that awakening about his grandmother brought shivers to Rudolf as he continued to look up at the sky, now filled with fast-moving clouds. His thoughts turned to his anxiety a few days later when he was able to speak to his grandfather while Luise was in the back yard of the apartment building hanging the wash. Hermann was reading the newspaper when Rudolf nervously broached the subject. The boy felt as if he was going to be sick to his stomach, but he had no choice in the matter: Now was the time to do it.

"*Opa*," he said in a timid voice while sitting at the table doing his homework.

Hermann looked over the newspaper. "What is it, Rudolf?"

"*Opa*, I am afraid to tell you something, but I must tell you anyway."

Hermann put down the paper, got up from his chair and walked over to Rudolf.

"What is it?" he said, frowning.

"*Mein Fähnleinführer* asked me to take a walk with him outside the *Heim* the other day. He wanted to talk to me."

Immediately, Hermann's big face took on a look that Rudolf rarely saw; it was so terrifying that Rudolf put his eyes down.

"What would that *pimpf* have to say to you?" Hermann demanded, his fists curled, ready to fight.

"*Opa*," the boy cried out, "he has noticed grandmother never comes to our parades on Sunday and that she has never been to the *Heim*."

"What business is it of his that your grandmother does not go to those things?"

Rudolf felt like he was losing control of the situation, but he had to explain this problem to his grandfather. The boy took a deep breath. "It is the duty of everyone to support the Fatherland, *Opa! Fähnleinführer* asked me why *Oma* was absent from these things."

"Rudolf…what was your answer to him when he asked you that?" Hermann demanded in a sharp tone.

"I said I did not know why she was not at the parades," Rudolf answered as the sweat began to form on his forehead. "Then *Fähnleinführer* told me I needed to tell her that as the grandmother of a proud Hitler Youth she *must* be at the parades and she *must* visit the *Heim!*"

There was a hard silence in the room. Rudolf looked up at his grandfather and said in a small voice filled with fear, "I know I cannot tell *Oma* such a thing because I know she…she does not like *Der Führer*, so I am pleading with you to talk to her. I want to stay in the *Deutsche Jungvolk, Opa!* I am afraid if she does not show up to these things, I will be thrown out."

Hermann stood by Rudolf for what seemed to be a very long time, thinking. The boy sat very still and just looked at his grandfather's tightly clenched hands, the welding scars showing white. Finally, Hermann reached over and patted Rudolf on the head.

"*Ja*, Rudolf. I will see what I can do."

In the days after talking to his grandfather, Rudolf's grandmother was extraordinarily quiet. She rarely spoke to either her husband or grandson and seemed to lose herself in her sewing. The household was one of tense unspoken feelings, something Rudolf never felt before, at least not at this new level of his grandmother's unhappiness. He was nervous at the Hitler Youth parade held the Sunday before his troop went on the camping trip, but Rudolf's heart skipped a beat when he eyed Luise and Hermann standing together as his troop marched through the *Marktplatz* in the heart of Bremen. He even allowed himself to show them a small smile as he passed in review and he saw his grandfather nod slightly to him.

The boy felt light as a Zeppelin as he proudly opened the door for Luise to enter the *Heim* to show her where he spent so much of his time. Much to his surprise, *Oma*, dressed in her striking new coat, even joked a little. As they climbed up the steps from the cellar where the workshop and showers were located, she said, "Rudolf, how privileged you are! From now on, you will no longer have to wait to take your Saturday night bath after your grandfather and I take ours. You can just come over here!"

Rudolf's thoughts jolted to the present when he heard his *Fähnleinführer* call the troop together to mete out punishment to the losing team. Everyone scrambled to their feet and they stood in strict formation as Ernst paced back and forth in front of the boys. Rudolf could see Ernst's jaw bulging as he gritted his teeth in anger, and his thick brows formed an angry bridge across his forehead. As they stood in formation, a strong, cold wind lashed out of the north and clouds began to amass now into dark thunderheads threatening heavy rain.

After a momentary silence, the leader yelled, "Separate into your teams!" and the boys scrambled to stand with their teammates.

"You!" Ernst pointed to Rudolf's team, but Rudolf jolted to a straighter stance, feeling as if Ernst was pointing directly at him. "What a miserable performance today. How do you expect to represent our great Fatherland when you can't even win a measly war game! Your punishment is this…you will stand here at attention until I tell you to go back to your tents."

With that comment, Ernst dismissed the other team and they all headed back to the relative safety of their shelters while Rudolf's teammates stood in the gathering storm. Only the *Fähnleinführer* remained to watch over them.

The boys stood at attention, each looking straight ahead, stretching their bodies as tall as they possibly could. Time passed slowly, more than an hour. The wind blew in heaving gusts, causing the trees in the surrounding forest to let loose of their colorful leaves like silky scarves in the wind. The sky was now nearly black except for a small patch of blue to the south that the racing storm clouds had not yet overtaken.

Rudolf stood as straight as possible and found if he bent his knees a little, his body had some leeway against the wind's ferocity. He heard some of his teammates mutter under their breath about their punishment, but Rudolf was determined to say nothing. He kept reminding himself to follow the orders of his leader; it was not for him to question those orders.

Hans, who was standing directly in front of Rudolf, began trembling. The older boy's clothes were still wet, Rudolf noticed, from the muddy battle in the woods and his shaking began to grow worse as time passed.

Ernst continued his vigil by walking slowly around the perimeter, periodically stopping to yell at one of the boys for slouching.

Suddenly, it began to rain, and some of the boys moved from their positions, expecting Ernst to dismiss them, but he did not. Instead, like an angry bull, he bellowed at them to stand at attention, and he strode within the ranks to personally antagonize any of them who showed a moment of resistance against his orders.

Although Hans was still standing, he was shaking violently now. Ernst walked up to him and slapped him on the back of the head, demanding he stand tall.

"*Mein Fähnleinführer*," the boy mumbled, "I do not feel good...I am sick!"

"Stand as I tell you or you will really understand what it is to be sick!" Ernst yelled.

Hans attempted to straighten up but he could not. Instead, he collapsed on his side into the mud. Ernst swore disparagingly at the boy and then he looked at Rudolf with a smirk on his face.

"You, Rudi...is Hans not your tent partner?"

"Yes, *Fähnleinführer!*" Rudolf yelled against the sound of the pounding rain.

"Good! Then you will stand twice as long in his place!" Ernst said.

"Yes, *Fähnleinführer!*"

Ernst ordered two of the boys nearby to drag Hans to his tent. The rain gained in ferocity and soon other boys began to fall into the mud, unable to take the punishment, only to be hauled ignominiously to their tents. Rudolf, knowing he could not bear such humiliation, gritted his teeth and stood tall in the rain. Never in his life had he felt such agony, the muscles in his calves burning as if he had stuck his legs into the campfire, but he knew this was the only way to prove that he could take the punishment. Besides, for Rudolf, it was unthinkable to disobey an order. He continued to stand at attention, his eyes straight ahead, and his back ramrod straight.

Rudolf could see Ernst was thoroughly wet and cold himself because the troop leader had his hands jammed into his coat pockets as he walked again through the ranks of the remaining boys. He finally dismissed each one individually, all except Rudolf, who continued to stand alone in the storm, and then Ernst retired to his tent without saying a word to him.

The boy was, at first, terrified when he realized he was alone. The earth-shattering thunder shook Rudolf to his core, and the deep gloom was only broken by lightening that crackled periodically in the forest like a camera's flash bulb. A dense mist began to form close to the ground, hiding the tents, yet above the mist the grotesque limbs of the trees swayed and moaned. Rudolf felt absolutely abandoned, and that feeling of fear he always dreaded clawed at his stomach.

Surely, *Fähnleinführer* will come out any minute to dismiss me, Rudolf believed. But Ernst did not come.

Rudolf entertained the idea of simply walking back to his tent and climbing in out of the rain. That idea only lasted a moment, however, when he realized this was his real test of courage, his *Mutprobe.* This was more courageous than jumping from the roof of the *Heim* into a canvass held by other Hitler Youth. No matter how miserable he felt at this moment, he would not falter. So he stood in the rain, unbowed.

An hour later, Ernst came back to check on him. The leader's face showed surprise that Rudolf was still there as if he expected to find him on the ground or back in his tent. He walked up to him, touched him on the shoulder, and said, "Dismissed!"

Rudolf smiled and saluted him with his arm held out in the proper position, saying as loud as he could, "*Heil Hitler!*"

Chapter 14

Late December 1944 - Early January 1945
Arizona

As if the new German offensive was not enough to trigger excitement among the Camp Papago Park prisoners, Rudolf heard whispers about a tunnel being dug by men quartered in Compound 1 A—one of the camp's five prisoner compounds that housed uncooperative POWs, many of them previous escapees. Since there were many rumors that roamed through the camp, Rudolf paid scant attention, his mind remaining on the possibility the Third Reich might indeed rise up to beat the Allies.

One day, while digging out the muck of an irrigation ditch, Helmut leaned over and said in a low voice, "Have you noticed the new *faustball* field?"

Rudolf nodded half-heartedly. He was not much into the sport which was an Italian version of volleyball; Rudolf's preference was soccer.

"Where do you think the dirt is coming from?" Helmut asked.

"I suppose the Americans are bringing it in," Rudolf answered, wiping his brow. He was hot from the labor even though the December day was cold. "I understand the camp commander has approved it."

Helmut pursed his lips together in a knowing way. "No, that's not where it's coming from."

Rudolf stopped his digging. "Where then?'

"From an escape tunnel in Compound 1 A."

"I heard about it, but I do not believe it," Rudolf said.

"It is true, Rudi! The tunnel runs from under the bathhouse, past the double barbed-wire fence to the edge of the canal. About two dozen men are planning to escape to Mexico."

Rudolf's jaw dropped. He looked quickly around to make sure none of the guards saw his surprised reaction, for he did not want to be the one that might alert them of the escape. As he slung mud to clean the irrigation ditch, all Rudolf could think about was the breakout and that he was not part of it.

A few days later, Rudolf and the work crew returned to the Feller farm, picking the last of the cotton crop; the remaining cotton bolls had popped open with the deep freeze.

Rudolf felt nervous as he dragged his sack to the scales at the end of day; he could see Bob Feller standing nearby waiting to weigh the cotton picked by each POW, and Rudolf was not sure what to say to him.

After such a display of discourtesy, Rudolf wondered what he could possibly do to make the situation right. He was unsure why he said what he did: it was as if his response to Bob's question about being anti-Semitic simply flung itself out of his throat, uncontrolled. That jolted him, and for the first time in his life, he felt as if he had no original thought of his own. His love for the Fatherland and all of its teachings about Jews suddenly became a painful jagged question mark in his mind. The image of *Oma* appeared to him suddenly, and he recalled what she told him many years ago—her voice choking with emotion—that the Hitler Youth was wrongly teaching him to believe all the problems of Germany were instigated by Jews.

When Rudolf handed Bob his sack of cotton, their eyes met, and Rudolf squared his shoulders. "Bob," he said, "I...I apologize for my behavior the other day. You and your family have been good to me and the other men. I had no right to say what I did."

Bob smiled warmly, and put out his hand which Rudolf readily accepted. "Hey, Christmas is coming. Say, how about you and Helmut coming for dinner?"

Rudolf looked confused. "Christmas dinner...?"

"We're Americans, not just Jews...we happily celebrate all the holidays!"

It was as if a great weight lifted off Rudolf. He laughed like a child. "Can we finish our discussion about the Hemingway book?"

"You bet! And be prepared for me to ask you lots of questions!" Bob said.

"That is only fair," Rudolf replied. "We will talk of many things!"

Christmas dinner with the Fellers never came for Rudolf and Helmut. Instead, the rowdy Battle of the Bulge celebration forced the commander to suspend all prisoner passes during the upcoming Christmas holiday weekend. He feared something was brewing among the restless Germans, and his intuition proved correct: twenty-five men from the troublemaker's compound disappeared through the hidden tunnel and escaped the night of December 23, a Saturday. Since no head count was done until Sunday afternoon—Christmas Eve Day—the escapees had hours of lead time over their captors.

Rudolf sat at the mess table on Christmas morning, his hands cupped under his chin. His bloodshot blue eyes looked like cracked cue balls and he suffered from a mighty headache, brought on by drinking too much of the citrus schnapps on Christmas Eve with Helmut; they had quietly celebrated Christmas as well as the escape of their fellow comrades, stretched out on their cots in the dark of their barrack, listening to the thundering rain.

"Do you think they will make it to Mexico?" Rudolf asked mournfully, wishing to the depth of his being that he were free like the escapees and on his way to a land full of dark-eyed senoritas, his sexual frustrations suddenly overcoming his desire to go home to Germany.

Helmut nodded negatively, slowly, as if his head hurt too. "They are dummies after all, Rudi! What is out there but desert, snakes, and starvation? Mark my words, they will be caught or give up because of this horrendous rain and then what...two weeks in the guardhouse with nothing but bread and water? As for me, I am happy here. You will not catch me doing such foolishness."

The Americans did not find the escape tunnel until the day after Christmas and local newspapers began printing angry editorials. Infuriated citizens accused the camp of incompetent management, expressing concern about the prospect of twenty-five hardened Nazis roaming the landscape with rape, murder or, worse yet, sabotage on their minds. Slowly, however, over the period of a month, with the aid of the FBI, local police, and members of the Papago Indian Tribe, the prisoners were caught—a ragtag bunch of starving and thirsty men whose only thoughts were to return home to Germany.

But during that month of hope for the escapees—every day— Rudolf listened intently to camp gossip, trying to learn the fate of his fellow POWs. Once in a while, he would see his friend from U-893, Fritz Kraus, who was housed in a different compound at the camp. The conversations between Rudolf and Fritz were usually short, slipped in during work details or when their compounds were involved in competitive soccer or *faustball* matches.

On a cold day in mid-January while Rudolf was using a pole-mounted pruning hook to pull ripe grapefruit off trees, he said to Fritz, "What do you hear about the men who escaped?"

Fritz grinned and pushed back a shock of hair that had fallen over his eyes. He put his hand in his pocket and pulled out a worn newspaper page with the photographs of the twenty-five men. Most of the pictures were marked with a cross.

"It's my way of keeping track of those caught and those who are still free," Fritz said, looking around to make sure no guards were watching, and then he handed the newspaper to Rudolf who stopped picking and quickly glanced at the men's pictures. His face turned sour when he saw how many had been caught.

"But, it was a nice try...don't you think?" Fritz asked after seeing Rudolf's face. "I wonder...what did the Americans *think* would happen when they put all the men into one compound who had escaped before?"

Rudolf shrugged. "I suppose they thought they could keep a closer watch on them."

"It was *stupid*, if you ask me," Fritz said. "Anyway, Rudi, listen to this…I heard the most amazing story!"

"What is it?" Rudolf asked as he reached as high as he could with the pole. A large grapefruit fell to the ground with a thump.

Fritz chuckled, barely able to contain his laughter as he picked up the fruit. "Last November, a group of high-ranking American officers toured the camp. They went into the troublemaker's compound—you know where the tunnel was dug—and a colonel actually planted his boots on top of the hidden tunnel entrance proclaiming there would never be a tunnel escape at Papago Park—the ground was too hard!"

Rudolf opened his mouth in surprise and began to laugh with Fritz. Both of them doubled over in mirth and eventually a guard walked over, warning them to quit horsing around. After the guard left, they continued to laugh at the stupidity of the Americans.

Chapter 15

December 1936
Bremen, Germany

With Rudolf's test of courage drawing nearer, he grew nervous about the character interview with Ernst and other Hitler Youth leaders; Rudolf knew he had to pass this interview if he were to become a permanent member of the Nazi organization. Every evening after he finished his homework and changed his clothes for bed, he began thinking about the interview and the conversation he had had with his grandmother. Troubled by her friendship with the Jew merchant, the silence of his room was small comfort for his overwhelming anxiety.

What would he say if asked about his family's support of the Nazis? Rudolf knew he would be able to say without a doubt his grandfather supported the Nazis—after all, it was his grandfather's decision to let him join the Hitler Youth, and it was his grandfather who made his grandmother come to the parades.

If he said anything detrimental about *Oma*, he knew she might be taken to a KZ, a concentration camp the Nazis established for political enemies of the Third Reich. If he lied about her, then he was committing a crime against the State. Rudolf felt as if his mind would wear out with his constant worry.

One particularly troubling night, Rudolf thought about one of the older members of the Bremen Hitler Youth, a 16-year-old Rudolf only knew by sight. The gossip was that the boy had reported his father to his Hitler Youth leader, saying his father openly swore at home against the Nazis. The leader reported the father to the Gestapo, and the father was sent to Dachau; as for the son, he received a promotion to squad leader.

The real question for his tortured mind boiled down to one thing: Was his *Oma*, this elderly woman who cooked, cleaned, and kept his *Opa* happy, an enemy of the State because of her hatred of all things Nazi? Surely not—she was an old woman, after all. What could she do to hurt Germany with her cranky opinions? And since his grandfather had pushed her to attend DJ events, she was more circumspect even in that regard.

After much thought, Rudolf knew the only solution for him was to lie. He had to admit his love for his grandmother despite her quick temperament and dislike of the Nazis. As for his committing a crime against the State—well, he was not prepared to even think about that.

On the Saturday morning of his character interview, Rudolf paid particular attention to his uniform, and he spent considerable time combing down the cow lick at the back of his head. When he came downstairs, Hermann looked up from the newspaper and smiled.

"Well, Rudolf, this is the big day. *Ja?*"

Rudolf nodded and nervously fiddled with the scarf around his neck, looking at his grandfather with big eyes.

"You will do well, I am sure of it," Hermann said. "Your grandmother and I are very proud of you, and we know you will pass this test with flying colors!"

The boy reached in his pants pocket to make sure he had his performance booklet which recorded his progress in athletics and Nazi indoctrination since his first day in the *Deutsche Jungvolk*. Seeing how nervous his grandson was, Hermann put down the newspaper and got up from his favorite chair to pat the boy on the back.

"Good luck, Rudolf!"

There was a knock at the front door and Hermann answered it. Standing in the hallway were several other boys from the DJ unit who came to pick up Rudolf.

"Go on now, Rudolf," Hermann said. The boy looked back at his grandfather and gave him a wan smile as he walked out. Hermann shook his big head and said to Luise as he closed the door, "Rudolf seems to be unnerved by this character interview."

"God only knows what goes on inside that *Heim*," she said with resignation in her voice.

The old man thought about that as he went back to his chair and sat down. Luise, who was standing at the sink drying dishes, looked over at her husband and gave him a sweet smile. Unexpectedly, a disturbing thought unsettled Hermann about his grandson's interview, and he glanced over at his beloved wife. A small tremor went through his large frame.

Hermann's mind whirled: She has done what I have asked her to do; surely, the Hitler Youth have stopped gnawing that bone. Yet, why else would Rudolf be so nervous? As he brushed aside the heavy feeling of anxiety, he reminded himself that everything was right with his world: He had a beautiful wife who could make a hearty meal from scraps of potato peelings if the situation called for it, he had a smart grandson who was in *Gymnasium*, and his work at the shipyard was forever challenging, particularly as the Nazis continued to build up the German Navy with new types of U-boats. He shook his head again, cleared his throat, and continued reading the Nazi propaganda in the morning newspaper.

Suddenly, Hermann put down the paper and said to Luise as if his abrupt thought would protect his family from harm: "You know, Luise, it is time we put the *Führer's* picture up in the living room."

Her answer was to drop one of her coveted porcelain dishes. As she picked up the pieces, a sour look shadowed her face.

Rudolf sat as straight as he possibly could in the blond-colored chair in Ernst's small office at the *Heim*. His back was to the window which overlooked the park where Ernst had taken him for a walk several months ago. It was mid-December now and the park reflected the cold, icy day: The trees were bare and the grass was brown and withered.

Ernst and two other Hitler Youth leaders were going through Rudolf's file. One of them complimented Rudolf on his excellent standing in his physical agility tests, running 60 meters in just under 12 seconds at the fall camping trip.

"Ah, yes, I remember you now," one of them said. "You were the one who stood so long in the rain!"

Rudolf nodded slightly.

Ernst smiled. Then he said, "Yes, Rudolf proved himself quite admirably that day, quite admirably."

The *Fähnleinführer* sat with his hands together, fingertips touching each other. "Well, Rudi, you have correctly recited all of the verses of the Horst Wessel song, and given us correct answers as to the history of the Nazi party. Now I just need to know a few other things about you and your family."

"Yes, *Mein Fähnleinführer*," Rudolf said.

The leader began moving his hands, tapping his fingers repeatedly together. Rudolf took a deep breath. He could feel sweat forming under his armpits.

"Why are you living with your grandparents instead of your mother and father?"

The question shook Rudolf, but he was determined to answer as correctly as he could.

"*Mein Fähnleinführer*, my mother and father died when I was very young. It was an accident, and that is why I live with my grandparents."

"What do you know about the accident?"

"Nothing…nothing more than that. My grandparents do not talk about it. I am not really sure what kind of an accident it was."

"How well do you think you know your grandparents?" Ernst asked.

The boy did not hesitate in his answer. "I am close to my grandparents, I believe as close as one can be with people who are so old."

There was a pause as the three leaders nodded at one another. One finally asked, "Are your grandparent's members of the Nazi party?"

"No," Rudolf said.

"Why not?"

"I do not know."

"What are the comments in your house about our great leader, Adolf Hitler?"

"That he has provided us with jobs and food on the table," Rudolf said.

"Who says that? Your grandfather or your grandmother?" Ernst demanded to know.

"My grandfather," Rudolf answered.

"What about your grandmother?"

Rudolf took in a deep breath, but did it slowly so that he would not look nervous.

"She is not interested in political matters."

"But when you first came to the DJ, she did not come to parades or to the *Heim*," Ernst said.

"That is true, *Mein Fähnleinführer*, but after you and I talked together, I spoke to my grandfather about it and she has been to the parades since then and to the *Heim.*"

"But why in the beginning did she not come?"

"Because she would rather stay home to cook and sew," Rudolf said, his voice growing stronger with each answer.

"Is there no other reason?"

"I know of no other reason."

Ernst continued to drum his fingers against one another, thinking. Then he said, "You have a friend named Lothar."

"Yes, *Mein Fähnleinführer*." Rudolf felt a pang of surprise.

"Why is he not in the Hitler Youth?"

"I do not know, *Mein Fähnleinführer.*"

"Have you talked to him about joining?" Ernst asked.

Rudolf thought for a minute. "I have talked about our activities, but he does not seem interested in joining."

"Do you know that just ten days ago, our beloved *Führer* decreed a law that has made Hitler Youth membership mandatory?"

"Yes, *Mein Fähnleinführer.*"

"And what are you going to do about it?" Ernst asked him in a snide voice.

Rudolf was silent for a moment. "I am going to discuss this with him today, as soon as I leave here, *Mein Fähnleinführer!*"

"Good, Rudi! Very good! We each have a duty to the Fatherland to make sure all German boys and girls are members of the Hitler Youth. You need to explain this to your friend Lothar."

A few days later, Rudolf stood on the second story ledge of the *Heim* and looked down at the older Hitler Youth members who were holding a large canvass for him to jump into. This was his *Mutprobe*, his test of courage, his moment in the limelight when he would become a full member of the *Deutsche Jungvolk.*

From this height, he could see the Weser River and the ships moving up and down its channel. The wind was blowing hard from the north and Rudolf felt his fear of heights begin to overtake him. Several other boys who were also on probation in the DJ were standing on the ledge, encouraging one another as their time came to jump.

Before he jumped, the conversation with Lothar entered his mind. Lothar had looked at him in a strange way when Rudolf broached Lothar about joining the Hitler Youth. "You are my best friend, Rudi," Lothar said, "but I have no interest in marching and playing war games."

"It is not a matter of marching and playing war games, Lothar!" Rudolf said in exasperation. "It is now the duty of every German youth to join. Don't you know about the new edict *Der Führer* just signed saying all German children must be a member?"

Lothar, who was sitting on the curb outside their apartment building with his sack of marbles, answered sullenly, "Yes, I know about the new edict. My parents are not happy about it because they need me to help them at the bakery. It will be very difficult for my family if I have to spend Wednesday and Saturday afternoons and Sunday mornings doing things they do not consider necessary like marching 25 kilometers."

Rudolf opened his eyes wide. "Lothar! It is your duty as a German citizen to join. This is more important than working in the bakery. This is…this is being a part of the Fatherland!"

The lanky boy got up wearily from his seat on the curb. "That is all fine and good for you to say, Rudi, but my family has food on the table only because we work daily at the bakery. We do not get paid regularly like your grandfather. We are in a different situation and as my friend, you must understand that!"

Rudolf's stomach churned. Why couldn't Lothar see how important this was…for Germany, for Rudolf's reputation in the Hitler Youth?

Rudolf pointed his finger in Lothar's face. "You must join, you must!"

Lothar grabbed Rudolf's hand and moved it away from him. Rudolf could see how mad he was because Lothar's face turned red and he suddenly swung his bag of marbles as hard as he could, hitting Rudolf in the arm. "Don't ever tell me again that I must join!"

As Rudolf jumped from the ledge the vision of Lothar's angry face came to him. It was the end of their friendship and he knew it. When he landed safely in the canvass, he could hear the members of his troop hollering with glee at his courage.

Later when he stood tall and received his coveted Hitler Youth dagger from Ernst inscribed with *"Blut und Ehre"*—Blood and Honor—Rudolf knew this was where he wanted to be.

His friendship with Lothar was a thing of the past.

Chapter 16

February 1945
Arizona

The excitement during the past six weeks kept Rudolf's mind off his confusion over his long-held Nazi beliefs. But after the capture of the last escapee—the longest holdout was the German leader of Camp Papago park, *Fregattenkapitän* Jürgen Wattenberg— and the disappointing failure of the German offensive in the Battle of the Bulge, Rudolf tried desperately to keep busy. During the day, he volunteered for any work crew he could and at night, he focused on teaching English language classes to the men in his compound. He longed to see Bob Feller again, to test his Nazi convictions against an American willing to talk about his own beliefs. That time would come during the spring planting of the cotton crop and he was preparing himself by reading books on democracy at the camp library.

The movies were another diversion for Rudolf, shown every other Sunday in the recreation hall. For the price of fifteen cents apiece, the prisoners were able to see American films, mostly westerns with he-men actors like Randolph Scott and Glenn Ford. Rudolf looked forward to the westerns—a distraction from camp life and a reminder of his favorite childhood author, Karl May, the German writer whose novels were akin to American writer, Zane Grey.

One Sunday, Rudolf and Helmut settled in for a couple hours of entertainment. Much to their surprise, the film was *Tomorrow, the World!* Rudolf recognized the words of Adolf Hitler: "Today we rule

Germany, tomorrow the world." He said to Helmut, "I don't think this is a western."

"No," Helmet said. "I think we are in for a political lesson."

The film opened with Germany at war. Because of the conflict, the parents of a twelve-year-old boy send their son to live in the United States with his uncle. Soon the American family is baffled by Emil's actions, and even though they try to make him part of their lives, Emil cannot get along with anyone, spouting Nazi racist propaganda. Eventually, Emil steals secret information from his uncle who works for the War Department. Caught and threatened with imprisonment, the uncle saves Emil, personally vowing to take the boy in hand. Only then does Emil reject Nazism.

An uneasy feeling engulfed Rudolf. The actor playing the part of young Emil spoke in a stilted German accent and had an arrogant demeanor. In a crucial scene where Emil dressed in his Hitler Youth uniform soon after arriving at his uncle's home, Rudolf slumped in his seat; an overwhelming feeling of shame descending upon him.

Rudolf pulled his handkerchief out of his pocket when the film ended and wiped his forehead, wet with sweat. Helmut looked at him and smiled, not noticing his friend's emotional reaction.

"We are monsters, are we not?" Helmut said jokingly.

"I suppose we are," Rudolf said, his voice sullen.

Rudolf spoke little as he and Helmut walked back to the barrack. When he got inside, he dropped down on his cot, unable to get the movie out of his mind. It was an exaggeration, Rudolf thought in defense of himself and the Hitler Youth, yet a sense of disquiet flowed over him, making him feel as if he were going to be sick. Trying to control his thoughts, Rudolf got up and walked outside again where he could see his fellow prisoners working in their small gardens, attempting to bring a touch of home to the barren camp. Many owned dogs, and some even raised chickens and rabbits.

Rudolf strode purposely past them, heading toward the double barbed-wire fence, near the Arizona Crosscut Canal, stopping abruptly as he came close to the barrier, and sat down in the dirt, facing the ever-present sandstone rock formation. He pulled a cigarette out of his pocket, sticking it in his mouth, unlit. Alone and desolate like the loathsome mountainous shape that lay before him, Rudolf tried to justify his involvement in the Hitler Youth at the age of twelve. He told himself it was a way to get out from under his grandmother's control, but he knew it was his passion for Germany and his idolization of Adolf Hitler that prompted him to embrace the youth organization with his whole being.

The only thing Rudolf felt sure of was that he never acted like an out-of-control Hitler Youth. His grandmother made sure he was home when he was supposed to be, not roaming the streets, or acting maliciously toward Jews. Yes, it was true he had written *Juden* on the walls of Jewish businesses along with other Hitler Youth when he thought no one was looking, but that is all he dared do—for in truth, Rudolf was more afraid of his *Oma* than he was of his Hitler Youth leaders. That she might find out he had done something wrong, simply struck terror to the core of his being. Even worse, was his uncompromising fear that she would discuss his errant behavior with his grandfather.

The only person he knew who acted like the character in the movie was *Fähnleinführer* Ernst Ackermann, the head of his *Deutsch Jungvolk* troop. Rudolf had heard him speak insolently sometimes to old Jews, and once Rudolf saw Ernst spit at a Jew fruit peddler who sold him an apple with a worm in it.

Rudolf remembered when Ernst had sternly questioned him about his grandmother; how terrified he was that his leader might learn his grandmother believed Jews were no different than other people. And now, here in America, he was friends with a Jew! What would *Der Führer* think of that? Rudolf noticed his hand shaking as he tried to light his cigarette.

Suddenly, everything seemed jumbled and mixed up, and Rudolf's disgust over his confusion caught in his throat. It seemed far easier to hold a single point of view: a closed mind brought less sleepless nights, yet he no longer wanted to be mindless and blindly accepting. He had done that and felt ashamed for it. Deep down in his heart, Rudolf recognized a small part of himself in the character of Emil.

A noise interrupted his reverie and when he looked up, he was startled to see the strange pock-like rock formation that sat implacably before him engulfed in a dust storm. It was moving fast in his direction. He knew he had no opportunity to run back to the barrack, and remembered when he began working at the Feller cotton farm that a fierce dust storm just like this one had engulfed the men. The guards had yelled for everyone to drop down and lay among the cotton plants until the storm passed. He could see the Arizona Crosscut Canal on the other side of the barbed-wire fence, but he had no way to get to it, so he crushed his cigarette quickly and curled into a ball, putting his forehead on the ground and pulled his jacket over his head, covering his mouth and nose with a handkerchief he quickly yanked from his pocket.

The maelstrom surrounded him; it was almost like swirling fog, but instead of mist, fine earth moved into every crevice of his body. He tried to hold his breath, thinking if he did the dust would stay out of his mouth, but finally he had to breathe and the dust cloaked his lips and tongue, seeping into his throat, choking him.

Amid the tempest, as he lay battered by the elements, his thoughts moved through landmarks of his life: standing on the sidewalk in Bremen's *Marktplatz* with his grandfather and grandmother, looking straight into the eyes of Adolf Hitler; jumping from the roof of the *Heim* as part of his induction into the Hitler Youth; and being captured by the Americans after U-893 sank off the East Coast of the United States.

Suddenly, a scene flowed into Rudolf's mind like the dust swirling around him: he was about sixteen years old and his Hitler Youth troop had been assigned the task of enforcing the nightly curfew in Bremen's *Marktplatz* area. The Gestapo, busy with more important war priorities in 1940, gladly put the task on the shoulders of the *Hitlerjugend*.

The troop marched through the *Marktplatz*, resplendent in their uniforms. Rudolf felt proud and grown up, as the troop strode past the tall statue of Roland. Rudolf remembered hearing a yell, and then about twenty boys surged out from behind the old gothic Town Hall with sticks and bricks, attacking the *Hitlerjugend*. The troop was caught off guard, and although they tried to defend themselves, the attack was fierce and some lay injured on the ground, crying uncontrollably for their mothers.

This was not supposed to happen to staunch Hitler Youth who played war games, and marched perfectly together, Rudolf thought. He managed to ward off several attacks, but then he came face to face with his old friend, Lothar, and he felt the shock of a direct punch to his nose. Surprised by the blow, he put his hand up and felt warm blood gushing through his fingers, flowing on his freshly pressed Hitler Youth shirt, staining it. Lothar stood for a moment and looked at Rudolf, a scowl on his face and then he melted into the crowd.

The boys, who attacked the troop, including Lothar, were jauntily dressed, in British fashion, carrying umbrellas and wearing scarves around their necks. Rudolf had heard of the Swing Kids, those who secretly gathered to watch American movies, dressed like English teens, and danced to nigger jazz, but he had not seen Lothar in a long time. He did not know his former friend was part of a group of juveniles, mostly boys, who hated the Nazis and flouted the law that all youth were required to join the *Hitlerjugend.*

Gestapo whistles filled the night air and the Swing Kids vanished. This was their neighborhood and they knew its nooks and crannies far better than the Gestapo. Rudolf knew its hiding places, too, but a sudden, cold fear flooded over him and he kept quiet, while the other members of the troop swore and pointed to where they thought the attackers disappeared. He stood where he was and pinched the end of his nose to stop the bleeding, trying to look angry like the other boys instead of fearful. He had heard what happened to Swing Kids: if caught, they went to concentration camps or worse—in some instances, they were hung.

Rudolf was not unmindful of that day long ago when he and Lothar were late to *Gymnasium.* Their teacher, Herr Braun, had physically punished Lothar, yet Lothar did not snitch on Rudolf, although he easily could have done so. Rudolf always felt grateful to Lothar for protecting him then, and he vowed to protect Lothar now; even though the Gestapo intensely questioned him, Rudolf maintained it was too dark to see the attackers.

As he lay on the ground, covered by sand, Rudolf could not imagine why the recollection of that night came to him. Finally, the storm passed; he opened his eyes and struggled to get up, dusting himself off as best he could, looking at the landscape that surrounded him. It was still the same—the forbidding fence blocking his freedom, the eerie rock formation, the ever present guard tower, but he was not the same. Something inside him felt different but Rudolf had no idea what it was.

He walked back toward the barrack, his head down, seeing nothing before him except his shoes as he automatically placed one foot in front of another, returning to his barrack, to an uncertain future. He found Helmut sitting alone on a stool he had made out of the skeleton of a giant saguaro cactus, a novelty among the Germans prisoners who took advantage of the camp's woodworking shop.

"You got caught in the sand storm, didn't you?" Helmut asked. "I have been concerned about you."

Rudolf nodded and sat down on the edge of his cot. "I had some things to think about."

Helmut got up and walked over to Rudolf. "I am sorry, my friend, to give you this," he said as he handed Rudolf a telegram from the German Red Cross. "It came after you went for your walk."

The young German sat still for a long time with the envelope in his hand, knowing the contents before he opened it: either one or the both of his grandparents were dead. He had no relatives except his grandparents, and he could think of no other reason that the German Red Cross would send him a telegram. He finally ripped it open and read that his grandmother, Luise Meier, had been killed during an Allied bombing raid on Bremen.

Rudolf crushed the telegram, and a roar came rushing out of his mouth from the depth of his being: "No! No! *No!*"

How could this happen at a time when he never felt so confused and forlorn? His eyes began to burn as the dust and the tears mixed together. He put his hands up to his face to ward off the flood, but it was no use as his body convulsed with uncontrollable sobs. Helmut, trying to comfort him, patted his shoulder. Finally, Rudolf uncovered his face and the startling blue eyes which made him look so alive were dimmed and swollen. He began to swear.

"Goddamn them! Goddamn the Allies! How could they kill a woman who never had anything to do with this war?" Rudolf demanded.

Helmut did not answer for a long time, and then he sat down on the cot next to Rudolf. "That is what happens in war, Rudi," he said in a quiet tone. "The men who make war only think about how powerful they will become, and how many countries they will rule, but there is little thought about the soldier who dies alone in a ditch or the peasants in the field who were doing nothing more than pitching hay or feeding the pigs when bombers strafe them just because they are there and considered the enemy, because they are simply German!"

Helmut took a deep breath and continued in a low, harsh voice, "The real reason for this, Rudi, is that we Germans wanted food on the table and political stability. Hitler told us he would make us masters of the world! And look at us now—we are masters of nothing."

Rudolf's face became inflamed, his fury building inside him like a stove stoked with too much fuel, ready to blow at any moment. He jumped up and ran to his foot locker, pulling out his duffel bag. He dug furiously inside it and came up with the small picture of Adolf Hitler he had purchased long ago at the Nuremberg Rally when he was so proud to be a Hitler Youth. He had carried it with him during his labor service in Russia, his naval training, onboard U-893 and jammed in his jacket before he jumped in the ocean as his U-boat slid into the sea.

He held it up and stared at it, remembering when he sat on his bed at home in Bremen doing his homework and his grandmother had come in with an armful of clean clothes to put away in the dresser. He had hidden the photo among his underwear because he could not think of anyplace else to hide it, and when his grandmother felt the metal frame, she pulled the picture out of the drawer, stared at it for a long moment, and asked, "Where did you get this?" an iciness to her voice that made Rudolf cringe.

"I bought it when I was in Nuremberg," Rudolf answered in a meek voice, wishing he could crawl under his bed away from her verbal onslaught.

"Humph!" she said, as she shoved the hated object back among his clothes. "Be careful, Rudolf…you are worshipping him as if he were Jesus Christ."

Now, with the death of *Oma*, the burning rage inside Rudolf erupted and he threw the picture on the floor, crushing the small frame and the glass under his heel—the glass grinding into the face of *Der Führer*. He stood looking at it with fury, then dismay. What had he done?

Suddenly, voices could be heard from outside and Helmut quickly shoved the broken pieces of glass under Rudolf's cot with his foot. "There are those here who would not like what you just did," Helmut whispered.

Rudolf knew that, and he sat down on his cot with a thump, his throat suddenly constricted with fear. Some months before, a murder had occurred at Camp Papago Park. A prisoner was suspected of treason for supplying information about his U-boat to American interrogators. Considered a traitor to the Third Reich, he was hung in a camp bathroom. The seven men involved in the murder had been court-martialed by the Americans and were awaiting execution.

Rudolf trembled when he considered what he had done in his grief for his grandmother. If others in the camp found out, would that they think him a traitor? Would he be killed for that simple, grief-stricken act? All he knew in this terrible moment was that his grandfather was alone and he wished with his whole heart that he was with him.

A few weeks later, Rudolf received a tear-stained letter.

"Your *Oma* was riding the electric streetcar in the *Marktplatz* near the statue of Roland, when the bombing began," his grandfather wrote. "She was with one of our neighbors, I think you remember Lothar Volkmann's grandmother, on her way to buy yardage for a new dress at a shop in another area of Bremen—*Oma* still complained bitterly about the closing of our neighborhood cloth store after all these years. Mrs. Volkmann told me everyone on the streetcar began screaming as the bombs exploded. Amid the confusion to get out and run to a shelter, *Oma's* dress caught on something, and she was unable to get herself untangled before another bomb exploded. Her last words to me that morning, as I kissed her goodbye, were that she hoped to receive a letter from you soon. She felt comforted you are in the care of the Americans."

The letter dropped from Rudolf's hands. He had a vision of *Oma* trying to get out of the streetcar, and he imagined the fear she must have felt as she tore at the dress she so proudly made; the vision came unwanted to his mind's eye, and Rudolf shook his head to ward off the mental picture, but he could not stop his eyes from overflowing with tears.

Chapter 17

May 1937
Bremen, Germany

Rudolf was not listening to his teacher, Herr Braun. Instead, he was thinking about a girl, a most beautiful girl he saw for the first time yesterday. It was during an embarrassing incident and Rudolf still stung from the shame of it, but no matter how hard he tried, he could not seem to shake the vision of her from his mind.

It happened in the middle of a rowing competition on the Weser River where all of his energy was focused on winning. Rudolf was in a dead heat with his opponent when he inadvertently glanced over at the left bank near the finish line and saw the dark-haired girl standing at the river's edge. She gave him a demure smile. In an instant, he lost his heart and the hard-fought race.

Fähnleinführer Ernst Ackermann stood with his hands on his hips as Rudolf forlornly pulled the boat from the water, and the boy glanced fearfully at his leader out of the corner of his eye.

"Rudi, what happened?" Ernst screamed in a fit of fury. "All you had to do was give it one more push and you would have won!"

"I...I don't know, *Mein Fähnleinführer*," Rudolf stammered, his face red from the dishonor of losing such an important competition with a Hitler Youth team from Bremerhaven, Bremen's port city located sixty kilometers away at the headwaters of the Weser River and the North Sea.

While Ernst continued his tongue lashing, Rudolf shyly looked past him, hoping to see the girl again. He spied her walking away from the river and, as if she knew he was looking for her, she turned her head for a moment and their eyes met. Rudolf tried in vain to bend his attention back to Ernst, but he stood frozen, his heart pounding thunderously in his chest.

Ernst stopped his harangue and grabbed Rudolf by the shoulder, physically shaking the boy. "Why are you not listening to me?"

"I am…I am listening!" Rudolf cried out, his blond features even more aflame with this new, strange feeling flooding his body, a feeling he could not control and was thankful Ernst's anger had distracted him.

At that moment, another race started and Ernst let loose of Rudolf, focusing his attention on the next competition. Rudolf stood steadfastly next to his leader, afraid to move for fear he would incur more of Ernst's wrath, but his thoughts were filled with the vision of the girl, her dark hair glistening like a crown as she walked away from him.

Herr Braun tapped his wooden stick on the top of his chair to remind his students of his unlimited power, saying in a measured tone, "*Ja,* the Third Reich is the most modern of the German empires, beginning in 1933 when our *Führer* came to power. Today, however, we will not focus on the Third Reich, but on the First and Second Reich."

The little man adjusted his bow tie and looked upon his own empire. Twenty 13-year-olds inhabited his school room, unruly boys entering the troubling zone of puberty—that most difficult time when their thoughts wandered to sensual subjects unless he kept a sharp eye on them. His attention was drawn to his star pupil, Rudolf Meier, who was staring down at his desk instead of looking at the map of Europe that Herr Braun had just pulled down over the blackboard.

"Rudi," Herr Braun called out. "Rudi, how long did the First Reich last?"

Rudolf jerked his head in the direction of his teacher, but Herr Braun could see Rudolf's thoughts were elsewhere. A dead silence pervaded the room.

"Rudi! I asked you a question. Stop daydreaming!" Herr Braun scolded.

Snickering permeated the classroom. Rudolf looked at his fellow classmates, his face troubled by the sound of the other students making fun of him. The teacher moved quickly from the blackboard to his desk to contain the outbreak of rebellion. Once there, he loudly rapped his wooden weapon on his desktop for immediate silence.

"Excuse me, Herr Braun. I did not hear the question," Rudolf replied, his voice cracking with the onset of puberty.

"Yes, I *know* you did not hear the question." Herr Braun said.

The teacher repeated his query with exasperation, and Rudolf suddenly jumped like a puppet from his chair and began reciting his knowledge about the First Reich.

"*Mein Lehrer*," Rudolf said. "I apologize for my inattention."

Herr Braun nodded in response. "Go on," he encouraged Rudolf.

"The First Reich, also known as the Holy Roman Empire, was a union of medieval states in middle and central Europe, including Germany. It began with the crowning of Charlemagne in 800, but the real time frame of the First Reich dated from 962 with the crowning of Emperor Otto I. It lasted until 1806, when Emperor Frances II disbanded it in response to the Napoleonic wars. Thus, the First Reich lasted almost a thousand years."

The boy sat down, his face bright red with embarrassment.

"Yes, you are correct, Rudi." Herr Braun said. "The Holy Roman Empire was a loose confederation of many smaller independent territories. Although it was considered an Empire, there was little desire among the various territories to expand across Europe. Now, can one of you tell me about the Second Reich?"

Lothar was the only one who raised his hand. He sat near the back of the class, as far away as possible from his former friend, Rudolf Meier. Grudgingly, Herr Bauer acknowledged the boy.

"Well…what do you have to say about our Second Reich?" Herr Braun nervously stroked his pointed beard, a sign he was unhappy with the majority of his students who were not prepared for the lesson.

"Herr Braun, after the First Reich was abolished, there were several attempts to unify the various German territories, but none succeeded until 1871 when it was created through the iron will of Chancellor

Otto von Bismarck," Lothar said. "Bismarck formed the Second Reich which was dominated by Prussia and ruled by the Kaiser. The Second Reich ended in November 1918 with the end of the Great War, and in 1919 it was succeeded by the Weimar Republic."

Murmuring filled the room with the mention of the despised Weimar Republic. Herr Braun looked sharply at Lothar for his transgression, but instead of becoming angry, the teacher responded by sadly shaking his head, acknowledging a chapter in the history of the Fatherland most people wanted to forget.

"Ah, yes, the Weimar Republic, created by that foul Treaty of Versailles!" Herr Braun shouted. "What it proved was that the German people are better off when they have a superior leader like Adolf Hitler. Democracy has no place in the Fatherland; that school of thinking based upon the falsehood that individual rights are more important than devotion to the State. No! It is the State that we all must give our hearts, minds, and utter dedication. If our State asks us to die for it... we will do so willingly!"

Herr Braun reached into his coat pocket and pulled out a white, pressed handkerchief, lovingly ironed by his dear mother, and mopped the beads of sweat from his brow.

"Now, since you brought up the subject of the end of the Great War, Lothar, we might as well look closely at the Treaty of Versailles. That dastardly document took from Germany almost fourteen percent of our territory which we held at the beginning of the Great War in 1914, not to mention all of our overseas possessions. Among other misdeeds, Alsace-Lorraine was returned to France and the Sudetenland to Czechoslovakia."

He moved to the map and outlined with a piece of chalk the various areas Germany lost. "What else, students, did the Treaty of Versailles take from our Fatherland?"

Johann, one of Rudolf's friends, raised his hand. Herr Braun smiled and nodded at the fresh-faced boy not yet showing the effects of puberty.

"Herr Braun, the Allies demanded millions in reparation for the Great War. It wasn't enough that we sought peace, they wanted to break our backs economically!"

"Yes, that is true," Herr Braun responded. "They wanted payment of 132 billion in gold Marks, made in annual installments—compensation for the damage of the Great War. We Germans were outraged by the huge sum of money, and our dear *Führer* promised in 1921—long before he came to power—that if he *did* come to power, Germany would stop paying the reparations."

The teacher mopped his forehead again. "In 1923, however, the German Republic could not pay the debt, and our enemies—the French and Belgians—in retaliation occupied the Ruhr, the main center of the Fatherland's coal, iron, and steel production. What happened next was unbelievable!"

The teacher raised his arm, flung the map of Europe back into its holder at the top of the blackboard with a loud clatter, and grabbed a piece of chalk. He began writing furiously on the board, at one point breaking the piece of chalk, pitching the small left-over piece over his head and picking up a new piece to finish his work. On the board, he wrote the figures "64 to 1," and "4,200,000,000,000 to 1," then he turned to face his pupils.

"Do you know what this is?" his voice rasped. When none of the students raised their hands, Herr Braun's frustration showed with the rising tide of his voice. "*This*," he yelled, as he banged the piece of chalk against the board and broke it once more, "is what we Germans were reduced to in those horrible years after the Great War because our enemies insisted we pay incredibly high reparations! In 1921, sixty-four Marks were worth one American dollar. In 1923, it was this!"

He underlined the long numerical figure with a great sweeping hand. "Here it is my students! A German in 1923, in order to be able to purchase anything worth one dollar in American money, had to have 4 trillion, 2 hundred billion in German Marks. Do you have any idea how many wheelbarrows it would take to haul around that kind of money in order to buy something worth one American dollar? Does this not tell you how worthless our currency had become, how hungry our people were? In response to the horrendous inflation, the government began printing 100 billion Mark notes!"

The teacher took a deep breath, readying for his final assault in the battle for the minds and hearts of his students. "It is hard to understand, but let me give you an example, one you can visualize. In November 1923, if a person had possession of one 100 billion Mark note, all it would buy was two glasses of beer. A loaf of bread cost 80 billion Marks. This happened because of that contemptible Treaty of Versailles!"

Rudolf stared at the blackboard. He tried to imagine what a stack of Marks that big would look like, but he could not. Somewhere in the back of his memory, he had heard stories from his grandparents about those days and remembered his grandmother lamenting the loss of a favorite French crystal lamp. It was her most prized possession, a wedding present from a wealthy aunt. When inflation became so unbearable and they had no money, his grandfather bartered away the Lalique lamp for a few mouthfuls of food and his grandmother forever mourned the loss of it.

Herr Bauer, Rudolf could see, was exhausted. He sat down on the corner of his desk, and straightened his bow tie which had become askew during his furious tirade. "*Mein Studeten,* this you must understand. Those times will never happen again because *Der Führer* would not allow the German people to suffer like that for a second time."

Then he said as an afterthought, "As for the Third Reich, which we are so fortunate to be part of, *Der Führer* himself said, 'There will be no other revolution in Germany for the next one thousand years.' "

Rudolf nodded as he assimilated the words of his teacher. *Der Führer* is truly our savior, he sighed. With that settled in his mind, he returned to his vision of the dark-haired girl.

Chapter 18

September 1937
Nuremberg, Germany

The sleek train pulled into the city of Nuremberg, touted by Rudolf's grandfather as one of the most beautiful of German cities. For one week in early September, this medieval showcase of Germany with its fairy-tale castle, huge stone gates, and stalwart turrets was host to the annual rally of the Nazi party, the *Reichsparteitag*, bringing hundreds of thousands of people to the city. The 9th Party Congress of 1937 celebrated "The Rally of Labor," a way to imprint upon the German people that unemployment was a thing of the past since the Nazis and Adolf Hitler came to power.

The train, filled with a thousand delegates, included members of the Hitler Youth, brown-shirted SA storm troopers, and members of the SS, Hitler's elite force dressed in their striking black shirts and pants. When the train halted, *Fähnleinführer* Ernst Ackermann yelled his command and all the Hitler Youth boys under his authority stood up in unison, including Rudolf. Each boy grabbed his backpack and, in short order, all were marching through the streets of Nuremberg's inner city where people lined five deep on the narrow sidewalks.

Rudolf's eyes opened wide with wonder when he saw the sea of flags fluttering in the breeze, and he could hear rousing martial music that came from military bands placed along the parade route. Every window and balcony was gaily decorated in floral garlands, and cheering people stood at their openings, waving to those marching below.

The fervor of the German people as they shouted to him and the other marchers made Rudolf's heart pound with excitement; there was so much activity going on around him that he felt like his mind had been taken over by a hive of bees—he could barely take it all in and march as perfectly as his *Fähnleinführer* expected.

Then, suddenly out of nowhere, a lovely young woman broke from the crowd and dashed to Ernst who marched at the head of the troop planting a kiss on his cheek. Rudolf, shocked that she would do such a thing, kept his eyes straight ahead and desperately hoped such an embarrassment would not happen to him.

As he marched the two miles to Camp Langwasser, Rudolf knew he was but one of eighty thousand Hitler Youth boys and girls carefully chosen to attend the *Reichsparteitag*—their selection determined by their athletic ability and adherence to Nazi indoctrination—and his pride showed clearly in the wide smile on his face and the way he squared his shoulders. The jubilation of the crowd infected his very soul and his delight at being a part of this national celebration reflected the mood of the crowd—Germany had truly regained its rightful place among the great powers of the world.

Before their train left for Nuremberg, Ernst told his troop how important their role was at the *Reichsparteitag*. "The Hitler Youth are the hope of this country and our great leader knows we are essential for the future of the Nazi movement," Ernst said. "He trusts us more than he trusts anyone. I know this because the Hitler Youth is the only one of the Nazi party branches that has the right to address Adolf Hitler with the familiar pronoun of *Du*. Of course, none of us would ever address him that way, but it tells us how special he thinks we are."

When the Bremen troop finally marched into the huge tent city, Rudolf knew exactly where his tent was located because of instructions he had received prior to embarking on the train; he marveled that every detail of the week's event was meticulously organized, down to the exact order of where he would march in the Hitler Youth formation to be viewed by *Der Führer* himself.

Rudolf easily found his tent, carefully placing his backpack in a corner, and then he sat down on the fresh straw piled in the tent's center. A few of his tent mates were standing outside talking excitedly to one another. Rudolf preferred, however, to sit alone inside and gather his thoughts. He was so keyed up from the march that his right eye kept twitching, so he laid back against the clean straw, hoping the earthy smell might calm him.

A vision of the dark haired girl appeared as his body relaxed. He never saw her again after that rowing competition in the spring, but she always came to his mind whenever he had a moment to himself. This was not often because of his chores, his homework, and his growing responsibilities in the Hitler Youth. Losing the boat race mortified Rudolf and it was not until a few days later that he gathered enough courage to ask his *Jungvolk* friends if they saw her standing on the bank, but none had. In a way, the girl was like an apparition because no one seemed to have seen her but him.

What was it, he wondered, that caused such a sensation in his body? He never felt like he did at that moment—oh, maybe a little when he woke up after a dream, but he never experienced the jolt of arousal like he did when she looked back and smiled at him. It was a moment he tucked into a special corner of his mind. She was beautiful, yes, but he pondered why he was so attracted to her. Maybe it was her dark hair, a halo of sorts. He searched his mind, but he could not remember anyone who had hair as dark as hers.

Viktor, a tall boy with a happy grin, stuck his head in the tent and laughed.

"Rudi, get up! What are you doing lying there like a sack of potatoes? Come, let's walk out to the entrance of the tent city; Ernst just gave us permission to go for half an hour. There are all kinds of things for sale there; I hope to find a souvenir to remind me of our time in this glorious city!"

Rudolf got up and dusted the straw from his clothes. He grabbed his backpack and retrieved a small coin purse. "I hope the souvenirs are not too expensive. My grandfather had to sneak me some money since my grandmother was not happy that the trip cost 25 Marks."

"Was it the cost of the trip," Viktor asked pointedly, "or is she is not happy about the time you are spending with the Hitler Youth?'

Rudolf, surprised Viktor would ask such an intimate question about his family, chose to remain silent, pretending to busy himself with the backpack.

Finally, Viktor said, "My father said it's a bargain since it includes lodging and all of our meals...but my family is not happy about all the time I spend at the *Heim*."

Rudolf put on a sour face. "My grandmother never thinks there is a bargain in anything. Especially since that merchant left..." His voice trailed off, not wanting to say something that might bring more gossip about his grandmother.

Viktor put his arm around Rudolf's shoulders. "It's bad enough living with parents, let alone living with grandparents," he commiserated.

Rudolf nodded, and the two boys headed down the long row of tents to the entrance decorated with swastika banners, gently lifting in the afternoon breeze. A large beer garden made festive with potted trees was surrounded by a multitude of food booths with *Wiener schnitzel*, potato dumplings and cucumber salad, German chocolate cake and apple strudel. Rudolf's mouth watered as he took in the delicious smells.

He had not noticed the hawkers earlier when he marched into the tent city with the excitement of the moment, but now he wondered how he could have missed so much. Peddlers filled an entire area, all of them dressed gaily in traditional German clothing to celebrate the festivities. There were so many souvenir items for sale that Rudolf was overwhelmed: small swastika flags, beer mugs emblazoned with the Nazi symbol, copies of Hitler's biography *Mein Kampf*, framed portraits of Hitler, and picture postcards galore.

Rudolf stopped to admire the display of postcards. One was especially handsome with the portrait of four revered Germans: King Frederick the Great; Prince Otto von Bismarck, Field Marshall Paul von Hindenburg and Adolf Hitler dressed in his WW I uniform. The inscription on the card read: "What the King conquered, the Prince formed, the Field Marshal defended, and the Soldier saved and unified."

"Look at this," Rudolf said to Viktor, handing him the postcard. "It shows *Der Führer* as the lowly soldier who has carried on our German heritage."

"How colorful it is! I bet your grandfather would like it. In fact, I think I will buy one for my father." Viktor pulled change out of his pocket and paid for the postcard.

The price was one Rudolf could afford, so he purchased it, counting his money carefully. With their allotted time running out, Rudolf and Viktor turned back toward the tent city when Rudolf suddenly eyed a small framed photo of Adolf Hitler sitting on a peddler's stand, its frame made of dark brass with a miniature swastika at the top. He stopped, picked up the item, and looked at the peddler, who was colorfully dressed in brown *lederhosen* with a red stripe down each side and matching red suspenders. On his head was a green Alpine hat with a red feather.

Rudolf asked the price, and the peddler said, "For you, the future of our beloved country, I will sell it to you for 10 *pfennig*." Rudolf pondered the offer for a moment. He could afford 10 pennies if he did not buy anything else except a strudel or two during his stay in Nuremberg, and he so much wanted a photo of *Der Führer* in his bedroom. *Oma* would not be able to scowl at it there because he would hide it in his dresser drawer; he could look at it before he got into bed.

With that in mind, he counted the money and stood sharply, raising his right arm as high as he could, saying, "*Heil Hitler*," to the peddler. Then he tucked the framed photo under his arm with a small, satisfied smile.

Rudolf could hardly believe his eyes. The sight of thousands of sailors and soldiers made him catch his breath—the sailors marching in their colorful Navy uniforms and the soldiers smartly goose-stepping—all passing before Germany's supreme leader, Adolf Hitler.

The Hitler Youth unit from Bremen was part of a district, or *Banne*, of 5,000 boys and girls selected to stand among 120,000 other spectators at Zeppelin Field to view the military march past. The huge 400-yard-long grandstand, located in the midst of the monstrous Nazi party rally grounds, was packed with enthusiastic flag-waving Germans.

As the military might of the Third Reich passed before the reviewing stand, Hitler stood with his arm raised in a tireless salute to his armed forces. Rudolf felt a thrill watching his *Führer* humble himself by saluting the men of Germany. He leaned over to Viktor and said, "I can hardly wait for our parade before *Der Führer!*"

Viktor nodded. "Do you think he will salute us like he has done today with Germany's *Wehrmacht?*"

Rudolf looked doubtful. "We are not soldiers like they are; we are just children after all."

"Yes, but don't you remember what Ernst told us on the train, about the Hitler Youth being very special to *Der Führer?*"

Rudolf answered with wonder in his voice, "How wonderful it would be if he did!"

When the march finished, Hitler sat down in the center of the reviewing stand, his generals gathered behind him. With his arms crossed and his dark eyes gleaming, Hitler watched hundreds of paratroopers drop from low-flying German aircraft amid the thunderous boom and smoke of anti-aircraft guns fighting a mock battle. To add to the excitement, armored tanks inched slowly across the huge field, their gun turrets turning ominously. At the end of the staged conflict, the leader of Germany stood and turned to the crowd. Suddenly, in an outburst of enthusiasm, the people greeted him in a resounding triple "*Sieg Heil*" with everyone's arm jabbing the air.

Rudolf never imagined he could feel such elation as he did at that moment. After being a part of the frenzied adulation of *Der Führer*, he came away from the military demonstration with a feeling he never had before. It was as if he had undergone a religious conversion; all he could think about was the possibility of seeing Hitler again.

In the evening, after a dinner of delicious soup served from huge cauldrons, Rudolf and the other members of the Hitler Youth stood near a mammoth bonfire in the center of Camp Langwasser and he saw the illumination of the sky from the one hundred and twenty *Luftwaffe* searchlights surrounding Zeppelin Field. Rudolf could hear the stir-ring "Badenweiler March," but he was unable to see the thousands of SS and SA members as they marched on the field carrying torches—an event deemed by party officials to be far too boisterous and political for Hitler Youth to attend.

Looking up at the sky, his voice filled with awe, Rudolf said to Viktor, "The searchlights make *Zeppelinfeld* look like an open air cathedral!"

Ernst, who was standing near the two boys, heard what Rudolf said, and interjected, "Yes, they are celebrating our *Führer.* He is our god. Not even Jesus Christ can come close to his greatness!"

Exhausted at the end of the day after so much excitement, Rudolf lay on the straw in his tent and thought about the events he had witnessed. The vision of the dark-haired girl did not come to him as it usually did. Instead, his mind was aflutter with images of waving red flags and black swastikas, men floating down from airplanes and smoke wafting up into the sky from pounding anti-aircraft guns—and when all of that drifted away, only the image of Adolf Hitler remained.

The "day of the Hitler Youth" dawned under a cloudy sky as eighty thousand German children made ready for their march into the Stadium of the Hitler Youth, and troop leaders meticulously checked uniforms for the final event. Rudolf nervously adjusted his scarf and looked around, noticing a slight buzz hanging in the air despite the demand by leaders for absolute silence. He longed to say something to Viktor, although he dared not with *Fähnleinführer* Ernst Ackermann pacing up and down the row glowering at everyone.

Within minutes, they were on their way, out of the camp, march-ing perfectly into the huge stadium, strutting into the heart of the Third Reich's political nursery school. It was then that hundreds of Hitler Youth flag bearers broke free of the formation and strode past the reviewing stand where high officials of the Hitler Youth stood. Next, the boys' and girls' sports units performed carefully-practiced maneuvers, their grand finale spelling out the name "Adolf Hitler" in the gigantic grandstand.

Rudolf's heart pounded with the pressure to perform perfectly. Infinitely proud of himself, he stepped flawlessly in place along with thousands of Hitler Youth lined up in perfect rows, twelve deep, the entire length of the stadium.

The multitude of children stood at parade rest with their feet apart and left hands on their belts, facing the twin grandstands adorned with Nazi symbols. Rudolf gulped when he saw the massive granite swastikas gripped by the talons of an enormous German eagle. He felt like he was in a dream, but it began to rain and he looked up for only a second into the wetness, realizing this was reality, not a hallucination. Ever obedient, Rudolf moved his head quickly back so that his gaze was fixed straight ahead—in sync with thousands of others—into the vastness of the Nazi pageant. The weather was of little consequence to Rudolf or any of the other determined youngsters who came to see their leader.

"*Achtung*!" boomed over the loudspeakers, and everyone froze to attention. Adolf Hitler stepped out on the speaker's platform, covered only that morning with a canopy because of the weather forecast. The children of Germany greeted their leader with a resounding triple "*Sieg Heil*!" and then they took their Hitler Youth daggers out of their holders and banged them in unison against their scabbards. Hitler gave a faint smile, held up his hands in a sort of benediction and the stadium became deathly quiet except for the sound of the rain.

Hitler's speech began slowly, carefully. He spoke of his meager beginnings and the hardships he faced, his voice quiet and controlled. The children listened, mesmerized despite the cold rain as Hitler told the story of his time in the military when he was temporarily blinded by a British chlorine gas attack and how depressed he felt as he lay in a hospital bed with rumors swirling that Germany was losing the Great War.

But then, *Der Führer's* voice changed. It became louder and rasping as he lifted his right hand into the air, pumping it up and down as he threw his words outward to Rudolf and the other youths who idolized his every utterance. He spoke of his fight to bring National Socialism to Germany and the many successes of the Nazi party. Then as the rain came down harder, Hitler spoke to the children about the weather:

"This morning I learned from our weather forecasters that, at present, we have the meteorological condition 'V.b.' that is supposed to be a mixture of very bad and bad. Now, my boys and girls, Germany has had this meteorological condition for fifteen years! And the Party had this meteorological condition too! It was a battle in which only hope could be victorious, the hope that in the end the sun would rise over Germany after all. And risen it has! And as you are standing here today, it is also good that the sun is not smiling down on you. For we want to raise a race not only for sunny, but also for stormy days!"

As if the storm did not exist, the eighty thousand Hitler Youths pumped their arms in rapturous salutes, yelling *"Heil Mein Führer"* until their voices were horse, tears mixed with rain streaming down their faces. Adolf Hitler brushed back his black hair from his forehead, smiled, and then raised his arm in salute to them, his favorite vassals. Rudolf looked at his tent mate, Viktor, who was standing in the next row, and they grinned at one another. Hitler did what they had most hoped for—a salute!

It was time for this glorious moment to end, but before they marched back to camp to ready themselves for their trip home, the thousands of children sang their anthem for Adolf Hitler:

Forward, forward call the bright fanfares
we march for Hitler through night and suffering with
the banner for freedom and bread.
Our banner means more to us than death.

For Rudolf, it was a moment he would carry in his heart the rest of his life.

Chapter 19

Fall 1942 - Spring 1943
Germany

I n the fall of 1942, when Rudolf was 18-years-old, the victorious Third
Reich spread from the northern tip of Norway to the shores of Africa,
from the British Channel to Russia's magnificent Volga River. It was a
glorious time to be German and to be in the military; the pride Rudolf
felt as he took the oath of allegiance as a member of the *Kriegsmarine*
felt like a spiritual transcendence, as if his soul were now an integral
part of the German Reich spreading its might throughout the world.

Once again, like that day more than six years ago when he swore
his oath as a member of the Hitler Youth, Rudolf stretched his lean
body to its limits, standing as straight and tall as he possibly could,
submitting for all to hear a holy pledge not to his beloved nation, but
to the leader of Germany:

"I swear by God this sacred oath that I shall render unconditional
obedience to Adolf Hitler, the *Führer* of the German Reich and people,
supreme commander of the armed forces, and that I shall at all times
be ready, as a brave soldier, to give my life for this oath," Rudolf said.

The new sailor was dressed in his all-blue German Navy Service
Suit with a shirt that sported a wide sailor collar decorated with three
white stripes. His white cap had a navy-blue ribbon around the brim
that flowed gracefully, touching the back of his neck. The uniform
was complete with a silk neckerchief and gray gloves. It was a windy,
cold day in Wilhelmshaven on the North Sea where he had completed
three months in navy boot camp, the *Schiffstammdivision*, and the

collar of Rudolf's Service Suit kept flying up in the wind as he stood stiffly along with the other young men who were prepared to give their lives to Adolf Hitler.

Rudolf thought about that oath many times while attending other *Kriegsmarine* training schools, never quite understanding why the oath meant more to him than many of his classmates—at least he felt that way because some of his classmates would look at him in silence when he reverently spoke of it.

His first training was at the Naval Signals School where he received general radio instruction, and now, months later, he was at the marine intelligence school in Flensburg-Mürwik where he was learning to become a *Funklaufbahn*, a U-boat radio operator. The days dragged endlessly while Rudolf studied to go to war, his impatience growing worse every day as the tide of the war turned in the winter of 1943 from its promise of world domination with Germany's February surrender at Stalingrad.

One evening not many weeks later, with the news that the *Afrika Korps* was withdrawing from Tunisia, Rudolf's patience came to an end. Suddenly, Rudolf slammed his fist on the study table in frustration. He had been studying for an examination on the Enigma, the highly-secret cipher machine that sent and received secret codes between U-boats at sea and U-boat headquarters on the coast of France, but the news had become too much for him. Cursing under his breath, Rudolf felt stifled by the burden of not having faced Germany's mortal enemies.

"Will I never be done with this?" Rudolf cried out. "I want to be at sea...now!"

Fritz Kraus, who shared living quarters with Rudolf, stared at his roommate as if he had lost his mind. "What's the matter with you, Rudi?"

When Rudolf did not answer, Fritz shook his head and then laughed. "You stupid *Schwein*! When you are heaving your guts out because you can't stand the rough sea in that floating metal tube, you'll wish you were still here in this comfortable room. I swear I do believe I have never met anyone like you—why are you so anxious to die?"

Rudolf expression changed from one of frustration to exuberance." Fritz, we are not going to die!" Rudolf said. "We are going to sink the enemies of the Third Reich, and it cannot be too soon for me!"

"*Mein Gott!*" Fritz replied, "Your love of the Fatherland is nothing short of amazing, Rudi. I joined the *Kriegsmarine* because I knew I would be drafted into the *Armeekorp*. I did not want to be cannon fodder, shipped to the Eastern Front, and die on frozen Soviet wastelands—but I'm not particularly happy either to be in the U-boat arm of the German Navy! They are slaughtering us! The British and Americans are sinking U-boats as quickly as we make them."

Rudolf straightened and his face became bright red. "Where did you hear such filthy propaganda?" he said. "The British and Americans are deathly afraid of our Wolf Packs, why else do they form such huge convoys to protect themselves from our U-boats? We are winning the battle of the Atlantic!"

Fritz, a short, slim man with a profusion of sandy brown hair, threw his pencil down in disgust, stood up, and leaned over the table toward Rudolf. His voice was low, so no one outside the room could hear. "Things are not so good, Rudi. I have family in Wilhelmshaven, aunts and uncles from my father's side of the family. There are rumors, lots of rumors in Wilhelmshaven."

"What are you talking about?" Rudolf said with anger. "Wilhelmshaven is a port city and many U-boat men pass through there, so there is bound to be plenty of gossip!"

"This isn't gossip! It's coming from top naval officers, friends of my family. They are saying many U-boats have been lost or captured since last July."

"What do you mean by *many?* A handful or so, maybe, but not 'many'!" Rudolf shook his head as if to ward off the bad news.

"More than a hundred," Fritz said with resignation.

Rudolf was silent, thinking. Then, in a venomous tone, he said, "I don't believe you!"

To that, Fritz threw himself on his bed. "I knew you wouldn't. You never question anything, for God's sake! Whatever the Third Reich says, you believe."

Rudolf put down his textbook on the Enigma machine and looked hard at Fritz. "I should report you to the Gestapo. You have told me these lies about the war ever since I have roomed with you!"

Fritz smiled. "You know you won't, Rudi. I'm the only friend you have around here. No one wants to associate with you because you're too Nazi. Members of the military are not supposed to be political—or don't you remember that?"

Rudolf screwed his eyes upward in a sign of resignation. "I have never understood why *Der Führer* made that promise to the military— that we cannot be involved in political activities or even vote! *Mein Gott,* just because we are in the military, that promise separates us from our beliefs!"

"Well, Rudi," Fitz countered, "Your beliefs hang on your sleeve! You need to keep your opinions to yourself...now, let's get back to studying the Enigma or both of us will fail. Then what will happen to us, huh? I dare say, we will be thrown into the clutches of the army and shipped to the Eastern Front."

Rudolf nodded, unhappily remembering his time a year ago when he worked for the Reich Labor Service to help clear the road to Stalingrad. He shivered internally; the Eastern Front was a cold, miserable spot on the face of the earth; the stench of death somehow filled his nostrils even now in this quiet room near the Baltic Sea, far from the Soviet Union, and he knew that he did not want to be there again. Floating in a U-boat seemed much more preferable than face-to-face war.

Rudolf looked at Fritz; he realized what his roommate said was true; he had made no friends during weeks of grueling training. In fact, he never had a close friend since his boyhood. Sadness filled Rudolf as he thought of Lothar and the loss of that friendship because of his obsessive desire to recruit him into the Hitler Youth. It was a mistake, a terrible mistake, and Rudolf knew he would always regret it.

A breeze came into the window, carrying with it the faint smell of spring's rebirth. Rudolf took in a deep breath and out came a mournful sigh: Rudolf was terribly lonely, much more than he thought he would be after joining the navy; Fritz, it seemed, was the only person who took an interest in him, who befriended him. He got up from the table and walked over to his roommate stretched out on the bed, and ruffled Fritz's thick hair. "OK, Fritz, let's see if we can learn this damnable Enigma!"

Rudolf reached for the envelope, his heart beating fiercely. His persistent study had earned him the top grade in his class and now his U-boat assignment was in hand. He looked over at Fritz who was already ripping open his envelope, so Rudolf did the same.

Fritz let out a shout. "U-893! I'm assigned to U-893 in Bremen!"

Rudolf stared at his notice, unable to speak for a moment while he digested his own assignment. It was also U-893, a new submarine just completed by AG Weser at the vast Bremen shipyard where Rudolf's grandfather worked.

"Fritz! Fritz! We are going to be together!" Rudolf said, slapping Fritz on the back. "You and I will be together on the same boat!"

Fritz laughed as he peaked at Rudolf's assignment. "Can you believe it?" he said with joy. "Well…I am going home with you!"

Rudolf nodded. Home to Bremen, where he could touch and smell the Weser River and perhaps even see his grandparents. He was to report directly to his commander at the shipyard where U-893 was berthed, ready for testing by its crew.

The young radio operators arrived a few days later at AG Weser with their sea bags slung over their shoulders. It seemed like a dream come true for Rudolf as he approached the large gate, wondering how many times he had walked through it with his grandfather. As a child, he was always excited to see the newest U-boat Hermann Meier was supervising; now he would serve on one of his grandfather's boats.

Rudolf stepped up to the gate and presented his identification papers, as did Fritz. The old guard recognized Rudolf, and a broad smile lit up his heavy face.

"*Ja, Ja*, if it isn't Hermann Meier's grandson!" the guard said as he clutched the identification papers of the two sailors. "You must wait a minute...I will call your grandfather!"

Rudolf, embarrassed by the attention, protested mildly, "But we must report directly to our commander."

The guard, who had worked at the shipyard many years, would have none of Rudolf's protest. "One minute with your grandfather, who has been waiting months for your return, will not get you into trouble with your commander, young man!" He picked up the telephone and dialed a number, smiling as he talked into the receiver, and winked at Rudolf who stood shifting nervously from one foot to the other.

Despite his concern about Navy protocol, a small smile came to Rudolf's face, and his bright blue eyes sparkled. It was a long time since he had seen his grandfather—over a year—and he was secretly happy about the guard's insistence.

The guard opened the heavy gate for them to pass through, and as they did, Rudolf caught his breath, for the familiar figure of Hermann Meier could be seen rushing out of the administration building half a block away. The young man clenched his jaw, trying desperately to harden himself at the sight of his beloved *Opa*. He brushed his hand quickly over his eyes as if he were flicking away a fly. Fritz and the old guard, seeing Rudolf's emotion, moved discreetly away, letting the men embrace in private.

Hermann put his big, scarred hands on his grandson's shoulders and held him at arm's length, his eyes also moist.

"Oh, you are a sight to behold in your Service Suit! Your grandmother will be beside herself until she sees you!" Hermann exclaimed, his booming voice sounded choked.

Rudolf hurriedly wiped his eyes, and he was silent for a moment while he soaked in the sight of his burly grandfather, still vibrant at sixty-six years old. Hermann's hair was graying now and his eyes were more crinkled around the edges, but Rudolf could see his spirit was still lively.

"I am so happy, *Opa,* to be assigned to one of your beautiful U-boats. What could be better than that?" Rudolf said with a mixture of pride and wistfulness in his voice.

Hermann just shook his head in wonderment and hugged his grandson again. Finally, Rudolf introduced Fritz to his grandfather. Hermann's firm grip as he shook Fitz' hand produced a pained look from the young sailor. Then Hermann nodded his thanks to the old guard, and he led the young men toward the wharf where U-893 sat in readiness.

For Rudolf, it was a step back in time. The smell of the mammoth two-hundred-acre shipyard flowed into his nose, the strong aroma of paint and acids had forever forged a place in his memory and it was as if he were a small boy again, hanging tightly onto his grandfather's hand, afraid of the shipyard's strange buzzing and banging and the unspoken threat of huge cranes lifting and swinging enormous girders high above them. As a boy, he worried that he might trip over the welders' compressed air hoses that lay everywhere, but his grandfather always guided him safely through this place of hulking steel skeletons, just as he did now.

On this day, Rudolf felt a sort of reverence as he passed the shipyard workers, each tipping their hat in a show of respect to Hermann who had worked at the yard since 1894, and to himself as well, now a member of the German Navy about to face war in an AG Weser U-boat.

Hermann Meier brought them to the wharf on the Weser River where U-893's blackness sat gleaming in the sun, its dark hulk causing Rudolf to suck in his breath. The boat was beautiful, as beautiful as the first U-boat he had seen as a small boy. The boat lay in wait for its commissioning ceremony, which would happen as soon as the entire crew arrived at AG Weser.

"Well, here you are, Rudolf: U-893. May God watch over you and protect you and Fritz and all the men who will live in her belly," Hermann said quietly. "I will bring your grandmother to the commissioning ceremony." He then touched Rudolf gently on the side of his face and turned away abruptly because his eyes overflowed with tears.

Frau Ida Leibling opened the door at *Franko-Alles* 30, one of the houses where officers and crew members stayed at the AG Weser shipyard while their new U-boat was going through its test run. She greeted Rudolf and Fritz with a lively smile and took their registration cards which she personally handed into SS headquarters in Bremen showing the crewmen's new address at the shipyard—a Gestapo requirement even though the sailors would only be in Bremen for two weeks or less.

She glanced down at the cards, making sure they were properly filled out and she noticed Rudolf's name. "Ah," she exclaimed, "you are Hermann Meier's grandson!"

Rudolf nodded, a blush spreading up from his neck. She gave him her manicured hand, nails sparkling with red polish. "Word of your arrival has come down from the administration!"

Rudolf stammered, "I…I am very happy to make your acquaintance, Frau Leibling!"

She shook her head, "*Nein, nein,* you are to call me *Tante* Ida! Everyone calls me Auntie, and you, especially, because I have known your grandfather for so long!"

Frau Leibling was the official "housemother" of the six-house compound at the shipyard. A woman in her late forties, she wore a stylish blue silk dress with wide padded shoulders, and it showed off her slim figure. Frau Leibling's hair was as up-to-date as her clothing; she sported a new permanent wave piled on top of her head.

She winked at Rudolf, which made him blush all the more and then she turned serious. "I must apologize to both of you. I am in dire straits these days what with the bombing of Bremen by those dreadful Allies! As you saw when you walked here from the wharf, four of my houses are destroyed and this one has just been rebuilt, in time for your stay. Still, I am sadly lacking bedspreads and some furniture which should be coming in from Holland any day. I hope you will be comfortable here despite this inconvenience."

Both young men nodded and Frau Leibling showed them to their room which also housed four other men. They stood looking at their temporary quarters, and Frau Leibling remarked as she left them to unpack, "Dinner this evening is at 8 p.m. Most of the crew should be checked in by then."

While putting away their belongings, Fritz said, "You have never talked much about your grandfather. I had no idea he was one of the supervisors at the shipyard. I suppose you have a job waiting for you here once the war is ended?"

Rudolf sat down on the bed. "I guess so, Fritz, but you know I never really thought about it. When I advanced from the *Deutsche Jungvolk*, I chose to become a member of the *Marine Hitlerjugend*. I guess I did that because of my grandfather's connection with the sea…building ships for so many years here at AG Weser. Much to my surprise, the *Marine Hitlerjugend* was more than just rowing competitions; we learned resuscitation, naval knots, information on signal flags, and of course, Morse code."

He ran his hand along his brow as if the motion itself would bring something to mind, something precious. "You know, Fritz…we would go out on small sailboats to the North Sea, and the beauty of the ocean somehow touched me, deep inside. Even if it was a miserable rainy day and the waves were running high, I loved it. That is why I joined the Navy, very much against my grandparents' wishes…yes, very much against my grandparents' wishes, although I really do not understand why." Rudolf's voice was melancholy.

Fritz gave Rudolf a quizzical look. "If you love the sea that much, why didn't you apply to become an officer? You graduated from *Gymnasium*, so you could have done that…you could have made it a life-long career."

Rudolf shrugged. "I want to fight for the Fatherland now—officer training takes too long. The war will be done before I can be part of it!"

"Ah, yes, you and the Fatherland again!" Fritz heaved a resigned sigh. "Well, at least you have a job waiting for you when the war is over. As for me, what is there to do in Braubach? It's a beautiful medieval town on the Rhine, but nothing ever changes there—and I do not want to become a tailor like my father! I have no idea what I will do after this is over."

Rudolf looked surprised. "You mean the war?"

"Rudi!" Fritz said, surprise in his voice. "Yes, I mean the war! Do you think it will go on forever?"

"Surely, we will never surrender. How could we? We are superior to all of them—the British, Russians and Americans, and *we* will win, not those inferior races. Besides, *Der Führer* promised the Third Reich will go on for a thousand years."

"He may have promised that, my friend, but that does not mean it will happen," Fritz said, a sad note in his voice. "I am afraid we are in for a terrible undoing."

"There you go again, Fritz," Rudolf said with a slight smile. "I am derelict for not turning you into the Gestapo."

Fritz nodded. "Yes, you are, Rudi. But tell me, does it not bother you that we must fill out these registration cards for the SS every time we go to another port? *Mein Gott,* no German can move throughout the country without having to notify the SS. It sticks in my craw!"

"I never thought about it," Rudolf answered, shrugging his shoulders.

"They don't have to do such things in America," Fritz said. "There is no SS there, scrutinizing every move."

Rudolf looked surprised. "How do you know about America?"

"Oh, my uncle, my mother's brother moved there after the Great War. I saw him once, when I was 12-years-old. He came home to visit, but he was terribly unhappy Hitler was in power and he said he would never come back again. He told us stories about life in America—oh so many wonderful tales of abundance and freedom; since then I have always dreamed I would go there too, but the war came and I had no money to get to America. So here I am," Fritz said ruefully.

"America is nothing but a mixture of races," Rudolf said with annoyance in his voice. "Their leader, Roosevelt is a crippled old man in a wheelchair."

Fritz scratched the side of his face, thinking. "Russia is a bunch of mixed races too, and they just beat the shit out of us at Stalingrad, my friend. I believe the will to protect one's homeland is far greater than whether or not we think we are a superior race."

Rudolf sighed, and closed his eyes as if to block the mental vision of a fallen Germany. The conversation upset his view of all things German. All he wanted was to be aboard the U-boat his grandfather helped build and fight the enemies of the Third Reich.

Luise Meier wore a new gray coat and a snappy gray hat with a turned up brim, framing her beautiful face, still remarkably free of wrinkles. Her blond hair, tinged with only a hint of gray, was pulled into a knot at the nape of her neck. She stood next to her husband, her purse clutched tightly against her full bosom, watching as the German flag rose for the first time on the deck of U-893.

Her grandson was somewhere on the boat's deck behind the conning tower along with fifty other crewmen as Commander Reinhard Weber viewed the flag ceremony from the ship's wintergarden.

Luise squeezed Hermann's arm. "I cannot see him," she said, her voice sad.

Hermann whispered in her ear, "They all look alike in their uniforms. I cannot find him either."

It was a nostalgic moment for Luise and Hermann, bringing them back many years to when their son, Erich, stood on UB-85 during its commissioning ceremony. On that fall day in 1917, the weather was cold and rainy, the ceremony short, much to the delight of friends and family who wanted nothing better than to get out of the miserable storm. When Erich stepped off UB-85 for a few brief moments to kiss them goodbye, Luise and Hermann could tell he was anxious to move on with his life. The couple only saw their son once again, and that was when he had become a determined Communist, brawling in the streets, much to their horror.

On this day, spring was in full bloom and the sun glinted off the Weser River. U-893 sat menacingly next to the wharf, ready to bring destruction and death to Allied sailors and their ships at sea. At the end of the ceremony, when the crew received the order to dismiss, most of the crew poured down the hatch into the boat for a bit of refreshment and conviviality before beginning the rigorous testing of the boat. Several of the crew, including Rudolf, walked down the ship's ramp to visit momentarily with friends and family who lived in Bremen and came for the ceremony.

When Luise spotted her grandson, taller and older now, she gasped involuntarily. No longer was he the silent little boy who came to her. Rudolf smiled, and Luise hugged him. She put him at arms' length then and just looked at him, shaking her head.

"Well, *Oma*, I have passed all the rigorous tests and I am a radio operator now." There was a hint of pride in his voice.

"Yes, Rudolf. You have worked hard to accomplish this and I am proud of you! Since you were a little boy, you have always tried to be the best. I know you will be the finest radio operator in the *Kriegsmarine!*"

Luise softly touched the silk neckerchief that decorated the front of his Service Uniform, and she looked up at her grandson with love in her eyes. She remembered those many years ago when she worried about what would become of him, this child who saw the unimaginable horror of rape and murder of his parents and dealt with it through silence. He had come through that, and now he stood before her, a man full grown.

"May Christ in His Heaven keep you safe from harm," she said, and then she did something she had never done before: She wanted to show Rudolf her love, something she had never done with his father, Erich, because it was not proper behavior between a mother and son, and she carried that grief in her heart all these years. Luise stood on her tip toes and kissed Rudolf lightly on the mouth.

After the commission ceremony, days were filled with testing and retesting all systems on the boat, making sure it was seaworthy. Before the first test run, Commander Reinhard Weber gathered the men together. It was a casual meeting, a signal to Rudolf that the man in charge of U-893 was not going to be a stickler for formality. A squat man, he sat with one thick leg hanging over the edge of the wharf, casually filling his pipe with his pudgy fingers. The crew congregated around him, straining to hear every word.

"Men—these are the objectives of the test run: To strengthen the boat in all areas for front line action. If there are any flaws in the boat, they should be noted and they must be fixed by the shipyard before we can get into this war."

There was a murmur from the crew and Weber nodded, adding, "Yes, that definitely means all of you must develop a thorough familiarity with the equipment so that when we are in a crisis, everyone knows what he must do, automatically without thinking!"

Oberfunkmeister Günther Reese, the Chief Radio Petty Officer, took Rudolf and Fritz in hand, shaping them slowly. Reese, a thin man whose clothes hung loosely from his lanky frame, was rigorous but fair in his approach to training the new men in correct procedures. At times, Rudolf noticed Reese seemed weary, but the young radio operator knew his superior had served in the German Navy since 1940 and he was not happy about having two untested radio operators onboard.

One night before dinner at Frau Leibling's boarding house, Rudolf stood within hearing distance of the Commander and *Oberfunkmeister* Reese and watched Frau Leibling hover between the two men, filling their wine glasses, chattering glibly. Suddenly, the Commander reached out and touched his glass with Reese's, impolitely disregarding the hostess. "To my lucky charm," he said.

Frau Leibling, her face showing a flicker of anger, laughed amiably to cover her embarrassment; Rudolf guessed she was unaccustomed to men ignoring her, but he was even more surprised to hear Reese respond to the Commander's toast with a tight smile. "I hope so, Commander! One must remember the sea is like a fickle woman. In truth, my luck is no better than anyone else's. "

The Commander, exuberant after a good day with no serious mistakes by the crew, smiled broadly, his pinched face radiant. "*Ja! Ja! Grossadmiral* Dönitz is a family friend; he did me a personal favor by assigning you to U-893!"

Later, Rudolf told Fritz about what he had overheard. "What do you think he meant by that?" he asked.

"The gossip is that every U-boat Reese served on returned safely to the base at Lorient," Fritz answered, referring to the big U-boat base on the coast of France. "He's considered lucky. I guess that's why the Commander said that."

Fritz lay on his bed with his arms cradled behind his head, a sober look on his face. Suddenly, he broke out into a bright smile.

"Say, Rudi! I hear we have one night's leave before we head out from Bremen. Let's find us a couple of whores."

Rudolf perked up but then his face darkened. "I can't do that, Fritz. I need to visit my grandparents."

Fritz sat up from the bed. "Tell me you are kidding, Rudi! This is our last chance to get drunk and have some fun before we go to war and you want to visit your grandparents? There is something seriously the matter with you!"

Rudolf became defensive. "I didn't say I want to visit them, Fritz! I said I need to visit them."

"Need! Want! What you need is to feel the exhilaration of sexual release. You're too tied up, Rudi. You need to loosen up."

Rudolf turned red. "It seems to me that you are always telling me what I need to do, Fritz. Are my friend or enemy?"

Fritz' eyes opened wide and he ran a hand through his thick hair. "I'm your friend, Rudi! I am! If I were not your friend, I would probably just tell you to go to hell because you're always behaving so…so goddamn correct!"

Rudolf dropped down on his bed. He did not answer Fritz because the other crewmen who shared their room came in after finishing a game of cards in the drawing room. Recently, Rudolf's dreams had become more erotic than he could ever remember; the dark-haired girl had come back to his reverie, although in his imagination, she was an adult now, but she always had that demure smile she gave him many years ago on the bank of the Weser River.

As the other men got ready for bed, Rudolf closed his eyes and thought about making love to her. Before the lights went out, he turned to Fritz and simply smiled. The other radio operator caught the implication and punched his pillow in exuberance.

Chapter 20

Spring – Mid-Summer 1943
Kiel, Germany to the mid-Atlantic Ocean

Judged to be in excellent working condition, U-893 left the AG Weser shipyard, slipping easily through the wide Weser River to the North Sea and then into the Kiel Canal for an eastward transit to the city of Kiel on the Baltic Sea. Once there, the boat was to stay overnight while fueled and a training officer was set to come aboard to put everyone, including the Commander, through a period of tough training.

All the crew, except for a small shipboard watch, had been invited by the Commander to join him for dinner at *Zum Patzenhofer*, a tavern in Kiel, not far from the harbor. Frequented by men of the *Kriegsmarine*, the tavern was dark inside, a cocoon away from the world at war, the smell of fried *schnitzel* wafting into the barroom from a hidden kitchen. A long mahogany bar stood along the wall, the mirror behind it reflecting the men of U-893 ordering their beers.

Rudolf and Fritz stood joking with their fellow crewmen, all crowding the bar, jostling one another in their comradeship. Their beer glasses full, the two radio operators headed to a private room off a hallway to join their Commander, passing three SS men drinking at the end of the bar and listening silently to the conversations of the crew. One of them reached out and grabbed Rudolf by the arm as he passed, spilling half of his beer onto the floor.

"I hear your Low German accent, sailor. I bet you're from that filthy place, Bremen!" the SS man growled. His big, sour face sported a u-shaped cut on his right cheek. He was much shorter than Rudolf, but built like a small freight car, compact and tight.

Rudolf looked at the mess on the floor and down into the glaring eyes of the SS man who taunted him. The sneer about Bremen, his beloved hometown, caused an instant anger that bubbled up his throat.

"Hold this!" he said to Fritz, handing him his beer glass, and he turned full-on to the troublemaker. "What is your problem with Bremen?"

"It's a town full of whores and lazy bastards just like you!" the SS man mocked.

Rudolf's mind reeled. He could not imagine why this man chose to insult him and his hometown, a man he did not know. But it did not matter as he reached out unexpectedly and grabbed the man's greasy hair with his left hand and landed a right-hand blow to the agitator's jaw, knocking him backward into the bar. The two other SS men jumped from their bar stools to enter the fight. Fritz threw the beer glasses at the assailants, and landed his own punch into the neck of the second SS man, stunning him momentarily. The barkeep yelled at the men to stop the melee, but other U-893 crewmen took up the fight, pummeling the three SS men senseless and turning over tables and chairs in their way.

"*Achtung!*" rang out the voice of the Commander who stood at the entrance to the private dining room. The crew immediately moved to attention.

"*Mein Gott,* I leave you alone for a moment and look what happens!" the Commander roared.

The moans of the three SS men were audible as Commander Weber marched into the room with his hand on his hips, a scowl of disapproval on his dog-like face. A deep silence enveloped the usual noisy barroom.

Oberfunkmeister Reese turned to the Commander and saluted, asking if he could have permission to speak.

The Commander took off his hat and scratched his head. "*Ja! Ja!* I would gladly welcome an explanation."

"Meier and Kraus did nothing to these SS *Schweine*! They got their beers from the bar and as they were walking past these three, one of them insulted Rudi, calling Bremen a filthy place. He deserved—all of them—deserved everything they got!" With that, Reese furiously spit on the floor, the spittle landing intentionally on the sprawled men.

The Commander looked down at the unconscious men with a scowl. He reached in his pocket, drew out a wad of Marks, and threw the money on the bar. "I hope this will take care of the damage," he said to the barkeep.

Weber turned to his crew. "Unfortunately, I see no solution but to leave and go back to the boat. When these men come to, they will report this to their superiors, causing great trouble for us, perhaps even delaying our mission."

He paused and then took more money out of his wallet, and walked up to the bar, handing it personally to the barkeep. "On second thought, this should keep your mouth shut."

There was a low murmur among the men, disappointed about the turn of events, but voicing approval of what the Commander had just done. The crew of U-893 were joined together now in a seamless unit, whether it was against the feared SS or the enemies of the Third Reich. A few of them even slapped Rudolf joyously on the back as they headed to the boat, but Werner Carl, a torpedo mechanic, called out, "This is bad luck! Our war patrol is doomed!"

Commander Weber heard Carl and turned on his heel to face the superstitious mechanic. "Keep those thoughts to yourself!" he snarled.

The silence of the night enveloped the crew while they walked toward the wharf, each sailor pondering the luck of U-893. Then, one man sang out, loud enough for everyone to hear, "*Ja*! At least we got a good fight out of it!" and the mood of the crew lightened as they climbed down the boat's hatch.

Early in the dim light of morning, using its diesel engines, U-893 left Kiel with a squadron of other U-boats and headed to the Bay of Danzig where there was less shipping traffic. There, off the coast of Poland, they could practice alarm dives, simulated emergencies in all departments, fire practice torpedoes, and experience the shattering noise of depth charges, barrel-shaped bombs that detonated underwater at a certain depth.

For Rudolf and the other radio operators, there was little rest during the training exercises; radio signals were constant. With each signal that came to the U-boat, the operator took the message down, decoded it, entered it into the signals log, and gave it to the Commander. Then the pattern reversed: The Commander's response was written down, encoded and then Morse code was used to send the message to U-boat headquarters.

Once the U-boats were in the Bay of Danzig, they formed a line and each boat dove one hundred meters into the sea. The loudspeakers of U-893 came on and Commander Weber announced, "Men! A torpedo boat on a parallel course to us is about to drop several depth charges set to explode at sixty meters. Remember, for those who are serving our Fatherland for the first time, this is only a test! True fear comes when we face the enemy."

There was a murmur among the crew as they braced themselves, but when the depth charges exploded, Rudolf was standing in the control room, his watch having just ended. He decided his strong legs could brace him from the shock waves; however, the discharge of the bombs threw him unceremoniously onto the metal grating, and Rudolf felt as if the universe itself had come to an end. A searing pain stabbed him in the shoulder when he hit the hard floor, and when he tried to get up, violent hammer-like blows to the hull kept him off balance. He stumbled and fell again, much to his embarrassment. Finally, when the boat stopped rocking, a noise Rudolf never imagined rumbled through the depths of the ocean. Like the voice of God, it was a resonance of sound that hung in the depths of the sea, making him realize death was more than probable aboard the submarine.

When he finally pulled himself to a standing position, he shook his head to clear it from the vast thunderous sound, yet Rudolf still felt the reverberation of the blast deep in the marrow of his bones. He jammed his hands in his pockets, so that the men in the control room could not see they were trembling; Rudolf never felt so frightened.

"What must it be like to be under real attack?" the young radio operator asked of no one in particular.

Konrad Glimpf, the Chief Engineer, stood near the conning tower. He looked at Rudolf with a stern expression and answered quietly. "It's hell."

The belly of the submarine had a warm feel to it and soft music came over the loudspeakers, music the men referred to as "Jewish jazz," melodies popular in America. At other times, the Commander ordered martial music to raise the men's spirits. The music flowed from a prized record player located in the radio room, and it was manned by the radio operators.

The U-boat's homey atmosphere included crates and boxes of provisions crammed into every corner, and long strings of German sausages and bananas hung from overhead piping. It made for cramped living in the metal tube, but the crew knew that despite long hours, their food was the finest in the German military. Delicious cooking filled the U-boat's space, and the cook, the *Smutje*, made sure coffee was on the stove around the clock. He even prepared a midnight meal for those coming off the late watch.

After passing all of the rigorous tests in the Bay of Danzig, U-893 headed west, back though the Kiel Canal, the North Sea and the English Channel. Slipping smoothly around the hump of northern France, U-893 stopped at the expansive U-boat headquarters at Lorient to take on provisions for its long voyage to the middle of the Atlantic Ocean. After leaving Lorient, the U-boat headed into the Bay of Biscay where the sea became harsh and angry. The bay, situated between the coast of France and Spain, was home to some of the Atlantic Ocean's fiercest weather. So many U-boats had been sunk there by the Royal Air Force that it was also known as the Valley of Death.

The rough sea played havoc with Rudolf and he could not keep his food down. He stopped eating, particularly when the boat ran on the turbulent surface which was at least four hours a day to recharge its batteries. However, Commander Weber often kept the boat on the surface many more hours than that to quickly reach his target destination in the Atlantic Ocean. Once there, headquarters would notify him by wireless where U-893's area of operations would be: America or Africa.

Rudolf's hangdog expression became a joke at the mess table. One day when the sea was particularly rough, he sat down to have a cup of coffee during the dinner meal, hoping it would settle his stomach. He watched as his crewmates wolfed down *Selmannoslabskaus*—a favorite seaman's concoction of corned beef, crushed potatoes mixed with beetroot, a fried egg and pickled herring lying on top of the entire heaped mixture with a dill pickle served on the side. Just the smell of it turned Rudolf's stomach. When he jumped up to find a bucket, the men laughed at him.

On his way back to the table, he passed *Funkmaat* Horst Hollmann, the boat's radio petty officer. Hollmann, who was next in rank to *Oberfunkmeister* Reese, smirked at the pale, young radio operator.

"Ah…so the *Selmannoslabskaus* did not agree with you!" Hollmann said, and he made a slight tsking sound.

Rudolf did not answer. His embarrassment at not yet having gained his sea legs caused him to feel uncomfortable with the joking of the crew. Hollmann's remark, however, set off a spark of anger that made him clench his fists. Rudolf disliked the older man from the first moment he met him, although he did not exactly know why. Perhaps it was Hollmann's all-knowing manner, Rudolf thought, and his rough way of criticizing much of what he did—so different from that of *Oberfunkmeister* Reese. He wondered about the relationship between the two petty officers—Rudolf noticed Hollmann and Reese rarely spoke to one another other than formal conversation about incoming and outgoing radio traffic.

When Rudolf sat down at the mess table, one of the men, Wolfgang Gertzner, pushed a gingersnap cookie toward Rudolf.

"Here," he said. "This ought to help your stomach."

"How do you know?" Rudolf asked.

"It's an old sea remedy. Ginger is supposed to help."

Rudolf smiled at Wolfgang. "How long will it take before I get my sea legs?"

"It's hard to say; every sailor is different," Wolfgang said, smiling. "You should know... you radio operators are also the ship's doctor."

Rudolf laughed, "Well, yes, I passed a short medical and first aid course, but I think we need to depend on *Oberfunkmeister* Reese if there is a serious medical emergency, certainly not me. I understand he has performed a successful surgery while on board a U-boat."

Wolfgang, who worked in the control room, nodded. "Let us hope that does not happen on this boat. Reese is good—and he is lucky—but his luck will run out one day."

"Why do you say that?" Rudolf asked with alarm in his voice.

Wolfgang shrugged his shoulders. "I suppose because no one can stay lucky forever."

Two small rooms in the middle of the boat on the starboard side, conveniently located near the control room bulkhead, allowed the radio operators to communicate easily with their Commander. One radio room held the wireless, the Enigma cipher machine, a typewriter, and the ship's valued phonograph. The other, called the sonar room, was where the hydrophones were located, the listening devices that picked up the sounds of other ships.

The Commander's tiny cabin sat on the opposite side of the corridor from the two radio rooms, his privacy shielded lightly by a green curtain. Rudolf quickly realized that whether he wanted to or not, he could hear all of Weber's conversations conducted above a whisper.

Rudolf worked the night watch after a disheartening day when U-893 spotted a large freighter against the horizon, finally catching up with the ship several hours later. After ordering the preparation of torpedoes, the Commander realized when he looked through the periscope that the ship carried the flag of Spain, a neutral country. He slapped the handles of the periscope back into place and cancelled the attack. The excitement on board for their first attack moved to deep gloom, and Commander Weber slunk to his small hideout, closing the green curtain with a yank.

Soon, however, Rudolf heard the Chief Engineer disturb the Commander's peace.

"Commander, there is a serious water leak in the conning tower." Glimpf said.

Weber pulled back the curtain, and when Rudolf looked up from his work, he noticed the Commander's face looked strained. "Then run the pumps and do whatever else you must to repair it!" he said.

"We will have to perform continuous vent blowing in the tower water condenser," Glimpf replied.

"Yes, yes—take care of it at your discretion!" the Commander said with impatience.

When Glimpf left, the Commander stood in the doorway of his cabin and cursed. "Those *Schweine*! I wonder if the idiots at AG Weser know what the hell they are doing when they build these U-boats."

Rudolf's ears pricked up when he heard AG Weser mentioned; he looked over at the Commander, his eyes wide with surprise. Weber caught Rudolf's look.

"Yes, Rudi, the shipyards say they build superior boats, but *all* of them develop problems. So who else are we to blame then when something goes wrong at sea? Most certainly not my men, so I must place the blame on the shipyard!"

Rudolf blanched, not knowing how to react to such blasphemy from his Commander about the company where his grandfather was almost a legend. Weber walked over to Rudolf and patted him on the back. "Don't take my comments personally, Rudi. We commanders have the right to curse anyone we want!"

The Commander's smile faded as he passed his hand across his forehead. "I have developed a bad headache. It is almost intolerable! Could you get me some aspirin?"

Rudolf quickly retrieved the medicine chest. He unlocked it and found a bottle of Bayer, handing several tablets to the Commander.

"Here, sir. I hope this helps," Rudolf said.

"Yes, I do too. Every once in a while I get one of these, and it makes it difficult to think properly! I need to lie down," he said as he turned to go back to his cubbyhole.

Suddenly, a jolt rocked the boat and lights dimmed. Weber dropped the pills as he rushed into the control room with Rudolf close behind. Rudolf stopped at the bulkhead and peered into the control room where he saw fire belching out of the auxiliary switch board and Glimpf screaming at the crew to grab fire extinguishers. Several men scrambled to grab them, and as they sprayed the dangerous fire, the men in the control room began coughing.

Rudolf saw one man fighting the fire fall to the floor, his body trashing in a convulsive fit. Another crewmember grabbed the fallen extinguisher and continued to work on the blaze. Coughing filled the room along with black smoke. Wolfgang Gertzner pressed his hand to his chest and struggled for breath. Finally, he yelled, "We need air! We need air! Our throats are burning!"

The Commander seemed stunned. Only after another crewman fell to the floor did he yell for the boat to surface along with loud cursing.

Rudolf ran back to the radio room, afraid he would get into trouble for not being at his station. The acrid smell of burned electrical wiring had floated past his station, spreading its poisonous tentacles into the other parts of the U-boat. Rudolf's throat felt as if he had swallowed hot tar; he could only imagine what the men closer to the fire felt. He could hear the continued commotion in the control room, and it seemed a long time before the fire was controlled and finally extinguished after the boat surfaced and the hatch was opened.

The Commander bellowed into the loudspeaker for *Oberfunkmeister* Reese to come to the control room to look after the fallen men. As he passed the radio room, Reese ordered Rudolf to come with him.

Two men lay on the metal grating. Foam filled the floor near the auxiliary switch board and the front of the power unit stood blackened, the inside damaged. Those still gasping for air were ordered onto the bridge.

"Get this man up top—quickly," Reese demanded, after a rapid examination. Rudolf and several other crew members lifted the fallen man up the tower to those who had already escaped to the bridge.

"The carbon dioxide from the fire extinguishers caused this, Commander," Reese said curtly as he stood upright and then pointed at the man lying on the floor. "He is dead."

Weber stood silent and morose by the chart table. After a long silence, he said, "At least it is the middle of the night, but we will be like sitting ducks when dawn comes. Glimpf, get this boat working as soon as possible!" he said, jamming his pudgy hands into his pants pockets.

Crewmen lifted the body of their fellow seaman and carried him to the aft torpedo room to be prepared for burial at dawn. *Oberfunkmeister* Reese and Rudolf returned to the radio room.

"I don't understand what happened..." Rudolf said quietly.

Reese looked around to make sure the Commander could not hear. He leaned over and whispered. "The Commander should have ordered the men to put on their diving lungs when he saw the fire. The filter on the breathing apparatus would have protected them from the carbon dioxide."

"He is not feeling well. He complained of a headache before this happened," Rudolf said as a way to explain Weber's actions.

"It does not matter," Reese countered, his face red with anger. "The *Kommandant* cannot let a headache interfere with his command of this boat!"

The boat ran steadily toward the mid-Atlantic, having been at sea for three weeks. Storm conditions rarely abated from a sea state of 6 to 7—wind at 33 to 37 knots and waves running from 20 to 25 feet. The boat pitched and rolled even when running underwater at periscope depth. At times, the winds were near gale force with the ocean heaped into great waves and white foam blowing in streaks along the direction of the wind. Despite the tremendous waves sweeping over the conning tower, lookouts steadfastly stood their watch on the bridge searching for adversaries, wearing harnesses attached to the inside of the bridge structure by a lockable clasp to keep them from washing overboard. In his cramped but cozy radio room, Rudolf often heard the lookouts grumble as they came off watch.

"The Commander is running the boat dangerously on the surface," a young midshipman complained, shaking water out of his sea boots.

"Since when does a midshipman know better than the Commander?" Otto Kölle, the First Watch Officer, retorted sharply. Kölle, known throughout the boat as a stern man, never rested his hawk-like eyes when he was on the bridge, constantly on the lookout for the enemies of the Third Reich. So far, his search had been futile except for the lone Spanish freighter.

"It just seems to me…" the midshipman countered, wiping his wet face with his hand.

"Commander Weber knows what he is doing," Kölle snapped. "We need to get to the staging area where we will receive our orders. If that means running on the surface twelve hours a day, then that is what we will do! Besides, a little sea water never hurt anyone."

The midshipman, a recent graduate of officer training school, made no further comment. He walked sullenly to his bunk as he took off his gray leather coat, shedding water like a Labrador retriever that had just jumped out of a lake.

Rudolf wondered about the midshipman's complaint, but he kept his thoughts to himself, holding fast to his firm conviction that no one should question the boat's leader. Although Rudolf greatly admired *Oberfunkmeister* Reese, he believed Reese's comment about the Commander's behavior during the fire verged on insubordination.

The days merged seamlessly with one another and a dull sameness set in. The ocean was not brimming with enemies like Rudolf believed, nor did the ship maintain its homey atmosphere as the human smells of the men crammed so tightly together took hold, along with mold on their food from the constant moisture inside the boat. Because of the bad weather, Rudolf rarely asked to go on the bridge to get a breath of fresh air, so day and night seemed indistinguishable.

Personal hygiene was impossible. Rudolf hated his beard, his face felt itchy and he scratched it incessantly, and his body odor seemed overwhelming, especially when he lay in his bunk. Rudolf would swab himself with alcohol, and when that ran out, sea water was the only alternative.

Rudolf slowly became accustomed to the pitch and roll of the boat, regaining his appetite. One day to everyone's surprise, the cook presented *Grüne Klösse* to the crew—green dumplings, made from potatoes. A regional German specialty, each man got three of the mouthwatering delicacies.

Wolfgang Gertzner soaked up gravy drippings with the scrumptious dumpling and crammed it in his mouth. "I wonder why the *Smutje* decided to treat us with such a delight?" he muttered to Rudolf.

"I don't know," Rudolf answered glumly. "There certainly has been nothing to celebrate—no good news from the wireless. The Americans have landed in Sicily."

Wolfgang thumped his hand on the table. "That's impossible! Our *Wehrmacht* will beat those *Schweinhunde* back to the sea!"

Rudolf nodded assent and then he looked around the table, asking loudly, "You know what *Der Führer* said about America, don't you?" No one took up his question, preferring to eat their dumplings in silence.

Rudolf, incredulous, looked around at his fellow crewmates and put down his fork. "None of you know what our leader thinks about America?"

"Well, why don't you tell us since you seem to have a knowledge of what Hitler thinks?" one of the crewmen responded snidely.

Rudolf ignored the tone of the other's voice and willingly took up the challenge. "He said it is a decayed country, a 'giant with clay feet.' I believe America will be handily defeated. It is a nation of mixed races and Jews. How could they have any backbone or will to fight Germany, a nation of pure blooded Aryans?"

The men at the table were silent.

Fritz Kraus, who just came off duty, sat down in time to hear Rudolf's tirade. He looked askance at Rudolf and interjected, "I think we all hope the best for our troops in Sicily and that they will beat back the Americans."

Rudolf opened his mouth to say more, but he suddenly caught the frustrated look from his friend, and closed his mouth with a snap. He looked down at his plate and picked up a piece of dumpling on his fork. The conversation changed to how soon the Commander would receive orders from headquarters about U-893's area of operations.

"I hope it is Africa," one of the men said, a piece of dumpling suspended on his beard. "It would be a wonder to see the native women with nothing covering their tits."

The men murmured among themselves, the vision of topless women suddenly as tasty as the dumplings, although they all knew there was no chance of landing on African soil; U-893's mission was to sink enemy ships.

"Do you think we might see some beautiful American girls sunning themselves on the beach if we are ordered to the American coastline?" another asked.

To that Fritz answered, "My guess is only the Commander will see such delights through the periscope, certainly not us U-boat *Schweine*!"

The enlisted men of the U-boat arm of the German Navy laughed easily at being called pigs. But the atmosphere changed quickly when Werner Carl stuffed the last of his dumplings in his mouth and growled, "Humph! We will be lucky if we make it back to Kiel considering everything that has happened already on this boat!"

The men, who had been so joyful at the beginning of the meal, finished in silence. Rudolf pushed his chair back from the table, ready to head for his bunk when he accidently heard one of his crewmates say to another, "That Rudi. He's a real Nazi."

He gasped and quickly turned his back, heading quickly to his bunk. For some odd reason, he felt wounded: he had never thought of himself as a Nazi, only that he was a proud German.

Orders from headquarters finally came through four weeks after the boat left the coast of France: U-893's mission was to play a deadly game of hide and seek along America's East Coast. At least we know where we are going, Rudolf thought as Weber handed him the decrypted message from U-boat headquarters. The orders gave the mission meaning, raising Rudolf's hopes that U-893 would be victorious. If *Der Führer* was right, and Rudolf believed he always was, the Americans would be easy targets because of their lack of will. Their freighters and war ships along the East Coast would be effortless kills.

The Commander took the loudspeaker in hand, a note of joy in his voice.

"Another week and we will be off the American coast. I have no doubt we will return to France with victorious pennants flying from the periscope, announcing our successes! However, on a more serious note, provisions have to last ten weeks," he said, "but we are lacking some foodstuffs that should have been put on board at Lorient. I have made a request to headquarters that before we get to our area of operations we be allowed to rendezvous with another U-boat heading back to France, one that can give us some of their provisions and take our letters to port!"

After four weeks, it was normal for the crew to have eaten the fresh fruit and the revered German sausage, but *Oberfunkmeister* Reese, who was responsible for ordering provisions for the boat, reported that he and the cook determined dock workers in France had shorted them on food. He shook his head when he spoke about it to Rudolf. "And they were Germans, too! The *Schweine!*"

"I don't understand it," Rudolf said.

"I do!" Reese answered. "They could take the provisions and sell them on the black market—to the French who are suffering from food shortages. Just imagine how much money those unpatriotic bastards put into their pockets with our food!"

Despite the beginning of food rationing, the crew was happy at last to know the American coast was their heading. The monotony of the mission, however, began to wear on Rudolf's nerves. Along with no action, he was privy to news on the wireless about Allied air raids on Germany, many directed at Bremen. The shipyard of AG Weser was a prime target of the Allies, but he also feared for his grandparents' safety because they lived in the heart of the city. His sullen attitude was noticeable at the mess table when he did not join in the crew's conversations. Fritz noticed his quiet manner more than anyone, and spoke to him about it.

"Not all war patrols have success, you know!" Fritz said. "Not every boat can have a Commander like Otto Kretschmer!"

Rudolf grunted—if only he had been on U-99 with Otto Kretschmer, Germany's top U-boat ace that held the record of sinking 39 enemy ships. He was lying on his back in his bunk, his eyes staring at the ceiling. "Perhaps what Werner Carl said was true. Despite having Günther Reese on board, maybe we are unlucky. The fight in the bar, the fire in the control room, no enemy ships…"

Fritz made a wry face. "Unlike you, Rudi, I will only consider this war patrol unlucky if we sink!"

One night, Rudolf was mournfully writing the day's events in the Commander's war diary, reporting no sightings of Allied ships. Suddenly, the Commander came out of his small compartment and looked hard at Rudolf.

"Why are you on watch again so soon, Rudi?"

"*Oberfunkmeister* Reese is not feeling well, Commander. He asked me if I would let him rest for a bit longer."

Weber rubbed his stocky hand over his beard. "Reese has not been up to speed for a few days. What is the matter?"

Rudolf looked dismayed. "I do not know."

"Have you been topside lately," the Commander suddenly asked.

"No, *Kommandant.*"

"The radio traffic seems light tonight. You may get a breath of fresh air. Just don't stay too long, in case headquarters decides to tell us the war has ended."

Rudolf looked askance at the Commander. Weber made a funny face. "I was kidding, Rudi! You must not be so serious…we must joke a little since there are no enemy ships in sight. This war is a grave matter, but it is not harmful to be lighthearted and hopeful."

"Yes sir!" Rudolf said. "Thank you, *Kommandant.*"

Rudolf quickly took off his shirt, keeping on his shorts and sail-cloth shoes, and went hurriedly through the control room before the Commander could change his mind, climbing easily up the tower and through the hatch. The four men on watch turned to look at him as he stepped out onto the bridge.

Otto Kölle, the First Watch Officer, nodded slightly. "A breath of fresh air, Rudi?"

"Yes sir."

"The sea is cooperating for a change," Kölle said. His binoculars locked to his eyes like a clamshell, as he scanned the horizon mercilessly.

Rudolf nodded. He took in a deep lungful of air, smelling to the core of his being the sharp tang of the ocean. There was little wind except what he felt on his face; the submarine was moving smoothly through the water and the only sound he could hear was the hum of the diesel motors. For a moment, Rudolf was back again on his small sailboat, facing into the wind as he tacked up the Weser River, heading for the North Sea. Suddenly, a deep ache filled his heart as he remembered home and his grandmother's pear cake because she always made the delicious treat for him after a long sailing weekend with the *Marine Hitlerjugend.*

The hatch opened and the Commander climbed onto the bridge, his binoculars around his neck.

"Feeling better, Rudi?" the Commander asked as he brought the glasses up to his face and scanned the horizon.

"Yes sir."

Suddenly, in a low controlled voice, Kölle said, "Large freighter at 180 degrees flying an American flag!"

Weber turned on his heel, his hands holding his binoculars steady. "Well," he said, breathless, "it's about time!"

Everyone on the bridge raced down the conning tower, the Commander the last one inside the boat, slamming the tower hatch lid shut. On Weber's command, the boat turned about and headed toward the enemy. Alarm bells shrilled, and all hands reported to battle stations as the vents opened and the boat dived to periscope depth. Rudolf ran back to the hydrophone room and saw a sleepy Fritz making his way down the corridor to take over the wireless. Rudolf placed a hydrophone on his head covering only his right ear. He needed the listening device to hear the sounds made underwater by the enemy ship, but he also had to hear Weber's commands.

Rudolf sat at the hydrophones and made a sweep of the area. The audibility was clear and he picked out propeller noises from the large freighter, now off the starboard bow, reporting it to the Commander.

When the merchant ship was within two miles, Weber's steady voice said, "Open tubes one and two!"

U-893 moved into firing range, and when the torpedoes shot out of their tubes, Rudolf reported to the Commander, "Torpedoes running!"

The boat's navigator held the boat's stopwatch and counted off the seconds as the torpedoes streaked toward their target. After three minutes there were two explosions in quick succession, then after a long pause, a blast shook the ocean and the sound of the freighter's propellers stopped. There was no noise for what seemed to be a lengthy period—but it really was only a few minutes—and then the fire reached the ship's boilers causing a horrific blast. Rudolf could hear the ship dying, bit by bit, piece by piece. The hair on the back of his neck stood up at the frightful sounds. He had never heard such eerie sounds as the crushing and groaning of metal upon metal, making him feel insignificant to the might of the sea.

Weber searched the area with the periscope, and then slapping the handles back into place, he roared, "Bring her up!"

U-893 bounced to the surface, water streaming off her deck. The Commander and other officers went up to the bridge to view the demise of the freighter. *Oberfunkmeister* Reese, gray faced, stood next to the radio rooms, monitoring the work of Rudolf and Fritz. Rudolf looked up at the Chief Radio Petty Officer.

Reese nodded. "At last it is done...our first success. The *Kommandant* has a heavy weight lifted off him!"

Rudolf felt exuberant, his face beaming, and then remembering Reese's illness he asked, "Are you feeling better, sir?"

"No, Rudi, I am not, but I am on my feet for the time being. This nausea has caused me great distress."

"Is there anything I can do?"

"No. It will either pass or it will get worse. I hope it is not what I think it is," Reese said, smiling wanly.

Rudolf was about to ask Reese what he thought the cause of his illness could be, but orders came from the bridge to broadcast an SOS for the freighter, giving the position of the sunken ship to anyone who might be listening to the wireless.

"Why is the Commander doing that?" Rudolf asked, incredulous.

"Probably because there are men in the sea, praying to God they will be rescued."

"But they are our enemies!" Rudolf nearly shouted.

Reese put his hand on Rudolf's shoulder. "They are not our enemies, they are our opponents. Our common enemy is the sea, Rudi. We will check if there are survivors and throw them a raft or two with provisions and then we will leave. If our time comes, Rudi, let us hope our opponents will do the same for us!"

Rudolf's sense of shame flooded through him and he put his eyes down to avert looking directly at his Chief Radio Petty Officer. He never thought about the enemy in such a way. The only time he could remember this shameful feeling was the day after *Kristallnacht* in November 1938 when roving gangs of Gestapo and SA members, the Brownshirts, destroyed hundreds of synagogues and thousands of Jewish businesses.

There was a synagogue behind the *Gymnasium* in Bremen, and Rudolf remembered walking to it after school with several other boys from his Hitler Youth unit to see the damage. On the ground was broken glass, and the door of the temple was smashed. The Torah, the text of Jewish laws written on a parchment scroll, was lying in the gutter with the strong smell of urine on it.

Rudolf's former friend Lothar was there, standing on the sidewalk. He looked over at Rudolf, peering directly into his eyes. "This is not right," Lothar said, sweeping his arm outward. "This is not right."

Rudolf was not sure what Lothar meant, but a disturbing feeling came over him; the sweep of Lothar's arm seemed not only to include the destroyed synagogue, but him and the other boys in their Hitler Youth uniforms

Chapter 21

Mid-Summer – Early Fall 1943
Mid-Atlantic to the American East Coast

The crew of U-893 celebrated their first successful sinking with a song as the *Smutje* carried pails of lemonade to the crew.

> *The Briton prattles "The world is mine",*
> *the people England's slaves,*
> *With German Sword resounds a "No",*
> *and we demand our rights.*
> *The U Boat fights for Germany's honor*
> *for right and freedom on the sea,*
> *Be on your guard, England,*
> *Be on your guard, England.*
> *Day in, day out, night after night*
> *the prey is stalked*
> *until finally the torpedo roars,*
> *despite the furious howls of the pack.*
> *The U Boat fights for Germany's honor*
> *for right and freedom on the sea,*
> *Be on your guard, England,*
> *Be on your guard, England.*

Fritz slapped Rudolf on the shoulder. "Two fewer torpedoes to bring home!"

Rudolf's mood had changed significantly. A bright smile peaked through his blond beard. Everything was good now; the beginning of a successful war patrol.

With time on his hands because *Funkmaat* Hollmann had taken over his watch, he sat down and wrote a triumphant letter to his grandparents. He told about the American freighter his grandfather's U-boat sunk, recounting the event in detail from the time he stood on the bridge until he heard the ship take its last breath. He hoped his grandparents would feel the same exhilaration he did. At the end of the letter, he wrote, "*Heil Hitler,*" then signed his name with a flourish, sealed the letter, and placed it in the mailbag.

They would meet up with the other U-boat in a few days and Rudolf's letter, along with those of the other crewmen, would eventually arrive in Germany after that boat returned to the submarine base on the coast of France. When he walked past the non-commissioned officer's mess, he saw *Oberfunkmeister* Reese also writing a letter. Reese looked up and Rudolf could see beads of sweat on his face, and that he was sitting in an odd position as if warding off pain. Reese halted Rudolf, waving his hand.

"Rudi, wait a moment until I finish this to my wife. Could you put it in the mailbag for me—it will save my having to get up. Walking is becoming painful."

Rudolf stopped and waited for the Chief Radio Petty Officer to finish, and a worried frown came over his face. Reese noticed Rudolf's concern when he handed the young radio operator his letter. "Well, at least the nausea has stopped, but the aching pain around my navel has shifted to my lower right abdomen. It is far more acute now, I am afraid."

"Can I do anything to assist you, sir?" Rudolf asked with, anxiety in his voice.

Reese avoided the question, saying instead, "I have spoken to the Commander... I believe he has ordered Hollmann to contact headquarters to see if we can meet up sooner with the other U-boat.

With luck, there will be a doctor on board, or at least a qualified *Oberfunkmeister* who can operate."

Rudolf's throat constricted and he felt an unwanted fear crawl through his body for this man who had shown great patience with his mistakes. "If I may ask, sir, what is it…?"

"Appendicitis, Rudi, I am fairly certain, although you should get to know the symptoms because you and Fritz may face this again as part of your medical duty. It is a tricky diagnosis—the pain does not usually localize itself as quickly as mine has—but I have had all the classic warning signs—nausea, sometimes vomiting, loss of appetite, and pain at first around the navel, then moving to the lower right stomach. There is also tenderness when you press and release here," Reese answered, putting his hand over the painful area.

"Cannot *Funkmaat* Hollmann be of help to you, sir? I mean… could he operate if…?" Rudolf's voice trailed off.

Reese did not answer immediately, his mind seemingly far away. Finally, he said, "Oh, no. Hollmann could not help me."

Rudolf walked away with Reese's letter and placed it in the mailbag. He felt anxious and wondered why Hollmann was unable to help Reese. Although he was uncomfortable around Hollmann, Rudolf recognized he was an experienced petty officer, and had served a couple of years on other U-boats. But surgery was another matter, even though instructions for surgery were often given over the wireless from a surgeon at U-boat headquarters. If Hollmann could not do it—or would not do it, which seemed implausible to Rudolf—the job might become the responsibility of either Fritz or himself if U-893 could not meet up in time with the other boat. The thought of performing surgery caused him to clamp his jaw so tightly that he felt actual pain. Medical duty was the one thing about being a radio operator Rudolf hated; the sight of blood made him physically ill.

After Reese had been carried gingerly back to his bunk, Weber ordered Rudolf to keep an eye on him. Rudolf placed a cold water bottle on Reese's stomach, and took his temperature. The reading was 99 degrees. Not good, Rudolf knew, but at least he was not burning with fever.

"There must be something more I can do." Rudolf said.

Reese slowly moved his head from side to side, pain etched on his thin face. "There is nothing I need, Rudi, nothing. Just pray the *Milch Cow* makes it here soon."

Word finally came through on the wireless that headquarters was directing a supply U-boat toward U-893 on its way back to the coast of France. The crew fondly called the supply boat a '*Milch Cow*' because it was laden with food, spare parts, and seven hundred tons of diesel fuel. In addition, there was normally a doctor on board a supply U-boat, a great relief for Rudolf. The estimated time for Reese's pickup and the transfer of foodstuffs was forty-eight hours.

Rudolf checked frequently on Reese, changing the water bottle and putting a cool cloth on his head, but those actions did little good and the Chief Petty Officer's temperature climbed upward despite the aspirin.

When it was Rudolf's time to take over the watch and Hollmann left the radio room area, he said to Fritz who was still on duty, "Reese is in bad shape, but when I asked him about Hollmann operating on him, he said, no…that Hollmann could not help him."

Fritz leaned over and whispered, "They despise one another."

"How do you know?"

"I was up on the bridge with the Commander and Kölle, taking a break. They were talking about it."

"How could Hollmann not aid Reese at a time like this?" Rudolf asked, incredulous. "I don't understand."

"They evidently served together on another U-boat, a couple of years ago." Fritz said. "Hollmann made a big mistake, according to the Commander. He neglected to change the direction of the auxiliary aerial located on the bridge to find the homing signal from a *Milch Cow* when their U-boat was running dangerously low on fuel, and Hollmann inadvertently gave the coxswain the opposite direction of the homing signal. The U-boat traveled several hours in the wrong direction, eating up fuel, and when Reese realized what Hollmann had done…well, you can imagine what happened. When the war patrol ended, Reese made sure Hollmann would never be promoted to Chief Radio Petty Officer."

Rudolf sucked in his breath. The mistake Hollmann made was easy enough to do; in fact, he could be doing it right now. With his heart suddenly thumping wildly, he carefully checked the bearing from the homing signal of the supply boat to make sure U-893 was heading in the right direction. It was, but in his nervousness, his armpits poured sweat so heavy, he felt like he was standing on the bridge in a heavy sea.

"I hope the weather stays good for the transfer," Rudolf said, his voice tight.

Fritz nodded, stifling a yawn. "I will get us some coffee. We need to be on top of this."

Hollmann had slipped away from his medical duties like an eel rushing into its hole on the sea floor, and Rudolf wondered why the Commander would let the Radio Petty Officer evade such an important responsibility. But this was no time to question the Commander's reasoning, Rudolf thought; it was a crisis after all, and he did hear the Commander call Reese his lucky charm. Although Rudolf was not especially superstitious, he knew the might of the sea could turn anyone's thinking into the realm of the mystical, even the Commander's.

Perhaps because the Commander knew the circumstances of their animosity toward one another, maybe the Commander did not want Hollmann to touch his lucky charm; even more plausible, Rudolf thought, was that Reese may have requested Hollmann be kept away from him.

Rudolf could see the Commander pacing between the control room and his private cubby hole across from the radio rooms, worry engraved on his dour face, his brows furrowed. Finally, he approached the two inexperienced radio operators. His big hand brushed his forehead as if he wanted to wave away the dire situation, but he said, "I have relieved Hollmann from duty until after the transfer of Reese."

Rudolf and Fritz looked at one another, a knowing glance between them. It was up to them now to make sure U-893 was moving in the right direction for the U-boat connection. The hours dragged, the young men relieving each other to check on Reese and catch a catnap, all the while keeping track of the homing signal of the *Milch Cow*.

Suddenly, alarm bells rang and the men on watch scrambled down the tower. Kölle pulled the hatch lid shut with a bang and yelled that an American destroyer was on the horizon off the port bow. He swore as he landed at the bottom of the conning tower. "They saw us and turned in our direction!"

"Are you sure?" the Commander demanded.

"Yes! The ship came out of a squall and it was fewer than four miles!"

The Commander yelled, "Dive! Dive!"

U-893's vents quickly opened and the submarine plunged into the sea at a steep angle. Rudolf had left the wireless room to check on Reese; he was caught off balance, falling against a metal ventilator during the crash dive, splitting the scalp on the side of his head. He lay on the grating, stunned for a few moments until one of the crewmen helped him back to the radio room, a difficult task at the steep angle of the submarine as it dived, trying to hide from the Americans in the ocean's depths.

Blood from the wound flowed down the side of his neck and onto his shirt, making him nauseous, but the feeling quickly passed as he pulled the shirt off and held it to his head, fumbling for the hydrophones and cursing under his breath. Fritz grabbed the medicine chest, found gauze and clumsily wrapped Rudolf's head while Rudolf tried to hear what was going on topside. Fritz then put on his hydrophones, and they could both hear spinning propellers growing louder on the port bow, reporting the noise to the Commander. It was not just one destroyer they heard, but three, coming in their direction, and Rudolf felt his stomach tighten as he listened to the ominous thrashing sound.

Soon the ships were close enough that everyone on board the U-boat could hear the propellers. One of the ships passed directly overhead, dropping depth charges with a resounding splash and then charged off at full speed to get away from the explosions.

"Cans dropping, sir!" Rudolf reported.

There was silence; everyone on board could hear the drops—eight in all. Every man on board counted quietly as the deadly charges began to sink.

"The *Schweine!*" the Commander muttered.

The sea exploded and shock waves shook the hull of U-893, breaking china used in the officer's mess, tossing anything in the boat not safely tucked away. The boat shook brutally, as if Neptune himself had pulled the vessel from the sea and vented his wrath on the sailors; then the terrible noise rumbled away. Rudolf's wound ached but the throbbing was unimportant compared to the fright he felt, and he hoped desperately he would not shit in his pants. He did not look at Fritz, afraid that his expression would show how afraid he was, but he could not stop his hands from shaking.

"All departments report damage," the Commander bellowed.

Several gauges had burst in the engine room, and a thin jet of water hissed into the control room from the hatch. Rudolf's heart stood still: his grandfather's boat had withstood the explosions with minor damage. The crew whispered cautiously to one another and all metal tools not in use were noiselessly tucked away. They all waited quietly, men at battle stations from bow to stern, straining to hear what was going on above them.

"Go to 260 meters," ordered the Commander, and the boat floated deeper into the sea, trying to escape.

The air was tense with anticipation. A disgusting smell permeated the boat; the shit bucket in the bow room fell over during the sharp incline of the dive. Adding to the odor was the sweat of fifty men, strong and musty with the anxiety of death hovering over them.

"All ships have stopped, Commander," Rudolf reported.

Weber grunted. He was chewing the bottom half of his lip.

Suddenly, the radio men picked up a chirping sound.

"Asdic, sir," called out Fritz.

The pinging of the destroyer's sonar came on slow at first, but then the noise came faster and faster as it honed in on U-893. The wolves were closing in for the kill.

"Go to 300 meters," Weber said, his voice a low growl, and the boat moved downward.

The thrashing of the enemy's dreaded propellers started up and once again depth charges were thrown overboard—this time, the destroyers dropped ten into the sea. Rudolf counted each one, know-ing he was not the only one doing so.

Rudolf had seen many German U-boat movies in his youth where panic reigned, but much to his surprise there were no sounds emit-ted by the crew, no crying out in fear during the attack; everyone acted in a professional manner, silently swearing or praying depend-ing upon each man, holding for dear life onto anything in the boat that would keep them from falling. Rudolf tried to calm himself as the boat rocked and shuddered; the sudden thought of dying becoming incredibly real, and urine ran down Rudolf's leg, much to his horror.

He tried to focus on the one remark that his Hitler Youth leader said again and again: "You are nothing. The nation is everything," but his love for Germany at this moment did not seem to help his feeling of terror; only the calmness of the other men kept him from embar-rassing himself.

The bow torpedo room reported that a torpedo had flooded through its outer cap; otherwise, U-893 held together under the bom-bardment with a few glass bulbs shattering. The creaking noise of the U-boat as its hull withstood the mighty pressure of the sea sounded like ghosts of dead seamen calling out; it was otherworldly, and Rudolf envisioned the pressure hull splitting with a great mound of water sud-denly rushing into the boat.

Now, it was a game: the Americans waiting for the U-boat to surface because the air in the boat was becoming foul and stifling hot, and the Germans waiting for their enemies to give up and leave the scene of the attack. Rudolf suddenly remembered Reese, but there was nothing he could do, not now while they were in battle mode.

Rudolf and Fritz could hear the boats overhead, moving back and forth, crisscrossing the surface where they thought U-893 lay sub-merged. Finally, the Americans renewed their attack, sure that their prey was still alive in the murky depths. Rudolf marveled at how the metal tube held together under such bombardment but he also won-dered if his hearing would ever be the same, the sounds of the explod-ing depth charges were so piercing and thunderous. Several hours of anxiety plagued the men as they waited for the next assault, the

air unbearably hot, every man stripped down to a minimum of clothing, when suddenly Rudolf and Fritz heard the start-up of one of the
destroyer's propellers. Miraculously, the ship was moving away.

Weber walked quietly to the hydrophone room, still munching on
his lower lip. "Where are the other two?"

"They are still there," Rudolf answered, "waiting."

"Hmmm," the Commander muttered. "Bring it up to periscope
depth."

Silently, U-893 floated up so the Commander could see the enemy.
As Weber viewed the battlefield through the periscope, Rudolf held
his breath, wondering what the Commander would decide to do.

Suddenly slamming the periscope's handles closed, Weber said,
"I'm tired of playing the sitting duck!" Without a moment's hesitation
he roared, "Both motors, full ahead!"

The boat charged forward, and Rudolf held his breath, but the
destroyers miraculously did not follow—U-893 was no longer their pri-
ority. The young radio men looked at one another and smiled as the
Commander growled, "Get us back on track with the supply boat!"

Finally, half a day late, U-893 met up with the *Milch Cow*. Reese was
conscious as two men carried him past the radio rooms and he offered
a small smile to Rudolf and Fritz who stood respectfully to see him,
and he was carefully lifted up the conning tower, where the officers
waited on the bridge to bid Reese farewell. The supply boat brought a
rubber raft to the side of U-893, and Reese was transferred in a calm
sea.

The loss of Reese affected Rudolf deeply: it was as if a shroud
dropped over him, dulling his sense of purpose. The man who had
stood up for him after the barroom brawl was gone from U-893. Perhaps,
Rudolf feared, Reese would not survive his appendicitis attack; he had
been without medical attention too long and his appendix might have
already ruptured, flooding his system with a fatal infection. Although
he said nothing to Fritz, Rudolf dreaded taking orders from *Funkmaat*
Hollmann, a man he never liked, and respected even less now because
of what happened to Reese.

Later during dinner, even with the taste of fresh food brought on board from the supply boat the men ate their meal quietly; there was none of the usual banter, none of the talk about sexual encounters or fantasies, only the clink of eating utensils as the men shoveled food into their mouths. U-893's lucky charm was gone and a feeling of doom permeated the boat.

U-893's luck ran out while lurking off the coast of South Carolina less than a fortnight later. The boat that had known the touch of Rudolf's grandfather was scuttled by her own crew—ingloriously sinking into the secretive womb of the sea.

It happened so quickly—the fog suddenly lifting at daybreak, Rudolf standing on the boat's bridge smoking a cigarette and the American plane roaring out of the rising sun, dropping its 600-pound depth charges and blowing a hole in U-893's pressure hull before she was able to dive. With the diesel room flooded, the diesel engines thrown off their mounts, and a significant number of batteries cracked—the alternate method a U-boat uses to propel itself through the water—Commander Weber turned to his Chief Engineer and said in a low voice, "We have no way to escape!"

And then came the most shocking moment of all—the Commander's order to abandon ship and scuttle the boat before the Americans could board her.

Rudolf glimpsed the guns of the destroyer firing toward the U-boat as he stood momentarily on the bridge before jumping into the sea, his heart pounding so hard he wondered if it would burst. "Goddamn them!" he swore as he hit the water and it was the sudden cold that forced the realization upon Rudolf that this disaster was really happening. When he surfaced, every fiber of his body kicked in as he took a gulp of air, and he knew he had to swim away from the boat; the muffled explosions telling him U-893 was sinking and the void created by the boat could suck him into the sea.

When he surfaced, Rudolf found the Commander and Glimpf floating not far from him, but the rest of the crew was scattered. Straining as much as he could, he could not find Fritz among the bobbing heads and the swell of the sea.

"Are you all right, Rudi?" yelled the Commander.

"I...I am." Rudolf answered forlornly. "And you, sir?"

"Yes, I am here, but it would have been better if I had gone down with my boat!"

Rudolf did not know how to respond to his Commander, so he nodded as if he understood, his chin hitting the top of his life jacket. He could see the outline of the American destroyer coming closer, and a mixture of pent-up anger and deep fear clutched at Rudolf, causing him to shake violently, his teeth chattering so hard that he was afraid the Commander would hear. Weber, however, was yelling at his officers to get the separated men to swim closer together.

Rudolf wondered what Weber was doing. Gathering the men together would only make it easier for the enemy to kill them; they were like sitting ducks, easy to pick off in their life jackets. Rudolf shook his head, trying to clear his senses; nothing seemed logical. The incompetent Americans had destroyed their boat and here he was floating in the cold ocean. Soon, they would kill him, too; he would never see his grandparents or the Fatherland again. He felt suddenly alone then, isolated from his crewmates who were raising their arms out of the water, yelling entreaties and rejoicing that the Americans would save them.

The destroyer moved smoothly toward the crew, and Rudolf viewed the huge ship with surprise; he had always assumed America was incapable of building anything equivalent to the might of the German Navy. The large destroyer loomed out of the water, and he saw men standing high on the deck holding guns aimed at the men in the water. Again, to his astonishment there were no shots fired. Instead, the Americans threw a rope ladder over the side of their ship and the men of U-893 began to climb aboard.

Rudolf floated in the water, waiting for most of his comrades to climb up before he did. He needed to control his emotions—fluctuating wildly from anger at the sinking of the U-boat to shame because the weak Americans had captured them, and then there was the joy of survival. Suddenly, he saw Fritz pull himself out of the water and climb up the side of destroyer. He took a deep breath; his elation that Fritz was alive lightened the heaviness of Rudolf's heart.

Once again, the last three men off U-893, Rudolf, the Commander, and the Chief Engineer, were the only men left in the water. "Go ahead," the Commander said to Glimpf and Rudolf. "I was the last off my boat; I will be last aboard this one."

Rudolf grabbed the rope ladder and pulled himself up. When he got onto the deck, a blond-haired sailor about the same age as himself handed him a blanket and a Red Cross parcel. Rudolf, surprised by the calm look on the American, expected anger on the face of the enemy; but there was none. Stunned from all that had just happened, he meekly followed his crewmates to the stern of the boat where he sat down on the deck and opened the package. Inside was a pair of underwear, pants and shirt, toothpaste and a brush. Everyone else was stripping to get out of their wet clothes and he did the same, all the while feeling the presence of the guards and their guns.

When he was dressed, he wandered among the men from U-893 and found Fritz leaning against the ship's railing smoking a cigarette.

He grinned at Rudolf. "We are alive, Rudi!"

Rudolf nodded, and he slapped Fritz on the shoulder. "Yes, Fritz! I am so glad to see you!"

The two men stood silently together, taking in the might of the United States Navy and its men. The ship looked new, with its deck guns polished to a high sheen, ominously reflecting the summer sun. Rudolf saw a few guards standing at the edge of the men from U-893, and although they were holding weapons, he could see that they were trying to talk to the Germans, offering cigarettes. Rudolf watched them carefully, the first time in his life he had seen Americans and he marveled that they really looked no different than the men from his U-boat.

Fritz shared his cigarette with Rudolf, and when he took a long drag on it, filling his lungs, he felt the smoothness of its taste.

"They are far superior to German cigarettes, don't you think?" Fritz asked.

"Yes," Rudolf acknowledged. "Real tobacco, isn't it?"

Fritz nodded.

Rudolf relaxed somewhat. Maybe it was the cigarette, he wondered, but then it occurred to him that he was alive after all, like Fritz said. He felt giddy for a moment, but then a sense of shame washed over him for he had not lost his life fighting for the Third Reich. Yet, despite that ingrained need to give his life for his country, he took a deep gulp of sea air, and knew he wanted to live.

He tried to hear what the American guards were saying to the crewmen, but he was not standing close enough. Rudolf realized none of the U-boat's officers were on deck, and he asked Fritz if he had seen them.

"They were taken into the ship," Fritz said, pointing to the door where they disappeared. "No doubt they are being interrogated."

Suddenly, the uncertainty of what lay ahead came to him, and his joy vanished. "What do you think they will do to us?" he asked Fritz.

"Who knows," Fritz said, shrugging his shoulders. "You could find out, Rudi. You speak English, after all."

Rudolf thought about that for a moment, fear rising in him. He was not sure if he should speak to the Americans without the approval of an officer, but since none of the officers were on deck for him to ask permission, perhaps he could help. He took another long drag on the American cigarette, tucked his anxiety away and walked over to one of the guards who stood casually with his rifle held across the crook of his arm. The guard, a tall man with thick eyebrows and big brown eyes looked at Rudolf.

"May I ask you a question?" Rudolf asked.

The guard's mouth dropped open. "Yeah, sure," he answered.

"Can you tell me what is going to happen to us?"

The guard scratched his chin. "Geez, a Kraut that speaks good English!"

Rudolf, not sure what to do, repeated the question. The guard yelled to another guard, who walked over to them.

"This guy speaks English," he said, motioning his thumb toward Rudolf. "He wants to know what's going to happen to them."

The second guard looked as surprised as the first. "Wait a minute!" he said, and he disappeared. The first guard dug in his pocket and brought out a cigarette pack, closely eyeing Rudolf as he did so, and thumped the Lucky Strike pack against the rifle butt, offering a smoke. Rudolf pulled the loose cigarette out, and put it to his lips as the guard jerked a book of matches one-handed out of his shirt pocket and handed them to the German. Rudolf lit the cigarette, cupping his hand to protect it from the wind, inhaled and looked the American in the eye as he handed back the matches.

"Where are you from?" the American said.

"I am from Bremen, in northern Germany, not far from the North Sea."

"I'm not sure where that is. I guess I never studied much German geography," he said. "I'm from Hollywood, California—you know, on the Pacific coast."

Rudolf nodded. "Is that not where all the American films are made—in Hollywood?"

"Yeah, that's right. Gosh, you probably know more about America than I do about Germany."

Rudolf laughed, thinking to himself that was probably true since Germans were superior to Americans. He studied the guard as he smoked. No German would stand with his rifle tucked into the corner of his arm while guarding prisoners, Rudolf thought. No wonder they are losing the war.

The second guard returned with a Lieutenant J.G., introducing him as Lieutenant Collins. Rudolf respectfully saluted the officer, and said, "Radio Operator Rudolf Meier, sir."

"I understand you want to know what is going to happen to you and these men," the officer said, waving his hand toward the other crewmen who gathered near Rudolf. "May I ask first how it is that you speak such good English?"

"I learned it in school," Rudolf replied. "I had a teacher who had lived in America."

"You don't have a hint of accent," Collins said, wonder in his voice.

"I know." Rudolf answered, "I had a tough teacher with many hours of drills."

The American thought about that for a moment, and then he said, "Do any of these other men speak English?" Collins asked.

Rudolf looked around at the men who were standing near him. He shook his head, "Not that I know of."

"Well, as far as I know, you're headed for America where you'll be held as prisoners of war. Right now, however, we're going to feed you."

"May I also ask where our officers are?"

"Oh, they're being entertained by our captain," Collins answered with a small smile.

Rudolf was surprised at the forthright answer. "Thank you, sir," he said, again saluting the officer.

The men of U-893 gathered around Rudolf as he told them what the American officer said. Wolfgang Gertzner slapped Rudolf on the back. "Well," he joked, "they wouldn't feed us and waste their food if they were going to kill us!"

"I supposed you are right," Rudolf said, and then he returned to Fritz who still stood by the railing.

"Well, well. So we are on our way to America!" Fritz said with a note of joy in his voice. "I wanted to come here years ago to see my uncle, but I suppose coming as a prisoner of war is better than nothing!"

But Rudolf was dour. "We have no idea how they are going to treat us; we are prisoners of war after all."

"Yes," Fritz countered, "that is true, and we would not be prisoners if the Commander had not had us sitting on top of the water like ducks in a pond. U-boats are supposed to hide underwater, after all, especially so close to the American coastline. I fault Commander Weber for our misfortune."

"That is insubordination," Rudolf warned, lowering his voice; still the reference to ducks came to mind when the Commander had called the crew together in the water.

Fritz looked at Rudolf with an impish grin, the one he always had when he was giving Rudolf advice. "Maybe it is, Rudi, maybe it is; but once again, you never question anything!"

Chapter 22

Late February – April 1945
Arizona

With the Third Reich fighting to its last breath, Rudolf finished reading *For Whom the Bell Tolls* a second time and thought deeply about its significance, often in the still of the night as he listened to the breathing of the other men in the barrack. He still felt confusion as to why Robert Jordan would fight for another country, but he began to delve into the nuances of Hemingway's character, slowing realizing that political allegiance was not the reason Robert Jordan fought—he fought to help the embattled people of Spain gain their freedom.

Rudolf wanted to discuss all this with Bob Feller, but he knew he would not see him until the planting of cotton after Easter when the men from Camp Papago Park would work again at the Feller farm. Wanting to be ready for their political discussions, Rudolf spent many hours in the camp library, checking out books he had never seen in Germany, books banned by the Nazis.

One day, as he ran his finger along the spines of library books, he noticed *All Quiet on the Western Front*, by Erich Maria Remarque. The title instantly brought up the long-ago memory of a tirade against Remarque by Rudolf's teacher Herr Braun.

"This descendant of French Jews," Herr Braun shouted to the class, "this Erich Marie Remarque wrote that patriotism in war is a thing of the past...such utter nonsense from one who calls himself a German! I, myself, attended one of *Der Führer's* book burnings and threw that piece of *zilch* into the flames!"

Intrigued with that memory, Rudolf pulled the book off the shelf, and turned it over, reading the back cover. As he did, from the corner of his eye, Rudolf noticed someone standing nearby. He turned and was surprised to see *Funkmaat* Horst Hollmann. Hollmann looked much older than when they served together on U-893, his hair grayer now and loose bags of skin hung under his pale blue eyes. Rudolf felt a sudden annoyance and wondered why the Petty Officer would be watching him, and then to his surprise, Hollmann gave Rudolf a thin smile and walked over to him.

"Are you finding anything of interest?" he asked.

"I was looking at this," Rudolf said, trying to control his voice, as he turned the book over, showing the front cover.

"Ah, yes," Hollmann said, "if I remember correctly our *Führer* banned that book."

"Did he?" Rudolf answered, trying to sound naive.

"Most certainly; the book is a lie," Hollmann said. "If anyone knows about conditions on the front, it is our *Führer* who served in the Great War and thoroughly distinguished himself."

Rudolf suddenly realized his Nazi officers and non-commissioned officers were taking note of the reading habits of enlisted men, making sure of their adherence to fascist doctrine. Rudolf smiled. He held tight to the book, feeling suddenly free, and said, "Then if it is a lie, I think I will enjoy reading it. It will be interesting to compare it with "*Mein Kampf.*"

Hollmann glared at Rudolf and then turned his back to him as if he were searching for a book himself.

The April sun browned the backs of Rudolf and Bob as they planted cotton. It was back-breaking work, bending down to the rich soil, quickly pushing three small cotton seeds about an inch into the dirt with their fingers. They repeated the process every four inches for the entire length of the cotton row, and then moved to another furrow, planting in the opposite direction.

Bob Feller worked alongside the men from Camp Papago Park, just as he had done the previous year. Although it was his last year in high school, Bob had been given time off by the school administration to supervise the planting of the cotton crop. His father, Vern, no longer rode in the old truck like he did last fall; his illness had incapacitated him enough that he was unable to leave the farmhouse.

Bob wiped his forehead with an old red kerchief grabbed from his back pocket. "Tell me, Rudi, what happened after you were captured? Where did they take you and the other men from the U-boat?"

Rudolf smiled at Bob. The American never failed to amaze Rudolf with his endless questions.

"We were taken to New York, where we saw your Statue of Liberty. I did not want to be impressed by her, but I admit I was. She was so beautiful standing there against the tall buildings of a great city—a city we were told had been destroyed by our *Luftwaffe*...but we saw otherwise." Rudolf's voice grew tight.

After a pause to grab more seeds from the bag hanging from his belt, Rudolf said, "We also saw docks filled with more supplies and ships than our German hearts could stand. Then, when we got off the ship, they cut our hair, deloused us, we were given new clothing and our identification papers. We worried about what would happen next, but they put us on a sleek train—not freight cars like in Germany— with men, who waited on us, black men. We could not believe the wonderful food we got while on the destroyer, but the food on the train was beyond imagination! We filled our stomachs with fresh fruit and good meat; the only thing we hated was the white bread!"

Bob brushed the soil from his hands and then filled his palm with more seeds. "Where did the Army take you after all that?"

"First, we traveled south to the interrogation center at Fort Hunt, near your Capitol, and we were there for several weeks while they questioned us. After that, we were sent to Ft. Blanding in Florida, again on a passenger train. We passed peaceful cities and farm land, and talked among ourselves about what we saw—not even a small reminder that America was at war like Germany except when we came to military bases. We saw that America is a rich country, so much land and production of food, forests beyond our imagination and industrial plants, but it was then we also noticed—what I said to you before—the separation of the black people from whites as we moved further south, and how the black people are so poor."

"Yes, I know," Bob said, with sadness. "I'm ashamed to say many white Americans treat Negroes shamefully, people who were brought here as slaves against their will. They are still treated badly, despite the Civil War that was fought to free them."

Bob stopped for a bit and straightened his back. "It's what we talked about before, you know, the Hemingway book. We—you and I—as members of the human race are diminished, *we* are less human even though we have nothing at all to do with others being treated badly—like the Negroes...like...like those people in the concentration camps Allied forces are finding as they close in on...Germany. Yet we *do* have something to do with it because we have said nothing or done nothing to stop such acts of disrespect and violence." Bob's voice shook a little as he said this, and he glanced quickly at Rudi out of the corner of his eye.

Rudolf stood up from his planting and looked at Bob. His voice was low so that the other POWs planting cotton could not hear him. "We have been shocked by the newsreels of the death camps. We call them 'bone films or *Knockenfilmen*.' At first, I did not believe them, none of the men believed them, thinking the films must be American propaganda to break those of us who love Germany. It cannot be true, we thought, but then we began talking to one another, remembering how this Jewish family or that Jewish merchant disappeared from the neighborhoods. I am afraid...I am afraid to say this, Bob, but some of us think it is true."

"How could it have happened, Rudi?" Bob asked, shaking his head.

"I have thought about it, in bed when all is quiet. Can it be that as Hitler Youth, as members of the military, we goose-stepped our way into mindlessness? It was drilled into us to obey, obey, obey...it seems that is what we Germans do best."

Silence stood between the two young men for a long while as they worked with the sun beating on their stooped backs and the smell of precious earth on their hands. Then Rudolf asked, "Has America never made mistakes?"

"Of course!" Bob answered readily. "Our treatment of the Negroes, but there are other mistakes. Our rounding up of the American Indians, putting them on reservations…no different than prisoner of war camps, in my view! And we didn't join the League of Nations after WW I! Maybe if America hadn't put its head in the sand with its desire to never be involved in another war, *this* war wouldn't have happened."

"In Germany," Rudolf said, "we believe Roosevelt deceived the American people; that he let Japan bomb Pearl Harbor so he could get America into a war with Germany."

Bob stopped what he was doing. "That couldn't be true, Rudi! In our republic, it's not the president who makes war—it's the people. Roosevelt didn't declare war on Japan…it was the vote of the United States Congress that did it. What Japan did to our naval fleet really burned us up…made us mad…and the American people directed their representatives to vote to go to war! But there's something else here, Rudi, something terribly important that I hope you can understand. In America, we are fighting and living and dying for only one thing: to be free."

"But what is freedom, Bob? What does it really mean?" Rudolf asked.

"Well," Bob said, "it's tough to describe, but I'll give it a shot. Freedom means I have the power to act or think or speak as I want. I can worship God anyway I want; I can openly disagree with the actions of my government without fear of going to prison; I can read any newspaper or magazine. No one keeps an eye on me and what I do, and there is no one standing next to me with a gun to my head as I cast my ballot."

Anger filled Rudolf's voice and his eyes turned steely blue. "Do you think the Nazis stood next to us with a gun as we voted for Adolf Hitler?"

"No, I don't think that, Rudi," Bob said as he fished around for more seeds, fumbling and dropping a few on the ground. He did not look at Rudolf as he bent to retrieve them. "But what I do think is that your people made a tragic mistake of putting all their faith in one man who controls every aspect of German life."

A long pause stretched between them as they continued their work and then Bob suddenly asked, "Are you a Nazi, Rudi?"

Rudolf look surprised. He gulped, but decided to answer as truthfully as possible. "Men in the German military were forbidden to be members of the Nazi party, but that has changed since the assassination attempt on Hitler almost a year ago—at least that is what we hear from the underground. Now, everyone is pressured to join the party, even my grandfather, I suppose, who had never been a party member. If you are asking if I believe—if I *believed* in the National Socialist party and its principles—then, yes, I was a Nazi in spirit. With my whole heart, I accepted as true that the *Führer* was the bearer of the people's will, and that only he knew what the people needed."

The young German put his head down in an attempt to hide his distress, bending over to plant the cotton, his face away from Bob, but then he gathered himself and looked at his American friend, straightening up to his full height. "I was wrong, considering what has happened to my beloved Germany."

Rudolf sat at a table tucked in a cozy corner of the camp library, reading Thomas Mann's *The Magic Mountain*. The renowned German author had moved to Switzerland in 1933 after Hitler came to power. Rudolf was curious about his point of view, long known to be anti-Nazi. Although the Nazi regime did not ban Mann's books—he had won the prestigious Nobel Prize for Literature in 1929—Rudolf remembered Mann's German citizenship was revoked in 1936 and he moved to California soon after.

The young radio operator sighed. It was a thick book, and delved deeply into philosophical arguments between the characters, all suffering from tuberculosis, and living together in a sanatorium high in the Swiss Alps. The book, a microcosm of European society prior to WWI, placed the main character, a young German man unsure of his outlook on life, between two experienced philosophers, a secular humanist and a totalitarian Jesuit. As these philosophers jousted for Hans Castorp's mind, Europe sank into war and Castorp, despite his illness, hurriedly leaves the sanatorium. As Thomas Mann wrote, Hans Castorp's change of mind about fighting in the war was "brought about by the thunder-peal."

Rudolf stopped reading. He placed the open book on the table, and then he sat back in his chair, thinking. He felt a kinship with Hans Castorp, a young man who tried desperately to understand his mentors' conflicting viewpoints. Although almost finished with the novel, a thought began to nag at Rudolf: Hans Castorp did not understand his reason for going to war.

His mind reeled. The conversation with his grandfather about not wanting to become a *Kriegsmarine* officer because it would delay his entry into the war hung over him like a thunder cloud. How incredibly foolish he was, swallowing whole everything that had been fed to him by his teachers and the leaders of the Hitler Youth.

Suddenly, a noise from behind startled Rudolf. When he looked over his shoulder, he saw *Funkmaat* Horst Hollmann.

"I see you are reading another book that our *Führer* disapproves of," Hollmann growled.

Rudolf did not answer, so Hollmann pulled up a chair and sat down. "There is talk about you, Rudi."

Automatically, the young man reached out, picked up the book, and turned to face his Petty Officer.

"What kind of talk?"

"Dangerous talk."

"Why should there be dangerous talk about me. I am nobody."

"You have been seen talking to that Jew farmer."

Rudolf thought about that for a moment before he answered, making sure his voice was steady, firm. "I work often at his cotton farm, and I speak English. No one else on the work crew really understands what we need to do, so I interpret for the farmer."

"You have long conversations with him, too long. Perhaps he is becoming a friend, huh?" Hollmann said, frowning.

"I am merely interpreting what the farmer wants the men to do," Rudolf answered.

"Be careful, Rudi, remember that in Germany, sentimentality toward Jews is committing treason. This war will be over soon enough and even if we lose, there will be those who will remember your friend-ship with that Jew when we return home."

Rudolf's face paled. The old fear grabbed at his bowels, that inner terror he could never explain, but he made no reply to Hollmann.

"And your grandfather, how is he doing now that your grand-mother was killed by the Allies?"

"My...my grandfather?" Rudolf asked wide eyed.

"Remember, Rudi, Germany has not surrendered. We will fight on to the bitter end. No one is free from the scrutiny of the Gestapo, not even your valued grandfather. I am sure his days are unfulfilled now that the AG Weser shipyard has been bombed extensively."

"The shipyard?"

"Yes, the shipyard is at a standstill, ruined by the Jew conspiracy that brought America into this war in the first place."

Hollmann got up from the table, reached over dramatically, yank-ing the book from Rudolf's hands. "I don't think you need to read this filth, do you?"

"No, *Funkmaat* Hollmann," Rudolf replied softly after a long moment. He looked down at his empty hands, and the dust of utter confusion dropped again over his soul.

Chapter 23

May – June 1945
Arizona

Hunger plagued Rudolf. He could actually see his ribs when he stood in front of the mirror in the camp bathhouse, and his stomach seemed to grumble louder than any thunder he heard rolling across Arizona's Sonoran Desert.

Helmut grunted as he looked over at Rudolf. "It is because of the *Knockenfilmen*. We who have been stuck for years in the middle of the desert picking cotton and citrus are being blamed for the *Führer's* concentration camps."

The war was over, and as more and more of the Third Reich's concentration camps were found by Allied troops—frozen-faced skeletal Jews and other non-Aryans looking blankly at churning newsreel cameras—the public outcry that German POWs held in America were being coddled forced the War Department to issue new food regulations: All meat was cut from POW diets except bologna and sausage. Vegetable sandwiches became the daily fare—chopped carrots mixed with cabbage, onions, prunes or mixed fruit.

Although Rudolf was hungry, he knew he was not as famished as other men at the camp because of the food Ruth Feller prepared for the Germans who worked in her cotton fields. She was one of the farm wives who took the POWs hunger in hand and supplemented their meager diet with hearty sandwiches of egg or cheese and homemade oatmeal cookies or fig bars.

As he caught his image in the mirror, Rudolf eyed his swastika tattoo. Maybe his grandparents were right after all; he never should have etched the Third Reich's symbol on his arm. With Germany's unconditional surrender, the swastika was now *verboten* in Germany. An unnerving question floated into his thoughts: How could he swim in his beloved Weser River with his shirt on?

Rudolf pulled one of his prized Chesterfield cigarettes out of his shirt pocket, lighting it after he left the bath house with Helmut. From the day Rudolf smoked his first American cigarette, Chesterfield became his addiction. Now, he smoked them sparingly, hoarding the three cartons he bought in the canteen just before the war ended. Along with sparse meals in the camp mess, the canteen carried little now except toothpaste and shaving cream. Gone were the treats the men longed for—candy, chewing gum—and the addictive cigarettes, which had become such a precious commodity that Rudolf hid them in a secret cache behind a wall board next to his cot.

The month of May neared its end, and the heat of the summer was already showing its blazing passion. As Rudolf and Helmut walked toward mess hall, they passed other prisoners carefully watering their withering vegetable gardens, a tiresome task after a day of manual labor in the growing fields or irrigation ditches.

Rudolf noticed Helmut was in a silent mood. "When do you think the Americans will let us have mail again?" he asked, hoping he could change his friend's frame of mind.

"Soon, I hope," Helmut said, his words sharp. "This is a sore point with me. I am worried about my family—all the bombing that happened in the last days of the war—worried to the point of sickness. Maybe we should complain to the Red Cross...it seems holding mail would be against the Geneva Convention! But what can we do? We are the losers, after all. Ravaging wolves are dividing Germany. The great three—Truman, Churchill, and Stalin are gathering together soon in Potsdam to decide what to do with us."

Rudolf nodded. There seemed to be nothing but bad news, nothing to take away the apprehension of being a prisoner of war in a country that was now the victor. He looked around and observed the absence of usual chatter among the men while they settled into their evening routine; a pall of quiet hung in the air as they gathered in the mess hall.

"Is something the matter? Why is everyone so quiet?" Rudolf asked Helmut.

"Something happened, Rudi...when we were in the bath house, I saw Werner Carl. He said the American guard—you know Tom McKay—hit him with the butt of his rifle while he was on a work crew today. I have never cared much for Werner, but still..."

Rudolf sighed, a knowing look on his face. "You know Werner. He has a nasty mouth. McKay is normally an easy-going fellow. Werner must have said something that made McKay angry. Besides, we all know camp guards are the scum of the American military—not good enough to send into combat against us, but OK, as the Americans say, to watch over us!"

Helmut shrugged. Just then, Werner pushed through the men to get to the front of the mess line, passing only a few feet from Rudolf who could see the nasty bruise on the side of his face. Werner's sudden celebrity gave him the opportunity to heap his plate with food and continue bad-mouthing the American guard.

"The *Schwein!*" Werner nearly shouted; he was the center of attention, and it looked to Rudolf that Werner seemed to revel in his injury. "All I said to McKay was that American prisoners of war were fed better in Germany than in *this* land of milk and honey. He swore at me and the next thing I knew, I was on the ground knocked out cold from the butt of his rifle!"

The men spoke quietly with one another. Some noted McKay had turned surly the past few days. Why would there be such a change, when he was normally amiable, Rudolf wondered. Everything seemed out of sync: first the restricted diet and now angry guards; so was this to be their fate?

Distraught, Rudolf walked to the camp library after dinner. He needed quiet time before he faced his class of students, more inclined now to learn English since Germany lost the war.

The library stocked newspapers from all over America; the number amazed Rudolf. There was the *Arizona Republic*, the *Los Angeles Times*, the *Chicago Tribune*, and the giant of them all, the *New York Times*. At first, like everyone else in camp, Rudolf believed the newspapers were propaganda organs of the American government, but after months of close reading, Rudolf realized each newspaper had its own point of view, many disagreeing vehemently with various government programs, even the direction of the war.

The sections with letters-to-the-editor also surprised Rudolf. Americans, he realized, were not afraid to express their opinions, questioning their government openly when something displeased them. Slowly, he began to trust the newspapers and distrust the news passed on to the enlisted men's quarters from the officers' compound where the illegal wireless honed in on news flowing out of Berlin. Now, of course, the only news from Germany was from the Allies.

Rudolf picked up a copy of the New York newspaper, about two weeks old. It was dog eared because so many POWs read it. He scanned the front page, and then when he opened the paper, he saw two different articles about prisoners of war.

Rudolf felt a jolt go through his body. He quickly looked over his shoulder, closed the paper, folded it under his arm and walked to a table in the far corner of the library. He sat down and read the first the article about thirteen hundred American soldiers arriving in New Jersey some spending months, others spending years as prisoners of war in Germany.

"One man told of how sick Americans were forced to march 500 miles through snow and rain from camp to camp," the article reported. "Another of eating cats and fighting for potato peelings when the ration of a bowl of sour soup a day became unbearable; a third spelled out slowly the name of a German officer who had left starving Americans by the roadside."

Another returning soldier showed a magazine to a reporter that pictured American girls shaking hands with German prisoners of war at a railroad station. The soldier, visibly upset, said his German captors did not shake hands: they used rubber hoses on American prisoners.

The returning Americans found it hard to believe stories of home-front fraternization with German prisoners.

Rudolf gulped. News of the treatment of American prisoners by Germany had filtered down to the guards. No wonder McKay hit Werner.

The second *New York Times* story reported on the last batch of three thousand German soldiers captured by American forces in Germany and sent to New York. One soldier was a frightened 13-year-old and another was a grizzled 65-year-old who fought in WWI. Although bedraggled and dirty, the men were healthy and well-fed, not emaciated like the American prisoners of war. Some of the younger soldiers, who admitted they were not yet sixteen, stressed to the American guards and reporters on hand that they were never members of the Hitler Youth.

The newspaper dropped from Rudolf's hands. With his beautifully-crafted swastika tattoo emblazoned on his arm and his years in the Hitler Youth, Rudolf wondered if he would ever see Germany or his grandfather again. Suddenly, because of his blind love for the Third Reich, the grim specter of spending the rest of his life as a prisoner of war loomed before him.

With the war over, camp gossip about prisoner repatriation grew as fast as the cotton at the Feller farm where Rudolf sweated in the June heat, weeding and thinning the bushy plants, wondering what would happen next.

An old crewmate from U-893, Wolfgang Gertzner, stood not far from Rudolf, chopping through thick weeds. Although he worked in the control room of the U-boat, Wolfgang grew up on a farm not far from the Polish border; hoeing was nothing new to him. He stopped for a moment, rubbed a callus with impatience, and said to Rudolf, "How much longer can the *Amerikaner* hold us?"

Rudolf did not look up as he hacked into a particularly thick weed. "We signed an unconditional surrender. There were no provisions in the surrender about prisoners of war. We are *kaputt!* They can do what they want with us."

"Surely," Wolfgang said, "we will be sent home before that bunch of hardcore Nazis and SS thugs the Americans have thrown together in Oklahoma. The rest of us poor bastards are just ordinary Germans conscripted in the military. What the hell are the Americans going to do with 370,000 Germans? Their soldiers are coming back now and need jobs."

Rudolf only grunted, and his silence forced Wolfgang to continue his conversation with another POW willing to gossip. In no mood to talk, Rudolf walked to an area empty of other workers; he needed to concentrate. His mind worked furiously, endlessly. Would his release depend on his cooperative work record? Rudolf knew that was not a problem because he always volunteered for work. But then he thought about his *Soldbuch* that he had surrendered to the Americans when he landed in New York. The fifteen-page booklet, carried by every man in the German military, included Rudolf's height, weight, birth date and birth place, and also gave information about his family, his military training, duties, transfers and promotions. The booklet documented Rudolf's reputation as an outstanding Hitler Youth, a source of great pride for many years; now he was terrified of those commendations.

The only blot on his Camp Papago Park record was his exuberant, drunken demonstration during the Battle of the Bulge celebration. Rudolf gnawed on his lower lip. Surely, his singing the German national anthem was nothing compared to others who tried to escape or boycotted work battalions. Still, Rudolf fretted.

Each morning, Rudolf and Helmut and a few other men showed up before sunrise near the camp gate waiting for Bob Feller. The Fellers needed fewer than a dozen men now to weed and thin the cotton, and camp guards no longer traveled along with the small work crew, trusting the prisoners to the supervision of the Fellers.

Rudolf and Helmut climbed into the cab of the truck with Bob, and the rest of the men jumped into the truck bed, all of them anxious to get to work before the heat of the day settled into the Arizona desert, each hoping the tedious work would move them one day closer to release.

Bob hunched over the steering wheel, a sullen look on his face, unusual because the young man normally greeted Rudolf and Helmut with a bright smile. Rudolf nudged him. "Are you not feeling well, Bob?"

"Oh, I'm OK," he said, but the sound of his voice betrayed him. He backed out of the pick-up area, and then yanked the shift into first gear with a grinding noise.

"How is your father doing?" Rudolf inquired.

"My mom and I are really worried about him, Rudi. He had a hard time breathing last night, but he seemed better this morning. Mom called the doctor. He should be at the house by the time we get there."

Rudolf nodded. The conversation about Vern Feller made him remember his grandfather, and for some odd reason, *Opa's* booming voice came to him. The letters from *Opa* contained tidbits of news, but nothing that really told Rudolf about his grandfather's situation. His last letter said there was no work at the shipyard—confirming in Rudolf's mind what Hollmann had said about AG Weser, much to his dismay. His grandfather also said he spent most of his time fishing on the Weser River, a surprise for Rudolf because his grandfather never liked to fish.

"I understand your concern," Rudolf said to Bob with a note of commiseration. "I worry about my grandfather. I cannot imagine him living without my grandmother."

Bob pushed into another gear as he gathered speed on the highway. Since graduation from high school in late May, the responsibility for the cotton crop had fallen completely to the young man since Ruth Feller spent her days caring for her failing husband, leaving the farm house only at noon to feed lunch to the men.

The sun began to rise and the desert sky moved from blackness to faint light, highlighting the outlines of strange arid plants with thorny branches against the pale backdrop. A jackrabbit jumped from the middle of the road toward the safety of the desert, the headlights making the animal's huge ears appear cartoon-like. The desert's smell wafted into the open windows, an unmistakable mixture of warm air, dust, and mesquite trees.

Something about early mornings in the desert called to Rudolf. It was not that he had overcome his loathing for such a bleak landscape, but there was a tang in the air that made him want to get up and out of the grim, dull barrack. The sky was always clear, not gray or foggy like that of the north coast of Germany, and it made Rudolf energetic. Today was a special day, as well. It was his twenty-first birthday.

Unexpectedly, Bob said to Rudolf, "I know you want to go home, Rudi, but what would we do without you and the other men? The soldiers coming home from the war aren't looking to pick cotton, so we are facing a real labor shortage."

Rudolf mulled over that remark for a moment. "What about using those people from Mexico or the Negro pickers?" Rudolf asked.

"My parents used Negroes before the war when there were groups of them that moved from farm to farm, but those pickers stopped coming with the draft and gasoline rationing," Bob answered, looking sideways at Rudolf for a second and then he returned his gaze to the road ahead. "As for the *braceros,* the Mexicans, they're coming over the border in droves, but they need to live on the land where they work and we're too small an operation for that. When the War Department set up the POW contract labor program...you know, when you guys arrived, it seemed the perfect way to keep the farm going. But then my dad got sick..."

Bob's melancholy infected Rudolf. The dead weight of hopelessness, the fear of never going home again washed over him like the cold North Sea. Rudolf wondered why he cared about this young man and his cotton crop, with everything that had happened to him and his family, but he did care—inexplicably.

"I think we are going to be here a long while, Bob," Rudolf replied, trying to reassure his friend. "By that time, I am sure you will be able to get other workers to keep the farm going. But, what about you? I thought you said you were going into the Army in a couple of months?"

"Yeah, well, I thought so too," Bob said, slouching further in his seat, his knuckles showing white on the steering wheel. "With my dad so sick, we asked for a deferment. I got it yesterday, but I...I really want to go, even though the war is over, I want to do my part."

Rudolf smiled faintly, a knowing smile. He understood all too well the inner need to serve one's country; to heed the deep call of drums and bright flags and crisp uniforms; to get away from cloying parents; to do whatever it is a young man has to do. He turned to Helmut and told him what Bob said. Helmut leaned forward, looked over at Bob, and then he said to Rudolf in German, "Tell him picking cotton is better any day than being in the military, ours or his!"

When Rudolf translated, Bob laughed. His joy was infectious, and they all began laughing together, the roar of their merriment reaching out through the open windows to the other men hunched in the back of the truck, who turned their heads, trying to discern what the ruckus was all about.

When they reached the Feller farm, Bob pulled up to the house, next to another car Rudolf did not recognize; probably the doctor's, he guessed. The men jumped out quickly, fetching their tools from the tool shed, and as they walked toward the cotton field, out of hearing range from the house, Rudolf stopped and looked back. Ruth Feller had come out onto the porch. A worried look enfolded her patrician face, and Bob jammed his hands into his pockets as his mother spoke to him, his head moving downward, as if he were closely examining the porch boards. Bob finally lifted his face to look at his mother, and she absent-mindedly wiped her hands on her gaily-printed apron, its brightness out of place somehow in that moment. They reached out for each other, standing with their arms entwined, their heads down. Rudolf turned away from the painful scene with his hoe sitting on his shoulder, and headed into the field.

After months in the cotton fields, the men knew what they needed to do: they spread out to hoe the weeds and thin the plants so the most robust could hungrily grab the rays of the sun. It was not until a few hours later that Bob appeared, looking ashen-faced.

Afraid to ask him directly about his father, Rudolf looked at him and said, "I see the doctor left."

Bob nodded, and then he stood for a moment, moving the toe of his shoe in the dirt as if the soil could give him some kind of answer. He looked up into Rudolf's face. "He's not going to get better, Rudi," he said, and turned quickly to check on the progress of the other workers.

At noon, the men gathered as always on the ditch bank under the big cottonwoods that soaked up the irrigation water and gave grateful shade in return. Ruth drove the truck to the shady spot and she and her son laid out hearty spam sandwiches and fresh lemonade on the tailgate for the hungry men, so eager for her homemade food, especially now with the cutback in their rations. Her ready smile was not as shining as it usually was, but she managed a small nod to each man as they went to the truck to get their lunch.

Rudolf's eyes met hers for an instant as she handed him his food, and he saw them fill instantly with tears. A look of embarrassment passed over her face, and she turned away from him, dabbing her eyes with the edge of her apron.

He ate his lunch with a heavy heart. Everything suddenly seemed utterly meaningless as he viewed Bob and Ruth, trying so hard to act normal. They were steeling themselves for Vern's death, but Rudolf knew only too well, there was no preparation for that loss, no understanding of its magnitude until reality set in, sometimes not for weeks, as it had been for him with the death of *Oma*.

Grateful for the break from the heat of the day, the other men also ate their meal in silence, knowing the family's circumstances as the news passed from man to man. While they ate, the heat formed a tent of stillness over the cotton farm, the buzzing of flies and mosquitoes the only sound in the quiet as the insects honed in on the food and the sweaty men.

After a while, Rudolf saw Bob open the door on the truck's passenger side, which faced away from the men. He pulled something off the seat and walked to the back of the truck, placing it on the tailgate, and then turned around with a mischievous grin. "Happy birthday, Rudi!" he said. Ruth stood beside him with a sweet smile.

Stunned, Rudolf got up from the ground and brushed himself off, his face red with embarrassment. The rest of the men surrounded him, slapping him on the back, sounding out their native happy birthday greeting of *"Herzlichen Glückwunsch zum Geburtstag."*

Ruth lit one candle, apologizing that she did not have more, and Rudolf blew it out, making a wish. Ruth handed him a knife and he cut into the cake; it was a dense cream cake made with sour cream—just like his grandmother always made for him. With food rationing so strict, Rudolf guessed that Ruth Feller did a lot of trading of her home-grown vegetables and eggs in order to get the ingredients for such a cake. When she gave him the first piece, she said, "Happy birthday, Rudi. I am sure your wish is to go home soon."

He nodded, took his cake to the ditch bank and sat down, feeling bewildered. Once again, the kindness of the Feller family overwhelmed him.

As he ate the wonderful cake, the desert landscape faded away, and Rudolf was a boy again, holding hands with his grandparents when they walked through the market square of Bremen on his birthday, toward the immense figure of Roland the Giant. His grandparents would stand Rudolf next to the tall statue and take a photograph, noting how much he had grown during the year by comparing his height with the birthday picture taken the previous year.

After the photograph, *Opa* and *Oma* would buy him an ice cream cone, something he looked forward to all year—no ice cream cone ever compared to the special one he got on his birthday. In the evening, his grandmother would proudly put out the cream cake she had baked especially for Rudolf, and his group of neighborhood friends would gather around the table, their small gifts in hand, waiting anxiously for a bite of her delicious dessert.

Biting into the cake made by Ruth Feller, its taste so familiar, Rudolf began to cry. The tears welled up, filling his eyes, dripping down his suntanned face. In an effort not to let the other men see his emotion, he turned away from them and wiped his eyes quickly with the back of his hand. Bob, who grabbed a piece of the cake after the rest of the men received theirs, walked over to sit by him. Rudolf looked up, shamefaced, his eyes red, and Bob simply patted him on the shoulder and sat down in the dirt beside Rudolf, leaning against a cottonwood.

"Life does not prepare us for such surprises, does it, Bob? Rudolf said with sadness.

"No...no, it doesn't." Bob answered, the cake sitting uneaten in his lap as he looked toward the farm house.

"What happens now? Everything seems so mixed up." Rudolf knew it was a pointless question, but he felt compelled, pushed from inside his very being to ask it, there in the heat of the day, at the edge of an Arizona cotton field, to a young American Jew.

"We must become one world!" was the young man's unexpected answer.

"What do you mean?" Rudolf asked, puzzled. He lowered his voice and hissed, "That is what Hitler wanted!"

"No, no...that's not what I meant," Bob said, brushing his hand through his thick, dark hair, turning his back from the other men sitting on the ditch bank enjoying his mother's cake. "I'm talking about a world of peace where no nation is isolated from the rest. But we can't solve the political problems of the world without first solving its economic problems. We—by that I mean America, Great Britain, and France—we created the economic mess that engulfed Germany. We caused the rise of fascism."

"You...you think that? How do you know such things?" Rudolf voiced surprise.

Bob grinned. "Well, I do a lot of reading. I'm really interested in politics; I hope one day to become a congressman. That's a farfetched dream, I know...." Bob's voice trailed off, and then he said, "Anyway, to get back to what I was saying, I happened to read a book written a couple of years ago, *One World,* by Wendell Willkie."

"There was a book with that name?" Rudolf asked incredulously.

"Yes! The book was a great success, millions of Americans bought it," Bob said, taking a deep breath to slow down his rush of words. "Willkie wrote about setting up an organization of world governments. I guess his idea took hold because a bunch of countries just met in San Francisco to put together the United Nations. It's going to be a reality,

Rudi! Imagine, nations discussing world problems and trying to solve them together."

Rudolf was silent for a moment, his mind reeling. "Do you honestly believe we can overcome this war? Germany and America...."

"Why, of course! If the human race can put its mind to do the horrors it does, can't the opposite be true? I believe that, Rudi; I know it!"

Rudolf leaned his head against the big cottonwood tree, the sweet taste of birthday cake in his mouth and the possibility in his mind that all things, even going home, was suddenly possible.

Soon, the men got up from their shady retreat and returned to work. Lighthearted, Rudolf's mood was better than it had been in weeks. His energy seemed boundless, and he chopped the weeds with ease. He began humming "Don't Fence Me In," the Bing Crosby song that was all the rage with Americans and popular with the POWs, who found humor in the lyrics and their particular situation.

Rudolf chuckled. The song was so American! "Oh give me land, lots of land under starry skies above...send me off forever, but I ask you please, don't fence me in."

What was it about Americans, he pondered, as he hacked at the wild plants choking the cotton. Perhaps it was their inborn sense of freedom, given to them willingly by their government. They seemed unafraid of going to war to right a wrong, and yet they were able to extend their hand in friendship to those they captured. More than anything, he noticed their conviction that no matter what troubles they faced today, tomorrow would be better. He wondered...could it be that Americans believed they had the ability to make the future better because they felt no fear of their government?

Rudolf stopped hoeing. A memory boiled over him like the desert heat as he stood in the field of cotton. It was 1936 and he was twelve years old, sitting at a kitchen table watching his grandmother dress the head wound of their neighbor. A policeman had clubbed Frau Schweiss because she would not voluntarily give up her deaf daughter to the Nazis for sterilization. The only person who had stood up to the policeman was an older neighbor, George Manheim.

Rudolf shivered despite the temperature: he clearly remembered the conversation that day. His grandfather reminded George Manheim that the policeman would report him to his superiors, but Manheim retorted angrily that Germans were silent about too many things, it was intolerable, the old man said, that the harmless, deaf girl would be sterilized.

That night, frightful noises floated down from the floor above them, and a terrified Rudolf climbed into bed with his *Opa* and *Oma*. The sounds were from Frau Schweiss and her daughter, Frieda, as they were dragged down the stairs; Herr Manheim was also taken away. They never returned, and no one—not his grandparents or the other neighbors—ever spoke about the incident.

How did it come to pass that Germans—his grandparents included—became afraid of their own government? Was it because, as Bob said, they allowed one man to do their thinking for them? Rudolf's head fell on his chest, and he was suddenly, horribly ashamed. *Der Führer* gave the people what they wanted all right, Rudolf realized—bread on the table and political stability; a full stomach and the Gestapo; conquest of Europe and Auschwitz.

All the optimism that had filled his head and his heart—there on the ditch bank eating his birthday cake—drowned. He had no idea how Germany could rise like a phoenix from the ashes of her battered soul. His beautiful country, so courageous and mighty to his childish eyes, was tainted now with the smell of death. Would that odor, Rudolf wondered, ever dissipate?

Suddenly, Rudolf heard a yell and he turned to look to the direction of the noise. It was Ruth Feller, standing on her porch and calling in a panic-filled voice for her son. Rudolf knew Bob was working at the other end of the property, far out of earshot. Rudolf, closer than anyone to the Feller house, ran to her, the hoe still gripped in his hand.

She sobbed, "Bob, I need Bob, Rudi! Take the truck. Please! Hurry!"

Dropping the hoe in the yard with a clatter, Rudolf ran to the truck; the keys were still in the ignition. Frantically, he started the engine and pushed the gear shift in reverse to back up the truck, but in his nervousness, he took his foot off the clutch too fast and it stalled. Rudolf sat for a moment and tried to calm himself, and then he started the engine again, slowly pushing the clutch as he shifted into gear and headed the truck toward the cotton field, following the dirt road that ran alongside the ditch bank, honking the horn, looking for Bob.

He could see his fellow prisoners look up from their work as he shifted gears recklessly, gaining speed, his hand plastered to the horn. Rocks flew from under the tires as Rudolf turned wildly onto the dirt road that ran adjacent to the last cotton row, the truck weaving a bit until he got it under control, and he could see Bob working among the men.

Suddenly, Bob looked up when he heard the horn, and a horrible look came to his face when he saw Rudolf. He threw his hoe down, sprinted toward the truck, and leaped onto the running board as Rudolf slowed. Bob clung to the truck door as Rudolf increased his speed, the dust of the road rising behind them, engulfing the green color of the fields, covering them with a dull haze.

Rudolf came to an abrupt stop in front of the farm house and Bob jumped off, losing his balance momentarily, but righting himself quickly, and then he made a dash for the steps. Ruth stood inside the screen door, waiting. She pushed the door open, and they stood together for a long moment at the threshold while Ruth lovingly brushed her son's dark hair away from his face, preparing him as only a mother could.

A deep jolt hit Rudolf. He never knew his own mother and in that instant, the longing for her burst out of him and he lowered his head to the steering wheel and pounded it with his fists in frustration. Why had he been deprived of such a treasure? And to realize it so clearly on this day was particularly galling. Twenty-one years before, he lay contentedly at his mother's breast, taking in her nourishment. Why did he never have her to treat him with such tenderness as Ruth treated Bob?

Rudolf sat in the truck for what seemed a long time. He could not bring himself to go back into the field to work, so he waited and smoked, his arm hanging out of the window, flicking the ashes of his cherished Chesterfields onto the dirt, the dull remembrance of loss filling his soul. Finally, when Bob appeared, his eyes swollen and face contorted with grief, he walked to Rudolf, and stood next to him with his head down, saying nothing for a while. Then, he said, "Can you get the men back to camp? I don't want to leave my mom...you know, alone with...."

Rudolf understood. "I will take them back," he said, looking up, squinting toward the setting sun. "You better call the camp to tell them we are coming."

Bob nodded. "Yes, I will...and Rudi?"

"Yes?"

"Thank you for coming to get me. I...I saw him before; well, you know, before..."

"I am glad of that, Bob."

Rudolf drove the truck to the field and found the men, gathered near the ditch bank as twilight fell. It had been a long day for everyone. From the cheerless look on his face, no one asked why they were late returning to camp. They simply piled in with their tools, and Rudolf took them to the shed where they put away the spades and pitch forks. With Helmut in the passenger seat, and the rest in the back of the truck, he speeded toward the highway, but slowed down as the county sheriff passed them on his way to the Feller home. The sheriff cautiously eyed the men, and nodded a sort of permission for them to continue on their journey.

Rudolf drove onto the empty highway, shifted the truck into high gear and turned the headlights on. Darkness spread over the desert, but the road ahead opened enticing possibilities. Taking a drag on his cigarette, he said evenly to Helmut, "We could head to Mexico."

There was a long pause then Helmut replied, "What's the use, Rudi? That *Polizist* knows who we are, and besides, the war is over."

Rudolf said nothing, and knew deep in his heart he could not betray Bob Fellers' trust; Bob had asked him to take the men back to camp, and that is what he would do. Rudolf sighed and reached over, turning on the radio. Bing Crosby's rich voice flooded the airwave with "Don't Fence Me In." Helmut made a funny noise and Rudolf looked over at him.

"I hate that song," Helmut declared, spitting out the window into the wind.

Rudolf pulled up to the guard gate at the entrance to Camp Papago Park; Tom McKay was on duty.

"Well, if it isn't Rudi!" the guard said with a sneer. "We expected you and your buddies to be headed toward Mexico by now."

Rudolf smiled despite himself, wondering if he should have ignored Helmut and turned south toward dark eyed *senoritas*, their hips swaying in time with his. "Well, McKay," Rudolf answered, "I thought about it, but I had no money to buy gasoline."

"Yeah, Rudi. I'd bet on the sunrise tomorrow that you Krauts all have money stashed up your asses," McKay said. "Anyway, you can park the truck over by the administration building. Major Kennedy is anxiously waiting for you boys." McKay picked up the telephone in the guard house to notify the major the men had arrived.

While Rudolf parked the truck, Helmut said, "What did I tell you? I knew they would have their snouts up, sniffing."

Rudolf grunted, climbed out of the truck along with the other men, and walked into the bright lights of the administration building. Major Kennedy, a man with bushy black eyebrows and piercing eyes, stood with a clipboard in his hands. The men filed into a perfect formation, saluted, and he checked their names off as each man identified himself. Rudolf had seen the major before, but only from a distance. The word around camp was that he was a 'by-the-book' officer, and because of that quality, the Germans respected him.

"Well, I'm glad you did the right thing and returned to camp," he said, speaking fluent German. "We've had enough excitement here for one day, and losing a truckload of men would not have made the commander happy."

Unsure of what to say, Rudolf held out his hand with the truck keys. "Here, sir."

"So, you're the one that drove them back?" the major's eyebrows went up with his question.

"Yes, sir," Rudolf answered.

"Your name again?"

"Meier…Rudolf Meier, sir."

"OK, Meier," he said looking at Rudolf, appraising him from the top of his dark blond head to the tip of his dirty shoes. "The rest of you can go get dinner. Meier, I need to speak to you."

The men looked at one another and then went out the side door into the compound where another guard checked them for contraband. Rudolf stood as straight as he could, expecting a tongue-lashing from the American officer. Instead, the major asked Rudolf to follow him into his small office down the hallway, and once there, the major set the clip board on his desk, pulled a pack of cigarettes out of his shirt pocket, and offered one to Rudolf. He searched around the desk for a lighter, lifting various folders and opening drawers, and finally found it in his pants pocket.

"Relax, Meier," the major said, lighting both cigarettes. "I just want to know what happened today at the Feller farm. That family has contracted for German labor since the program began, and they have been very reliable. It came as a bit of a surprise, to say the least, when this Bob Feller called to say you men would be late returning to camp and that one of you would be driving. Highly unusual, I must say. He gave no other explanation."

Rudolf relaxed a little as he breathed in the smoke. "Sir, Mr. Feller…Bob's father, died today. It happened late in the afternoon, and there was no one there except Mrs. Feller and her son. Bob did not want to leave his mother alone…so he asked me to drive the men back to camp."

"I see," Major Kennedy said, slowly taking in the information. "Was Mr. Feller's death sudden? I mean to say, it wasn't an accident or anything like that, was it?"

"No, sir. He had been sick for some time."

The major flicked the ash off his cigarette into a nearby ashtray. His bushy eyebrows knitted in thought. "Tell me, Meier, how is it you know so much about the Feller family?"

Rudolf considered the question for a long moment, and took another drag on his cigarette, his blue eyes looking straight into the major's face. "I have worked often at the Feller farm. They have been kind to me."

"Why did you not try to escape?"

"To be honest, I thought about it, but the war is over. I want to go home and escaping might delay that."

"Hmmm," the Major said as he picked up Rudolf's file and thumbed through it. "I see you were quite involved in the Hitler Youth, Meier."

Rudolf's face reddened. So they knew.

"Yes, sir. I was."

"I also see you have been teaching English classes to men in your compound."

"Yes, sir."

The major leaned up against a desk. "Tell me, Meier, if you were sent home to…where are you from, by the way? I didn't notice that in your file."

"Bremen, sir, on the Weser River."

"Ah, yes, Bremen! I have been to that beautiful city—that is before the war, of course. I remember well the statue of Roland. What do you think you will find when you return home?"

"I…I don't honestly know, sir," Rudolf said, taken back for a moment by the question. "My grandfather has written that Roland still stands because of the brick bunker built around it. I have heard there was a lot of bombing."

"Yes, there were many air raids over Bremen," Kennedy said. "With the Focke-Wulf aircraft factories and the valuable U-boat shipyards, Bremen was a very attractive target. I regret to say there was much bombing of the civilian population. A portion of the city was firebombed."

Rudolf looked down, his throat dry as tissue paper and the American cigarette suddenly unpleasant. So this is how it felt to be the loser. He flicked the ash into the ashtray with a vicious little movement caught by the sharp-eyed major.

"Yes, my grandmother was killed by Allied bombs," Rudolf replied in a low voice.

"I am sorry to hear that," Major Kennedy said as he closed Rudolf's file and placed it on the desk. "So…when you return to Bremen, what will you do?"

Rudolf wondered why this man was so interested in him, but he tried not to show intolerance of an American officer who obviously had thoroughly reviewed his file. "I hope to take care of my grandfather the best I can."

"With your knowledge of English, you could be of use, Meier."

Surprised, Rudolf asked, "Of use, sir?"

"America wants to occupy Bremen and Bremerhaven," Major Kennedy said. "The British captured those areas, but America needs access to the North Sea. We are—shall we say—pressing the British for that…ah, opportunity. What I mean in that with your English language skills you could be of use to the military government in Bremen. You have a good record here—despite your days in the Hitler Youth. Bringing the men back to camp shows the mark of a man who can be trusted."

"…Thank you, sir," Rudolf sputtered, perplexed by the attention of the American officer.

There was a long silence between them and then Rudolf—trying to take the major's attention away from him—said, "If I may ask, sir, you mentioned there was some excitement at the camp today."

"Ah, yes, that! Well, I'm sure you know about the new newspaper, *Der Ruf*, distributed to all the POW camps. There was a fight between those in the camp who believe it is Jewish propaganda and those who want to read the truth about what is happening in Germany."

Rudolf raised his eyebrows. He had seen the slick German-language publication available for five cents at the canteen. Just as the Allies yanked the noose on Germany, the bi-weekly newspaper had been quickly distributed to all POW camps. Rudolf heard rumors that hand-picked German POWs published *Der Ruf* under the auspice of the War Department, and from the very first, the newspaper had raised a lot of questions among the men. Those of different political persuasions took sides: Nazis boycotted it, anti-Nazis defended it, and neutrals, like Rudolf, bought the newspaper.

The major smiled momentarily. "We know the men can be disagreeable at times with us but they are not normally that way with one another. An NCO was seriously hurt in an ugly fight today. In fact, you may know him. It was *Funkmaat* Horst Hollmann. He served on the same U-boat you did."

Rudolf's jaw dropped and a stunned look crossed his face. Hollmann!

The major noted Rudolf's surprise. "A committed man, that Hollmann, a man who will never change his belief in National Socialism despite the destruction it has brought on Germany. But...you are not like him...are you Meier?" The major's voice changed, its softer tone probing delicately, pointedly, into Rudolf's psyche.

The question hit Rudolf like a blow to his solar plexus. Involuntarily, he bent over a little, his breathe expelled with no effort of his own. He realized this officer knew a great deal about him, and he was suddenly afraid.

"I have tried to understand the difference between National Socialism and your democracy," Rudolf answered, his eyes down.

"Well, Meier, that's not a bad start. Not bad at all!" The major suddenly stood up, ending the conversation. "I can imagine it has been a difficult day. You may go now."

The young German stood straight and saluted. It was the salute of an enlisted man to an officer, hand to forehead, not the old prideful Nazi salute with an arm raised hailing Adolf Hitler, forbidden now with the unconditional surrender of the Third Reich.

Rudolf headed out the door to the compound, and stood rigid while the guard searched him for contraband. A sense of doom flowed over him, so intense that he thought his knees would buckle. He summoned all the strength he could, not allowing his body that urge of collapse in front of an American guard, and for a fleeting moment he remembered standing in the pouring rain in a German forest, trying to prove he had the mettle to be a Hitler Youth.

Rudolf cursed as he moved aimlessly toward the mess hall, to food, but he was not hungry; the end of the Third Reich finally penetrated his soul and pent-up grief surged through him. He stopped only yards from the building, bent over with his hands braced on his knees, and threw up into the desert sand, gagging on his vomit.

The Nazi salute that frightened the world was gone now. No more panzer divisions rolling through the sands of North Africa, or *Luftwaffe* strikes over London; the terror of the seas, the German U-boat, would never lurk again along the East Coast of America or patrol the North Sea, nor would the blood-red flags emblazoned with the black swastika wave menacingly over the Reich's Chancellery in Berlin or the rest of the world, for that matter. Above all, *Der Führer* was dead, by his own hand.

What was to become of the German people, Rudolf wondered, his body shaking with cold panic. And what then was to become of him?

Chapter 24

July 1945
Arizona

The guard, a flat-faced corporal with a habit of cracking his jaw, drove Rudolf and Helmut into the heart of Phoenix to the Culver Street Synagogue. The corporal said little on the long trip, except to mutter as he walked the Germans into the Jewish house of worship that he would be waiting for them.

"Don't get any ideas about leaving here without me," he said in a sullen tone, stationing himself resolutely near the entrance.

A man dressed in a dark suit stood in the foyer and introduced himself as a representative of the Feller family. He put his hand out to the two German men. "I am Simon Feller, Vern's nephew. Ruth and Bob are pleased the camp commander allowed you to come."

The men nodded silently and each shook Simon's hand.

Simon walked over to a small table in the foyer filled with yarmulkes—thin slightly-rounded skullcaps—and said, "I hope you won't mind putting these on. It's a sign of respect for God."

Both men obliged, but it was a clumsy moment as the Germans, dressed in their clean but shabby camp uniforms, took off their caps and donned the skullcaps. Simon led them into the sanctuary and walked them to their seats. All heads in the synagogue moved collectively from left to right, following the German prisoners of war as if they were watching a basketball game. A small buzz rose from the congregation when Simon seated them behind the row reserved for relatives.

Rudolf had never been in a synagogue except to peer into the one in Bremen desecrated during *Kristallnacht.* His nerves were on edge, and his hands shook a little as he settled into the seat. For some unknown reason, he wanted to yank the strange cap off his head and throw it to the ground, but he did not move a muscle because it seemed as if a thousand eyes pierced his back. He caught Helmut's furtive glance, which calmed him a bit; at least he was not alone.

At the front of the synagogue, Rudolf saw Vern's closed coffin, made of plain pine with the Star of David etched on it. He tried to locate Ruth and Bob Feller, finally spotting them in the center of the front row. They were dressed so different from what they wore on the farm that Rudolf hardly recognized mother and son. Ruth wore a black silk dress and a string of pearls adorned her neck. On her head was a small black felt hat with a veil that dropped over her eyes.

Bob's dark suit and tie made him look older than his years. A yarmulke covered his head, and the sight of it jolted Rudolf. For the first time, he realized Bob was a Jew. Bob may have told Rudolf he was a Jew, but Rudolf never saw Bob as one until that piece of cloth covered his friend's head. In Rudolf's mind, infested with fascist teaching, Jews were bankers, merchants, and shop keepers, not farmers who labored in the field. Now this young man, whose friendship Rudolf embraced, came unexpectedly into sharp focus.

Bob turned his head and nodded solemnly at Rudolf. Rudolf's eyes met those of his friend, and he wished desperately they were planting cotton and talking, sharing ideas. Oh, how he did not want to be in this place that seemed so foreign, *so* Jewish.

The memorial service began, and Bob turned his face back to the rabbi who stood at a lectern at the front of the synagogue.

"The Lord is my shepherd," the rabbi said, pausing to look into the crowd, but he did not look toward the Germans and the synagogue's pressure-cooker atmosphere dropped dramatically.

Rudolf noticed the rabbi was a big man, not unlike his grandfather, although he wore a full beard. The German prisoner of war shifted uneasily in his seat. Why had he always envisioned a rabbi as old, small, and dark skinned? This one was exactly the opposite—middle-aged, large, light-skinned, and his beard was golden brown. He appeared energetic and full of life, not someone who stared squint eyed over an old piece of parchment. Maybe this rabbi was different because he was an American, just as Bob was an American.

The psalm was the same that Rudolf had heard as a boy when he attended Lutheran services with his grandparents, and he felt comforted because of its familiarity. After the psalm, the rabbi recited a scriptural passage in English, and then a tall man, in his mid-forties, with dark hair tinged gray at the temples, stepped up to the lectern.

"I am Jesse Feldman, a long-time friend of Vern's, and I am here today to honor him and to tell his family how much respect this man held in the community."

The man looked directly at Ruth and Bob and smiled. "Vern and I went to high school together back in the Bronx, in New York. He was a different man than most of us. We wanted to be accountants or merchants. But Vern, from an early age, loved the land, the feel of the soil, the warmth of the sun. Vern tried to be what his parents wanted—for a while, at least. But when he was twenty, he took a train going west, and ended up in Phoenix, where he worked any job he could to save enough money to buy his farm. Vern loved Phoenix so much that he enticed the rest of the Feller family to move here, and then he bribed me and I followed him here too."

Jesse looked down at his hands for a moment, and then said, "Vern made friends easily because he had a wonderful way about him. He could relate to the troubles of others and because of that empathy, he gave of his time to those who needed it—people of all faiths and creeds and nationalities. Many a roof in this community was repaired by Vern, many a field was plowed for a fellow farmer who was sick, and Vern provided food from his garden for those in need; that is why I see so many people here today to show their respect, people who are not members of this synagogue."

There was a pause, and then he said, "More than Vern's love for his farm and his community was his love for his wife Ruth, a school teacher who willingly became a farmer's wife and his son Bob, his pride and joy. I know that this fine young man will follow in his father's footsteps," Jesse said, his voice choking.

He stopped for a moment as if to gather his thoughts and then said with sadness, "Vern Feller will be greatly missed."

Jesse stepped down from the lectern, and Rudolf could see Ruth bring a handkerchief to her face with Bob leaning over toward his mother to console her. Abruptly, a sense of shame flowed over him; his disquiet about Jews and their strange rituals had displaced his sorrow for Bob and Ruth. How could that happen, when he felt such respect for this family?

Rudolf shuddered. He realized that his reaction to Jews was automatic, like turning on a light switch when one enters a dark room. Rudolf's chin, chiseled with its deep cleft, fell against his chest. Could his friendship for the young man remain now that he saw Bob clearly as a Jew?

The rabbi returned to the lectern, asking anyone who had lost a loved one to stand and recite with him the Prayer for the Soul of the Departed known as the Mourner's Kaddish. Rudolf looked down at his trembling hands as he listened to the alien Hebrew sounds flowing from the rabbi's mouth. Suddenly, Rudolf realized everyone had stood at the rabbi's request, except for himself and Helmut, and suddenly he understood what it was like to be ostracized, to be alone among many. He did not know how much of this he could tolerate; he felt feverish, almost as if he had contracted some sort of sickness when he walked into this place filled with Jews. All he wanted was to leave.

The ceremony ended after the rabbi made several announcements about the burial and visitation with the family. Rudolf felt surprised that the funeral finished in so short a time, and he lingered in his seat. Helmut gave him a nudge and Rudolf looked around as the synagogue emptied, his mind filled with perplexing thoughts. What he expected at a Jewish funeral was far different than what actually happened. He assumed the scroll—the Torah—would be brought out with great flourish, candles would be lit amid the intoning of multitudes of prayers, and loud wailing would fill the house of worship. Instead, it was quiet and dignified.

He got up quickly and moved with Helmut to the foyer, where they put the skullcaps back on the table, and looked at each other furtively, as if taking them off relieved them of a great burden. The Fellers were nowhere to be seen, but the corporal stood ready at the entrance, scowling.

"Just like you two to be the last ones out, giving me heartburn! Besides, what the hell are you Krauts doing here anyway with all these Jews?" the corporal sneered. And then he cracked his jaw.

The days of summer moved slowly, with little change in the lives of the prisoners. Gossip about repatriation never stopped swirling like a dust storm around the camp. With no concrete news for the POWs, there was nothing to make the hot days and nights move faster except the furious games of soccer between compounds—the only release for men trained to make war.

One hot July evening, Rudolf walked victorious off the soccer field after having scored the winning goal, his bronzed, lean body glistening with sweat. Fritz, who played on the opposite team, sat glumly on the bench with a broken wrist.

Rudolf grabbed a towel and wrapped it around his neck, mopping the moisture on his face. He grinned at Fritz, and then sat down next to him.

"For once, luck was with me! The field was wide open and your goalie was slow."

"If I had been there, you would not have had a chance!" Fritz growled as he lifted his right hand, wrapped in a cast like a white flag of surrender.

Rudolf dug into his pocket and pulled out one of his remaining Chesterfields. He lit it with a match, inhaled, and handed it to Fritz, who took it awkwardly with his left hand.

"Have you heard anything?" Rudolf asked.

Fritz made a face. "I suppose you know who the *Amerikaner* are sending home first—fifty thousand 'useless men'—the sick, the insane, and the die-hard Nazis. Maybe I can go home now because I broke my wrist in a soccer game. I'm useless, too. How can I pick fruit or cotton or dig out an irrigation ditch?"

Rudolf nodded and Fritz handed back the cigarette.

"Yes, I know. We are still here because we are 'useful,' Fritz," Rudolf said. "The farmers need us; not enough Negroes have come home from the war. Believe me, they will find something for you to do, even if it is to clean toilets."

Fritz heaved a sigh. "Still, Rudi, it is difficult for me to understand that hardened Nazis are going home first. I tell you that article in *Der Ruf* was such a blow, I felt as if I were going to be sick! So what if that American general tries to salve our wounds by saying the Nazis will have no privileges and are not going back as free citizens? They are going *back*, goddamn it!"

"Yes...to the coal mines of France and Germany. I would go work in a coal mine, for that matter; at least I would be closer to my grandfather."

The men sat quietly as they watched the start of another soccer game, smoking the cigarette down to a nub. When Rudolf crushed it into the ground, he asked Fritz, "I thought your American uncle was trying to help you."

"It was of no use, after all his effort. He tried to convince the War Department he would take me in and teach me to be a good American. Their answer was that no prisoner of war could remain in America."

"Hmmm," Rudolf said, as he tugged at the towel around his neck. "The only good out of this is that officers and NCOs like Hollmann who do not work in the fields like the rest of us might also be sent home first. Hollmann—that *Schwein*—he should have died after that fight in the canteen! Unfortunately, he did not."

"Yes." Fritz nodded. "I have never forgiven him for refusing to help *Oberfunkmeister* Reese. For all we know, Reese died."

Rudolf made no comment. He was afraid of Hollmann. He did not want to admit that to Fritz, but he was. On a rational level, Hollmann's threat that word would get back to Germany about his friendship with Bob Feller seemed improbable now that the Third Reich was in ruins.

But on a deeper level—that small part of Rudolf still beholden to Nazi authority—believed he was in peril.

Just as the soccer game moved into the second half, Helmut Kessler sat down on the bench next to Rudolf.

"Where have you been, Helmut?" Rudolf asked.

"I have been in the library, putting together these petitions," he said, as he showed Rudolf a sheaf of papers.

Rudolf—his attention caught up with the possibility of a score by the opposing team—ignored Helmut until the older man nudged him.

"What is this?" Rudolf asked, barely glancing at Helmut's papers.

"This is important, Rudi! They are petitions renouncing our allegiance to National Socialism, and our pledge to support the creation of a democratic Germany."

Rudolf gulped. "*Mein Gott!* Why are you doing that?"

Fritz heard Rudolf's outburst and looked at Helmut.

"What a good idea, Helmut!" Fritz said after he read the petition. "Give me your pencil and I will sign it. Since I cannot stay in America and live with my uncle, I might as well sign your petition. To a new Germany!"

Helmut handed him the pencil. "Would you consider passing the petition around your compound?"

"Yes, of course."

Helmut handed several sheets to Fritz, and then looked at Rudolf. "Well, what do you think, Rudi?"

"You are making trouble for yourself...."

"Yes, I know. But the war has ended and we must take destiny into our own hands. I am not afraid of those Nazi officers and NCOs who think they run this camp. I am not a Nazi and have never been one. I simply served my country in the German *Kriegsmarine*, like many men here. Why are you so afraid, Rudi?"

Rudolf did not answer. Instead, he looked at the soccer game, his face as hard as stone.

Rudolf returned to his barrack after hammering English verbs into the heads of his fellow prisoners. The night was especially hot, and Rudolf saw cots set up outside the building, the men hoping to catch even the smallest whiff of wind. Rudolf found Helmut inside the stifling barrack with his dog-eared petitions spread helter-skelter on his cot, the floor, and his footlocker, rifling through the papers trying to discern who signed them and who had not.

"Helmut—maybe we will sleep better if we move our cots outside like the others," Rudolf said, pulling off his shirt.

"Yes, it is warm tonight. Let me put these papers away first," Helmut said. He gathered them together and placed the petitions in his footlocker, carefully locking it.

Helmut looked exhausted, Rudolf noticed, as they struggled with the cumbersome folding beds, finally setting them up a small distance from their comrades.

"I am surprised at the number of men who are afraid to sign the petition," Helmut said quietly as he sat on his cot, "even you, Rudi." After a long, thoughtful pause, he said, "Perhaps you are right. The Nazis have a stronger hold here than I want to believe. The Americans have been lazy in this regard and have let the Nazis control the camp to maintain order, and those of us who are neutral remain under their thumb."

It was true, Rudolf knew. He heard talk in the library while preparing for his class. At the center of the commotion, was Hollmann—apparently recovered from his injuries—pounding loudly on a table, expressing his displeasure at the petitions, and scoffing at the Allies' control of Germany. Other men listened to him, nodding agreement.

"Germany's historical destiny that *Der Führer* promised and that the German people believed in has not vanished!" Hollmann nearly shouted. "Yes, the future seems bleak, but the Fatherland will come back...and the world will soon forget what happened to the Jews. No one really cares about them anyway. If they did, the Allies would have opened their doors to the Jews when we asked, years ago, before the war! Instead, they quietly let us incinerate them, and now it is our fault."

A sense of shame flowed over Rudolf as he tried to concentrate on his class preparations. His mind turned to the Jews in the synagogue on the day of Vern Feller's funeral. He admitted to his nervousness around them, but except for their strange rituals, they appeared no different than anyone else. Was that cause to kill them?

Thinking about Hollmann's outburst as he lay on his cot under the black velvet sky, Rudolf wondered if he mentally defended the Jews because he disliked his former U-boat officer, or if his friendship with the Feller family interfered with his reasoning. Jews were responsible, after all, for Germany's economic devastation between the wars: Hitler said that a thousand times. Nothing had changed, except the Fellers were different. Or was he different? A deep sigh escaped him as the perplexity of it all overwhelmed his thoughts and he pulled his cot closer to Helmut's so they could talk quietly.

"Will we ever go home?" Rudolf lamented.

Helmut chuckled. "How many times have you asked me that, Rudi? We will go home, but I believe it will be later rather than sooner."

Rudolf's mind raced. "Helmut—I cannot believe what terrible luck has befallen Germany! We have lost two wars, and *Der Führer's* dream of building a superior race has blown up in our faces."

"There is no such thing as a superior race, Rudi!" Helmut said with a snort. "The trouble is we Germans believe our own propaganda! We were damned good at goose-stepping, but what else did we do except terrorize the world?"

Rudolf did not answer, so Helmut continued. "Our American friends listen to their own propaganda as well. They are supposed to always be happy-go-lucky, kind, and honest. We, their captives, know otherwise. While I admit the Americans have not been bad to us, neither have they been as good as their newspapers report. Our food rations are sparse, and we have no news about our families. That said—I still want to bring my family here and become an American."

Rudolf ignored Helmut's outrageous desire and plunged on, "We Germans are *kaputt!*"

"Yes, we are, Rudi," Helmut answered, with a note of sadness. "What else can we do now but imitate those who beat the shit out of Germany? Democracy is the only way out."

Rudolf silently considered Helmut's response. Democracy did not work in Germany after the Great War. Could it work now with Germany bleeding and on her knees? His teacher, Herr Braun, said the Treaty of Versailles forced democracy upon Germany, but the history of the Weimar Republic was *verboten* under the Nazis, so he knew virtually nothing about it. It seemed foolish to Rudolf that a group of men talking endlessly with each another, like those in the American congress or the British parliament could ever work in Germany as effectively as a strong, take-charge leader like Adolf Hitler.

Rudolf stretched out, tired now after hashing over his country's fate; it all appeared to be utterly confusing. He looked up at the starry night, and listened to the howl of coyotes in the distance. It was an eerie sound, and the hair on the back of Rudolf's neck stood up involuntarily when he heard their cries. Still, sleeping under the stars was far better than the cramped barrack that smelled of men's sweaty bodies, and being outside reminded Rudolf of his many outings in the German countryside with the Hitler Youth.

As the night turned cooler, Rudolf slept deeply, dreaming of the day so long ago when he saw the dark-haired girl standing on the bank of the Weser River. She was there again, fully-grown now, tempting him, smiling at him, calling to him. He rowed furiously to reach her, and he felt water from the river splash onto his arm, but she disappeared into a thick fog that enveloped the river bank.

Rudolf woke suddenly with a strange sense of unease. The moon was bright, almost giving a feel of daylight. He sat up and felt his arm. When he brought his hand up, there was a wet, sticky feeling on his fingers. Startled, he realized it was blood, and then he felt his arm again, running his hand up and down, looking for a wound, wondering how he could have injured himself. There appeared to be no injury, yet curiously, blood was on him.

He looked over toward Helmut, whose head lay at an odd angle. Rudolf rolled over and stood up; he moved to Helmut, calling his name softly, but there was no answer, only the cry of the coyotes in the desert beyond the barbed-wire fence. Rudolf peered closer at Helmut and saw something reflected in the moonlight, something strange, dark. He put his hand out, tentatively, fearfully, and drew it back quickly. Finally, he gathered the courage to touch Helmut's shoulder, to shake him. Then Rudolf jerked his hand away, seized with terror: His hand dripped with blood.

Someone had cut Helmut's throat.

Rudolf's old fear took hold: that inexorable tide of fright he felt deep inside since he was a small boy, sweeping over him like the ocean covering a U-boat as it plunged rapidly into its forbidding depths.

Rudolf dropped to his knees, moaning. His forehead fell forward onto the desert sand, and he did not care at that moment if he lived or died. *Mein Gott...*was it Helmut who had called out to him and not the dark-haired girl? He beat his head again and again against the cruel earth, where it seemed that love was always lost and pain flourished; he blamed himself for dreaming about a girl he never knew. If he had not been so sound asleep, he could have saved his friend, stopped the bleeding somehow. Guilt tore at Rudolf's soul.

Helmut was dead, gone. How could he survive the rest of his internment without him? And then, he began screaming.

Rudolf opened his eyes. The walls around him were different than his barrack, painted white with a dull sheen. Not sure of where he was, he sat up suddenly, and then he heard a woman's voice, soothing and calm, "You mustn't move quickly, young man."

"Where am I," Rudolf asked, his fear causing him to speak automatically in German. He put his hand to his chest because his heart felt as if it were going to burst.

A tall woman, her graying hair pulled back neatly into a knot, came to the side of his bed. Her smile was warm and confident. "Do you speak any English?" she asked as she placed one hand on his shoulder in a comforting manner and with her other hand, she began taking his pulse. A frown came over the nurse's face as she counted the beat of Rudolf's blood flowing through his arteries.

"Yes." Rudolf said.

"Good," she replied, finally placing his arm gently on the sheet, and Rudolf could see she mentally noted his pulse rate. "Lie down, please. You need rest. You've had a terrible jolt to your system. Do you understand?"

"Yes," Rudolf nodded. He looked carefully at the nurse; a halo of light seemed to surround her head, but then Rudolf realized it was her starched, white-as-snow cap.

"The doctor will be here soon to speak to you. Are you comfortable?" she asked, covering him while he settled his head back onto the pillow.

"Yes, except for…" he moved his hand to his chest. " I feel pounding, here, as if my heart is going wild."

"I know," she replied, her voice reassuring. The nurse moved to the end of the bed and picked up a clipboard with a pencil hanging from a string. She made several marks on the attached paper and carefully put the clipboard back.

"What's wrong with me, why am I here?" Rudolf asked with a note of alarm in his voice.

"Dr. Wilson will be here shortly. Try to rest; if you need me, just push that button on the cord here," she said showing him the bell cord before she left the room, her starched uniform rustling like dry leaves.

Rudolf tried to rest like the nurse told him, but the more he thought about his throbbing heart, the faster it seemed to beat. He could hear voices in the hallway humming against the drone of machinery somewhere distant, and the sharp odor of disinfectant filled the room, a smell not unlike what his grandmother used when she scrubbed the floor of their small apartment. He tried to think. Why was he here? Had he been hurt in a soccer game? But he knew he did not play last night because of the English class. Everything seemed muddled. There was the moonlight and the mournful wail of coyotes, and talking to Helmut. Then, he had a dream…

Suddenly, a wild, painful cry sprang from Rudolf's throat, and the muscles in his arms and legs tensed. He gasped for air, feeling as if someone's hands were gripping his throat, choking him. The nurse ran into the room and a doctor followed, holding his stethoscope from thumping against his chest.

The doctor moved hastily to Rudolf's side. He was a middle-aged man with glasses that framed his large, dark brown eyes. He spoke to the German in a quiet, calm tone, but there was no response from Rudolf except his wheezing for air, and a look of fright covering his face. The doctor turned to the nurse. "I thought he might get through this without another attack, but apparently he's still in distress. Get me the phenobarbital."

He quickly injected Rudolf and then kept his hand on the young man's pulse for a long time. "Finally," the doctor said with relief, "his heart rate is dropping."

The nurse stood anxiously by the doctor's side. "I've never seen anyone like this."

"Hmmm, well…there's lots of documentation from the eighteen hundreds about female hysteria," the doctor remarked, adjusting his glasses, "but there isn't much about hysteria affecting men."

"You mean those women who fainted a lot?" the nurse said, a smile playing coyly at the edges of her lips.

"Well…yes, but it was fashionable then to feign hysterics," Dr. Wilson said. "This young man is experiencing real physical symptoms. The murder of his friend obviously brought on his hysteria, but my guess is that there is something deeper going on, some other internal distress."

The doctor stood by Rudolf's side, watching him closely as his body slumped, his eyes closed, and his breathing slowly returned to normal. "Keep an eye on him, nurse," the doctor said as he walked out the door, nearly bumping into Major Kennedy.

"Ah, Major Kennedy… Rudolf Meier just had another hysterical attack, and I gave him a sedative. I'm afraid he'll sleep for some time."

Kennedy frowned and his bushy black eyebrows made a thick line across his forehead. "Nuts!" he exclaimed.

"I'm sorry; he was very agitated," Dr. Wilson said, fingering his stethoscope.

"How can I carry on this goddamn investigation without talking to the only one who may have seen something?" the major said. "He's been here two days."

"Yes, I know," the doctor said, "but you would not have been able to speak with him anyway in his disturbed state. The only thing we can do is notify you when he wakes up."

"Alright, I'll be waiting," the major snorted. "And I don't care what time it is!"

Late in the afternoon, Rudolf opened his eyes. He lifted his head, and looked around the room. Everything felt out of kilter and the room shifted irrationally on its own. He closed his eyes again to ward off the dizziness, and then covered his face with his hand to block the light coming in through the window. Although he did not move his body, his mind worked furiously: Helmut was dead. Now he remembered the blood, his own screaming, the other men crowding around him, and the American guards trying to question him before they brought him into the hospital.

The nurse's voice floated into his brain. "Young man, you need some nourishment."

Rudolf moved his hand from his face and opened his eyes. It was the same nurse who took his pulse earlier. Now she stood next to him with a tray and she set it on a small table next to the bed as he watched her. From somewhere, she grabbed another pillow and placed it under his head, raising Rudolf's upper body enough so that she could spoon the thick beef and barley soup into his mouth. He was still dizzy, although not as much as before, and the food tasted delicious; Rudolf suddenly realized how hungry he was.

She watched him carefully as she fed him. "Are you feeling better?" she asked.

"A bit," he said.

"Good, you will need strength before the major comes."

"The major...?"

"Yes. Major Kennedy. He ordered us to notify him the moment you woke up, but Dr. Wilson told me to feed you first."

When the soup was gone, she began feeding him chocolate pudding, and when he finished, she asked if he would like a cup of coffee.

"Yes, that would be good," he said, giving her a slight smile.

She nodded, picked up the tray and took it out of the room.

With his stomach full, a sense of wellness flowed over Rudolf now that the incessant thumping of his heart had stopped. He half-closed his eyes and waited contentedly for the coffee, but his reverie was broken when the major strode purposefully into the room.

"At last you are awake," he said in German as he grabbed a chair and set it down next to Rudolf. The young man made no response, but simply looked at the American officer, wondering what he had done to deserve facing this man again who seemed to know too much about him.

"The doctor said you are better."

"Yes, sir, somewhat," Rudolf answered cautiously.

"I need to ask you some questions," the officer said as he pulled a piece of paper from his shirt pocket. Rudolf could see the scratching of comments made helter-skelter on the sheet, some actually written sideways.

Rudolf desperately did not want the American officer to question him about Helmut's death, but he knew there was no way out, so he gave a slight nod. Then he saw the nurse return with the steaming coffee. She set the drink on the table next to his bed, and said to the major, "I would be happy to get you a cup, sir."

"Huh...? No thanks, nurse," he replied offhandedly as he continued to scan his notes.

Rudolf waited impatiently for the officer to begin his questioning, but Major Kennedy did not look up from his scribbles. The German sniffed the coffee's enticing aroma, but he was unsure if he could be so bold as to pick it up from the tray.

Finally, Major Kennedy looked up. "All right, Meier. Tell me how you knew Helmut Kessler."

Before answering, Rudolf looked longingly at the coffee. The officer, sensing his need, picked it up and handed it to him.

"Thank you, sir," Rudolf said, taking several big gulps. He cradled the cup in his hands, trying to infuse his body with its warmth, as if the heat would fortify him somehow against the major's questions. "Although we both served on U-893, I did not know him until we came to this camp. We lived in the same barrack, and we often worked together at the Feller farm."

"How is it you came to sleep outside your barrack two nights ago?"

"Two nights ago? I…I thought it was last night. Have I been here that long?"

"Yes. You don't remember?"

"No…I…I lost a whole day…?" his voice trailed off.

"Why were you sleeping outside?" the officer pressed Rudolf, ignoring his question.

"We often sleep outside, sir. In the summer, it is too hot to sleep inside that stifling building."

"So it was not an unusual thing to do?"

"No, sir."

"What were you and Kessler doing before you pulled your cots outside?"

"I was teaching English in the library and came back to the barrack to find Helmut sitting inside going over papers," Rudolf said.

"What kind of papers? The officer's eyebrows rose with curiosity.

"Helmut had…well, he had a petition going around the camp." Rudolf stopped and took another gulp of coffee.

"Yes? A petition…what sort of petition?" There was a note of irritation in the major's voice.

"It was a petition Helmut started. It…it renounced National Socialism and supported the creation of a democratic Germany."

"Really?" the major said. "Well, that's interesting…tell me, what did you think of his petition?"

Rudolf's hands began to shake, creating small waves of coffee spilling over onto the sheet that covered him. Major Kennedy looked sharply at the cup, reached out, took it from Rudolf's hands and placed it firmly on the tray.

"It's alright, Meier," the major said, changing the direction of his questioning. "I understand Kessler was a good man."

"Yes, he was, sir. He worried constantly about his family. They were his whole life." Rudolf's voice broke and his eyes abruptly filled with tears. Major Kennedy looked at the young man for a moment, and then he quickly got up, walked over to the door and closed it.

Rudolf turned red with shame. He pressed the palms of his hands over his eyes as if that action would stop the tears, but it only made him look like a little boy. The major stood by the door, gazed at the ceiling with a vacant stare, and waited for the crisis to pass. Some minutes later, with Rudolf again in control of himself, the officer walked back to the bedside and sat down.

"What did you think about the petition, Meier?"

Rudolf took a gulp of air, like a drowning man. "I told Helmut he would be making trouble for himself."

Major Kennedy pursed his lips. He remained quiet for a time, his eyebrows knitted together and then he asked, "I take it from what you just said that there are men in this camp who would be upset by Kessler's petition?"

The fear that Rudolf intimately knew finally crawled out of his belly and made itself visible on his finely chiseled Aryan face. Although the German made no outward movement to answer the probing question, the American officer glimpsed Rudolf's inner terror.

Rudolf's expression unnerved Major Kennedy; the mere sight of it made his upper body jolt suddenly as if he put his finger unwittingly in a light socket. Attempting to regain his composure, the major reached into his shirt pocket and took out his fountain pen. He moved slowly, cautiously, unscrewing its top. He made another scribbled note on the paper, using his hand as a pad, and then he got up from the chair, walked around the room, hands jammed into his pants pockets. The major finally stopped at Rudolf's bedside and asked, "Did you…sign the petition?"

The German's blue eyes nearly bugged out of his head. "No!"

"Is that because you still believe in National Socialism?" the officer asked in a caustic tone.

Rudolf's chin fell to his chest. "I believe in nothing at this moment. All I want is to go home and take care of my grandfather. Please, please! All I know is that I woke up and looked at Helmut and realized when I touched him that his throat was cut and he was dead!"

A stony look crossed over the major's face, and he leaned closer to Rudolf. "Meier, who killed Kessler?"

"I do not know."

"Yes, I think you do."

"No, no! I do not."

"What are you afraid of, Meier?"

"Nothing."

"Yes, you are. I just saw your fear; you know I saw it."

Rudolf looked down at his hands and realized how tightly clenched they were. He consciously relaxed them, a movement not unnoticed by the major, and then the German took a deep breath. "I swear to you I do not know who killed Helmut."

"Who threatened you, Meier?" the major countered.

"No one."

"If no one threatened you, then why are you so afraid?"

Rudolf did not answer and he did not look up. Finally, after what seemed like a long time, the major put his pen and paper back in his pocket, and got up with a sigh. "Those petitions. What did Kessler do with them?"

"Before we moved the cots outside, he put them in his foot locker."

"Are you sure?" The major's voice was tight with disappointment. "Kessler's foot locker was empty when we searched it."

Rudolf's head popped up and his eyes opened wide. "It was empty? Major Kennedy, I saw him lock it!"

"Did he talk to you at all about the petition? By that, I mean, were men signing it?"

"Not many, sir. Helmut was in fact concerned that so few had signed it. On the night he died, he told me he thought the Nazi officers have a stronger hold on Papago Park than he previously believed."

"Do you think that, Meier?"

Rudolf's hands clenched again, and he glanced toward the door, its closure giving him confidence that no one else heard his words. He took a gulp of air. "Yes, sir, I do," he said softly, and the dizziness he felt earlier returned with a vengeance.

Rudolf's mind rummaged through endless thoughts of Helmut while he lay in the hospital bed; most were wishful thinking about what he could have done to save his friend's life. He sighed deeply and felt grateful for his time in the hospital, away from probing eyes and ears. Rudolf envisioned the gossip that was probably swirling around the camp like a mischievous dust devil invading every nook and cranny. He knew the men had nothing better to do than talk about Helmut's murder and the democracy petitions. No doubt, those idle conversations included questions about him, and Rudolf wondered how he would deal with those once he returned to his barrack.

The Feller farm beckoned Rudolf; it had become a sanctuary to him. He could talk to Bob about ideas he never even considered before he came to America while laboring amid the verdant cotton, forgetting his troubles. While the unending brown landscape of the Sonoran Desert burned his eyes, the green of the cotton plants gave him some small sense of his Germany.

A knock on the partially open door brought Rudolf out of his somber thoughts and a familiar face peaked into the room.

"Hi," Bob Feller said.

Rudolf smiled. "I was just thinking of you and the farm."

Bob walked to the side of the bed and looked down at Rudolf. The young man broke out in a big smile. "You're OK?"

"Yes, OK, as you Americans say," Rudolf nodded.

Bob stood awkwardly, looked around and finally pulled a chair to Rudolf's bedside.

"Major Kennedy called to tell us what happened."

Bob's remark stunned Rudolf. "Major Kennedy?"

"Yes…he told us you were in the hospital, and what happened to Helmut. Oh, gosh, Rudi! Mom and I have been terribly upset."

Rudolf took a deep breath; he would never be able to forget the memory of the grotesque angle of Helmut's head as it lay in the pool of blood. Not knowing what to say because his emotions lay so dangerously close to the surface, he answered, "I am anxious to be working at your farm."

"Yes, and we are anxious to have you back!"

"How are you and your mother handling the farm without…?" Rudolf's voice dropped off at the thought of Vern Feller.

"Mom is having a rough time of it. She misses my dad terribly, and so do I, but I'm busy, awfully busy, Rudi. The farm is running me ragged. This year, it looks like a top grade crop. If it turns out like I think it will, maybe we will be able to hire a manager so I can get my law degree at the University of Arizona. I still have to go into the military, but with the war over, maybe the draft board will give me a student deferment."

For a brief second, the sharp sting of jealousy jolted Rudolf. He realized the future lay bright in front of Bob, while he merely waited endlessly to go home to a broken Germany. There was an awkward silence and then Rudolf said, "I think the doctor will release me tomorrow. I should be back to work soon."

"You know, Rudi, it's a funny thing," Bob said. "You're one of the best workers we have, yet I don't need you at the farm to work as much as I want you there because we always have so much to talk about! I miss our conversations; I miss listening to a different point of view."

"Yes," Rudolf acknowledged. "I understand… I feel the same."

Bob stood up. "Well, I need to get back, but I wanted to see you. Mom and I…well, we've been worried about you. What happened to Helmut seems impossible to believe. I'm really sorry, Rudi. I know he was your friend. More than that, he was a fine man."

Rudolf nodded. He pursed his lips to stop any show of emotion.

"Oh, I almost forgot, Rudi. I brought you this book. I talked to you about it that day we celebrated your birthday…the day my dad died."

Bob handed it to Rudolf. Its spine was deep red, and the bold letters said, *One World.* It was written by Wendell L.Willkie.

Rudolf took it gingerly, gratefully, and turned it over. On the back cover was the face of the author, the man who ran against President Franklin Roosevelt in 1940. Rudolf smiled and the two young men shook hands. He was keenly aware that no one had visited him while he recuperated from the shock of Helmut's brutal murder; no one, not even his friend Fritz had expressed sympathy for the loss of Rudolf's friend. No one that is, except a Jew.

Chapter 25

August - November 1945
Arizona

The heat of the August day brutalized the men as they worked in the Feller cotton field. Not even the noon rest under the cottonwood trees gave them any respite from the sweltering temperature. The Germans, worn thin by the unremitting heat, worked halfheartedly. They were especially despondent with the latest news—broadcast throughout the camp by the new public address system—atomic bombs had obliterated Hiroshima and Nagasaki, and then a few days later, Japan surrendered. The men spoke to one another in hushed tones about the ascendency of America in the world order. The attack on Japan had supplanted the vaunted strength of the Third Reich in their minds and it was a bitter pill to swallow.

As if the blast of the sun and America's technological brilliance were not enough to disturb them, in mid-afternoon a new member to the work crew stumbled upon a large rattlesnake hiding in the lush cotton undergrowth.

Rudolf heard Karl Schmidt scream when the snake struck his leg; he ran toward the youngster in time to see the snake slither away from the point of its attack, heading to the ditch bank. The reptile, at least four feet long, was seeking another place to hide, and as the other men rushed to help Karl, Rudolf followed it and cut its head off with a sharp swing of his shovel.

He watched, fascinated, as the snake's body writhed in its death throes, and then he scooped it up and threw the headless viper into the irrigation ditch. When Rudolf turned back to the field, he could see the youth sitting in the dirt crying, holding his leg. Bob was already by his side, comforting him.

Ruth, who had driven to the field to bring more water and lemonade for the men, saw the commotion. She grabbed her first aid kit from the truck and rushed to the injured worker.

"Don't move!" Ruth said, as she tore the leg of his trouser, but he continued to squirm, fearfully looking around for the snake. When she realized Karl did not understand what she was saying, she called to Rudolf: "Rudi, tell him not to move!"

Rudolf went to Karl, knelt down on one knee, and touched him on the shoulder, reassuring him that the snake was dead and Ruth Feller was trying to help him.

Using a clean white cloth, she washed the bite with water that one of the men brought from the truck. Then she took another cloth from her well-assembled kit that containing assorted bandages, mercuricome, and healing salves, and carefully wrapped the youngster's leg.

With Karl still whimpering like a child, Rudolf said to Ruth, "He is one of the last prisoners to come to the camp."

"He looks very young," she replied. There was sadness in her voice.

"He told me he is seventeen, but I believe he is younger," Rudolf said.

"My God, he's just a boy!" Ruth said as she got up from her task. "My guess is that he is not much older than fifteen." She brushed her hands and turned to her son. "Bob, get this youngster to the camp hospital. It's a deep bite. I don't like the look of it."

Bob grunted. "Rudi, put Karl in the front seat with us, and tell the men to hurry."

Rudolf yelled to the men and they all ran to the truck, jumped into the back, dropping their tools by the side of the dirt road.

On their way back to camp, Rudolf spoke quietly to the youngster and then said to Bob, "Karl cannot believe this has happened to him. He was so glad you Americans captured him that he felt nothing would ever go wrong again in his life. Now he thinks being bit by a snake is a bad omen."

Bob pressed his foot on the accelerator in his hurry to get to the hospital, and brushed a lock of his thick, dark hair away from his face. "Tell Karl plenty of people get bit by rattlesnakes and they go on to live a healthy life."

"How do you know?" Rudolf asked.

"Oh, I was bit by one when I was about ten years old. I foolishly stuck my hand into the woodpile. I was pretty sick for a while, I must admit, but I'm still here. Tell him he's going to be OK."

Half an hour later, after dropping the rest of the men off at the camp entrance, Bob drove to the hospital building. Rudolf waited with Karl in the truck while Bob went inside to get help. He soon returned with two German orderlies carrying a stretcher. Rudolf and Bob watched while the men lifted the terrified youngster onto the stretcher and carried him inside.

With Karl in good hands, Bob climbed back into the truck. "I'll see you tomorrow. I hope we can make up the work we lost today," he said, a frown on his face.

Rudolf nodded, and looked up at the gathering clouds. "Maybe we will be lucky. We might get a summer storm this evening."

He slapped the side of the truck as it passed him, and then he turned toward his barrack. Immediately, Rudolf saw Horst Hollmann standing near his compound's entrance, a smirk on his face. Rudolf's heart began to race, but he kept his eyes down as he passed his former U-boat officer.

"I see you are still hanging out with that Jew farmer," Hollmann said, loud enough for Rudolf to hear, but Rudolf just kept walking.

Later that evening, Rudolf sat on his cot that he had pulled outside from his stifling barrack. He wore only his underwear and his rag-tag canvas shoes in a vain effort to cool his body from the relentless heat. This was the small moment of time before lights out when he could smoke, read, and think. These days, he spoke little with his fellow inmates, trusting no one since Helmut's murder. He still taught English and played soccer but his only real pleasure was to submerge himself in books; Rudolf found they were the only way to escape the drudgery of his existence and his fear of Hollmann.

The odd rock formations near the prisoner of war camp stood in stark black silhouette against the fading blue sky and Rudolf gazed at them with a dull hatred. The rain never materialized, but he could see lightning strikes in the surrounding desert. Before night spread its wings, he had been reading the book given to him by Bob, but now the lack of light forced him to put *One World* down. Rudolf realized the book was one man's look at the world embroiled in war, gathered while traveling thirty-one thousand miles around the globe in the fall of 1942. From information gathered on that journey, Wendell L. Willkie believed a federation of nations working together could secure world peace. Without that foundation, he said peace would never prevail.

Rudolf lit his Chesterfield and drew in its taste slowly, his head thrown back, his eyes closed, savoring the flavor. Smoking kept his hands busy whenever he found himself with nothing to do except think. Absentmindedly, he pushed his fingers through his hair and wrinkles burrowed the bridge of his nose. What did peace really mean? Although Bob passionately believed the newly chartered United Nations could achieve world peace, Rudolf was not so sure.

He reached over, yanked off his shoes, and put his feet up on the cot with a thump. Peace was only a word bandied about by world leaders, and world peace seemed even less of a reality after the Potsdam Conference. Carved into pieces like a gigantic pie, Germany was now at the mercy of the Allies. Was that the world peace Willkie dreamed of? Rudolf kicked the book out of his way and it fell onto the ground.

Rudolf sighed; imagining world peace seemed impossible. He knew his imprisonment in an American prisoner of war camp, surrounded by barbed wire and guard towers, affected his attitude. Disconsolate, he laid his head down on the pillow and flicked away the stub of his cigarette, wishing sourly that it would land in dry brush and catch fire. At least that would cause some excitement, something to change the dull monotony of days passing ever so slowly with so little news about what was happening at home.

❖

There was silence throughout the room as the film ended. When the lights came on, Rudolf and Fritz lingered while the rest of the men got up to leave.

"It is only a story," Fritz said with determination. "Surely it cannot be true."

Rudolf raised his eyebrows. "A German wrote it."

"Does that make it true?" Fritz asked.

"No, but it cannot all be a figment of her imagination. I want to believe that it is nothing but lies, but I have to admit it sent chills up my spine," Rudolf said, finally getting up from his chair and heading toward the door to the compound.

The American film, *The Seventh Cross*, based upon a novel written in 1939 by German writer Anna Seghers, gave a first-hand account of German life in 1936; three years after the Nazis took control of the country. As the film unfolds, seven German men escape from a concentration camp; after their escape, the camp commander erects seven crosses where he vows each man will hang when recaptured.

Only one escapee survives—George Heisler, a Communist, a man worn by oppression and fear of his fellow countrymen. But through luck and fortitude, he finds a web of ordinary Germans who refuse to bow to the Gestapo: the woman tailor who supplies him with clothes and money, the Jew doctor who mends the escapee's torn hand and does not report the incident, a former friend who puts his wife and children in jeopardy to help him, and a lonely barmaid who hides him from the Gestapo. Heisler calls them, "The people who healed me."

Heisler escapes to Denmark, but the crux of the film is also about the change in the lives of those who realize they can individually fight Nazi terror.

Rudolf kept thinking about the film as he crossed the dirt yard and walked toward his barrack. The main character seemed so downtrodden, and so afraid. Rudolf shuddered. He empathized with the character of Heisler, portrayed by American actor Spencer Tracy.

Although Rudolf's fellow countrymen never personally betrayed him, Rudolf saw Helmut's murder as a betrayal. The lack of trust Rudolf carried now was like the burden of a pack animal forever crushed under the weight of treachery. He felt its load daily—in his barrack, the mess hall, the cotton fields, never sure who to confide in among his fellow Germans. Did he make a mistake to say what he did about the film to Fritz? Surely not, he hoped with all his heart. Rudolf's only solace was to remember George Heisler's words: "There is a God-given decency that will come out in them if given half a chance. That is the faith we must cling to…the only thing that makes our life worth living."

Rudolf sighed as he entered his barrack and sat heavily on his cot. *The Seventh Cross* reminded him that he had but one trusted friend— Bob Feller. He had another at one time, Lothar Volkmann, Rudolf remembered ruefully, but that friendship had ended badly. His hand moved across his forehead as if to wipe away the memory. What *was* he thinking? Looking back, Lothar seemed to be the only one who would not swallow the Nazi line; he was true to himself. In fact, Lothar would be the kind of person who would help a person like George Heisler.

The underlying question hit Rudolf as he unbuttoned his shirt. Would he, Rudolf Meier, have aided George Heisler? His youthful passion for Adolf Hitler and Nazi Germany was akin to being in love, Rudolf realized. He was so sure of everything then. Now he was unsure about everything, even how he would have acted had he known some- one like Heisler.

Rudolf laid his arms across his knees, looking down at the floor. Alone in the barrack, Rudolf's inner tension wrapped itself around him like a straightjacket, closing him down emotionally. When men he worked or played with spoke optimistically of going home, he would stare vacantly ahead. What was there to go home to except an aging grandfather? Who would hold him in the night and keep the horrid memory of Helmut's blood from splashing on him?

Suddenly, he realized he had not received a letter from his grand-father in the last mail delivery. Rudolf reached up with his left arm to rub his right shoulder at the base of his neck; the muscle was stiff with anxiety. In the years since Rudolf's capture, his grandfather had never failed to send a weekly letter—he could count on it like clock-work. Rudolf unconsciously rubbed his neck muscle harder. Was *Opa* alive and if so, where was he living? Even though Bremen had been severely bombed, his grandfather never said anything about the damage. He wrote instead about old neighbors and his trips to the AG Weser shipyard to have coffee with men he had known for years. There was no work to be done at the yard except the clearing of rubble, and Hermann was too old for that. The letters always ended with *Opa's* continuing hope that Rudolf would be home soon.

A thought jolted Rudolf. What would he do once he was home? How would he make a living? He never considered this until now because his focus was always to get back to Germany. Perhaps he could go back to school and get the education his grandparents expected of him before he joined the *Kriegsmarine*. But now it occurred to him that such schools probably did not exist because Germany no longer existed, at least not the Germany he remembered.

Rudolf lay down on his cot. His worry about his grandfather aggravated his nervousness and he reached for a cigarette, but stopped himself; his stash was low. He fell into a fitful doze and woke with a start, his body covered in sweat. Disgusted with himself, he got up, grabbed a towel and headed to the bathhouse for a shower.

August became September, then October, and finally November, and still no word from the War Department about repatriation. Then, suddenly, *Der Ruf* announced that all German POWs would be returned to Europe by March 31, 1946.

"Well, at least they have told us something," Rudolf said to Fritz as they walked toward the soccer field on a nasty November day, the wind howling from the north, the dust obscuring the rock formations.

"Yes," Fritz said, his head bowed against the wind. "It is something. Not much, mind you, but something."

The day before Thanksgiving, Rudolf prepared for the celebration with the Feller family. He washed his clothes, polished his shoes, and then spent what little money he had on a haircut. Sitting in the barber's chair, Rudolf thought about the conversation with Bob when he was invited for Thanksgiving. Bob had punched Rudolf in the arm and said, "The girl I'm dating has an equally good-looking sister, Rudi! They're both coming over."

Rudolf smiled sheepishly. It seemed impossible to him that he might be near a woman again, let alone an American. "I am not sure I would know what to say to her," he said.

Bob made a funny face. "It hasn't been that long since you've spoken to a female!"

Rudolf looked down at his feet. "Except for my nurse when I was in the hospital and your mother, I have not spoken to a woman in a long time."

Bob slapped Rudolf on the shoulder. "Believe me, with your handsome mug—face, I mean—I don't think you'll have any trouble!"

The two young men laughed and Rudolf said, "Then it will be a feast for the eyes as well as the stomach."

Looking forward to the wonderful day ahead, Rudolf headed to the canteen to buy the latest issue of the camp newspaper, *Der Ruf*. When he got there, he saw men standing outside the building talking excitedly, waving *Der Ruf*. One of them shouted, "The goddamn Americans! Isn't it enough that we have been slaves for them? Now they are sending us to the French!"

"What?" an astonished Rudolf asked no one in particular.

"See for yourself! *Der Ruf* has the story," the man said in an angry voice.

Rudolf's hand shook a little as he gave his five cents to the POW at the cash register. It was Wolfgang Gertzner who had served in the control room of U-893.

Wolfgang handed the paper to Rudolf with a shrug. "At least we might see pretty French girls."

Rudolf took the newspaper outside and opened it to a screaming headline: "War Department to Send POWs to France." Rudolf read the article with his heart thumping hard against his chest. To his horror, he read the War Department had signed an agreement to ship German prisoners held in America to France to form labor battalions. More than 375,000 German POWs—men moved from American holding pens throughout Europe—were already clearing rubble and mining coal for the upcoming winter.

A prisoner standing close to Rudolf took the newspaper and ripped it up, his fury etched across his face. "It seems to me there is little difference between Germany's Nazis and America's democracy. Either way we have been sold as slaves."

Rudolf's eyes blurred. He could not focus on the page, so he moved next to the canteen building and leaned against the wall, trying to steady himself. He held the newspaper close to his face, as if deeply absorbed; something his grandfather did when he got into a heated discussion with *Oma*, only with Rudolf it was a way to hide his ever-present anxiety. The loud conversation between the men went on for some time, but Rudolf heard little of it; the sting of American betrayal coursing through his body as if he had wandered into a nest of hornets.

The next morning, Rudolf prepared himself for Thanksgiving with little enthusiasm. When Bob picked him up, his disconsolate face prompted the American to ask what was wrong.

"I am not going home to Germany, Bob. Perhaps you have heard. We are all being sent to France."

"Yes, I know, Rudi," Bob said.

"It's not fair!" Rudolf nearly shouted. "France declared war on Germany, after all, and we took up their challenge, beating them at their own game. Besides, we did not destroy France. It was you Americans who bombed it, trying to destroy us!"

Bob did not respond to Rudolf's remark. Instead he said, "I'm truly sorry, Rudi."

Rudolf looked over at Bob. He had known him now for more than a year. He was a man now, no longer a youngster who asked probing questions. Bob's dark hair, slick with Brylcreem, had a deep shine; he wore tan pleated slacks, a white long-sleeved shirt and a hand-painted tie. Rudolf realized how shabby he looked. His dress *Kriegsmarine* uniform was at the bottom of the sea along with U-893, so he wore the denims issued to him as a POW—both shirt and pants plainly marked with the ever-present PW. His one prized possession, the gray leather U-boat jacket, lay across his lap.

"Perhaps I should not have come with you today," Rudolf said suddenly.

Bob opened his mouth to say something, but instead pulled over to the side of the road and turned off the truck's motor. "Rudi," Bob said, "when Mom and I heard the news, we couldn't believe our ears. We felt that we had to do something, so my mom made a few phone calls...to important people we know in Washington, D. C. She also called Major Kennedy."

Rudolf shook his head as if wax filled his ears and he could not hear properly. "Your mother... she called Major Kennedy? What for?" he asked, suddenly afraid of what these American Jews might have said to make trouble for him.

Bob brushed away Rudolf's misgivings with a wave of his hand, "Well, because we feel you could be better used by the American military in Germany! You speak such good English, Rudi! What a crime it would be to send you to France to work in a labor battalion. We know you have been responsible for helping the men understand what we needed them to do on the farm. The guards certainly couldn't do it, but you did! You're the one who helped us when my dad died—finding me, taking the men back to camp. Gosh, sakes! You could have driven off to Mexico, but you didn't!"

"I thought about it," Rudolf admitted, his voice sullen.

"Of course you did! But you didn't *act* on it, and that's what matters. The major suggested my mom and I write a letter to the camp commander, recommending you as an interpreter. He also said he would commend you to the commander."

Rudolf sat very still, mortified that Bob might have discerned his quick prejudiced reaction, but a look at the American's face revealed nothing of the kind. Once again, the Fellers' kindness overwhelmed him; their recommendation might come to nothing, but hope permeated his heart.

Suddenly, the future seemed brighter, and the wonderful Thanksgiving feast was waiting for him. Maybe, just maybe, there would also be a smile or two from that pretty girl.

Chapter 26

December 1945
Arizona

More than a week passed before Major Kennedy summoned Rudolf who was relaxing in the library after eating in the mess hall, reading the *Arizona Republic*. One of the guards came into the room and tapped him on the shoulder; it was the same gum-popping corporal who stood watch at the Phoenix synagogue while he and Helmut attended Vern Feller's funeral.

"Hey, Meier, Major Kennedy wants to see you."

Rudolf, surprised, looked up at the corporal. He put the paper back in its rack, and followed the guard to the administration building.

When they arrived outside the major's office, the corporal tapped on the door, opened it a crack and announced Rudolf. Rudolf stepped inside and smartly saluted the major who was sitting at his desk, smoking.

"Come in, Meier, come in. Please, sit down."

Rudolf sat on a hard metal chair in front of the major's desk with an expectant look on his face.

The major smiled. "I'm assuming Bob Feller spoke to you about the recommendation from him and his mother."

"Yes, sir."

The major paused while he pulled a pack of Lucky Strikes from his desk drawer and offered one to Rudolf.

"Thank you, sir," Rudolf said, taking one. The major flipped open his black Army-issued Zippo lighter, and the German bent over the desk to reach the flame.

A long silence developed as the major eyed Rudolf through the pall of smoke. "OK, Meier, I'm sure you're sitting on pins and needles."

"Sir?"

"Oh, sorry. That's an American expression for someone who is anxiously awaiting news."

Rudolf let out a deep breath. Knowing how things moved in the military—even the German military, Rudolf assumed he would not hear anything for weeks.

"Yes, sir, although I do not know what I am waiting for exactly."

"Well, this is how it is, Meier. The Fellers believe you would be a good interpreter for the American Military Government now operating in Germany."

Rudolf looked down at his lap. "I am not really sure why they have said that."

The major deeply inhaled the cigarette smoke, and then eyed it with disgust as if its taste suddenly turned foul. He impatiently stubbed it out.

"Well, I have a pretty good idea. The most important reason, to my way of thinking at least, is that you can be trusted. You showed that when you did not attempt to escape with the Feller truck."

"I could do no less. They have been good to me, sir."

"Well, Meier…the commander and I have discussed your record at length, and we believe you deserve a break."

Rudolf's head popped up. "Sir?"

"There's a new program, the Eustis Project that will begin in a few weeks," Major Kennedy said. "It's a six-day reeducation program for select German prisoners of war, about 20,000 men out of the 370,000 held in America. You'll need to fill out a questionnaire, Meier. This *Fragebogen* is quite lengthy. If you understand the history and more liberal political traditions of Germany before the Nazis took over, then the War Department will admit you into the program and transfer you to Ft. Eustis, Virginia where you will learn the meaning of democracy and the values of America.

"When you graduate, you will be shipped directly to Germany and work for the American Military Government. I do not know where your station will be in Germany or what kind of work you will be doing. Still, you will be home, after all and not picking up rubble."

Rudolf took a huge gulp of air and his head buzzed. A feeling of buoyancy took hold of his heart. "This is good news, Major Kennedy! I am so grateful—I must admit, I...I was worried about my Hitler Youth record."

"Yes, well, we realize almost all German youngsters were forced into the Hitler Youth. That doesn't mean you were a member of the Nazi party. You had no choice, for God's sake!"

Rudolf did not change expression even though he felt his stomach flip. If given the chance, he would have joyously joined the Nazi party, but the German Navy prevented that error in judgment. He stammered, "I am also concerned about—you know—about Helmut Kessler's death."

The major smiled. "We are still investigating his murder, Meier, but we believe you had nothing to do with it."

The young German sat quietly, trying to comprehend what just happened to him. Then he asked, "What do I do now, major?"

"I suggest you go to the library and study as much as you can about your country's history," the major replied. "There are plenty of books there on that subject. You're a smart fellow, Meier. I know you will be able to answer the *Fragebogen* correctly. Then sit tight. You'll have your orders fairly soon after that."

Rudolf reached over and stubbed his cigarette out in the ashtray on the major's desk. He stood up, saluted, and asked, "May I be excused, major?"

"You are excused Meier."

As Rudolf turned to go, the major said, "Meier, I hope you realize this would not have happened without pressure from Mrs. Feller and her son. Perhaps you do not know this, but the Fellers are one of the most influential families in Phoenix. Their personal contacts go far beyond this measly camp."

Rudolf stopped and turned. "No, sir, I did not realize that. Thank you for telling me."

The major got up then, walked around his desk and reached out his hand to Rudolf. A look of disbelief overtook Rudolf's face, and then he gripped the major's hand.

"Thank you, sir. I appreciate everything you have done," Rudolf said.

"Good luck, Meier. I hope you keep in mind that you can make Bremen—and Germany, for that matter—a beautiful place once again. You, and other young Germans like you, can do that, I know you can. *Auf Wiedersehen!*"

Not many men at Camp Papago Park passed the *Fragebogen*. It was a thorny questionnaire for the prisoners, men who knew less than nothing about their country's history except for what they had learned from their Nazi-indoctrinated teachers. Few could describe the ideas of the German philosopher Fichte, name the first president of the Weimar Republic, or identify one of the characters of Mozart's *Magic Flute.* Despite his intense study, the questionnaire gave Rudolf a headache as he endlessly searched his brain for answers. But Rudolf passed, much to his relief.

After the *Fragebogen,* a terse interrogator interviewed him for over an hour, asking questions about his family and his service in the *Kriegsmarine.* Rudolf felt like a child again under the scrutiny of his Hitler Youth leader; it was demeaning, and he admitted to himself the American officer was as hard-headed as a German.

With a bathroom break and a cup of coffee, Rudolf was almost through the arduous process. Then the Americans placed him in a small, cheerless room that reminded him of the cramped radio room on U-893. Another interrogator placed sensors on his body and asked endless question about his years in the Hitler Youth. All he wanted was to go home to Germany, so he lied and he failed.

Rudolf's special status with the Fellers allowed him a second chance, and the major took him in hand, personally coaching him. The second time around, Rudolf answered with care—yes, he once believed in Hitler, National Socialism, and that Germans were racially superior; yes, he did think newsreels of the German concentration camps were American propaganda. Finally, after sleepless nights and encouraging conversations with Bob while picking the ripened cotton, his orders to attend the reeducation classes came through.

Fritz was the only one he told in camp. While the two shipmates watched a heated soccer match, Fritz gave Rudolf a thump on the back when he heard the news. "You made it!" Fritz said. "I knew you would, you *Schwein!* Long ago, when we studied together, I believed you were destined for something better. Unfortunately, I failed the *Fragebogen* miserably."

Rudolf put his head down so Fritz could not see the emotion that came to him so easily these days. "Yes, we have been together a long time," he said as he reached into his pocket and pulled out a piece of paper. "This is my grandfather's address. If you get the chance, write me there. I will get it somehow."

Fritz took the paper and tucked it away. "Rudi, be careful. We both know the Nazis run this camp. Whoever killed Helmut is still here."

Rudolf's voice was low against the piercing yells of men rooting for their favorite team. "Yes, I will not be sleeping much until I go."

Why had he chosen not to trust Fritz after Helmut's brutal murder, Rudolf wondered, remembering Fritz had expressed his anti-Nazism when they both had attended marine intelligence school. But Rudolf knew distrust among the men was a fact of life. Prisoner of war camps were like war zones of their own; they changed everything, even one's faith in a friend.

As the day drew closer to his transfer, the War Department issued Rudolf a barracks bag made of cotton with a drawstring, several woolen blankets, a first aid kit, and eating utensils. Nothing else was to be taken back to Germany—not radios, cameras, field glasses, tools, cigarette lighters or foot lockers.

Rudolf packed sparingly—clothes, letters from his grandparents, and also the publication *Kleiner Führer durch Amerika*, a "Brief Guide through America." It was a colorful booklet issued by the War Department as a learning tool to describe America's geography, natural resources and political institutions. Rudolf coveted the propaganda booklet as a souvenir to take home.

On his last day of work, as the sun took its time to lighten the morning sky, he climbed into the old farm truck with Bob. Rudolf felt a mixture of emotions: happiness and sadness bound tightly together like the all-too-familiar tightly-bound cotton boll and cotton seed. Bob reached out and put his hand on Rudolf's shoulder. "Mom and I are glad for you. You will learn about America and our democracy. More important, you are going home."

"But it will never be like what I have learned from you," Rudolf said with remorse.

Bob cocked his head to the side, quietly taking in the compliment. Then he laughed. "Just imagine, Rudi, your last day picking cotton. I wish it were so for me!"

Rudolf looked out the window, trying to compose himself, focusing on the winter landscape. He bit his lower lip. The scene before him changed little even in the dead of winter, only the mesquites were bare of leaves, their black branches standing resolutely against the cold sky. This desert panorama was so different from Germany and his dislike for it still lingered, but Rudolf knew he would carry the memory of this place with him for the rest of his life. He glanced then at his friend.

"Bob, you know and I know that this farm is merely a stepping stone for you. You will achieve all your dreams. I count on it," Rudolf said.

The Fellers' cotton crop had fulfilled Bob's prediction; it was bountiful. Many men worked to pick it, and once again, guards travelled to the Feller farm with the prisoners, watching them carefully as they worked. Escaping inside America was preferable to the prisoners now; no one wanted to clear rubble in France.

As the long day came to a close and Rudolf weighed his sack with more than a hundred pounds of cotton, Ruth Feller stood next to the scale. She leaned over, kissed Rudolf faintly on the cheek, and handed him a thick package of oatmeal raisin cookies.

"A little something for the train ride to Virginia."

"Thank you," he said.

The vein in the cord of Rudolf's neck stood out, and he was unable to look Ruth Feller in the face. She reached out and touched him, a stroke of affection. He glanced down at her then, remembering the first time he saw her. Through the long months, despite great difficulties, she always showed kindness. Now, he knew how much he would miss her, so he bent down and returned the kiss. She smiled softly and then moved away, her eyes glittering with tears.

When the truck finally delivered Rudolf at the end of the day to Camp Papago Park, the other men jumped out quickly and moved off to their barracks, leaving Rudolf and Bob alone. They climbed from the truck and walked toward one another.

"I am not sure what to say," Rudolf lamented.

Bob had his hands jammed in his pockets like the day his father died. "I will miss you terribly, Rudi."

"Yes," was all Rudolf could say. His emotions forced him to remain silent.

"We will meet again, I know it," Bob said. Rudolf only nodded. They clasped hands fiercely, and Bob climbed into the truck, backed it up quickly and was gone. Rudolf stood watching him until he could no longer make out the taillights in the winter dusk.

The $50 check crackled stiffly in Rudolf's hands. It was a government-issued check from the canteen credits he had earned while working in the fields of Arizona. An American millionaire could not have felt richer than Rudolf at that moment. He folded it carefully and placed it in the bottom of his shoe for safekeeping.

As he settled into his assigned seat on the sleek train, his heart raced in time to the diesel engines warming up for their run across the American southwest, through New Mexico and Colorado, and then northeast to Chicago. The railroad car smelled new, like his future, and as he waited for the train to pull out of the train station in Tempe, he chatted amiably with men he knew from the camp who were also on their way to Fort Eustis. Suddenly, a disturbance at the front of the railroad car caught Rudolf's attention; he heard his name called out, above the noise of the engines. Someone pointed to him and Rudolf recognized the guard Tom McKay sprinting down the aisle. Rudolf's breath caught in his throat.

Mein Gott! Why him, why now, Rudolf thought, just when Germany was within his grasp.

McKay rushed to Rudolf and reached into his pocket, pulling out a letter. "Meier! Goddamn! I'm so glad I made it in time. Here!"

Rudolf's hand shook as he took the letter, looking up at McKay's hang-dog face. It was from his grandfather!

"It just came, and I knew you would want it," the guard said proudly.

Rudolf sat speechless, unable to respond. McKay bent down to Rudolf and hoarsely whispered, "Major Kennedy also wanted me to tell you that he arrested Horst Hollmann last night. He's charged with the murder of Helmut Kessler. I doubt if that Nazi will ever see the Fatherland again!"

McKay slapped Rudolf on the back and held out his hand, which Rudolf shook with all the strength he could muster, trying to convey his appreciation. "Hey, good luck, Meier!" McKay shouted, and he ran to get off the slowly moving train.

Rudolf let out a deep sigh and closed his eyes. After he had watched Bob Feller drive away last night, he had walked to the camp graveyard and in the dying light, he found Helmut's gravestone; a lone jackrabbit startled him as it hopped across the tumbleweed-strewn graveyard. The coyotes began their nightly songfest in the distance, and he shivered slightly—their sound made him remember that terrible night

Helmut died. He had come before to this place, but now he wanted to say goodbye, so he bent down on one knee and gently touched the marker.

"If it were me, Helmut, I would want to be home in Germany, but I know you loved America, so perhaps this is where you should be," he said softly.

Now, as the train moved out of the station blowing its whistle, Rudolf remembered his heated conversation with Helmut about America. Helmut was right after all: the vaunted strength of the Third Reich was a brutal nightmare, not a vision.

Chapter 27

January 1946
Ft. Eustis, Virginia
Camp Shanks, New York
Statue of Liberty

A thousand men moved quietly into their seats for the opening lecture of the six-day reeducation seminar, Rudolf among them. For the first time in many months, freedom was within his grasp; he could physically see it at Fort Eustis—only three strands of barbed wire stood between him and the Virginia countryside. There were no guards, no dogs, no towers, and no floodlights at night. He could smell freedom, too—the coolness and greenery of Virginia filled his nostrils and replenished his soul, bone dry from the parched Sonoran Desert.

Colonel Alpheus Smith, a big man, strode to the lectern. He looked at the sea of men and smiled. Then he said in a calm but sure voice, "American democracy is not perfect."

Rudolf sucked in his breath, shocked that the commander in charge of the Fort Eustis Special Projects Center would admit such a thing; no high-ranking officer of the Third Reich would ever say that about Hitler's National Socialism. But then, Rudolf remembered with unease that freedom of expression was *verboten* in Nazi Germany.

Nervous laughter filled the room as the colonel waited for his words to sink into the minds of the prisoners of war. "The trouble," he continued, "isn't with democracy. It is with some Americans. Even though there are a few bad Americans and a few bad things in America, they haven't spoiled democracy and they can't spoil it. Democracy is the best thing in human society."

Rudolf's attention wandered for a second as he looked around at the other men in the room with their shapeless blue-black uniforms. Only the stenciled 'PW' appeared on the denim sleeves and legs. If there were German officers here, he did not know it for the denim gave no hint of name or rank. Rudolf realized the Americans had successfully achieved equality with anonymous clothing, not an easy task among Germans so aware of social and military status.

There was no deliberate philosophy that carried the day in America, the colonel said, other than the ability to solve a conflict by finding the middle ground. "Through the use of compromise, differences of opinion are built into real advantage, since they enable men to examine a problem from many sides and to understand all alternatives involved in making a choice."

At the conclusion of the lecture, Rudolf moved to a table at the end of the room where he grabbed a cup of coffee and a donut slathered with sugary glaze. Standing beside him was a man that Rudolf guessed to be in his forties—his hair, gray at the temples, gave him an air of distinction. The older man nodded as he picked up a gooey donut with a fork and placed it on a plate. He said to no one in particular, "I do not suppose this could be considered strudel."

"No, I don't think so," Rudolf answered with a chuckle.

"I have dreamed of it, you know—real German strudel," the man said.

"My favorite was the kind with apples," Rudolf replied.

"Ah, *Apfelstrudel!* My heart, and my stomach cries for it!"

Rudolf smiled. "In the apartment where my family lived, there was a family of bakers," he said, suddenly remembering Lothar's family. "People would come for miles just to taste their apple strudel."

The older man nodded. "And where was that?"

"Bremen."

"Bremen! I was there once, with my bride. I remember so well, the statue of Roland and that magnificent plaza where the old town hall stood. It was a wonderful city. But of course, I would think it perfectly grand because I was there on my honeymoon with my Anna."

"Where are you from?" Rudolf asked politely.

"Rehna."

Rudolf's eyebrows furrowed as he tried to remember his geography of Germany.

"It is about 40 kilometers southeast of Lübeck," the older man said as a way to refresh Rudolf's memory. "We were but a small farming community."

Rudolf looked surprised. "You speak as if it is no longer there!"

The man looked down at his empty coffee cup and then dropped the remainder of the sugary donut into it, as if its taste had turned bitter. He placed the dishes on the table with a clatter. "Who knows what is left of Reyna since the Russians took it. I have not heard from my Anna in a while," he said, his voice low.

Rudolf immediately jammed his hand in his pocket, his fingers searching frantically for his grandfather's letter brought to the train by the American guard; he wanted to make sure it was there, tucked safe against him. The feel of the paper reassured him *Opa* was still alive, and he remembered how buoyant he felt when he read the letter as the train pulled away from Camp Papago Park. He looked quickly at the older man, and seeing his distress, he put down his cup and plate. "I am Rudi," he said, extending his hand.

Surprised, the other man cupped Rudolf's hand in both of his. "Rudi, I am Gerhardt."

They stood together for a moment, each man warming to the other through their mutual worry, and then they heard the call to gather for the open discussion sessions.

"I am in group ten," Gerhardt said, pulling a piece of paper out of his pocket.

"Good. I am in the same group," Rudolf said.

When they found their assigned area, Rudolf and Gerhardt sat next to one another. They were part of a unit of fifty men gathered around their leader, Frederick, who was also a prisoner of war. Rudolf judged Frederick to be in his late twenties. He noticed a deep scar ran from the corner of Frederick's mouth to the edge of his jawbone and Rudolf wondered if it was a battle wound.

Frederick introduced himself to the group while lighting a pipe. "Just so you know—I was scrupulously cleared to work for the Special Projects Division because of my strong belief that National Socialism ruined our beloved Fatherland." After saying that, he eyed the men carefully through the puff of smoke and then crossed his lanky legs.

"So, to begin…Colonel Smith made some significant points in his lecture about 'The Democratic Way of Life,' so let's get down to what you think," Frederick said. "I want you to voice an opinion, and I know this may be difficult. As Germans, we have been trained to listen to our leaders and not give our own point of view, but that is all changed now."

A collective murmur rose from the group. Gerhardt was the first to raise his hand and Frederick acknowledged him with a nod.

"The colonel admitted democracy is not perfect. He said the trouble is not with democracy but with some Americans. Cannot that also be true of National Socialism—that the problems were with some Germans? National Socialism worked in Germany until we gave the Nazis too much power. I think it can work with restraints."

Another man piped in, "But the colonel was not speaking about *how* democracy works, you know, the day-to-day running of the government. He was saying there may be bad Americans and bad things that happen, like how they treated their Indians—but that democracy itself—the idea of it cannot be spoiled. Unfortunately, National Socialism is rotten to the core. We cannot resurrect it—and I doubt if the Allies would let us resurrect it!"

"I agree," said a slim man who wore round glasses that made him appear owlish. "Democracy is about freedom of the individual. National Socialism was always about what the government would do for us—about social programs to put food on our table or provide jobs. From food and work, then the Nazis moved into every area of our lives, controlling what we did and how we thought. The problem as I see it is that we Germans do not know how to think for ourselves; we have always been told *what* to think. If that is the case, then how can democracy succeed in the new Germany?"

"Say, how about this," another man said as he took a long puff on his cigarette. "Why don't the Americans, Russians, British, and French pull all their troops out of Germany and let us Germans figure out our own destiny? Let us 'slug it out' with one another, as the Americans put it. If it comes to civil war, then…so what? We should have done that long ago."

Rudolf raised his hand and then rubbed the deep cleft in his chin as he spoke. "But that is what happened before the Nazis took over! There were fights in the streets throughout Germany every night between Communists and the Nazis. When Hitler came into power, the German people breathed a sigh of relief because the structure of society was maintained; there was no more lawlessness. We Germans respect order, and look what we got for it."

A rueful laugh escaped from Frederick. "Say, here's something to think about! How is it American democracy runs without strict, unbending principles? I find that the most interesting aspect about this country. It seems that Americans have the ability to talk to one another, to work things out."

Another man said, "I think the American political system is an attitude of mind. There is an acceptance of compromise that we do not have in Germany."

"And in that spirit," Frederick said as he looked at his watch, "let's compromise and go to lunch!" The sound of laughter filled the air as the group stood up, their chairs scraping collectively against the floor. Rudolf smiled. It was good to hear merriment again.

The afternoon's lecture covered the Constitution of the United States, with the speaker emphasizing how the freedoms named in the document created a land of opportunity. There was another round-table discussion, and then the men watched the film, *Abe Lincoln in Illinois*. When it ended, Gerhardt turned to Rudolf. "If we had such a man in Germany, we would not be here now."

A faint smile came to Rudolf's lips. "We are an ill-fated lot, we Germans. We lost the Great War; we starved in between the wars; and we blamed it all on the Jews, like the people in the South blamed everything on the Negroes. I wonder—if we had an Abraham Lincoln, instead of Adolf Hitler, do you think he would have emancipated the Jews?"

"I cannot even fathom it," Gerhardt replied, scratching the end of his nose.

The days passed quickly with lectures, discussions, and films. In the evenings, after dinner, the men attended Protestant or Catholic services, and then they freely gathered again despite the late hour. The fertile ground of the Virginia countryside, where the seeds of democracy had been sown so many decades before, seemed to pull the prisoners of war together into small clusters, on the steps of the barracks, near the closest coffee pot, or in the corner of a deserted classroom. They talked about the idea of democracy into early morning, rolling it around on their tongues and storing bits and pieces of its principles into the recesses of their minds.

Rudolf could hardly wait for each day. Perhaps it was the engaging conversations between men who had previously kept their mouths shut and their boots highly polished. It was as if the blackboard of his soul, so filled with the scribbling of National Socialism, was being erased, albeit slowly, and rewritten with the inscriptions of American democracy.

One morning, he arose particularly early, his mind feverish as it worked over various American ideals and democratic concepts. He dressed quickly, walked to the mess and grabbed a cup of coffee, happy to see there was no one around to interrupt his thoughts.

Holding the cup in both hands for warmth, Rudolf stepped out a side doorway in time to view the sun rise through a fine mist hovering over a dense green pasture. The field, just beyond the fence surrounding the military compound, was dotted with sleek, well-fed horses. He walked to the fence line, awestruck by the horses' majesty and realized they were thoroughbreds, not the ordinary stocky work horses that graced the German countryside.

Suddenly, out of nowhere, he saw a figure moving across the field, carrying a bridle and saddle. A lustrous black horse stopped grazing as the person walked up to it, and willingly accepted a treat; then it surrendered to the bridle and saddle. In no time, the rider expertly climbed onto the animal and began leading it through its paces, slowly circling the field, moving parallel to the fence line of the military installation.

Rudolf sipped his coffee unhurriedly, fascinated as the horse and rider came closer. He realized it was a young woman. She wore an outfit that he had only seen in magazines—glossy black leather boots, tight tan breeches, a snug-fitting dark jacket with a black velvet collar, and a small-brimmed hat covered her brunette hair that was pulled into a bun. Without warning, she reached back to the horse's rump, gave it a sharp slap with her riding crop, and the animal broke into a gallop.

The girl dashed past Rudolf, and then she expertly turned the horse away from the fence toward the pasture. To Rudolf's surprise, she quickly circled back and halted the horse directly in front of him.

"Hello," she said, reaching down to pat the horse. "You've been watching me."

Rudolf heart stood still. He guessed her to be about fifteen years old, her young womanhood just coming into flower, her face glistening creamy white with nothing accentuating her luminescence except a touch of pink on her full lips. She looked at him with startling lavender eyes. That she would even stop to talk to him—a German prisoner of war—was unnerving. He opened his mouth to answer her, but found he could only stammer, "Yes...yes. I have."

She smiled brightly. "Isn't Jack beautiful?" she asked, leaning deeper over the horse's fine neck, staring straight at Rudolf, and then she laughed, a full-throated sound that sent a thrill through his entire body. "Oh, Jack's not his full name, because he's a thoroughbred, but I call him that—you know like the children's nursery rhyme—Jack be nimble, Jack be quick, Jack jump over the candlestick!"

Rudolf's eyes scanned the majestic animal, but his vision quickly returned to the girl. He nodded, mute with the girl's splendor.

"Are you tongue-tied?" she asked, cocking her head, her eyes boring into his.

"Tongue-tied? I do not know that word," he said, his face flushing.

"Oh, yes, I forgot...you're one of those Germans learning about American democracy, aren't you? Well, anyway, 'tongue-tied' in American means you're too excited to speak."

She was more beautiful than any female Rudolf had ever seen. Trying to keep her from moving away, wanting to bask a few moments longer in her radiance, he asked, "How do you know about us?"

"Oh, we're a pretty small community. Word gets around."

Stupefied, Rudolf repeated her words. "Word gets around? What do you mean?"

"Well, I know that you and the other men are here because you're the last hope of Germany. It would not be right if we sent you home without explaining who we Americans are and what we believe in."

Rudolf's body moved unexpectedly; he had expected a frivolous answer from one so beautiful but instead he had received a swift blow to his German ego. Momentarily stunned, he gathered his thoughts and then asked, "How do you know this?"

She smiled, and the light of her splendor turned his insides to jelly. "My father is the commander of Ft. Eustis," she answered. The girl patted the horse again, and made a small clicking sound in the corner of her sensuous mouth, pulling on the reins and turning the horse away from him. After a moment she looked back and waved; Rudolf could not help but return her farewell, but there was a strange, gnawing feeling in his gut: He never before this moment regarded himself as the last hope of Germany.

On the fifth day of the "six-day bicycle race"—a term the men used for the fast-moving reeducation program—the lectures covered the failure of Germany's Weimar Republic. The main speaker, much to Rudolf's surprise, was a high-ranking German officer. He was tall, with the bearing of a Prussian aristocrat, and he had fought in the North Africa Campaign with German Field Marshal Erwin Rommel.

Rudolf leaned forward, anxious to hear this man who was a member of the vaunted *Afrika Korps*. What made him even more interesting was that he was also a prisoner of war, just like the men in the audience.

"Germans are not good at compromise, we know that," the officer said. "The failure of the Weimar Republic is a prime example of that lack of ability. We can lay the blame on the aristocrats, on the intellectuals, or on the Jews; but let us be truthful here. The German people, ordinary people, showed the world that they were incapable of surmounting the difficulties of forming a democratic state and society."

There was dead silence in the lecture hall, but the speaker looked directly at the thousand men and did not flinch. "We Germans have given the excuse that we were 'little men,' powerless to stand up to the Nazi takeover of the German Republic. But we let it happen; we wanted order. Once Hitler was in power, we saw factories switch from farm equipment to tanks, shipyards that no longer made luxury liners, but instead produced U-boats. We saw—and heard—ordinary citizens notify the Gestapo if anyone acted differently. They pointed their fingers at other Germans who stood up for a Jew or did not have a picture of *Der Führer* hanging in the living room."

Rudolf looked down at his hands, suddenly uncomfortable as the memory of his grandmother flooded over him. He did not want to listen to this, but all he could do was clench his hands in frustration.

The German officer pressed on: "Germans may claim powerlessness or ignorance as to why the Nazis did what they did, but deep within us, each one of us knows otherwise. There is no other way to move forward from our awful past, and we must acknowledge that the tragedy of the Third Reich was our own fault."

When the officer finished, he gathered his notes and walked away from the lectern, but the men in the audience sat hushed and they did not move from their seats. They had read the accusations against Germans in American newspapers and had seen the devastating newsreels of captured concentration camps, but no German had spoken in such a direct manner, particularly a German officer.

Gerhardt looked at Rudolf. "I knew we could not get through this without someone laying guilt on us, and to think it is one of *us*! Surely, he must be a collaborator."

"I did not expect it," Rudolf said, his face red with anger. "I thought we were here to learn about democracy. We all know what happened. Why must we be continually reminded of it?"

Another man, sitting beside Gerhardt leaned over and said, "Perhaps we are continually reminded of it because we keep sticking our finger into the fire. When will we learn?"

Rudolf shot the man a look of distain; the stranger got up, and moved into the crowd that began to disburse. Finally, Rudolf stood, his anger cooled somewhat and looked around. He saw other men whose facial expressions reflected his own, but he realized there was no recourse for either himself or for the other shaken Germans except to grab a cup of coffee and head for the discussion group.

When Rudolf got to the table, Frederick was already there, waiting. In an attempt to get the sour-faced men to speak, Frederick said, "That officer only reminded us what the world is saying. We might as well speak of it ourselves or it will fester and Germany will never recover."

Rudolf's arm blasted up with a vengeance, his distress sitting plainly on his face. "Most of us here were children when the Nazis came to power! We only followed orders! We were not responsible!"

Frederick coolly packed his pipe with tobacco, but his voice betrayed the warmth of his feeling. "Maybe so…but is that not exactly the point? I carry the memory of my father remaining silent when the Gestapo came for the Jew family that lived in the basement below us. They had done nothing wrong, but I am willing to guess they died in Auschwitz. And you—did you not witness such a thing?"

A sickening feeling engulfed Rudolf. His grandparents never said anything about the young mute girl, her mother, and the elderly neighbor that the Gestapo had dragged down the apartment stairs in the middle of the night, never to be seen again. He stared at Frederick and said quietly, "Yes, I saw it happen, but what could I do? I was but a child."

Frederick smiled, put the pipe to his mouth and took a long inhale while lighting it. "Yes, you are right, you could do nothing then. The problem is that children carry the ways of their parents. We learn silence. We hear a racial slur. Those behaviors are like a cancer that has not yet exploded in our bodies. If you realize those hideous actions now, then you can work to ensure you do not repeat them, that you do not pass them on to your children."

Rudolf fidgeted uncomfortably in his chair. When the discussion group ended for the day, a sense of relief flooded over him.

The next day, the final hours of the crash course, the lectures focused on the future, not the past. The answer for world peace and economic security was Wendell Willkie's *One World,* and his international vision of world politics infused with American values.

Rudolf was resolute, however. His attitude had not changed since he kicked Willkie's book off his cot at Camp Papago Park. "I am concerned," Rudolf said to his discussion group, "about Russia in the new world order. I do not believe internationalism will work with Russia."

Frederick looked up from his notes, his eyebrows raised quizzically. "As Mr. Willkie said, we need to learn to work with Russia after the war."

Rudolf bristled, and raised his hand again. Frederick called on him with a sigh. "How can that be possible when there is so much animosity between the Germans and Russians? The Russians control half of Germany now. Are the Americans going to stop them when they are on the move to take the rest of Germany—as we know they will!—and then all of Europe?"

There was silence among the group, and Frederick reacted by sitting back in his chair and fiddling with his pipe. "I am told that the American military does not believe Russia is going to push its sphere of influence." When there was no response, Frederick leaned forward. "Your function, as you step back onto German soil, is to serve as goodwill ambassadors for the American cause. America and her democracy will prove itself to the German people with you as the standard bearers. Russia's communism can never spread where democracy has seen the light of day."

Rudolf gulped. Now he understood why he had been sent to Ft. Eustis! It was not merely to learn about democracy; he and the others were the first line of American propaganda in the new Germany. Rudolf was not sure if he liked that—he was not sure if he liked that at all.

The room, crowded with men slapping each other on the shoulder in congratulation, smelled of cigarette smoke, coffee, and chocolate cake. Rudolf stood awkwardly, trying to eat the cake and protect his prized graduation certificate tucked under his arm.

When he finished, Rudolf moved outside into the refreshing chill of Virginia's winter. He leaned against the building; one leg tucked behind him and pulled the certificate from under his arm. He examined it closely. He moved his fingers across the embossed paper like he was caressing a beautiful woman, finally satisfied it was real. Despite his misgivings, this was his ticket home; this was his future. He took in a deep breath, the cold air filling his lungs, and thoughts of home warmed him: hugging his grandfather as he jumped off the train in Bremen, making love to the dark-haired girl, and swimming again in the Weser River.

His reverie ended when Frederick walked over to him. "I'm glad you were in my group, Meier. You presented me with some tough questions, making me squirm. You've been thinking a lot about democracy, haven't you?"

Rudolf nodded. "When I was in Arizona, a young American tested my thinking every day. We had some lively conversations. I miss him already."

"Tell me, Meier. Did you get anything out of this…this six-day bicycle race?"

Rudolf look surprised. "Yes. I did, particularly at first. However, I must admit the lecture by the German officer made me angry. Maybe what he said was true, but I am not prepared to swallow it whole. I need to think about it. And, you?"

"I am embarrassed to be a German," Frederick said.

Rudolf gulped. It never occurred to him to feel embarrassed about being a German. The Fatherland had so many good qualities—hard working people, a culture of music and art that was beyond compare, and great scientific achievements, so great, in fact, that the Americans and Russians raced to conquer Germany just to capture rocket scientists like Wernher von Braun.

"Are you going home?" Rudolf asked Frederick in a small voice.

"I'm not shipping back to Germany," Frederick answered as he stamped out his cigarette, "until these reeducation classes are finished—we have twenty thousand more men to go through this process. But as soon as I can, I want to immigrate back here. There is nothing for me in Germany; I want to become an American. Take my advice and do the same."

Frederick reached out to Rudolf and they shook hands. "Good luck to you, Meier," he said and then walked away. Rudolf stood frozen, trying to fully understand Frederick's meaning, but he knew deep inside, in his heart, that he would never feel embarrassed to be a German.

A few days later, Rudolf stood on the dock at the main port of embarkation, Camp Shanks, New York. Before him lay the Hudson River and the ship that would take him home.

Thousands of men waited to be processed, and the line moved slowly past the dock-side processing desk where a waiting officer checked off each man's name.

As he stepped up to the desk, Rudolf's heart thumped so hard, he was afraid the officer could hear it.

"Rudolf Meier, Camp Papago Park," he said in his perfect English. The officer looked him over. "Say, how do you spell that—M-e-y-e-r?"

A small line of perspiration formed on Rudolf's upper lip. "No sir, it is M-e-i-e-r," he replied as the officer looked through his rooster, a wait of eternity for Rudolf. Finally, this man who controlled his return to the Fatherland looked up. "OK, here it is," and he made a check on the paper. "You're cleared to go on board."

Rudolf strode joyfully up the gangplank of the United States hospital ship *Frances Y. Slanger*, his heavy barrack bag hoisted jauntily on his shoulder, his cap pulled down tight on his head to keep it from flying away as the winter wind whistled off the Hudson River.

Once on deck, he walked to the bow of the ship and looked down the river toward Manhattan. He could hear the bustle of the port, the hum of diesel engines from tug boats moving ships smoothly out into the flow of the river, and shrieking sea gulls following in their wake hoping to find a tasty morsel. When the engines of the hospital ship began to rumble under his feet, there were yells from the American sailors and clanking of the anchor chain as it was hoisted into the ship's bowels. Finally, leaning over as far as possible, he could just barely see the gangplank as it was pulled away from the side of the ship.

Slowly moving out into the Hudson, a blast of the ship's whistle sent goose bumps up Rudolf's spine. Two men stood nearby, men Rudolf recognized from the Fort Eustis seminar. He nodded to them, but they paid no attention because of their heated argument.

The older of the two said, "Why are you crying, you *Schwein*! I, for one, am happy to be leaving!"

The other wiped his tears from his face with the back of his hand. "What is there to go home to? Devastation! How will we make a living to feed our families? I believe we are kidding ourselves if we think the Nazis are no longer there. I am afraid to go back! Somehow they will find out I attended this democracy school!"

"Such foolishness!" the first man retorted. "All you need to say is that you were forced into it! Besides, it would be all to the better if the Nazis are there, waiting, biding their time! Remember, the party brought order out of chaos, created jobs and all of us, the ordinary German, had many benefits. The Americans will do nothing for us, wait and see!"

The man who had been crying became angry. "Freedom! That is what we did not have! The Nazi party was exalted above the family, our churches were destroyed, and we became a nation of anti-Semites! Yes, the Jews were responsible for our troubles between the wars, but Hitler exploited our fears!"

The other man scoffed, "Tell me, this country that you love so much, this America—there is no welfare for the people, no help to the poor. Freedom does not put food on their tables! Only a strong leader like Adolf Hitler does that. This democracy they taught us about—it will be nothing by the time Stalin gets through with it!"

More men crowded together at the bow as the ship moved farther down the Hudson, toward the Statue of Liberty. They buzzed with excitement at America's symbol of freedom, but Rudolf only stared at it, holding tightly to the cord of his sea bag. To his surprise, he bitterly remembered when he first viewed the American icon, on the deck of an American destroyer. It did not represent freedom to Rudolf, as the bile of resentment crept up his throat. It represented a country that had imprisoned him and then tried to jam the value of democracy down his throat. The only real freedom Rudolf remembered was sitting on the ditch bank of a cotton farm discussing democracy with a Jew.

Then, he bowed his head; conflict raging within him. Bob was not just a Jew; he was a young man who had reached out to Rudolf and became his friend. Everything they talked about on that ditch bank tested Rudolf's love for the Fatherland; everything the Feller family represented caused Rudolf to analyze whether he was a decent, caring human being. Because of them, he was standing here, now, on this ship. Because of them he was not going to France to work on a labor battalion like so many thousands of other POWs. Perhaps the German officer was right: he had to accept his portion of guilt for the bloodshed of the Third Reich, for the killing of decent people like the Feller family.

Rudolf stepped away from the bow, pulled his bag onto his shoulder, and headed toward the mess where he could get a cup of coffee to shake off the chill and then he would find his bunk.

He did not look back at America's symbol of freedom; it reminded him this moment of his loneliness for Bob Feller and the American's happy grin. He was going home now, home to his beloved Germany, and that was all he dared care about.

Acknowledgements

This historical novel would never have come to fruition without the help and encouragement of many people.

In 2007, about six months after I began writing *The Swastika Tattoo*, I joined a writing group in Sedona, Arizona, headed by novelist Willma Gore. At that time, she was but 85 years old and holding court with several groups of writers. Now she is well over 90 and her energy and tough standards have never failed to amaze me, her encouragement a beacon in the dark of night when I never thought I would finish this novel.

In that group were two writers who I also wish to thank: Anne Crosman and Lin Ennis for giving me much needed feedback.

While in Germany doing research for this book, my husband and I spent several days with a former U-boat officer who had been held many years in Canada as a prisoner of war. Volkmar König and his wife, Dorothee, opened their home and their hearts to us. Herr König provided me much-needed background information.

To Jak Mallmann Showell for his gracious help at the U-boat Archive in Cuxhaven, Germany; and to Ken Dunn for lending his technical eye to my writing

To my sons, Chris and Steve Brailo. They have always been an unflagging cheering section. Even when they were small, they gave me the inspiration to continue writing. To my delight, they are men who do not judge a person by the color of their skin.

To my mother for her life-long encouragement.

Finally, and most importantly, to my husband, Joe. He has lived through my struggles with this book, always giving in to expensive trips, the loading of heavy baggage, and driving harrowing roads in foreign countries. I could not have done this without his continual love and encouragement.

About The Author

Geraldine Birch has enjoyed a long career as a newspaper reporter, having worked a decades-long stint as a freelancer at the *Los Angeles Times* and for various community newspapers in Southern California.

A reporter, editor, and political columnist for the *Sedona Red Rock News* in Arizona, Birch was recognized with a first-place award by the National Newspaper Association for her political column, "Gerrymandering."

Her historical novel, *The Swastika Tattoo*, was inspired by her interview with a German submarine officer and recently won an honorable mention in the Reader's Choice international book contest.

Birch currently lives with her husband in Arizona.

A Conversation With Geraldine Birch

Q: Why did you write this book?

A: I was at the Burton Barr Central Library in Phoenix about ten years ago. While there, I happened upon the Arizona Room which is a research section with materials about the history of Arizona. In it, I came across old news articles about Camp Papago Park, a prisoner of war camp for 1,700 German U-boat officers and crewmen located in the 1940s on the outskirts of Phoenix, Arizona. I was astonished that the United States had German POWs and the more research I did, the more fascinated I became with the subject. Ultimately, I found that there were more than 500 camps throughout the United States during WWII, housing approximately 370,000 Germans.

But it wasn't just the POW camps and the use of German labor that caught my interest. My field of study is political science. I have always been interested in the difference between fascism and democracy and why a country chooses one political system over another. I try to explore this in *The Swastika Tattoo* with my fictional character Rudolf Meier, who is a confirmed fascist from the young age of 12 years old.

Q: This book is also about U-boats, the term used for German submarines. It's not a usual subject for a woman to write about. How did you do your research on that?

A: I traveled to Germany where I was escorted through U-995 with a former U-boat officer. Herr Volkmar König gave me a thorough tour of the boat and explained many of its functions. In addition, I also went to Chicago to see U-505, a gem-like German submarine at the Museum of Science and Industry.

Walking through those two U-boats gave me the feel of the closeness of the quarters and how small the two radio rooms were. After reading many books about U-boats, watching German U-boat movies and documentaries, I felt I could give an adequate description of life on board.

That's not to say that I didn't have a lot of questions about day to day survival and technical aspects of U-boats. Soon after I began writing this book, I posted a complicated question on www.uboat.net and received a knowledgeable response from Ken Dunn, a man who has made the study of U-boats a beloved avocation. Through many emails, the reading of the section of the book on my fictional U-boat U-893, and with much advice, Ken gave me a thumb's up.

Q: What do you want the reader to come away with after reading *The Swastika Tattoo?*

A: This is a book about intolerance of other people and cultures. Prejudice and intolerance are infused in us at a young age. As children, we are like small radar stations, picking up racial slurs and intolerant body language from our parents, relatives, and family friends. Prejudice moves then from generation to generation, unchecked unless we are taught differently. Nazi Germany is a prime example of intolerance; Jews especially, but also Catholics, homosexuals, and anyone who might have had a physical or mental handicap. The Hitler Youth and the classrooms of German school children were nurseries for intolerance.

Intolerance did not just live in Germany during the Third Reich, it is alive and well in Europe with the influx of African and Turkish people who are looking to make their life better. It is also alive and well in America. It seems that whenever the economy has a serious setback, people want to place the blame on those who look different or come from a different culture.

Our government and political parties aren't much different. Democracy is a messy business and always has been. The Greeks, so proud of their democracy, voted to kill the philosopher Socrates because he posed questions no one in the young democracy wanted to answer.

Americans are talking less and less to one another. It is easier to shout slogans or pithy sound-bites on both sides of the political aisle rather than working on a compromise. My hope is that with *The Swastika Tattoo*, readers, especially young adults, will begin to look inward and realize we are all human beings, no matter what our skin color, no matter where we came from.

Hopefully, with that realization, respect for others will begin to flourish. And from there, a democracy that works.

Study Guide For High School Students
Short Summary

The Swastika Tattoo is mainly written from the point of view of the main character, Rudolf Meier, a German prisoner of war whose love for his country is as visible as the swastika tattoo on his forearm.

This historical novel takes place in two different parts of the world: Arizona and Germany.

The novel opens with Rudolf working on a cotton farm on the outskirts of Phoenix. Arizona. He is a German prisoner of war housed at Camp Papago Park in east Phoenix along with nearly 1,700 other German submariners. The chapters in Arizona are during the time frame of September 1944 to early 1946.

As part of the back story, the second location is northern Germany in a beautiful medieval city called Bremen, not far from the North Sea. This is where Rudolf lives with his grandparents, Hermann and Luise Meyer. It is there that he grows up, attends school, and joins the Hitler Youth, an organization begun in Nazi Germany to teach German youth the core beliefs of fascism under Germany's leader Adolf Hitler. In addition, there are several chapters where Rudolf trains as a radio operator on a U-boat (a German submarine) and his time at sea. These chapters are from the period of 1936 to 1943.

Because the chapters move back and forth between Arizona and Germany, rather than describe each time frame separately, this synopsis will relate what happens in Arizona, then Germany, then return to Arizona.

In Arizona: It is September 1944 and Rudolf is laboring in an Arizona cotton field. A year earlier, he was captured along with the submarine crew of U-893 off America's East Coast, interrogated at Fort Hunt in Virginia, and sent to a POW camp in Florida. Then when Camp Papago Park opens, he and other U-boat men are all sent to Arizona. Because he is the only one who speaks English among the other German POWs, the son of the cotton farmer, Bob Feller, approaches Rudolf with a question that reverberates through the prisoner's mind during the long months he is held in captivity: Why do the German people still believe in their leader Adolf Hitler? The question infuriates Rudolf, who firmly believes the glory of Germany is because of Hitler, *Der Führer*. At this point in time, Germany and America are still fighting, but America is on the offensive.

Rudolf is wary of Bob Feller. But when the teenager goes to great effort to find a small Bible lost in the cotton field that belongs to Rudolf's bunkmate, Helmut, his attitude softens. When Rudolf and Helmut are invited to the Fellers' Thanksgiving dinner, Rudolf feels conflicted in his acceptance, but when he sees the same porcelain on the dinner table that his grandmother cherished in Germany, he feels drawn to the family. As Bob brings Rudolf and Helmut back to the camp after the sumptuous dinner, he gives Rudolf a book by the American author Ernest Hemingway, *For Whom the Bell Tolls*, saying, "…it's about a man who stays true to himself amid the crisis of war."

In Germany: These chapters begin in May 1936. They tell the story of Rudolf's upbringing by his grandparents, Hermann and Luise Meier. Luise hates Hitler because Nazi thugs killed Rudolf's parents who were Communist agitators (a fact unknown to Rudolf). After the visit of Hitler to Bremen (Rudolf believes the leader of Germany looked directly at him), Hermann, who is a supervisor at one of Germany's largest U-boat shipyards, decides there is no other way for 12-year-old Rudolf to rise in Germany's social order than to join the Hitler Youth, much to Rudolf's joy and Luise's dismay.

Rudolf is deeply conflicted during these years of indoctrination by his teachers and the Hitler Youth—he loves his grandmother, but he hates her overt anti-Nazi behavior. He is also confused not only by his grandmother's friendship with a Jewish merchant, but by the refusal of his best friend, Lothar, to join the Hitler Youth—conflicts he must somehow resolve. His fear heightens when his Hitler Youth leader wants to know why Luise does not attend Hitler Youth functions. He lies; covering up for his grandmother, fearing she could be sent to a concentration camp, but he is worried to the point of sickness that he will be caught lying. Rudolf proves his mettle, however, by standing at attention for hours in a driving rain storm while on a camping trip with the Hitler Youth, but he finally loses Lothar's friendship because of his attachment to the youth group. Rudolf becomes more attuned to Nazi philosophy when he is selected to attend the Nazi Party's annual rally in Nuremberg and he marches before his idol Adolf Hitler, a moment he will never forget.

As Rudolf moves into adulthood, he joins the German Navy and is trained as a U-boat radio operator. In that cramped boat, he comes face to face with his lack of humanity, not understanding his fellow crewmen and their compassion for enemies of Germany after the sinking of an American ship. When he is given an order to send a signal of distress for the Americans floating in the sea, he shouts that they are the enemy. However, his superior officer reminds him the real enemy is the sea and Rudolf had better hope if U-893 is in peril and sinking that the Allies will also act humanely.

The men he works with on the U-boat are apolitical while Rudolf is considered to be a Nazi because of his outspoken love for the Third Reich. Conflict arises on the U-boat because of Rudolf's dislike for a superior officer, Otto Hollmann, but nothing is resolved because the boat is discovered by the Americans and destroyed by a bomb. After escaping the sinking boat, Rudolf and most of the crew are rescued by an American destroyer.

The novel returns to Arizona, where, despite himself, Rudolf becomes emotionally attached to Bob Feller, even when he realizes, much to his dismay, that the Fellers are Jewish. It is Bob who teaches Rudolf the meaning of democracy and individualism as they work together in the cotton fields testing each other's point of view. The unexpected death of Bob's father forces Rudolf to make a hard decision about escape from the POW camp, and when he returns instead to Camp Papago Park, Nazi officers, particularly Otto Hollmann, take note of his friendship with a Jew, threatening him.

As Rudolf waits longingly to be returned to his beloved Germany after the end of the war, his friend Helmut becomes infatuated with the freedoms he sees in America. When Helmut is brutally murdered, Rudolf believes he may be the next target of the hard-core Nazi officers who control the camp. He suffers a hysterical collapse, not only because of the murder of his friend, but because his core beliefs about Nazi Germany have been shattered.

As days turn to months, word finally comes that all 370,000 German POWs in the United States are being sent to England, France, and Belgium to clean up the war's rubble instead of being returned home to Germany. Rudolf is furious. But miraculously, through the influence of the Feller family, Rudolf is chosen to attend reeducation classes in Virginia for a select 20,000 German POWs who are then quickly sent home to Germany as standard bearers for democracy. However, the tough political and philosophical discussions at the seminar among the German POWs cause much emotional tension for Rudolf; he's just not sure democracy will work in Germany or that he even wants it to.

Finally, bound for Germany on an American hospital ship, as he views the Statue of Liberty, Rudolf listens to his fellow POWs argue the merits of democracy versus fascism, and his internal conflicts bubble again to the surface. Rudolf is well aware of the influence of a Jewish family on his life, but now all he dares care about is that he is going home.

Major Theme
Intolerance

The Swastika Tattoo is an exploration of intolerance, which is the refusal by someone to accept people who are different than they are. These differences could include race, point of view, beliefs—religious or political, lifestyles, or social standing. The main character, Rudolf Meier, is deeply schooled in intolerance toward Jews which he learns from his teacher, Herr Braun, and from his peers in the Hitler Youth.

Rudolf's grandfather, Hermann is a practical man. Although he is not a member of the Nazi party, Hermann is very aware that the Nazis run Germany and if his grandson, Rudolf, is to get ahead in the world, he must be part of the new German social order. However, because of his social background, rising from a mere welder at the great AG Weser shipyard in Bremen, Germany, to a supervisor, it is well known in the neighborhood that Hermann Meier is capable of living in a better area, but he prefers to stay among the people who are his long-time neighbors and friends. Thus, Hermann Meier is shown as a man of tolerance except when he learns that the head of Rudolf's Hitler Youth unit is the son of a day laborer. Hermann is unhappy that his grandson is exposed to people who he considers beneath him socially and thus they are unacceptable.

Rudolf's grandmother, on the other hand is intolerant in a different way. Luise is unable to forgive the Nazis for killing Rudolf's father. Luise Meyer's intolerance is toward the Nazis in general and the head of Germany, Adolf Hitler, in particular. She harbors such hate toward him that she calls him a terrible name and refuses to place Hitler's photograph in her home—a way of showing during the Third Reich that Germany's leader is revered by the family.

However, Luise is tolerant toward a Jewish merchant who has been her friend for many years. When she learns that the merchant is leaving Germany because of racist policies toward Jews by the Third Reich, she is angry. She tells Rudolf that Jews are people just like everyone else and although they have different beliefs, they are only trying to lead a decent life and take care of their children. When Rudolf hears his grandmother say that, he is stunned and extremely upset, believing that Jewish people harm Germany—at least that's what he's been taught.

Rudolf shows his intolerance throughout *The Swastika Tattoo*. In the opening chapter of the book, Rudolf is intolerant toward the teenager who is the son of the cotton farmer where Rudolf and other German prisoners of war toil under the Arizona sun. When the teenager, Bob Feller, asks Rudolf why the German people still believe in Hitler, he wants to physically strike out against the young man. To Rudolf, the question is blasphemy. He believes no one should question the German people's love for their leader, Adolf Hitler.

Not only is Rudolf intolerant of the Americans who have captured him, he shows his bigotry when he learns that the Feller family is Jewish. After giving the usual Nazi harangue about Jews in Germany, he realizes later that Bob and his family have been extraordinarily kind to him and the other prisoners and he begins to reassess his thinking. He remembers the wonderful Thanksgiving dinner that he and his friend, Helmut, were invited to at the Feller home. It is there at that dinner, that Rudolf sees the same china on the holiday table that his grandmother prized so much at home in Germany, and he begins to realize what his grandmother said may be true—that Jews are no different than anyone else.

One scene in particular, exposes Rudolf's intolerance. That is when he and Helmut have been invited to the funeral of Bob's father, Vern. The funeral is in a Jewish synagogue. Believing all the stories from his teachers and the Hitler Youth, Rudolf feels unnerved to walk into a place filled with so many Jewish people. He doesn't want to hear what he considers the garbled sounds of Hebrew, but he is amazed to find that the Rabbi, the head of the congregation, looks no different than anyone else and that only a few words of Hebrew are spoken at the ceremony. Once again, Rudolf re-assesses his thinking by reading books given to him by Bob that tell about human decency, democracy, and individualism.

When Germany loses the war to the Allies—America, Great Britain, and Russia—Rudolf is inconsolable. He has a difficult time understanding why his country, which he fervently believed to be infallible because of its leader Adolf Hitler, could possibly be defeated. As he comes to grips with this loss, he begins to feel the intolerance of his German officers who have warned him to keep away from his Jewish friend Bob Feller. It is only when Helmut is murdered, that he begins to understand the power of his officers over the men in the camp, and he suffers a hysterical collapse.

Finally, through the kindness of the Feller family and their influence with people high up in the government in Washington, D.C., Rudolf is picked as one of 20,000 German POWs to attend a reeducation seminar in Virginia. The seminar is a crash course in democracy. This opportunity to leave the camp in Arizona enables Rudolf to escape the possible retaliation of his officers for being friends with a Jew.

Upon graduation from the democracy reeducation program, Rudolf is cleared to return to Germany. As he stands at the railing of the American ship that will bring him home, he sees the Statue of Liberty. He suddenly becomes conflicted and judgmental once again of the Americans who held him in captivity for 2½ years. But, then he remembers the Feller family, their kindness, and all they have done for him. As he turns away from the great symbol of freedom, unable to assess everything that has changed him—including that his closest friend is a Jew—all he can dare think about is that he is going home.

Historical Terms of World War II*

Adolf Hitler - an Austrian-born German politician and the leader of the Nazi Party. Hitler was chancellor of Germany from 1933 to 1945 and dictator of Nazi Germany (as *Führer*) from 1934 to 1945. In April 1945, he committed suicide in a Berlin bunker as the Allied armies encircled the city.

Allies - the countries that opposed the Axis, which included Germany, Italy, and Japan during WW II (1939–1945). The three major Allies were Great Britain, Russia, and the United States.

Battle of the Atlantic - the longest continuous military campaign in World War II, running from 1939 to the defeat of Germany in 1945. At its core was the Allied naval blockade of Germany, and Germany's subsequent counter-blockade. The Battle of the Atlantic pitted U-boats and other warships of the *Kriegsmarine* (German Navy) and aircraft of the *Luftwaffe* (German Air Force) against Allied merchant shipping.

Bolshevik Communists - a faction of the Marxist Russian Social Democratic Labor Party (RSDLP) that broke away from two other labor parties in 1903. Bolsheviks were the majority faction in a crucial vote, hence their name. Ultimately, the RSDLP became the Communist Party of the Soviet Union

Camp Papago Park - a prisoner of war (POW) facility located in Papago Park in the eastern part of Phoenix, Arizona, during WWII. It consisted of five compounds, four compounds for enlisted men and one for officers. The camp housed about 1,700 U-boat officers and crewmen. The property now is divided between the Papago Park Military Reservation, belonging to the Arizona National Guard, a city park, residential neighborhoods and a car dealer's lot.

Dachau - the first of the Nazi concentration camps opened in Germany, located on the grounds of an abandoned munitions factory near the medieval town of Dachau, about 16 km (9.9 mi) northwest of Munich in the state of Bavaria, which is located in southern Germany.

Enigma Machine - electro-mechanical rotor cipher machines used for the encryption and decryption of secret messages.

Fatherland - a beloved reference to Germany.

Fascism - a radical authoritarian nationalist political ideology.

First Reich - also known as the Holy Roman Empire. The First Reich was a complex of lands that existed together in a loose unit from 962 to 1806 A.D. in Central Europe. It lasted nearly a thousand years. The empire's territory was centered on the Kingdom of Germany.

Fort Hunt - a US military-intelligence facility located in Virginia where German POWs were interrogated upon capture by the United States. The facility is no longer in existence.

Geneva Convention - the Geneva Convention comprise four treaties that establish the standards of international law for the humanitarian treatment of the victims of war, including prisoners of war.

Gestapo - the official secret police of Nazi Germany and German-occupied Europe.

Great War (WW I) - a global war centered in Europe that began in July 1914 and lasted until November 1918. It was predominantly called the World War or the Great War prior to WW II.

Hitler Youth - a paramilitary organization of the Nazi Party. It existed from 1922 to 1945. The *Hitlerjugend* or HJ was the second oldest paramilitary Nazi group, founded one year after its adult counterpart, the *Sturmabteilung* (SA). It was made up of the *Hitlerjugend* proper, for male youth ages 14–18; the younger boys' section *Deutsches Jungvolk* for ages 10–14; and the girls' section *Bund Deutscher Mädel* (BDM, the League of German Girls).

Hereditary Health Court - also known as the Genetic Health Court. These courts decided whether people should be forcibly sterilized in Nazi Germany.

Horst Wessel song – Kaiser Horst Ludwig Wessel was a German National Socialist activist and an SA-*Sturmführer* who was made a posthumous hero of the Nazi movement following his murder in 1930. He was the author of the lyrics to the song "The Flag on High," usually known as "the Horst Wessel Song," which became the Nazi Party anthem and Germany's co-national anthem from 1933 to 1945.

Mendelssohn - Felix Mendelssohn was a German composer, pianist, organist, and conductor of the early Romantic period (early 19th Century). Mendelssohn was born into a prominent Jewish family.

National Socialism - referred to in English as Nazism, National Socialism was the ideology of the Nazi Party and Nazi Germany. It is a variety of fascism that incorporates biological racism and anti-Semitism as it tenets.

Nazis - shortened word for people who belonged to the National Socialist Workers Party and believed in the ideology of National Socialism. Its leader was Adolf Hitler.

Nuremburg Laws - laws that classified people with four German grandparents as "German or kindred blood." People were classified as Jews if they descended from three or four Jewish grandparents. A person with one or two Jewish grandparents was a *Mischling*, a crossbreed of "mixed blood." These laws deprived Jews of German citizenship and prohibited marriage between Jews and other Germans.

Potsdam Conference - held at Cecilienhof, the home of Crown Prince Wilhelm Hohenzollern, in Potsdam from July 17 to August 2, 1945. Participants were the Soviet Union, the United Kingdom and the United States. The three powers were represented by Communist Party General Secretary Joseph Stalin, Prime Ministers Winston Churchill, and, later, Clement Attlee, and President Harry S. Truman. The division of Germany was decided at this conference.

Reich Labor Service - The *Reichsarbeitsdienst* (or RAD) was an institution established by Nazi Germany as an agency to reduce unemployment, similar to the relief programs in other countries during the 1930s. During the Second World War, young men served in the RAD prior to military conscription and they were used as support for Germany military forces.

Rhineland - Historically, the Rhineland refers to a loosely defined region embracing the land on either bank of the Rhine River in central Europe. The remilitarization of the Rhineland by the German Army took place on March 7, 1936, when military forces entered the Rhineland. This was significant because it violated the terms of the Treaty of Versailles and was the first time since the end of World War I that German troops had been in this region.

Richard Wagner - a German composer, conductor, and theatre director primarily known for his operas. His music was a favorite of Adolf Hitler.

Ruhr - an urban area in North Rhine-Westphalia, Germany. An important industrial area occupied by the French in 1923 as a reprisal after Germany failed to fulfill World War I reparation payments as agreed in the Treaty of Versailles. The German government responded with passive resistance, letting workers and civil servants refuse orders and instructions by the occupation forces. Production and transport came to a standstill and the financial consequences contributed to German hyperinflation and ruined public finances in Germany.

S.A. Brownshirts - the *Sturmabteilung (SA)* (or also known as Brownshirts) functioned as the original paramilitary wing of the Nazi Party. It played a key role in Adolf Hitler's rise to power in the 1920s and 1930s. Their main assignments were providing protection for Nazi rallies and assemblies; the disruption of opposing political parties; and the intimidation of Jewish citizens.

SS - the *Schutzstaffel* (SS) a major paramilitary organization under Adolf Hitler and the Nazi Party (NSDAP). Built upon the Nazi ideology, the SS under Heinrich Himmler's command was responsible for many of the crimes against humanity during World War II (operation of concentration camps). It was one of the largest organizations in Nazi Germany. After 1945, the SS was banned in Germany, along with the Nazi Party, as a criminal organization.

Second Reich - the unification of Germany under the proclamation of German Emperor Wilhelm I in 1871; also known as the German Empire. The Second Reich ended in 1918 with the defeat of Germany in WW I, and the abdication of the Emperor.

Battle of Stalingrad - a major and decisive battle of World War II in which Nazi Germany and its allies fought the Soviet Union for control of the city of Stalingrad in the southwestern Soviet Union. The battle took place from August 23, 1942, to February 2, 1943, and was marked by constant close-quarters combat and lack of regard for military and civilian casualties. It is among the bloodiest battles in the history of warfare, with the higher estimates of combined casualties amounting to nearly two million. The heavy losses inflicted on the German army made it a significant turning point in the whole war. After the Battle of Stalingrad, German forces never recovered their earlier strength, and attained no further strategic victories in Eastern Europe.

Swastika - the swastika was adopted as a symbol of the Nazi Party of Germany in 1920. The Nazis used the swastika as a symbol of the Aryan race. After Adolf Hitler came to power in 1933, a right-facing and rotated swastika was incorporated into the Nazi party flag, which was made the state flag of Germany during Nazi rule. The swastika has become strongly associated with Nazism and related ideologies such as fascism and white supremacies in the Western world.

Swing Kids - a group of jazz and swing lovers in Germany in the 1930s and 1940s. They were composed of 14- to 18-year-old boys and girls in high school, most of them middle- or upper-class students. They sought the British and American way of life, defining them in swing music and opposing the National-Socialist ideology, especially the Hitler Youth.

Third Reich - also known as Nazi Germany is the common name for Germany when it was a totalitarian state ruled by Adolf Hitler and his National Socialist German Workers' Party (NSDAP). On January 30, 1933 Hitler became Chancellor of Germany, quickly eliminating all opposition to rule as sole leader. Under the "leader principle," the *Führer's* word was above all other laws. Top officials reported to Hitler and followed his policies, but they had considerable autonomy. The government was not a coordinated, cooperating body, but rather a collection of factions struggling to amass power and gain favor with the *Führer*. In the midst of the Great Depression, the Nazi government restored prosperity and ended mass unemployment using heavy military spending and a mixed economy of free-market and central-planning practices. The return to prosperity gave the regime enormous popularity; the suppression of all opposition made Hitler's rule mostly unchallenged. Hitler predicted the Third Reich would last a thousand years.

Treaty of Versailles - one of the peace treaties at the end of World War I. It ended the state of war between Germany and the Allied Powers. It was signed on June 28, 1919. Although the armistice, signed on November 11, 1918, ended the actual fighting, it took six months of negotiations at the Paris Peace Conference to conclude the peace treaty. Of the many provisions in the treaty, one of the most important and controversial required Germany to accept responsibility for causing the war along with Austria and Hungary, to disarm, make substantial territorial concessions, and pay heavy reparations to certain countries. This would prove to be a factor leading to World War II.

U-boat - the Anglicized version of the German word *U-Boot*, itself an abbreviation of "Unterseeboot" (in English, "undersea boat"), and refers to military submarines operated by Germany, particularly in World War I and World War II. Although at times they were efficient fleet weapons against enemy naval warships, they were most effectively used in an economic warfare role (commerce raiding), and enforcing a naval blockade against enemy shipping.

Weimar Republic - the name given by historians to the federal republic and parliamentary representative democracy established in 1919 in Germany to replace the imperial form of government, the Second Reich. It was named after Weimar, the city where the constitutional assembly took place.

Werner von Braun - was a German-American rocket scientist, aerospace engineer, space architect, and one of the leading figures in the development of rocket technology in Nazi Germany during World War II and, subsequently, in the United States. His crowning achievement was to lead the development of the Saturn V booster rocket that helped land the first men on the Moon in July 1969.

Wolf Packs - refers to a naval tactic against shipping convoys used by German U-boats during the Battle of the Atlantic.

*Various sources have been used for these historical terms: *The Faustball Tunnel, German POWs in America and their Great Escape,* John Hammond Moore, 1978; The *Rise and Fall of the Third Reich,* William L. Shirer, 1950, 1960; *The Third Reich, A New History,* Michael Burleigh, 2000; and Wikipedia.

German Words and Their Meaning

Chapter 1

Baumwolle:	Cotton
Der Führer:	The Leader
Führerprinzip:	The Leadership Principal
Wehrmacht:	German military forces
Unterseeboot:	Submarine, known as U-boats
Amerikaner:	American
Mein Gott:	My God
Faustball:	Volleyball
Schnitzel:	A thin cutlet of veal, seasoned, dipped in batter and fried

Chapter 2

Wunderbar:	Wonderful
Opa:	Grandpa
Enkel:	Grandson
Kapitänleutnant:	Lieutenant Commander
Kriegsmarine:	Term for the Germany Navy during the Third Reich
Oma:	Grandma

Chapter 3

Gymnasium:	High School
Sieg Heil:	Hail Victory
Heil Hitler:	Hail Hitler

Chapter 4
Pimpf: A nobody, or a squirt (meaning a small person)
Marktplatz: Marketplace

Chapter 5
Ja, Ja: Yes, yes!
Fregattenkapitän: Commander

Chapter 6
Reichsmarine: Term for German Navy under the Kaiser
Kaiser: Title of German emperors (e.g. Kaiser Wilhelm I)
Du dummer Idiot: You stupid idiot

Chapter 8
Das Volk: The people
Jungvolk: Young people
Gestapo: Secret state police
Schweinhunde: German swear word
Mutter: Mother
Vater: Father

Chapter 9
Deutsche Jungvolk: German young people
Lederhosen: Leather trousers
Fähnleinführer: Troop leader
Reichsführer: German leader
Mutprobe: Test of courage; daring
Heim: Home

Chapter 10
Geschlechtsverkehr: Intercourse
Schwein: Pig

Chapter 11
Der Stümer: The Attacker
Juden: Jewry

Chapter 12
Hitlerjugend: Hitler Youth
Deutschland, Deutschland
über alles: Germany, Germany above all
Misthaufen   Shit heap

Chapter 13
Dummköpfe: Idiot, fool
Zeppelin: A large gas-filled buoyant airship

Chapter 17
Mein Lehrer: My teacher
Mein Studeten: My students

Chapter 18
Reichsparteitag: Rally of the Nazi Party held in Nuremberg in the fall
Du: You
Weiner schnitzel: Breaded meat with an accompanying sauce
Mein Kampf: "My Struggle," Adolf Hitler's autobiography
Pfennig: Penny
Banne: A Hitler Youth district composed of 5,000 boys and girls
Luftwaffe: Air Force
Zeppelinfeld: Zeppelin Field
Achtung: Attention
Heil Mein Führer: Hail my leader

Chapter 19

Schiffstammdivision:	Ship Master Division
Funklaufbahn:	Radio operator
Afrika Korps:	Africa Corps
Armeekorp:	Army Corps
Franko-Alles 30:	An address
Marine Hitlerjugend:	Marine Hitler Youth
Nein, Nein:	No, no
Tante:	Aunt
Oberfunkmeister:	Senior Radio Petty Officer
Grossadmiral:	Grand Admiral (Commander-in-chief of German U-boats)

Chapter 20

Schweine:	Pigs
Smutje:	U-boat cook
Selmannoslabskaus:	Seaman's concoction of corned beef, crushed potatoes mixed with beetroot, a fried egg and pickled herring lying on top of the entire heaped mixture with a dill pickle on the side
Funkmaat:	Radio petty officer
Kommandant:	Commander, Captain
Grüne Klösse:	Green dumplings
Kristallnacht:	The Night of Broken Glass - November 1938 when Nazi Brownshirts and Gestapo destroyed hundreds of synagogues and Jewish businesses

Chapter 21

Milch Cow:	Milk cow

Chapter 22
Zilch: Nothing
Knockenfilmen: Bone films, referring to newsreels of the German concentration camps

Chapter 23
Kaputt: Broken, ruined, destroyed
Soldbuch: An ID booklet every German soldier or sailor carried
Herzlichen Glückwunsch zum Geburtstag: Many happy returns
Polizist: Policeman

Chapter 26
Fragebogen: Questionnaire
Auf Wiedersehen: Farewell, goodbye

Chapter 27
Apfelstrudel: Apple strudel

Glossary

Benediction - a blessing

Blasphemy – profane or mocking speech, writing, or action concerning God

Cacophony – harsh, jarring sound

Communist – a member or supporter of a political ideology where government controls the economy and a single, often authoritarian party holds power. The ultimate objective is a higher social order in which all goods are equally shared by the people.

Contraband – goods forbidden by law to be imported or exported

Creed – a brief statement of religious belief

Deferment – to postpone or delay

Delouse – to rid of lice

Demeanor – outward behavior or conduct

Dogma – a doctrine or belief

Enmity – hostility; antagonism

Fortnight – fourteen nights; two weeks

Foyer – an entrance hall or lobby

Humanist – an outlook that gives prime importance to human rather than divine matters

Ignominious – to bring on shame or dishonor

Instigate –to urge on or to incite some action

Jesuit – a member of the Society of Jesus, a Roman Catholic order founded by St. Ignatius Loyola in 1534.

Repatriation – send back to the country of birth or citizenship

Resonance – prolongation of a sound by vibration

Sabotage – to deliberately damage or destroy especially for military or political advantage

Scabbards – a sheath for holding a knife or other large blade

Schnapps – strong alcoholic liquor

Secular – activities or attitudes that have no religious or spiritual basis

Spawned – referring to an offspring with contempt

Swarthy – having dark skin

Totalitarian – a government or state where one group maintains complete control

Transcendence – beyond the range of physical human experience

Transit – the carrying of people, goods or materials from one place to another

Vassal – someone who is dependent or subservient

Yiddish – a language used by Jews in central and eastern Europe before the Holocaust. It was originally a German dialect with words from Hebrew and several modern languages and is today mainly spoken in the U.S., Israel, and Russia.

Naval Terms

Morse code - a method of transmitting text information as a series of on-off tones, lights, or clicks that can be directly understood by a skilled listener or observer without special equipment

Starboard – the right side of a boat (facing the bow)

Port – the left side of a boat (facing the bow)

Coxswain - the person in charge of a boat, particularly its navigation and steering

Suggested Essay Questions

Analyze the relationship between Rudolf and his grandmother, Luise. What happened in the past to make her so anxious about Rudolf joining the Hitler Youth and why does Rudolf not understand her feelings?

Discuss the concept of family in Nazi Germany.

Hermann Meier is highly respected by his neighbors. Why is this true?

Discuss the concept of fear as presented in the novel. What are Luise and Hermann so afraid of after their neighbors are dragged off by the Nazis? What is Rudolf afraid of regarding his grandmother and her relationship with a Jewish merchant?

Analyze the impact that the Hitler Youth has on Rudolf. Although he believes it is a way to get out from under the scrutiny of his grandmother, what does his membership in that group do to his way of thinking about anyone who was not a pure-bred German?

Discuss the concept of education in Nazi Germany. What was the responsibility of the teacher, Herr Braun, besides teaching reading, writing, and arithmetic?

Discuss the issue of social status in Germany. Rudolf's grandfather is well aware of his social status at the commissioning ceremony of

U-28. Why was Hermann Meier so surprised that the owner of AG Weser would speak to him at the commissioning ceremony?

How did this view of one's place in society allow the principal of *Führerprinzip* to rule its social structure?

Trace the theme of the Swastika Tattoo throughout the novel and analyze what the Nazi symbol really means to Rudolf.

Trace the development of Lothar Volkmann, Rudolf's childhood friend, from a playmate to someone Rudolf no longer understands. What lessons did Rudolf learn from Lothar when he thought about him years later during his time in the POW camp?

Rudolf matures considerably though the course of the novel— from a 12-year-old boy who idolizes Adolf Hitler to a seasoned sailor and prisoner of war. What developmental changes did he go through and what caused the changes?

When a member of the United States Armed Services takes his or her oath of enlistment, it is an oath to support and defend the Constitution of the United States. What is different from that oath and the one that Rudolf takes as a member of the Hitler Youth and the German Navy?

When Rudolf is a radio operator on a U-boat, he is considered a Nazi by members of the crew. What has he done to make his shipmates say that?

Discuss the major theme of the book, intolerance.

Why does Rudolf believe the Americans are inferior to Germans?

Analyze the relationship between Rudolf Meier and Bob Feller. How does this relationship change throughout the book? What are the causes of the change in their relationship?

After Rudolf sees the beautiful Meissen china on the Thanksgiving table of Ruth Feller, why do his feelings begin to change toward the American family?

Why do you believe Rudolf does not understand the underlying concept of Hemingway's *For Whom the Bell Tolls*—fighting for the rights of other men because of a moral code that envelopes all of mankind, not just one race or country?

Oddly, Rudolf brings up the prejudice of Americans to Black people. What is the reaction of Bob Feller to this accusation?

Rudolf was incredibly upset by the movie *Tomorrow the World*. What was it about that movie that made him so distraught?

Discuss the symbolism of the sand storm that Rudolf is caught in at the prisoner of war camp.

What is the reason Rudolf never questions his leaders, no matter what they tell him to do?

Discuss the prisoner of war camp, Camp Papago Park, as if it were a character in the book. What is the character of the camp?

Why does Rudolf hate the desert landscape of Arizona?

Although the German POWs are repeatedly trying to escape from the camp, why does Rudolf does not escape when he has the opportunity?

What revelation does Rudolf have after he suffers from a hysterical collapse?

When Bob asks Rudolf if he is a Nazi, what is his answer?

Discuss democracy as Rudolf believes it to be in the beginning of the book. At the end of the book, after his reeducation training in democracy, what does he think about democracy?

CPSIA information can be obtained at www.ICGtesting.com
Printed in the USA
BVOW09s1959291214

381230BV00016BA/709/P